The Hiber Nation

Book One

Sleep

Benjamin Thomas Allen

Copyright © 2022 Lee Russell writing as Benjamin Thomas Allen

All rights reserved. No part of this publication may be reproduced, stored or transmitted in any form or by any means, electronic, mechanical, photocopying, recording, scanning, or otherwise without written permission from the author. It is illegal to copy this book, post it to a website, or distribute it by any other means without permission.

This is a work of fiction and is the work of the author's imagination. Any resemblance to actual places, events or persons, living or dead, is entirely coincidental.

Lee Russell asserts the moral right to be identified as the author of this work.

For my wife - she knows all I would want to say to her

Benjamin Thomas Allen is the pen name of the writer Lee Russell.

Lee lives in the South of England with his family.

The Hiber Nation - Book One is Lee's first book and he very much hopes that you enjoy the world he has created.

Table of Contents

Table of Contents	5
From the Author	7
Chapter One	8
Chapter Two	19
Chapter Three	27
Chapter Four	38
Chapter Five	49
Chapter Six	57
Chapter Seven	63
Chapter Eight	70
Chapter Nine	79
Chapter Ten	89
Chapter Eleven	104
Chapter Twelve	108
Chapter Thirteen	115
Chapter Fourteen	122
Chapter Fifteen	129
Chapter Sixteen	140
Chapter Seventeen	150
Chapter Eighteen	155
Chapter Nineteen	165
Chapter Twenty	177
Chapter Twenty-One	186
Chapter Twenty-Two	199
Chapter Twenty-Three	214
Chapter Twenty-Four	222

Chapter Twenty-Five 231
Chapter Twenty-Six 243
Chapter Twenty-Seven 249

From the Author

Thank you for taking the time to pick up this book. I really hope you enjoy the adventure that you are about go on. I intend to take you into world inhabited by peoples of The Hiber Nation. This nation is unique in its geography and lifestyle. It is my intention that you will use your imagination to decide where this nation is and also "when" it "was". You may think this book and its subjects are set in our past or our future, or some other world. I would rather you enjoy this adventure using your own narrative, filling in any gaps that I have left with your own personal answers. In due course, I may, of course help you with these issues, but I believe your imagination will, if you let it, provide a fulfilling "guide" more than my rigid direction on these things.

I have had the Hiber Nation in my thoughts for many years. Over time I slowly began to understand its geography and how the only way for the Hiber people to survive extremes of winter was for them to sleep through the deepest of winter. You may want to reflect upon the idea that the verb "Hibernate" may well have come from some distant memory over the millennia in recognition of this country and her people. Hibernation, in our current context, generally relates to the winter response of a number of animals across our earth. However, what if all living beings undertook such a period of sleep? Is it that far beyond science or our imagination. If you have picked up this book, I guess not.

The culture, living conditions and behaviours of the Hiber Nation slowly developed in my mind and I came to be envious of some of their way of life. In an age where we are aware of our finite resources more than ever, the Hiber Nation appears to have come to terms with their existence without destroying their wider habitat or environmental eco-system in which they are located. However, as with all things, there are threats that come to the fore. On a physical plane, the neighbouring nation - I have called it "Tukerland", appears a threat to the whole existence of the Hiber Nation and their communities. You may well think otherwise and that is your right. But I have brought out of my musings a narrative that parallels the tension on a number of levels that our own nations have faced in our recent history and continue to face today. So, please join me on this adventure. Love those characters you love, and dislike those you dislike, it is your choice. I only commend you to remain committed to the journey.

Lee Russell (writing as Benjamin Thomas Allen)

Chapter One

It was late in the evening. Jandray was sat at the table and had started to plan for the following day. The home he shared with his mother was in the capital community of the Hiber Nation and was warm and comforting. The trees that his home was made of were formed from a living network of walls, floors and ceilings, and also still very much alive. Under the careful cultivation of the Hiber gardeners, homes were weaved, rather than built, into amazing constructions that allowed numerous rooms to be built at ground level, further down into the ground within its roots and also amongst the wide branches. The oldest houses within his community had existed for many hundreds of years. Hiber trees continued to grow for three seasons out of four. However, in the winter season their leaves and branches took on the appearance of glass as they entered into their own sleep for the coming winter. Jandray's home had been planted many generations ago. It wasn't large, as the homes within the Hiber Nation were able to expand or contract depending on need. However, it was spacious enough for Jandray and his mother. It also benefited from amazing views of the capital's community which hosted the home of the King and Queen of the Hiber Nation. This impressive palace stood at the centre of the Paltir community, the first and largest of the communities across this nation.

Each of the main twelve communities across the Hiber Nation had subtly different tree varieties. The leaves and branches had a diversity of colours so that if you visited each community you would note the distinct changes in hues as you passed through the community. Only in Paltir, the capital community, also home to the Queen and King were all the varieties found within the same community. And the 'Royal' palace, oldest of the old, was a rainbow of different hues and colours across its vast structure. The trees gave most generously of their energy. They were treated almost as living people, and were certainly the oldest living entities in the Hiber Nation. It was the amazing biological flexibility of the trees that allowed the Hiber Nation to build without destroying the beautiful essence of this most natural gift to the landscape. The trees shed huge branches each year. From these branches, the communities were able construct virtually all the other material needs that were required in such a bucolic environment.

The trees also grew intensely flammable cones that were used for heat. It was one of the great mysteries of the Hiber Nation that such a tree existed to provide for nearly all its basic protection and living requirements. As a result, the trees were revered across the generations. The trees never died, they continually replenished and renewed themselves. As they got older, their branches became as hard as any rock. They became so strong that wooden fire hearths could be made without any damage to the overall structure. The intense weave of the branches allowed light into buildings in daylight, but also allowed any smoke to filter to the outside. That said, the fire cones were such that there was almost no smoke, only a scent of fresh air and clear water (if you can imagine that smell). Over centuries the careful management by the Hiber gardeners had allowed magnificent structures to be built. These gardeners also cared for the tree nurseries across the whole country to allow an infinite growth stock.

Autumn was weaving its patchwork of colours across the trees and Jandray's home had started to prepare itself for winter. The leaves were changing to a subtle golden hue as they prepared to host water that would then enable them to become like crystal during the long Winter months. It was still a number of weeks away, but Jandray had lots to do before "the Winter Sleep". His lessons on the reasons for this event needed to have impact on the teenage children under his care. He looked back to his childhood. It was the spoken word, passed down the generations, that ensured he was able to pass on this knowledge to his wards. He wondered if any of those in his current class would want to teach future generations? He certainly did not have any idea that this would be his future when he was their age. It comforted him that he could still remember his childhood. However, it was tinged with sadness. Whilst he still had the loving kindness of his mother, Tasren, he had no memory of this father. He knew nothing of his father, not even his name. When he tried to discuss the subject with his mother, it had caused her to cry silently. She would not talk about him at all, other than to say that he was a loving, kind, humble man who had great integrity and that Jandray should hold onto those qualities all his life.

Jandray, despite the love of Tasren, still felt the gap, one that only a father's love can bring to a relationship. As he grew up, he saw his friends with their parents and could see that they responded to both their mother's love and their father's love and care in different ways. A father brought a different, but no less important love into the relationship. As he grew, Jandray began to understand the differences, and he knew that he would always have a missing part, both in his heart, and perhaps, in his character. Despite this he also knew that as he was growing up his mother gave her all as she tried to fill the void that she could also see. He wasn't unique, there were a number of families who lived with only one parent, some who had no parents and were cared for by extended family members. It was a key part of the Hiber culture that nobody was outside of a wide and nurturing network. Jandray could see it in children within his school. A reflection of true community where everyone mattered, everyone was cared for, and everyone took part in the Winter Sleep.

He built up the fire in the hearth and as the fresh scent filled his mind his thoughts returned to the matter at hand; that of preparing his new class for the annual Winter Sleep. When a small child, it was enough to know that your parents, wider family and everyone around you took part in the sleep. However, as a teenager, it was natural to become curious, even resentful, that half your life seemed be in some form of suspended animation as a result of the sleep. The fact that it meant that the Hiber Nation could survive winters where nothing could live, in a land totally covered by metres of snow and ice didn't really count. Even the fact that the sleep seemed to have a regenerative effect on people, so that there was very limited ill-health and life-spans were extensive, did not seen to make the difference with some teenage thoughts.

That said, the excitement created by the annual selection of the HiberWatchers was immense. These two individuals, chosen from the whole Hiber Nation, became celebrities in their own right. Only two were chosen each year and they could only hold this role for one year. Anyone could apply to be in the selection, and many did. But it remained the case that only two would have their names engraved on the the cataract that froze in winter to become the Ice Wall. Each winter as the waters took on their crystal ice form, it was covered with hundreds of names, going back generations. No one knew how the names were etched on the ice and how they appeared each winter All they knew was that the names etched on that wall were there for all to see as soon as the winter sun reflected onto the frozen wall.

The successful applicants would become the HiberWatchers and would meet the Queen and King and also the Elders of each Hiber community. The Queen and King were directly descended from the earliest folk of the Hiber Nation and their family had regularly provided the HiberWatchers in early generations. However, as time moved on it was decided that the privilege of being a HiberWatcher should be shared across the whole population. Whilst the Queen and King were formal titles, they were only first amongst equals and were part of the Hiber Elder Council which governed the Hiber Nation.

Jandray returned to his thoughts about the HiberWatchers and the forthcoming selection. People across each local Hiber community could nominate themselves. In some very rare years, a local community had the privilege of having both HiberWatchers chosen from their community. It did not happen very often as there were twelve main communities. But when this occurred it was cause for special celebration. Each HiberWatcher gave a solemn vow to remain awake and protect all the people of the Hiber Nation during the Winter sleep. The final selection was totally random. The member of the Council who placed their hands into the selection chest took it as an immense privilege. They were given the honour of adding the HiberWatcher's name to the illustrious list of HiberWatchers throughout Hiber history.

It had been many years since the selection had brought the two HiberWatchers from the same Hiber Community. As the selection was totally random, and many of the Hiber people applied,   it was no surprise that the chance of this special event occurring was limited. Jandray had never experienced this special situation. His mother was always very quiet when asked if she had seen such a celebration. Jandray found this odd, but never seemed to find the time or the inclination to ask further. In his own mind Jandray wasn't too concerned. He had, in his younger years, put his name into the selection, but as he grew older he was less and less interested in the celebrity status it brought. Though he should have been married by this stage of his life, he felt it more important to be able to care for Tasren in her older age. Whilst it was likely that any kind of ill health was many years away for Tasren, she would still get frail. The Winter Sleep helped, but it was not a miracle cure for the ageing of the body that came to everyone.

Jandray felt that the children under his care were his "adopted" children for a period of time. He could carry out a surrogate parent role, without being a biological parent of any of them. This surrogate role was embedded in Hiber culture. Whilst each community was distinct, their children were hosted across twelve schools, one in each community. So Jandray had children from every community in his class. It was felt that this continued mixing of children from the earliest of years would ensure that each community learnt about the individual differences of each region of the Hiber Nation. Friendships formed at school would last a lifetime and so would the unbreakable network that kept the nation whole and in unity. It was fairly simple to know the community of ones home and one's birth as there were no surnames in the Hiber Nation. You were simply given a name and were "of Paltir" or any of the other eleven communities.

In his early years as a teacher, when he was barely older than his students, Jandray felt it was odd to have this parental responsibility. Each student had host families but he was their "anchor", their key link to their home family. However, over the years he had found this very rewarding and he kept in touch with many of his pupils as they grew and left his care. He had even seen one of his extensive cohort of ex-students become a HiberWatcher. He had been so proud that he, perhaps, had been an influence on this student, to the point that they had applied for the selection. Jandray would never forget her name - Sartora. She was a quiet girl, highly intelligent and intensely curious. After her role as HiberWatcher, she had gone on to be an important part of Hiber Nation's ruling elite with direct access to the Elder Council. It was widely thought that Sartora would be an Elder one day.

Occasionally, Sartora would pop into the school, which was always a cause for excitement amongst the students. She would always make point of coming to see Jandray. Sartora's own child was in Jandray's class. Altera reminded Jandray of her mother at her age. He made a point of showing no favouritism. That cannot be said of Sartora though. She had ensured that Altera was in Jandray's class when it came to the final years of her education. It was very unusual for two children from the same community to remain within their community school. The one child from the local community normally was the offspring of a member of the local council, and there was almost an unwritten view that this child was highlighted for leadership. It meant that the child had extra responsibilities to ensure that the other eleven students were welcomed and understood the community. It also meant that the child, whilst having the benefit of staying at home during school terms, had to be hosted in turn by each community during holidays.

How Sartora had managed to convince Elder Farrender to allow Altera to remain had never been revealed. Regardless, it was a source of quiet pride for Jandray that Altera was in his class. It was a shame that in recent visits to the school Sartora did not seem at all happy. The usual glow in her eyes and the lilt in her voice seem tempered with some hidden sadness. Jandray had no idea why this change had taken place. There were rumours that Sartora and her husband were estranged, but these were only rumours. Tasren had taught Jandray to treat such rumours with little respect. The most important thing was that whatever problems Sartora was facing right now it did not seem to have negatively impacted on Altera. She was growing into a well adjusted adult and her friendship group in school was extensive and positive. The only difference this meant was that Jandray had thirteen students in his class, rather than the normal twelve. Some would say that this was unlucky, but Jandray had no time for such views. There were twelve communities, twelve mountains, and also Queen Mountain - that made thirteen - the logic sat well with him.

Jandray heard a quiet rustle of leaves and Tasren appeared at the entrance to the main room where Jandray was sat with his reflections. She always tried to give him space and time to himself, often telling him that it was no life to be still living with his mother. However, they both knew that Tasren was as devoted to Jandray as he was to her. There was never any conflict and both existed in an atmosphere of peace and quiet. "How are things progressing this year?" said Tasren. Such a wide question could have drawn many answers, but Jandray was aware of the real question that Jandray was asking as she asked each year. What she really meant was "Are you going to enter the selection this year?" It was a routine that took place between every year and Jandray gave the same answer "Mother, you know that I have no intention of entering my name in the selection." At this point, both would smile and Tasren would the say "Well, you never know, it could be the making of you." The immediate retort was "Mother, you have already made me what I want to be." A hint of remorse seemed to reflect in Tasren's eyes and then it was gone. "Ah well", she said, "perhaps one day."

After this short conversation Tasren informed Jandray that she was off to her bed, commenting as she always did that "the number of Winter sleeps in front of me is reducing each year", to which Jandray would reply "and you will keep saying that for many years to come." Jandray then returned to his thoughts and continued to plan how he was going to address the seriousness of the Winter Sleep to his students. How was he going to ensure they saw beyond the excitement, the celebrity…. The Ice Wall? And it was a serious matter.

The Winter Sleep was fundamental to the survival of all within the Hiber Nation. It really was a matter of life or death. Perhaps he would use the example of the trees, and how they also went to sleep each Winter, to arise stronger each Spring, and they did this without anyone to watch over them. No one knew how long the trees had been part of the Hiber Nation, all they did know was that they existed far into the past, appearing not long after the first land was formed. The only thing older than the trees was the land itself. And the most obvious manifestation of this land, other than the Ice Wall, were the mountains that circled the Hiber Nation. And one mountain in particular was located at the centre of the Hiber Nation. It was acknowledged as the Queen of all mountains.

The Queen Mountain was higher than all other mountains in the Hiber Nation. The wide circular mountain range that made an impenetrable winter barrier around this land were collectively called the Winter Watchkeepers. It was from this name that the HiberWatchers derived their name. The HiberWatchers would protect the Hiber Community as the Winter Watchkeepers did the Queen Mountain. No one really knew how high each of the Watchkeepers summits were. They stretched into the sky and it was permanent winter at their highest slopes. The most intrepid Hiber explorer had only navigated a tiny proportion of the mountain range and it's truly vast height. There were twelve mountains that formed this range, and from these mountains, the twelve Hiber Communities grew and flourished. Each mountain provided the rich and abundant soil that fed the nation And the Queen Mountain towered above the whole mountain range. If the height of the each of the "Watchkeepers" could not be guessed, the height of the Queen Mountain appeared infinite. On and clear day, the true size of the Queen Mountain was almost beyond comprehension.

A giant lake circled the Queen Mountain like a natural moat. This lake was fed by the melting snow of the twelve mountains and the Queen Mountain herself. In turn, this lake and its rivers helped irrigate the lowlands of the Hiber Nation. In Winter, a "bridge" of ice formed across the lake. This bridge allowed all the Hiber Nation and all living animals to enter into caverns at the centre of the Queen Mountain. Looking from above, it would have been clear that the Queen Mountain and the Winter Watchkeepers were a range of dormant volcanoes, with the Queen Mountain being the mother of them all. Over millennia, the Watchkeepers had created the lava and the ash which eventually created the rich soils that fed the Hiber Nation. And the Queen Mountain, so majestic in stature, still harnessed a volcanic warmth within it massive caves that allowed the Hiber Nation to survive the harshest of winters.

As Tasren settled into her night-time routine, Jandray felt that it would be many hours before his mind would be ready to rest. Just thinking about the vastness of the subject, and how to distill it into a discussion with teenage students never got any easier. Like all things, some students were completely disinterested in the history of the land. Some loved the concept of the HiberWatcher and the celebrity status it brought, but thought nothing more about the wider story that unfolded each year.

The miracle of three months sleep followed by the awakening and the new growth that Spring brought each year was an amazing subject. However, other students focussed on elements such as how all the wild animals and birds knew when to sleep also. The more inquisitive wanted to know where they slept. They were to learn that the Queen Mountain had many caverns in which each strand of life's rich diversity had a winter sanctuary. Some marvelled over the trees and how they turn almost to glass; how each survived the intense winter intact. Jandray would encourage those students in particular to think of becoming tree gardeners when they finished their studies. Tree gardeners were highly sought after within all communities. Their skills were at the centre of Hiber life.

Animal husbandry for the benefit of producing meat to eat didn't exist in the Hiber Nation as all life was deemed sacred. Animals were kept in agricultural and also domestic settings. Some of these animals willingly gave their strength to pulling farming tools, removing tree branches that had been shed and a range of other agrarian tasks. Other animals gave of their milk. Hiber cheese was renowned for its flavour. However, many animals were wild and roamed free. They had no fear of people, and people had no fear of them. Only one breed of animal had the ability to survive the full winter awake. This animal was known as a Watch Hound. They were small population of loyal but ferocious hounds that had thick coats that helped them stay warm in the deepest of winter. However, even they couldn't stay outside for long in deepest winter. Their key role was companionship for the two HiberWatchers and to help identify any potential threat to those at sleep. The Watch Hounds had their own hierarchy and no-one knew (other than perhaps the Hiber Key keepers), how they somehow managed to carry out their own selection to choose two hounds who would remain awake with the HiberWatchers, whilst their kindred also slept.

The other key work in the nation was that of crop farming. Over generations the Hiber Nation had carefully cultivated the soils around each community and it provided for the majority of their needs. Plants were cultivated from which all their clothing and other coverings were derived. Crops provided the food for each table. Any excess was carefully stored and limited amounts of surplus crops were traded with the country beyond the border of the Hiber Nation. This country was due south and their inhabitants did not sleep in winter. They didn't need to as the winters further south were not as severe. However, this meant that their communities were in need of extra food in winter and the Hiber crop was very sought after. Only a few Hiber leaders were chosen to liaise with this outside nation. Not in a disparaging way, the people of this country were just called the 'Long Eaters' as they needed food all year round.

Jandray was forbidden to discuss the Long Eaters with his students. It was generally accepted that those of the Hiber Nation were no better than these people, but were distinctly different. The culture of the Winter Sleep, the husbandry of trees and crops and the sacred nature of all living things were not shared by this other land. What little Jandray did know about the neighbouring country was that there always seemed tension amongst the Elders of the Hiber communities if trade was discussed. Not that Jandray ever attended Elder meetings, it was just what he had heard. Some within the Hiber communities wanted more trade with the Long Eaters, some wanted less. All that Jandray wanted was continuing peace. In the annals of Hiber history, there was mention of conflict over the years, where the Hiber Nation had been attacked. However, this history was rarely discussed and any attempt to learn more was discouraged by the Elders and by the Hiber Library Key Keepers. These history keepers literally held the keys to the Hiber library. Those subjects were for another day thought Jandray. No use thinking about a country he couldn't visit and Elder conversations that he couldn't join!

Jandray's eyes began to feel as heavy as new winter snow and he knew he must at least have a clear plan for the next few weeks of lessons. He decided to start with harnessing the excitement that surrounded the selection for the HiberWatchers as this would gain his students interest. He would then use this subject to cover the key issues about preparations for the Winter Sleep, together with slowly unpacking with his students the potential for their future careers. Whilst it was their parents, Elders and their wider community who would ultimately choose for them he could, at least, have an input into this within his role as teacher in the Hiber community. At the cross-community teaching events that he regularly attended he had discovered that many teachers did not think that this was their role. In fact he had been at odds with the Teaching Council on occasion when he had stretched too far the curiosity of his students. How many times had he heard an Elder say, "teachers for teaching, farmers for farming, gardeners for gardening." Whilst Jandray was fully aware that living in community meant personal sacrifice for the greater good there was a risk to a curious mind if it wasn't given access to a diversity of thought. He had been fortunate. His mother had let him decide what he felt he could contribute most to the community. Ultimately, it was teaching that fed his desire to foster curiosity and awareness amongst his "flock". He felt each student who had truly explored the options would be far better at their chosen role than a student forced into one by his parents or his community.

As he started to formulate the lessons he was reminded of an ancient poem that his mother used to sing to him. He could only remember a few lines now and he was sure that the history of this poem would be in the library. However, he had never found it despite the active support from the Key keepers. Perhaps it was a good start to the subject matter. He would see:-

"The HiberWatchers watch, and the sleepers sleep

The Queen protects them all in her keep

Winter falls, and deep cold it does bring

And the world will refresh when we wake in Spring"

Chapter Two

The Hiber Elder Council was still in session as Jandray was preparing for sleep. In reality, they were thinking more of their beds than they were of the subject at hand. They could be forgiven for this basic need of rest. Since early in the morning they had been discussing plans for the Winter Sleep. It seemed ironic to Queen Torcas that the subject of sleep was preventing all of them from having any. She looked to her left and smiled as she saw that her husband King Nilan was stifling a yawn. "Don't make it too obvious that you are tired" she quietly said to Nilan, "some may think you are not interested." "I was interested twelve hours ago, and I will be interested tomorrow" he equally quietly replied. "But I must say, that my interest level right now is more fixed on a warm hearth, a late supper, and the warmth of my wife laying next to me." Even at their age, Torcas and Nilan remained totally in love with each other. They were as committed to each other as the day they had fallen in love. Their long years had seen both sadness and loss, but overall, it was a marriage they celebrated every day. They were equals, their titles meant very little to them. However, their role within the Council was of utmost importance to them.

There were sixteen members of the Elder council, which included the Queen and King, one Elder from each of the Hiber Communities, and the two Hiber Library Key Keepers. The Key Keepers did not have voting rights but were there to pass on their wisdom and also to research issues raised when necessary. As the ones who protected the library they were essential to the recording of decisions at Council in order for there to be a Hiber record of whatever was decided. In Hiber culture, all votes needed unanimous agreement to be passed. This was a fundamental aspect of their community. Everyone's views were important and all opinions were equally valid. Community was about the greatest good for all the community. It was accepted that this didn't always mean that everyone agreed. However, the key issue was that everyone agreed that a united view was a most critical aspect of Hiber society. Anything else would begin to fracture the strength of a community that had survived for generations. Each Elder was both a leader for the Hiber Nation and a servant for their community. They were chosen for their willingness to collaborate rather than compete.

That's not to say the Elders always agreed with each other. Whilst the communities of the Hiber Nation were harmonious, they were not perfect. Individual personalities meant that some Elders naturally sided with each other and deep seated rivalries, sometimes generational, often got in the way of the right thing to do. It was fair to say however, that in the main, after exhausting all the options, the Council generally came to unanimous decisions. This meant that bruised personalities and trampled hopes had to be part of the life of an Elder. An Elder could be any age and it was not, necessarily, a life time appointment. At any time an Elder could step down and nominate a successor. Generally speaking this only happened when an Elder felt that they wanted to retire. Occasionally, an Elder resigned when they had felt so strongly about an issue which was not agreed upon by the Council. The Hiber culture dictated that a majority view was not sufficient, all Elders fell in line and made a decision unanimous when a majority view was reached. The wiser and, perhaps, the more humble Elders accepted this. Those with strong and less than humble characteristics found this much harder to do.

The current Council had been notified that Elder Farrender had decided to step down from her role at the end of Autumn. This would mean that a new Elder would need to be approved. A side debate had already commenced on who would be the new Elder. What made this event a great deal more interesting was that Elder Farrender was the Elder for the Paltir community in which the Queen and King had always been based. Farrender had been Elder of the Paltir community for many years and had provided wise counsel over all that time. She never put her own community before that of the other eleven communities, a failing that some Elders seemed happy to make. She voted with her heart for the whole country. "Strength is found within difference, and success is made in full community" were her watchwords. The Queen and King had made no secret of their sorrow that the loss of Farrender would be to the Council, and they had actively sought her advice on a potential replacement. With her trademark humility all Farrender would say was "our community has the wisdom to make the decision and the humility to live with its consequences", or in other terms - the community will make the right choice and will have to live with the decision if a mistake was made.

It was widely known that Lorsern was a one of the frontrunners for the role. Lorsern was highly intelligent, and had a reputation for making difficult decisions in his role in the local Paltir council where he served under Farrender's leadership. However, if truth be known, Farrender had real reservations about this man. Whilst he always said the right thing and whilst he did work hard for the local community, he was also, by Hiber standards, incredibly self-seeking. Thankfully the weaknesses in his character had not been passed to his son Maltas. Maltas was in the same class as Altera, both in under Jandray's care. Farrender had heard that Maltas was quiet and considerate, most unlike what she saw in his father. What was the making of difficult situation in Council was that Farrender felt that Altera's mother, Sartora, would be the natural successor to her. However, Sartora was very young in comparison to the ages of the other Elders. Whilst the other Elders would not have a direct choice in the next Elder for Paltir, and neither would Farrender, it was natural that they would bring their individual influences to bear on those making the decision.

And so there would be two different selections this year. Not only would the whole Hiber Nation see who had been selected for the two HiberWatchers, the Paltir community represented by Farrender would also vote on a new Elder. All three names would be announced at the same time with the new Elder leading their community into the Winter Sleep as their first leadership role. This event was due to take place at one of the two key festivals of the year. In early Winter, just as snow began to fall, there was the Winter Festival. The first winter snow also coincided with the ice bridge starting to form. All of the Hiber Nation became coated in a frosting of snow, and the trees stared to take on their crystal form.

Farrender's attention was suddenly brought into stark focus as she heard one the other Elders, a man called Delcant, begin to speak. Delcant represented the Decinter community, which was closest to Tukerland, the only populated nation that bordered with the Hiber Nation. As Farrender, and indeed all the Council had begun to expect, he was starting to expand on his longstanding narrative, that of extending trade with Tukerland. "We cannot delay progress any more" said Delcant. "Yet another year will pass and we will not have had any movement on this issue which is so important to our nation." A murmur went across the room of the council and Farrender looked closely to assess who was in agreement and those, like her, who were cautious and concerned about Delcant and his motives. Farrender stood up as he talked. As with established etiquette, she looked at the Queen and King to seek permission to enter the discussion. King Nilan nodded to Farrender and she opened her reply with question, "Progress for who Elder Delcant? Progress for the Hiber Nation, progress for Tukerland, or progress for Elder Delcant's personal desires?" A tense atmosphere fell across the room. It was not at all like Farrender to speak so bluntly to anyone, especially to an Elder.

For a few short moments Delcant remained silent although his face betrayed the anger that was within his impending reply. "Elder Farrender must withdraw her question, and especially apologise for her slanderous accusation that I am somewhat benefiting personally from this trade. If she cannot substantiate this absurd diatribe, she should withdraw the accusation." Farrender was in no mood to withdraw any aspect of her question. She knew that other Elders around the room had also heard the rumours of Delcant living a life beyond the humble existence expected of an Elder. "My question was in three parts, and we need an answer to each. Two of them are for open discussion in this forum, but I guess the final question can only be answered by Elder Delcant. Information I have from sources I am not prepared to reveal has indicated disturbing activity in some parts of the Decinter community. The most obvious one is pressure on the tree gardeners to extend the home of Elder Delcant and to use saplings from other communities. One could almost assert that Elder Delcant was trying to usurp the immense building we currently sit in!"

Elder Farrender had impeccable sources across all communities which, to be fair, most of the Elders also had. The impression on the faces of some of the Elders gave indication to an unsaid agreement that they too had heard of this activity. "This is nonsense", said Elder Delcant, "Bring direct evidence to me of such activities and I will gladly answer to this. Rather, I think it is the jealous rant of an Elder soon to go into retirement." Perhaps Elder Delcant should have stopped there but he couldn't help to try to elevate his position. "In fact", he said, "there are those local leaders within the Paltir community who feel that perhaps the Queen and King should move their home around the communities on frequent basis."

Queen Torcas and King Nilan looked at each other and could see the subterfuge behind Elder Delcant's answer. All Elders knew that the Library and the proximity of the Paltir community to the Ice Bridge and the Ice Wall had made it a natural "capital" for the Hiber Community. There had never been any elitism about this. The Paltir community was the first community to exist and the eleven further communities had grown and had been planted from this "First Community". Everyone had accepted that the "First family" from which the King and Queen were descended did not denote a level of superiority, rather that it signified the genesis of their whole nation. However, the Queen and King also had excellent sources across their communities and they knew that Elder Delcant had begun to try and grow and extend his own home within the meeting place for the local Decinter community. Elder Farrender had echoed their own private concerns; that Delcant was starting to create dissension within the Hiber Nation.

Elder Caltan, from Nicenter, the nearest neighbour to Decinter community stood to speak. It would be no surprise if Caltan supported Delcant and that is exactly what he did. "Dear Council members, I wish to add my concerns to that of our eminent Elder Delcant. There is no truth in these vile rumours that Elder Farrender has so malevolently posed in her question. I also request that she withdraw the question." "So", thought Torcas, "is this how it was going to be?" Generally speaking the Elders, if there were any fractures in agreement, tended to split geographically. Perhaps this was understandable. Those closest to Tukerland had most to gain from trade. However, they also had most to lose should Tukerland ever wished to invade the Hiber Nation. Such conflict had not existed for many generations but Torcas and Nilan knew, through the extensive teaching from the Key Keepers, that this had not always been the case. "The Long Conflict", as it was known, had taken many lives. Infants had no idea that the true meaning of the term "Long Eaters" had come from this war and some of the untold atrocities that the warriors of this country had brought to the battlefield. A shiver ran through Torcas as she thought of the impact that conflict would bring. Suffering to both the Hiber Nation and Tukerland. A level of suffering and loss that had to be avoided. She needed to bring the conversation back to a central point that all could agree on before positions became entrenched.

"Elder Delcant, I am sure that Farrender was just voicing concerns she has heard, and in no way wished to challenge your integrity", said Torcas staring pointedly at Farrender. "Whilst Farrender has a right to ask the first two questions, I would think that, on reflection, she will happily withdraw the third question." Torcas knew that Farrender would immediately acquiesce, she was wise enough to do so and close enough a friend to know that Torcas needed this for the unity of the council. "Queen Torcas, in view of your request and your wise words I do withdraw the final part of the question…. for another time." Elder Delcant had started to look triumphant as Farrender had started to speak but then his anger returned. "For another time" he slowly repeated, "For another time, what kind of answer is this?" Before Farrender could respond, King Nilan stepped in. "Elder Delcant, your concerns about Farrender's accusation are very valid." Delcant immediately started to smile. "So, I will personally arrange a visit to your community to re-assure you that I will ensure that Elder Farrender fully withdraws her question when it is shown that her sources are wrong." The smile immediately left Delcant's face.

"A masterstroke", Torcas thought to herself. Elder Delcant had walked and talked himself into a personal visit from the King. Elder Delcant had realised this too and was attempting to formulate a reply. All he could say was "Of course the King will be most welcome." Farrender, wisely, and not without a great deal of satisfaction, sat down and said no more on the matter. "Now that this has been agreed" stated Queen Torcas, "The key issues we do need to discuss are that of the HiberWatcher Selection and the election of a new Elder for the Paltir community. In view of the unfinished business between Elder Farrender and Elder Delcant, I suggest that, breaking with tradition, we move the election of a new Elder to Spring. All agreed?" As she looked around the room, the Queen saw that most were in agreement. "A formal show of hands then Elders please." Eleven of the Elders agreed immediately. Only the hand of Elder Delcant remained firmly by his side. King Nilan slowly focussed his attention towards Elder Delcant's direction. His piercing blue eyes held steady as he searched Delcant for an answer. The King stood and started to speak. "It has been our desire to always have unanimous agreements within Council, despite any disagreements on that journey. Elder Delcant do you want to be the first Elder to break with that tradition. Is that part of the progress you are seeking at this Council?" Elder Delcant realised that he was quickly going to be at odds with most of his Elders as he saw the disappointment and anger starting to build. "Not at all,

King Nilan, I apologise for giving that impression", as he, very unwillingly, raised his hand.

"Excellent" said the Queen as she also stood up. "In order for full unity to be restored, and to ensure that Elder Delcant and Elder Farrender are on the same page on this, I recommend that Elder Farrender join the King on his visit to Decinter. This way she can be the first to apologise to our esteemed Elder Delcant when he proves her concerns unfounded." "Absolutely" was the immediate reply from Elder Farrender. "I am at your command and I promise, before this Council, that I will be the first to admit my concerns are unfounded at the appropriate time." Delcant and Farrender's eyes met fleetingly. Both of them knew that Farrender would not be needing to apologise, and that Delcant needed to get back to his community as soon as possible to assess his next options. "Shall we agree a date for the visit?" said King Nilan. Delcant replied, "time is getting short, perhaps this can wait until the Spring also?" At this Queen Torcas smiled indulgently and said, "Elder Delcant, surely you don't want this matter of your integrity to sleep with you over Winter, how about two weeks from now?" The lack of reply from Delcant was taken for consent and King Nilan said "So, that is settled then."

It was now getting late. Whilst the excitement of the dissension between two long-standing Elders had kept energy and attention levels high it had not created a positive environment for further discussion. The final unanimous agreement was that the Council meeting would end without further issues being discussed, and that they would all return to their communities to prepare for the Selection and for the Winter Sleep. All Elders were keen to see how their local leadership groups had driven the local plans in their absence. Moving all twelve communities into the safety of Queen Mountain was a significant logistical matter. Regardless of the fact that this migration was an annual event, factors such as population increases, and changes in harvest yields meant that it had unique challenges each year.

As the Elders began to slowly leave the council chamber Elder Delcant purposefully walked over to the Queen and King. They were in conversation with the Key

Keepers ensuring that an accurate record of the meeting was prepared and stored in the library. "Can I assume that the usual agreements on limited trade with Tukerland can still take place amongst the communities closest to them geographically? Decinter is always the main conduit for export of those stores that will not survive in our barns over Winter, and I had plans to progress this upon my return from Council" said Delcant. "Of course", replied King Nilan. "I can join you and see first-hand how those negotiations take place. It has been a few years since any from the First Family have joined you in those meetings. It will show the Council's support to you and this will be essential, going forward, if trade does change in future years." He smiled at Delcant, turned sharply and left the chamber. "Elder Delcant" said Queen Torcas, "This has been a great meeting for you. Not only has King Nilan agreed to ensure the concerns of Farrender are addressed as soon as possible in order to minimise any harm to your reputation. In addition he will be able to support you in the discussions with the Tukerland leadership. You must be so pleased." An enigmatic smile appeared on her face as she was saying this. For Elder Delcant it was quite the opposite. It couldn't have been a worse outcome. However, he was nothing if not persistent, and he knew that Farrender would step down in Spring. His plans were delayed, damaged slightly but by no means at an end. And, he thought to himself, that when Lorsern took over the Eldership of the Paltir Community things would look very different. Now he had to concentrate all his considerable influence to make that happen. "Of course", he replied to Queen Torcas. "Your wise intervention ensures unity and I am in your debt." Silently, he said to himself, "And you will all be in mine soon enough when my plans reach fruition."

Chapter Three

Tukerland's ruler was meeting with his warrior leaders ahead of their normal trade negotiations with the Hiber Nation. Sargern, the Leader of Tukerland, was a large and intimidating man. Tukerland had always valued athleticism over intellect and Sargern fitted this stereotype entirely. Neither was Tukerland a democracy. Sargern had seized control and subsequent rule of this land through force. That was over twenty years ago and Sargern had now started to look for possible usurpers in the making. He had no doubt that history would repeat itself and a young pretender would challenge him for the rule of this country. Sargern had always felt it was better to be feared that liked and his inner circle helped perpetuate that fear within the wider leadership. Sargern was loyal to his warrior elite and became blind to their weaknesses and their excesses. But if that loyalty was ever put in doubt, that bond was severed, usually at the head!

However, to the wider nation he was viewed with great respect, and even a form of love. He had achieved this by ruthlessly putting down all rebellious factions across Tukerland. What had once been a nation of warring states was now a strong, and on the face of it, a united nation. It would probably never be as united as its neighbour, The Hiber Nation, but at least Tukerland regional clans were not killing each other on a regular basis as had been the case in the past. Peace itself had caused a new problem. Over the years, war had kept the population of Tukerland within its ability to feed itself. War had a habit of reducing hungry mouths to feed. Peace had brought a larger population than had ever been experienced in Tukerland and this was a hungrier population as well. This was the main subject of today's meeting.

As he looked around his Warrior Hall, based within his palatial enclosure, Sargern knew that as his athleticism and sheer size started to diminish with age he would need to use more than just brute force to remain in power. For this reason he had started to include within his warrior leadership those who could bring what he lacked; diplomacy and an acute and strategic mind. He also expected these members of the group to identify any warriors who were getting ideas about replacing him. Several promising warriors has lost their heads in drink only to lose their head in reality when their intoxicated bragging had reached the ears of Sargern. In reality he was the least worst option when it came to being united as a country. Most people, who had any ability or inclination to do anything about it, saw that Sargern kept an effective control and hold over the warring nature of the Tukerland clans, and had done so for 20 years. No one was starving and no region had to face the fear of their greatest risk to life being their own neighbour. If Sargern chopped a few heads off here and there, then that was for the greater good as far as they could see.

Very few people in Tukerland knew what a real community, built on supportive leadership and equality, could be. Yes, they knew that they had a neighbour called the Hiber Nation but their wider knowledge of this country and its culture was relatively unknown. Schools, as they existed in Tukerland, pursued martial subjects as well as ironmongery and farming. Girls went to school and they had equal rights in that they could follow martial subjects too. Over the years, Sargern had realised that women were just a capable and equally as dangerous as men. For that reason a number of them had also lost their lives at his hands. And even more at the hands of his wife Baltock. She was, in all respects a warrior Queen, and Sargern a warrior King. Sargern had refused that title as he felt that his killing of the last King dictated a time to make a change. He felt that future leadership should be on merit not bloodline. However, that view was becoming more and more unpalatable to him as he realised that his strength would fade in time. Perhaps he had been too hasty in removing the title of King.

In some respects, Baltock was the only person that Sargern was afraid of. His other challengers over the years had been strong but had ultimately been despatched. Baltock professed her love for Sargern, but he knew that this love was dependent on him remaining as ruler. If Tukerland had been ready for a warrior Queen to lead them then he had no doubt that Baltock would have been a very real enemy. However, she was as clever as she was strong. She knew that her time had not yet come and that Sargern was a necessary partner in her plans. She was younger than Sargern and could bide her time and whilst she did, she would ensure he provided children that would be her protection when her strength also began to fade.

Sargern and Baltock had four children, three men and one woman. The youngest was called Saltock. He was now nineteen years old and was a disappointment to Baltock. The other three children had already took their places in the warrior elite. They loved their father and did his bidding. Saltock had proved able in martial skills, but was slighter in stature than his brothers. That said, he was still an imposing figure. His tall and wiry physique made him look more like a twin to his slightly older sister. That was where the similarities ended. His sister, Balger, was considered a loner and an unfeeling individual. Her whole life she tried to emulate her mother and had taken some of the worst traits of her mother. She had taken the strength of her father but without any thought at all to the need to have a loyal network around her. In fact, other than her mother, whom she idolised, the only person that sparked any level of interest in her was Saltock. He had no idea why she liked him but he was grateful for this fact. Saltock was highly intelligent and was someone who could make friends easily. He put people at ease with his humility and his humour. He could, on occasion, even make his sister smile.

Now that Saltock was nineteen years old it was time that he took his place amongst the warrior leaders that surrounded his father. It quickly became apparent to Sargern that his son's intellect would be essential in progressing a positive relationship with the Hiber Nation. Saltock had already met the main negotiator, an elderly man called Delcant. Whilst Delcant was always friendly, sycophantically so, there was something about him that made Saltock uneasy. One of the strengths of the Tukerland ruling elite was that they spoke as they found and generally there was little subterfuge in their dealing with anyone. In the main, this was encouraged by all. It wasn't perfect because it also had the habit of creating tensions. However, these tensions were usually quelled by Sargern. This straight speaking manner was always encouraged by Sargern, up to a point. He was happy to be challenged on anything other than his right to lead. As long as a warrior avoided any hint of challenge to Sargern's authority they could speak freely and were encouraged to do so by Sargern.

Having experienced this level of candid discussion within his own warrior colleagues, experiencing Delcant's approach to negotiation made Saltock uncomfortable. He had grown into a man who was not only highly intelligent but also a man of integrity. He knew that the failings of his father and mother, perceived as strengths amongst many people, would not maintain peace forever. He could see that Sargern was increasingly worried about challenges to his leadership. He could also see that his mother had characteristics similar to Delcant. She could be incredibly devious in her dealings with people. Those she couldn't tame with fear such as those who had Sargern's trust, she gained with a friendship that was not at all real. Saltock could see how she manipulated those around her, all to further her own ambitions. Saltock was concerned that his mother would only remain loyal to Sargern as long as he was the leader of Tukerland. When he learnt that Sargern had chosen him to meet with the Hiber Nation representatives, he was both intrigued and alarmed at this thought. Did his father also suspect Baltock's loyalty and was keeping her near to him, or was he placing Saltock to watch over Grasby the lead negotiator? Either way, he reflected on how he could maintain his own personal integrity in the discussions.

Sargern raised himself slowly from his seat at the head of the table. As the men and woman around him noticed they began to fall silent, a standard mark of respect that was expected by Sargern. No one wanted to be the last person to stop talking as this would lead to displeasure being displayed by Sargern. And displeasure from Sargern could be life-limiting. "Warrior Leaders of Tukerland" Sargern exclaimed, "as is usual at this time of year, we need to discuss our plans to feed our fellow warriors and their kin during the winter period ahead, whilst our neighbours in the Hiber Nation take the easy option and sleep through winter." Sargern waited as the expected laughter that followed such a retort built and then subsided. "We do not have that luxury as we do not have the facilities to enable a long winter's nap!" Further raucous shouts commenced and then faded away. "And, over the years, none of our communities would have the confidence that our erstwhile colleagues in neighbouring clans wouldn't have killed us all in our sleep!" Whilst this was said in a jovial manner by Sargern the older ones present in the meeting nodded in agreement that there was a great deal of truth in that statement.

Sargern continued, "However, we are stronger than we have ever been. Peace reigns amongst our Tukerland clans and the Hiber Nation remains a peaceful neighbour." Sargern paused to take a long draught from his oversized cup which was, in reality, a large jug. "And why would we want to lose valuable drinking time by sleeping more than we needed to?" At once all the warriors jumped to their feet and raised their cups and other drinking utensils in the air. Not many succeeded in sitting back down without spilling great deal of the alcoholic beverage contained within. Tukerland beer was drunk at every meal and had grades of strength. The Evening beer was particularly strong. Beers for breakfast were commensurately weaker and this was watered down for the younger members of the community.

Baltock looked around her and then at Sargern. "Husband", she shouted above the mayhem around them, "you have lost none of your skills at warming up your leaders" and she smiled indulgently at him. "Perhaps we should get them to the matter at hand before the evening wears on and our leaders will be too intoxicated to agree to anything." Sargern turned to Baltic and said, "There is a benefit to having our leaders too drunk to remember what they agreed to. They are too proud to admit later that they cannot hold their drink. I have got my way many a time with the support of a good amount of drink being consumed by those I have been 'encouraging' to my way of thinking. And you have also used that particular skill against me on more than one occasion too." Baltock just smiled knowingly at Sargern and retorted, "Perhaps husband, perhaps.... But I would never say you couldn't hold your drink, you always remain in full control of your tongue and your views." Whilst this was not necessarily true, Baltock still ensured her husband's ego was stroked. It was one of the many ways she ensured the longevity of her control over him.

"You are quite right" Sargern replied, and at that he called the meeting back to order. "Leaders of Tukerland, despite my making light of the situation, we do have important things to discuss." At this point, Saltock began to take more interest. He had casually joined in the jovial nature of the meeting at this point. If any had carefully watched him they would have noted that very little alcohol had reached his lips, but much had been spilt. This meant that those who were serving the leaders, and those seeing his cup being re-filled, thought he as as intoxicated as they were. In fact, he was totally sober and ready to speak when called upon by his father. Whilst he couldn't rouse their joviality in the same way as his father, he was a very popular young man and knew he would have their ears when he needed them.

"My son, Saltock, is joining the small group who have been chosen to meet with the Hiber Nation, to discuss plans for trade before the Hiber Nation's annual sleep." To maintain the manufactured sense of this event being a weakness of the Hiber folk, he continued, "Before they get too sleepy, we must agree transactions to increase our store of food. And I for one would not be a pleasant person if I lose out on my regular stock of Hiber cheese!" A grunt of general agreement met this statement. The trade from the Hiber Nation brought a great deal of high quality produce to add to the general food produced in Tukerland. "And we, as the best brewers of beer anywhere in our two countries, have had an excellent harvest. I know the Hiber Nation will want a good stock for both their Early winter festival, and for it to be laid down ready for their Spring Awakening." Again the nods around the room gave assent for Sargern to continue. "The fact is that if we do not agree in good time the trade for this year, the winter snow will be amongst us. The pass into the Hiber Nation via the Decinter route will be closed as the snow and ice closes off their country and their trade goods to us. To all purposes, Hiber will be dead to us, as will anything that tries to remain outside of their Queen Mountain's protection."

"With your indulgence I will ask Saltock to take you through our plans for the meeting." All those present agreed. Only one person was unhappy with the indulgence. Warrior Grasby was a longstanding member of the warrior elite. He was the same age as Sargern and, at one time, had felt he could have been the leader of Tukerland. However, his martial skills were no match for Sargern, even though his intellect was more than a match. Over the years he had decided that friendship would bring him more than enmity. He had slowly built his way into Sargern's inner circle of advisors and was, perhaps, one of his closest advisors. What Sargern didn't realise was that he also had the ear of Baltock. Grasby wasn't a friend of Sargern, there was only one person in the room that could be described as that.

Warrior Nirtan was also the same age as Sargern. He had a proud demeanour balanced by a humility that was rare amongst the Tukerland warriors. However, he was a skilled fighter and was also thought to be one of the most intelligent leaders within Sargern's inner circle Little was known about Nirtan's family, it was said that he was an orphan that had grown like a weed amongst the wandering peoples displaced in the wars prior to the peace that Sargern now rigidly enforced. Nirtan's only companion was his servant - Mortarn. As this was a warrior leaders meeting, Mortarn was only present to serve his master his beer. In reality, Mortarn was watching everything that took place, and he would discuss the whole meeting with Nirtan late into the evening.

Grasby had plans, big plans, plans so audacious he felt that it would launch him into being the only possible ruler of Tukerland. He would force a return to the basic instincts of this warrior nation, and it would bring long term prosperity; to his country and to him personally. All that was needed was the time, the energy and the spark. Sargern was getting too comfortable with peace. Grasby could seen that in the way that he was starting to trust more and more decisions to others. And he could see it in the increased amount of revelry and drinking that Sargern enjoyed. Whilst he was still more than a match for many of his age, and even for most men much younger, it was clear that Sargern could also perceive that his hold on this highly combative warrior elite could only last for a finite time.

There was a period when none of the warriors would have supported these views. But vitriolic words, dripped into conversations at appropriate times, had started to gain traction for Grasby. It would only be a matter of time before he could start to put real plans into action. In his meetings with Delcant at the negotiations in recent years he had found a similarly devious individual; one who only had a heart for his own advancement. However, Grasby knew that whatever benefit he would gain from the traitorous Delcant in the short term, he would also sweep Delcant aside in the longer term. Delcant was devious and self-seeking. With being from the Hiber Nation, however, he had not got the long history, or the 'pedigree' as Grasby liked to think, to truly make decisions that could lead to many deaths. Grasby was old enough to remember the times before peace was achieved in Tukerland. Unfortunately, he was also old enough to have turned those memories into romantic ideas of heroes and epic battlefield victories. He had forgotten the pain and loss that had been visited on many people as a result of these battles.

"Let me listen to what Saltock has to say", said Grasby quietly to himself. "Saltock may have his uses if I can bend him to my will", he thought as he sat quietly listening and smiling to himself. Grasby was equally aware that he could also be making a big mistake. Would his estimation of Saltock be incorrect and have consequences beyond what he could imagine? If so, they would significantly, possibly terminally, impact on his plans to seize the leadership of Tukerland. If the worse came to the worst, Saltock would have to go the same way as his father would go, painfully to death!!

Saltock surveyed the meeting. Many of those present had known him since a child. Most liked him, but he was unsure how many respected him. He knew that his position was only assured because of his father. He didn't want to let Sargern down and he also knew that his mother would be assessing his every word and would not be at all happy if he did not get his plans across clearly. If only this meeting was like the Hiber Council that he had heard rumours of. What would it be like to raise an issue and then have an informed discussion followed by a vote? This was not at all how things would happen here. Those who supported a view would try and shout down those who didn't. It wasn't unusual for meetings to deteriorate into outright fighting if a subject was not settled. Meetings could become tense and violent very quickly. Only the intervention of Sargern, on one side or the other, tended to return such events to relative calm. Then those who had lost would nurse grievances to be aired at a difference time.

Saltock commenced his prepared speech. "Our plan is to meet the Hiber Nation representatives at the Decinter community in the near future. Following this meeting we will seek as much produce as they are prepared to provide us. Coinage will not be exchanged. Rather, we will barter our beer and also our expertise at making farming tools provides us with a welcome outlet for such implements." During the generations of conflict that had taken place across Tukerland their craftsmen had become very skilled in forging weapons of war. When peace finally arrived these crafts were changed into forging tools for use in construction and farming. There was still a large amount of weapons held by Tukerland warriors but they were mainly used for civic occasions nowadays. As the Hiber Nation had never shown any hint of aggression during all this time those weapons had only ever been used on their own people. It was at an early age that a great sadness took hold of Saltock every time he remembered that the greatest craftsmen of previous generations used their art to create instruments of war. It was, he felt, one of the greatest gifts of peace; that these craftsmen could now develop instruments that help feed and plough and build, rather than weapons to maim and kill.

"With the permission of this group, and with the support of you, our Tukerland warrior elite, Grasby and I will oversee these discussions. I am sure that we can bring a very positive exchange between to our two nations." It was not the way of this group to politely clap to show their support. However, they showed their agreement by banging their vessels on the table, thereby ensuring even more beer was spilt. "As you know", he continued, "there is a limited amount of time to progress all of these issues. Whilst we can survive Winter, the Hiber Nation will have to have all agreements in place and the exchange taking place in last week of Autumn. As indicated by my father this will allow the beer to flow at their Winter festival." He paused momentarily before he added, "Although that will be a pitiful amount of beer by our standards." This was cause for another extensive round of raucous laughter and clattering of mugs and jugs. Sargern watched his son and realised that he knew how to manage this group. It was essential to encourage them to believe in the culture of Tukerland and to ensure they continued to see the Hiber Nation as a country to deal with, but one that was without threat to Tukerland.

Grasby looked on at the general agreement that Saltock was receiving from those present. He knew it wasn't the time to challenge the approach that Saltock had laid out. What he needed to do was destabilise the forthcoming meeting, he needed to precipitate a crisis where the trade negotiations faulted or became stuck in disagreement. Grasby was sure he could create this situation. He had already discussed this with Elder Delcant. Both were aware that a direct approach to challenging established trade protocols would be too great a step for the hesitant

Hiber Nation and Sargern would not want to create what he would see as unnecessary conflict. But Grasby was very sure that his devious nature, supported by the snivelling Delcant, could create an impasse. When that occurred Grasby could use the opportunity to bring his much bigger plan into operation. At the same time it would also potentially sweep Sargern and Saltock away in a very bloody coup. It was all a matter of timing. That timing would have to be carefully managed and the time was drifting away as surely as winter snows would fall in just a few weeks time.

Saltock was concerned that Grasby had said very little during the meeting. He did not trust Grasby at all and had been certain that Grasby would try and belittle his plans. The fact that he had not done so was all the more worrying. Saltock was not the only person in the meeting who thought this too. Nirtan had very similar concerns. He had expected that Grasby would use the meeting as an opportunity to grandstand as an elder statesman of Tukerland, one who would, at the very least, maximise a situation that would make it look like Saltock was a minor part in the negotiations. He would subtly ensure that he received the plaudits as the "fatherly" guide to Saltock. The fact that Grasby had not challenged Saltock's plan and had remained very much silent was something unexpected. It could only mean that Grasby had some other equally distasteful plan in mind; one that would only serve to enhance Grasby standing amongst the Warrior rulers. Sadly, as he looked to Sargern, it was clear to Nirtan that his intoxication had meant Sargern had missed this aspect of the meeting. Looking across at Baltock, Nirtan saw nothing in her face and manner to betray anything of what she may have been feeling.

What no one in the meeting was aware of was the blossoming friendship between Saltock and Nirtan. In Saltock, Nirtan filled an intellectual gap that this father could not. In Nirtan, Saltock was the son he had never known. Nirtan's friendship with Sargern had meant that he had known Nirtan since he was born. Sargern had been interested in his youngest son, and loved him, but his attention was always more focussed on his elder two sons, who were of similar stature and physical prowess as Sargern. And Baltock, while it was clear she loved Saltock, favoured her daughter, Balger.

Nirtan planned to meet with Mortarn in the morning when they would compare their recollections of the meeting and would discuss their concerns. Mortarn was the closest person to Nirtan, and Nirtan looked upon him as a brother. In the warrior hierarchy of Tukerland Mortarn was just Nirtan's servant. But only Nirtan and Mortarn knew their true history. That history needed to be kept a closely guarded secret. At some point Nirtan thought that he may decide to tell Saltock, but that time had not yet arrived. After Nirtan and Mortarn had discussed all the possible options he would then seek a meeting with Saltock. Within the Tukerland warrior elite, there would be no surprise at Nirtan and Saltock meeting. Everyone knew that they were friends. Sargern encouraged it and, in his mind, it meant that Saltock had a protector should anything happen to Sargern. Sargern had no doubt that Nirtan was absolutely loyal to him. He had proved it in battle many years ago and had saved Sargern's life on more than one occasion. During these battles Nirtan had ample opportunity to let Sargern's life end and step into a leadership role but he had never done that. Over the years, Nirtan had always been at his right hand, ever the friend and his most loyal subject.

Had they known what each was thinking, Grasby and Nirtan would have agreed that time was slipping away. It was not long before the negotiations took place. Nirtan was not part of the group visiting the Hiber community. However, it was possible that he could send Mortarn with Saltock as his hand servant. He was sure that Sargern would approve. Mortarn would be his eyes and ears and could report back at the conclusion of those negotiations. Time would bring a conclusion to Nirtan's concerns about Grasby, for good or for ill. He couldn't shake off the feeling that it wouldn't be for the good of the Hiber people, nor for Tukerland in the long run.

Chapter Four

As usual Altera was first to arrive at the classroom. She had a thirst for knowledge that mirrored her mother's when she was her age. Living at home meant that she was up as early as her mother and father who were off to work within their community. All the other students, other than Maltas who lived in Paltir also, were with their host families. Altera still wasn't certain that her mother's pressure to keep her at home was the right idea. It made her look like she was being treated differently and she felt it could make her look weak. Was she being kept at home because her mother thought that she couldn't cope with living with a host family for most of the school year? The compromise of her living with host families during school breaks did allow her to visit her neighbouring communities, however. Secretly though, Altera was pleased that she was at home. Whilst host families across the Hiber Nation were very caring, and the homes themselves were very similar in style, there was nothing quite like being at home.

Altera worked hard to befriend all the students in her class. She felt that she was almost a host in her own right. She would support homesick students just by being there for them. Her home became a refuge for all the students in her class. Her mother didn't mind this and her father was rarely present. She wasn't quite sure what was occurring between her mother and her father. There was never any conflict; there had to be proximity for this. The times that her mother and father were together in the home had become less and less in recent times. Her father did not show much attention to Altera and, to her knowledge, he never had.

Over the years Altera had learnt to manage without that fatherly support and her mother was so loving that it didn't really matter to her. Since she moved into the latter years of her eduction Jandray had become a surrogate father to her. Whilst he cared for all those in his class it was very clear to Altera, in only small ways, that she was special to him. She thought it must be because her mother had been in Jandray's first class. At that time there was barely an age difference between them. Now fifteen years had passed and Jandray had taught many classes. He had a reputation for being one of the best teachers across the whole of the Hiber communities. On many occasions he had been asked to take on a supervisory role within the wider school network. On each and every occasion he had declined. The only thing he did agree to take on was to Chair the Hiber school network. He valued visiting each school across the twelve communities and always arranged the Hiber teachers conference that occurred each year.

The next pupil to arrive in class was Maltas. Maltas was the image his father. He was athletic, intelligent and had the same thick dark hair as Lorsern. However, whilst similar in the physical sense, Maltas was the direct opposite of this father when it came to other characteristics. Maltas was humble and friendly, whilst his father was arrogant and aloof. Maltas was happy to be the friend of anyone and everyone, regardless of status, whilst his father focussed his attention on those who could support him in the local Hiber Council. Maltas was happy to be one of the crowd, where Lorsern made no secret of wanting to succeed to the Elder role when Farrender stood down. Maltas was best friends with Altera, whilst Lorsern and Sartora were totally and implacably at odds on all things. Perhaps this enmity between their parents had made them think carefully about their own friendship. Logic would dictate that Maltas and Altera would follow those fault lines. However, as soon as they had met, Maltas and Altera realised that they had so much in common that a deep friendship grew. It was totally platonic, there was never any thought of it developing further in that respect. Both knew that and both were very happy with this. They both had grown deep feelings for each other but they were bonds of friendship only. Perhaps because Altera and Maltas both had distant fathers, they found a common bond. In addition, both saw Jandray as the father they wished they had.

Slowly the other eleven students arrived into class. In the Hiber Nation, thirteen was not unlucky. In fact, as there were thirteen mountains in total within the Hiber Nation, the group had begun to see themselves as a once in a lifetime group of friends mirroring the thirteen mountains. As a result they created a name for their group - 'The Mountain Keepers'. Their informal meeting place was Altera's home. All the students enjoyed each others company and all saw Maltas and Altera as their natural leaders.

Jandray walked in the room and the students took their seats. The register was opened and Jandray went down the list. He didn't need to really as it was clear that everyone was present. However, he liked the tradition of repeating everyone's name and in the early days of a new class it ensured he remembered them. He knew that there was nothing more upsetting to a child in a new school environment than the teacher not even remembering their name.

"Maltas", "Here", was the immediate reply

"Altera", "Here"

"Fantred, "Here"

"Findren", "Here"

"Alspeth", "Here"

"Maylen", "Here"

"Junstern", "Here"

"Larpan", "Here"

"Antos", "Here"

"Calpir", "Here"

"Ocsend", "Here"

"Corprind" "Here"

"Dasbran", "Here"

"Thank you class" replied Jandray as he smiled at them all. How he managed to connect with each of them with one smile was a mystery to Altera. She watched Jandray intensely. His smile was genuine, warm and seemed to be just for you. She was not sure how he did this. What she was certain of was that he made everyone at ease. Whatever was on their minds at a particular time the permanence of his smile and his clear love for his role and for his students was obvious for all to see. If there was any jealousy it was from other students who wanted to be in their class. It wasn't that Jandray's class had the best results, or that they won the most awards. There were other classes and other teachers who took many of those accolades over the years. It was just the Jandray accepted a student as they were. If their strength was from the land, he would encourage this, if it was with trees, he would foster this interest, and if it was with organisation, he would nurture that interest. No one was left behind in Jandray's class. Everyone had worth as much as everyone was different. Jandray ensured that these differences were not seen as weaknesses, rather they were a cause for celebration.

"And so, the matter at hand" said Jandray. "The next few weeks we will study the history of the Winter Sleep; why we have it, what it means to our community, and the general logistics that are needed to ensure we all wake in Spring." Jandray continued, "Whilst you have all taken part in these events since you were born it is important, as you move to adulthood, for you to know more about our culture, our environment and the lands beyond our Mountain protectors." Jandray looked across at Corprind and Dasbran and said, "As Corprind and Dasbran will know more than most of you, our nation borders with a country called Tukerland. Whilst we are not encouraged to discuss the history of Tukerland, I feel it is important that you are aware of the trade that takes place between our nations each year. Now this has not always been the case, with trade only commencing a matter of a few years ago. The elder members of the Hiber Nation remember a time when Tukerland was a country at war, and it was only in recent decades that peace has reached that country."

Jandray stopped and reflected about where this conversation was going. He had, perhaps, already said more than the Elder Council would have approved. They did not want children to be curious about the world outside the Hiber Nation. Jandray could see their point. It was only within recent generations that Tukerland had achieved an element of stability. In the past there would have been little benefit in discussing a nation that had more interest in killing each other than anything else. Over the years it only the fact that the warring factions did not have the ability to come together to wage war on the Hiber Nation that had kept them safe from attack.

However, Jandray was sure that some of those in Tukerland viewed the vast natural resources of the Hiber Nation with eager eyes.

Jandray worried that, in time, these warriors may do more than just look at the prosperity of the Hiber Nation. He was connected enough across the communities to be aware that this fear of being subject to aggressive attention by a united Tukerland was very much in the minds of the Elder Council. Jandray pushed these fears out of his considerations and continued, "But in recent decades a positive trade has flourished between Tukerland and our nation. Our harvests are plentiful but our winters are harsh. Whilst we store enough for any risks to future harvests, there is still plenty that we can share with our neighbours. Not least because we don't eat during the Winter Sleep. As you may be aware, the citizens of Tukerland enjoy a milder winter and they do not have to enter such sleep. As a result, they need food throughout the winter." Looking around the class, he could see that his students were listening carefully. Even their parents did not talk so candidly of Tukerland, so it was exciting for them to hear, albeit in limited form, the details that Jandray was expounding.

Dasbran looked at Jandray and indicated his request to speak. Jandray noticed and said "Please Dasbran, do add to the discussion." "It is as Teacher Jandray has said" Dasbran haltingly began to speak. He had always been the quiet one of the group. Jandray knew that he came from a family where his grandfather, Delcant, was the Elder of the Decinter community. Jandray knew Delcant and was not impressed with his fawning nature with those who he felt could benefit him. He also knew that Dasbran's father was being groomed by Delcant to take his role on at some point. Even at this early stage, this brought pressure onto Dasbran, who was the grandchild of, and in time, potentially son of an Elder. Dasbran had no desire to be part of the ruling group in Decinter. His passion was the mountains. He knew every aspect of the mountain under which Decinter nestled. He had even, at risk of being punished, climbed into the high peak of Decinter mountain. No one knew this. Last summer, when the snow had retreated to its highest point, he had climbed high enough to see the homesteads on the Tukerland plains below the mountain. He had seen trees being chopped down to make the homes. He had also seen animals in large pens being herded into covered barns, and had seen carts leaving from the other side of those barns, with no obvious movement within them. He hadn't told anyone about this. If he had, they would have known he had climbed where he should not have, and he would have been in trouble.

Jandray was aware of Dasbran's passion and had encouraged him to climb the lower hills of Paltir Mountain with him. When the two of them did this, it was clear to Jandray that Dasbran was a much more proficient mountaineer than he. However, the fact that Jandray had recognised this interest in Dasbran meant that he had started to grow in confidence with the class. To the point that Dasbran said, "The Decinter community, along with the Nicenter community, and to a degree, the Octurn community, are the closest to the Tukerland border. Well, to the inhabited parts of Tukerland that is." Dasbran took a deep breath and could feel his confidence slipping. "Go ahead Dasbran", welcomed Jandray, "Please continue, I think you are in a perfect position to update the class." With this encouragement, Dasbran continued, "My grandfather is the Elder of Decinter." He said this without any element of pride, in fact it was almost with sadness in his voice that he continued, "He is one of the main trade negotiators with the Tukerland leaders each year. I don't get to see him much as it takes a lot of his time up, but he does speak with my father about it often."

Dasbran was very aware that he was almost invisible when Delcant visited his home and spoke with his father. For that reason, Delcant was not as careful as he would usually be when discussing trade issues with his father. It was not that Dasbran understood much about a lot of what was said, but he was intelligent enough to notice when the conversation became excited between his father and grandfather. Dasbran wasn't sure how to continue. He knew that the discussions were private, but he also wanted to help his fellow students understand about the trade. He carried on. "All I know that is different this year is that my Grandfather feels that there is much more trade that could take place between our two nations. I think he feels that we are too hesitant in our relationship with the Tukerland people. He was here in Paltir for the Elder Council recently and he said that the Queen and King took such interest in his views that King Nilan is going to join him in the negotiations this year."

A silence had descended over the room. Many of the students had never heard Dasbran speak for so long. Most knew of his family, but there was never a hint of boasting about his connections. It was not uncommon for family members of Elders to be in Jandray's class. Jandray was highly regarded and a number of Elders pushed for their loved ones to be hosted within the Paltir school, as it was also close to where the Elder Council met. On a family level it meant that their child could be visited after the Elder Council ended. And, for Elders who were ambitious for their offspring, it placed them in the community which was central to the Hiber Nation. Not all Elders wanted their family to be in Jandray's class, and Delcant had actively tried to have Dasbran placed with a different teacher. Delcant was aware that Jandray valued friendship, integrity and unity above accolades; not a value set that was high on Delcant's list of priorities. That said, at least Dasbran would be in the same class as Maltas and Altera. Delcant thought that Dasbran could join up with Maltas whose father was close to Delcant, and he could keep an eye on Altera. If he had known of the friendship between these three, and indeed between all the students, Delcant would have been very disappointed indeed.

Jandray stepped into the conversation, "Thank you Dasbran for that very interesting update. Perhaps you all may wish to keep that information within this class at the moment." Corprind in his characteristic blunt manner said, "Dasbran, you best listen to that advice. I wouldn't want to be on the wrong side of your grandfather or my father. Delcant is not known for his mild temper down in our community and my father seems to follow his directions - more's the pity." Corprind was as open in his emotions as any student that Jandray had met. He had no guile, and said exactly what he wanted to. His father was the Elder of Nicenter and was influential as he was needed to help with the export of grain and other arable crops to Tukerland. Sadly, Corprind's father seemed to be under Delcant's influence. Jandray always felt that those who worked the land had an ability to see beyond politics, but this was not the case for Corprind's father. Land was forever, politics and those who played it were as short-lived as the winds in Spring as far as Corprind was concerned. Without realising that he had given an insight into the unsightly character of another Elder, Corprind then sat back down. If he had been more politically aware, Jandray thought, Corprind still would have felt the same about the land. His friendship and loyalty to Dasbran was also more important to him than any risk of slighting an Elder, even it was his father. And the truth was the truth, to Corprind's mind. Delcant wasn't well liked by most reasonable people who had the misfortune to come into his area of influence.

"Thank you Corprind for your bluntness of advice to Dasbran. I am sure he will take it on board, without saying where that advice came from. You would also be advised not to upset your father, who is close to Elder Delcant I think", advised Jandray. "And so", said Jandray, "who knows what the main items for export to Tukerland are, and as importantly, what do we get in return?" A number of hands raised at this point. Whilst all the students were friends, there was still a healthy rivalry in getting Jandray's praise and attention of the wider class. "Maylen, what can you add?" Maylen was a confident young woman, and Jandray felt she was destined to work with farm animals. She had a natural ability to bring calm to a situation, learnt no doubt at her mother and father's hands in their work with those domestic stocks which eased the labours of farmers and artisans across the communities. "Well, I do know that many of our grain crops are sought after by Tukerland. Especially, the grain that they use to brew their beer. But I also know that they regular seek export of livestock which is always refused." "Very interesting", replied Jandray, "does anyone know why only food crops are exported?"

Antos raised his hand. "Please explain" said Jandray. "Well, its like this. Here in the Hiber Nation we value all life. Our animals are true friends in that they give their strength to our ploughs and transport. They give wool for our clothing and they help the nutrients of our soil. In return they ask for very little, other than not to be seen as a crop themselves." This was an excellent answer thought Jandray, he couldn't have said it better. "Do go on." Antos paused and looked at his classmates. "Those in Tukerland see animals as a source of food. They raise them to kill and eat them. They would dearly love to harness the breeding stock of our animals to produce more food. My Father said the Long Eaters not only should eat less, but should also realise that to eat another being, even though they may look like dumb animals, is not something the Hiber Nation would ever support. And for that reason, livestock export will never be agreed."

"Let's look at things from the Tukerland perspective now", replied Jandray. "What can they export to us, that we don't already have in abundance?" The strength of this particular class, felt Jandray, was that none were harnessed with a fear of looking stupid in front of their peers. This class was the closest group of students he had ever taught. And he didn't think that this was all down to him. It was clear that the friendship between Maltas and Altera, in a situation where one might have assumed would be conflict due to their parents dislike for each, had set a new standard. Similarly, Dasbran and Corprind were connected through their familial links to Elders. All those in the class were in agreement, whether consciously or not, that if Maltas and Altera could look beyond their differences, then so could all of them. Jandray thought that this was an example of the truest form of community that the Hiber Nation could aspire to.

Ocsend raised his hand and said, "Teacher Jandray, the main export from Tukerland is beer. I should know, my father does drink quite a lot of it." A ripple of laughter spread throughout the room. Ocsend's father, Ertin, owned an inn within the Octern community which, like Nicenter and Decinter was situated on the border with Tukerland. Ertin's hospitality was renowned, not only in Octern, but throughout the Hiber Nation. Whilst the trade negotiations always took place in Decinter, there were many who wished it could take place at Ertin's Inn. He was a brewer and was utilised to check the quality of the Tukerland beer. Hiber beer was brewed throughout the communities, but the Tukerland beer was also popular too. At Ertin's Inn, it was said he had all twelve varieties of Hiber beer along with a number of varieties of Tukerland beer. Not many could taste a mug of each in one evening and remain standing.

As Jandray forced his mind to drift back from some very memorable evenings at Ertin's Inn, he reminded himself that he was fortunate indeed to have an extended role that allowed him to visit all the communities. If Ertin's Inn had been big enough to host the Hiber Teachers Conference he would have had it there. Sadly it wasn't, but that was, perhaps, a good thing. It meant visiting the Inn was a real treat. "Yes", agreed Jandray, "you are quite right." As laugher erupted across the class, he suddenly realised that he had agreed that Ertin drank heavily. He smiled, but he knew he had to say something to recover Ertin's integrity. "What I meant to say was that Tukerland beer is the main export into our communities, not that Ertin is a drunkard. Quite the opposite, a kinder and more hospitable host could not be found across the whole of our nation." Ocsend blushed with pride and took a mental note to inform his father of Jandray's kind comments.

"Whilst there are twelve excellent varieties of beer to be had across our nations, the yield is quite low. This serves to create a gap in demand which the Tukerland exports help to fill. And, may I add, none of you are old enough to be enjoying this pleasure at the moment!" Jandray continued, with a hint of humour in his reply, "However, as you will have observed, our Winter Festival and our Spring Awakening is a cause for celebration. Our negotiators will want to arrange a sufficient stock of beer is obtained to ensure these festivals pass with the normal amount of fun for all."

Findren raised her hand, "It is felt that Tukerland tools are superior to the ones that we use. They use iron rather than wood, and my father told me that once they honed their skills into farming and construction equipment, instead of weapons, they became very adept at making high quality implements." "Absolutely", immediately replied Jandray. "Tukerland tools are renowned for their toughness and longevity. Many agree that they are superior to the wooden ones we have traditionally fashioned, and they are highly sought after. I am sure that the export of equipment of these sorts will be high on the list of our negotiators."

Fantred suddenly took the conversation in an all too sombre direction when she asked, "What if Tukerland wants more than we can give them? Whilst we are not encouraged to know much about this nation, my community is concerned that they are still warlike in nature, and may take what they want if we do not give what they need." This was a fair point, thought Jandray, and one that probably sat very heavily on the Elder Council, so it was no surprise that this concern filtered through to students. Fantred will have heard these concerns raised when she was at home, raised by her community, and maybe from her immediate family, reflected Jandray. Maltas was also very aware of these concerns. However, his father held an alternative view that more trade should take place, and that the Hiber fears of Tukerland were outdated and were restraining opportunities for both nations. Maltas was also aware of the influence that Delcant had over his father and that Delcant was hoping Lorsern would be come the next Elder of Paltir. But, perhaps, despite all his arrogance, his father was right; Maltas hoped so. It was what made his father popular, telling communities they had nothing to fear was always a good way to extend your influence. "My father says that we have nothing to fear from Tukerland, and that increased trade would benefit both our nations. As many of you will know", he continued, "I don't automatically follow my fathers views or loyalties, but I do hope he is right, for all our sakes." Most of the students were fully aware that Lorsern was disappointed with Maltas on many levels, not least his friendship with Altera.

Jandray felt that he needed to step in as the mood had cooled considerably, and it would soon be time for the lesson to end. He did not want it to end in such a fearful way. "Again, I find I am in agreement with our students", he said as he smiled at them. "Fantred has raised concerns that many within our communities feel, whether they voice them or not." He looked over to Fantred and said, "Thank you for having the confidence to speak in daylight, what many fear as they talk in the evening, it is to your credit that you raise this." He then looked over to Maltas, "And Maltas, I really do hope that your father is correct in his views, the last thing we need is fear of conflict, especially as we move closer to our sleep over winter." Jandray should have stopped at this point but something made him add, "And so much can happen whilst we sleep unawares of the outside world, that we only pray that Queen Mountain and our HiberWatchers keep us safe during this period." Jandray then remembered his actual intention was to lighten the mood in the class, so he quickly added, "It is a burden indeed for the Elders and for the HiberWatchers, I wouldn't want their job for all the beer in Tukerland."

The students smiled at this point, as they all knew that Jandray had never been seen intoxicated. But his intention had been realised, and their spirits raised. Little did any of them know how prophetic Jandray's word would be.

Chapter Five

The meeting of the Mountain Keepers society was about to began. Altera's mother and father were working late, and the thirteen students had Altera's house to themselves. The discussions of today's lesson were still very much in their minds. Thankfully, Sartora had left plenty of food and refreshments for them. She was fully aware of this "secret society" that Altera and Maltas were leading. She had no intention of stopping them practice their leadership skills. She knew from Jandray that he also was aware of this 'society' and had told Sartora that this class was as close as any he had ever taught. The students had no idea that both Jandray and Sartora were fully aware of their meeting up, and that quietly they approved of their doing so.

There was still a buzz around the students as they thought of what they had discussed in class today. Trade with Tukerland was not something that most of their parents talked about. In fact Tukerland was not a subject often raised. When it was, there was a generally a negative overtone to such discussions. Altera thought that Jandray had been very astute in bringing in both sides of the wider issues of trade, even though it brought out a level of fear for some of the students. At their age, however, most of the students revelled in the excitement of the discussion. They were, perhaps, still not mature enough to understand the risks of living next to a nation that had martial skills at its core. Fantred had really raised the level of interest when she had moved the discussion to what would happen if Tukerland wanted more trade than the Hiber people were willing to give.

Alspeth was looking carefully at the walls of Altera's home. "You know", she exclaimed to no member of the group in particular, "If you look carefully, you can see the subtle differences of the trees in each community." Alspeth, like many of her kinfolk was keen on tree gardening. This was no surprise to many of her friends, as she was always talking about trees and, on occasion, she had been seen talking into branches of trees. If they were not such a close group of friends, Alspeth would definitely have been a loner. If truth be told, she felt more comfortable in the company of trees, or at a tree nursery than she ever felt in a group of people. "The trees are all connected within our communities", she said. "Once established, I believe that their roots all link in with each other. Our older folk say that there are stories of some tree gardeners being able to talk to a tree and the faint whisper of the conversation could be heard by gardeners in other communities. Also, there are rural myths that tell how the trees talk to each other and this is how they know when to sleep in winter and know when to wake in Spring."

Maltas was listening carefully. "Wouldn't it be something if the group could communicate through the trees when they were all back in their home communities. It would be an amazing extension of our secret society" he mused. He put these thoughts to the back of his mind as the students slowly began to think more about the HiberWatcher Selection than their stomachs. Sartora's generosity in leaving such lovely food had satiated their appetite. They slowly gravitated towards the hearth, where Altera had built up the fire. It never ceased to amaze Maltas that living trees could not only provide shelter, but could also shed cones that that gave them warmth. He could barely comprehend that the older branches the trees discarded could become so hard that fires could be lit on them and they would not be damaged. Alspeth could, no doubt, give him the full reasons for this, but now was not the time to raise that subject. Whilst it interested him, many students just accepted the environment around them without question.

"Tonight is an opportunity to discuss the HiberWatcher selection" said Altera. "It isn't far off and in a few short weeks the two HiberWatchers will be chosen. At the same time the two Watch Hounds will be found to keep them company. Even now, our animal experts are looking out across the Watch Hound packs to establish if any are growing a coat suitable to protect them through winter." "It is such a shame that only adults can be HiberWatchers", said Larpan. "Can you imagine having your name on the Ice Wall for all to see?" he said. "Even more so, can you even comprehend being awake all Winter, to protect our communities?" As he said this, he could see that all the students were thinking of what it must be like. Each year in Spring, those who had been chosen as HiberWatchers seemed to have been changed in subtle ways. Whilst it was the HiberWatcher code not to discuss anything about their activities, it was clear that something had moved within their soul. After being a HiberWatcher, many of them disappeared into the rural highlands of their communities for a period of time. It was almost like they had been so used to enforced loneliness that it was a shock to be surrounded by people again. The HiberWatcher training was carried out in secret. Only the Hiber Key Keepers knew what took place in that training

Only two students in the group were related to a HiberWatcher. One was Altera, whose mother had been a HiberWatcher, the other was Junstern. Just after she was born, Junstern's mother, who was called Jalper, was selected as a HiberWatcher. At the time, it was thought strange by some that a new mother would choose to put their name forward for selection. However, Junstern's mother would say afterwards, "Giving birth to Junstern was the best gift given to our family. Both my husband and I agreed that the most appropriate gift we could give in return was to offer to protect our communities, as those who had protected and provided for us whilst I was pregnant." Junstern told the group, "My mother always assumed that it would be my father that was selected. However, as it turned out, my mother's name was pulled out. She had the full support of my father, who was so pleased that she had been given this honour." "Did your parents not worry about what was ahead?" said Calpir. "I think I would be so worried if either my mother or father was chosen, what if something had happened to them?" "I was too young to know anything about it", said Junstern "But as I got older my grandfather did sometimes say that whilst it was a huge source of pride for his daughter to be chosen, he went into the Winter Sleep more troubled than he had ever been before." As she thought back to this chat with her Grandfather, she continued, "However, my Grandfather was old enough to remember the conflict that took place in Tukerland when he was younger, so perhaps that was the reason for his worries."

Altera did not add to the conversation as her mother had rarely mentioned about being a HiberWatcher, and she thought that this may have been the source of why her mother and father were more and more estranged. However, the mention of Tukerland seem to drag them all back to today's conversation, for which Altera was grateful. She did not want to be seen as taking away from Junstern's pride in her mother. Whilst no one wanted to say it, they had all been, to a greater or less degree, moved to reflect on what would happen if Tukerland returned to its warring ways. Just as Jandray had done in lesson today, so Altera did at this secret meeting "Let's have confidence in our negotiators as Maltas has encouraged us to do. Let us be reassured that the peace that we enjoy will continue." Her soothing words seemed to have the desired effect, the mood uplifted again, and all thoughts returned to the HiberWatcher Selection.

It was time to include the whole group in a plan that Maltas and Altera had been discussing. Did they have a right to do what they had discussed? Probably not. Would it be beneficial to the person concerned? They had thought so. "Here goes" thought Maltas as Altera slowly stood up, turned slowly and looked at everyone in the meeting. "Who is the most trustworthy person we know, and who would made the best HiberWatcher in the Hiber Nation?" she said, with more than a hint of nerves in her voice. Just the thought of what Maltas and she had been discussing made her both excited and extremely nervous. Before any of the group could answer, Maltas added, "And who deserves their name on the Ice Wall; more than anyone we know?" A hum of voices started to build around the room. "Before anyone shouts out, let's have our own selection" said Altera. She handed each of the group a piece of parchment and a pencil. "Write down one name, and it cannot be your own!" she said with a serious look on her face. This was at odds with the real selection process as entering into it was entirely voluntary by the person concerned. "After you have made a choice, put it in the pot that I am passing round and then we will see."

There was a flurry of activity. Maltas could see that some wrote a name immediately, others took their time and stared into the fire as if hoping that some kind of inspiration could come from there. Finally, everyone had written a name, the cup had been passed round and placed back in the middle of the group. "Now," said Maltas. "Pass the cup back round. Be careful not to pick out your own piece of parchment and get ready to read the name written on it." The cup went first to Dasbran. "Dasbran, please read out the name and then pass to your left" said Maltas. There was an expectant atmosphere in the air as Dasbran slowly lifted a piece of parchment out of the cup. He looked at the name and the looked at his friends "Jandray" he exclaimed. He then passed the cup round. It was no surprise that Corprind was sat next to him. He carefully reached into the cup and his fingers curled round another piece of parchment. As he opened the parchment, he smiled and said "Jandray." Next to Corprind was Ocsend. He too pulled out a piece of parchment. A wide smile spread across his face. "Jandray" he almost shouted. And the cup continued to pass round the group. Every time a name was brought out, it was followed by "Jandray." Every time, the name read out was getting shouted louder and louder.

The cup finally returned to Maltas. There was only one piece of parchment left. As he carefully opened and smoothed the parchment out, he looked at all of his friends and said quietly "Jandray." There was uproar. Immediately the group started to chant "Jandray", "Jandray", "Jandray." They jumped to their feet and continued to shout his name. Maltas and Altera looked across the circle of friends into each other's eyes. They had hoped that their friends would have felt the same as them, and they had been proved right. "So" shouted one of the group; it was difficult to hear due to the general mayhem taking place. "So, what do we do now? Teacher Jandray has always made it clear the he would never put his name into the selection." This had an immediate effect on the group and they slowly began to sit back down. "It was a great game Maltas" said Larpan, "but it changes nothing."

Maltas and Altera gazed at the gathering around them. "Not necessarily" said Altera. The selection is totally open and anyone can walk up to their selection post and put their name in the selection jar. As you know, these jars are then brought to Paltir and the contents then placed in the HiberWatcher chalice. They are not checked individually before they are placed in this chalice, so each of us could place Jandray's name in our own community selection. This would give a much greater chance of Jandray being chosen." The impact of what Altera was saying slowly dawned on the group. "But, this would implicate all of us in this issue. We would have conspired to alter the random nature of the selection, won't that get us all into trouble?" said Alspeth, in a quiet and nervous voice. "Totally", said Maltas. "It would mean there was no going back for us, regardless of the outcome. If we were found out, we would bring disgrace upon our families. But, I for one, will sleep much better knowing that the best person we know is one of the HiberWatchers this year. Especially with the fears that we are all thinking about what is happening, or could happen, with Tukerland."

Altera spoke up, "We cannot, and will not, do this unless all of us agree", her voice becoming more confident as she said the words that would possible connect them more than they had ever planned when they set up this group. At first, it was just for fun, to have secret meetings, discussing nothing of import. Things were changing rapidly. The Mountain Keepers would have to be a real secret society, with a really big secret to hold. Altera continued, "This takes our group beyond anything that anyone imagined. We also risk losing the respect of Teacher Jandray if he ever found out that we had been instrumental in tipping the selection in his favour." In his normal blunt manner Corprind said, "I think we should do it. I am amongst those who lives closest to Tukerland. I don't believe what my father says, and I don't like his support of Delcant. I feel the fear that some of our braver families mention when they think my father isn't listening." Dasbran looked across at Corprind and nodded his agreement. "It's all well and good that my Grandfather, and Corprind's father, is saying all is well. But sadly, I have to agree with Corprind in that his father follows Elder Delcant too closely I think. I love my Grandfather, but equally I know just how very persuasive he can be."

Corprind continued, "Elder Delcant has ensured that my father is very much under his command when it comes to all aspects of Elder business." After a brief silence Dasbran then said, "But I have seen Tukerland with my own eyes, I have seen how they chop down trees, and I have seen their animals herded into barns. What I didn't see was any live animals come out. If we are to maintain the culture and care that our nation has known for years, we must do anything we can to ensure that we all remain safe from Tukerland. If Teacher Jandray, as a HiberWatcher, can play even a small part in that, then he gets my vote; even if he doesn't know what we have done, and even if it fractures the trust in which he holds us all."

The group were unused to Dasbran speaking so passionately. They had all seen him grow in confidence under the tutelage of Jandray, and they could note a maturity in his voice and his words that even Dasbran wouldn't have thought possible. "Let's put it to a vote then" replied Larpan. "If it is unanimous we go ahead, but if not, we will have to re-think this. If we want to maintain our unity, it must be unanimous, just like decisions made by the Elder Council." All present nodded their agreement. "Do you want a secret vote, or a show of hands?" said Altera, adding, "I don't think it fair that anyone should feel any pressure on this." The students began an animated discussion about this and Jandray, at the very least, would have been pleased that his students had learnt to talk carefully and with due respect for everyone's views - even if he hadn't liked what they were talking about.

Maylen pulled the group back from their discussions. "I, for one, would have wanted a secret vote. However, I cannot get out of my head the vision of those animals being taken to slaughter, so I will not object to an open vote" and raised her hand. At this, it was like a wave occurring around the room. All hands were raised, except that of Altera. She could feel twelve pairs of eyes looking at her. The selection for Jandray had been primarily her idea and now the enormity of what they were about to do was very real. She had taken this group from a harmless group of friends, into a society with a huge secret to keep. And with this thought she raised her hand. "So", exclaimed Maltas, "It is unanimous." The group did not know how to feel, and for a moment they were lost in silence.

Maltas broke the silence when he said, "This weekend, we are all back in our own communities, prior to the Winter Festival that culminates in representatives from all communities arriving in Paltir for the final day of the festival and for the outcome of the selection. As you know, whilst each community will have their own festival, a good number from each of our homes will come to Paltir to witness the selection. If the snow falls as we normally expect, the movement of all our communities into Queen Mountain will commence shortly afterwards. We will all be able to enjoy the snow, whilst it is still manageable to do so. However, we will then all be subject to our local councils who will ensure we are safe in the caverns before the full winter snow begins."

"What we need to do" advised Altera, "Is to try hard to be together in Paltir on Selection day. By then, we will all have put Teacher Jandray's name into our local selection. Just remember, our plans are likely to still come to nothing, many within our communities will put their name into the selection. There is no guarantee, even with many more votes than anyone else, that Jandray's name will be pulled out in the final selection." Dasbran raised his hand and the group encouraged him to speak. "What we have not considered is what if Jandray refuses and says that he didn't put his name in for selection?" Corprind, in his normal straight speaking manner replied, "Well, we will just have to cross that particular ice bridge when, and if, we come to it." At that, the tense atmosphere was broken. "We leave this matter to Queen Mountain" Maltas said. "If she agrees with us, then nothing will prevent Jandray being a HiberWatcher this year."

The group decided that it was late enough, and Altera's mother and father would, no doubt, be home soon. None of them wanted to return to their host families later than what was allowed, so they said their goodbyes to the warm home and comforting hearth in front of them and went their separate ways. It really would be out of the hands of the Mountain Keepers society as soon as they placed Jandray's name in each selection post. All would have to wait and see. And Jandray, preparing for his bed, would have had a troubled night's sleep if he had known what could possible lay ahead for him, if the Mountain Keepers society saw their wish come true.

Chapter Six

King Nilan began to prepare for his visit to Decinter to take part in the trade negotiations. He was reassured that Farrender would be at his side throughout the following days. Farrender had been the Hiber Nation's main negotiator with Tukerland for many years. She was highly respected in the Elder Council and, it was said, was also respected by the Tukerland trade representatives. But, if this was to be her last time in this role, Nilan would have to observe the event very carefully and think how all Farrender's skills could be replaced by a new Elder next year. Nilan had little time for Lorsern, the subject of discussion at Council. From all he had seen, he had not been very impressed with him. However, what troubled Nilan about Farrender's favoured choice was the rumours of estrangement between Sartora and her husband, who was called Torpast. Whilst it was not necessary to have a partner if you were chosen to be an Elder, it was absolutely critical that your partner was in support of you if you did have one. Farrender had never married and she was everything an Elder could be. Her community was her family, and everyone in it was viewed as part of her extended family. He also knew that Farrender had a special fondness for Sartora. He could see the mother and daughter relationship that had built up over the years. Ultimately, Nilan trusted Farrender, he did not trust Lorsern; and that was enough for him. He would support Farrender's nomination of Sartora; and he would hope that she and Torpast had a future together.

Including journey time and the trade talks, Nilan would be away for a couple of weeks. It would be a very pleasant journey to take in Autumn. The trees would be turning various shades of gold and Nilan would pass through a number of the twelve Hiber communities on his way to the most southerly part of their nation. They would travel on horseback, with only a limited amount of provisions to enable them to travel light and fast. A number of wayside inns would be used and, as he was a late addition to the trade delegation, he was very happy that Farrender had already arranged accommodation. With typical humility, Nilan refused any offer to alter the journey plans or the accommodation chosen.

Nilan, if he had known, would have fully agreed with Jandray in that he would have preferred to stop at Ertin's Inn. Sadly, this was not on the most direct route between Paltir and Decinter. Before he had become King he had spent many a pleasurable evening at Ertin's Inn. However, when his father died, Nilan had to put some of his pleasures to one side to concentrate on leadership of the Hiber Nation. Part of this sacrifice included that whenever he travelled it was expected that he was hosted by the local Elder. This was not too much of a sacrifice, other than when he had to visit Decinter. Nilan did not like Delcant, they were totally opposite in personality and character. In addition, because he was King, even though the Elder Council held the ultimate authority, Delcant's fawning nature was in overdrive whenever Nilan visited.

King Nilan was pleased that his late addition to the delegation meant that he would be able to ride on horseback to the meeting. There were rumours that all the mountains were connected by tunnels that had been formed many thousands of years in the past. However, over the years, the knowledge of these tunnels and their routes had been lost and many people thought of them only as myths and fantasy. It reminded him to speak with the Library Key Keepers in order to look again at the potential of these tunnels actually existing. If they did, it would be a great opportunity to explore, and could even be critical to the safety of the Hiber Nation if there was any risk of conflict with Tukerland. Many in Tukerland viewed the Hiber mountains, and certainly the caverns within Queen Mountain, with a level of fear and suspicion.

For a couple of days Nilan could leave some of these thoughts behind him. Whilst, no doubt, he and Farrender would spend time discussing options for the trade meeting, there would still be plenty of time to relax and take in the spectacular surroundings of his nation. Wherever you were the mountains appeared to be close. It was their vast size that created this feeling. In reality there were many miles of rich arable land surrounding each community before you reached the lower slopes of each mountain. And then, at the centre of the nation, Queen Mountain towered supreme over all the other twelve mountains. There was no way of knowing how far

Queen Mountain stretched into the sky. All that could be said is that her vast shape filled the horizon wherever you were in the Hiber communities that surrounded her. The lower slopes of Queen Mountain were almost as high the peaks of each of the Watchkeeper Mountains around her. It was truly awe-inspiring to try and grasp the immensity of this landscape. Yet, it was a productive landscape. Surrounded by the circle of mountains, with Queen Mountain in the middle, the land was protected from adverse winds and weather for most of the year and Hiber farming provided abundant crops. Refreshing pure water flowed down from the mountains and provided all the needs of both the land and the communities.

Nilan wondered what it would be like to see this land in winter. Even though his ancestors had been HiberWatchers, as King he was now forbidden from entering into the selection. In the early winter he had a flavour of what the land would look like as it was bathed in the early snowfall, turning the nation into a wonderland of glistening ice. The trees, by early winter, would be almost fully converted from verdant growth into hard and impenetrable structures of ice. But to see the land slowly disappear under hundreds of metres of snow, like a massive protective blanket, would be a thing to behold. All that was left of the nation was the twelve Watch Keeper mountains surrounding what would be taken for a land of winter wilderness where nothing lived; with Queen Mountain towering over a desolate but majestic landscape. And it would remain that way until Spring heralded the thaw and life would begin again. He envied the HiberWatchers, and even the Watch Hounds that kept them company, for the beauty that they would experience during the Winter Sleep.

Queen Torcas came into the bedchamber where Nilan was packing his clothes. "Husband", she said softly. "I am going to miss you when you are on your journey to Decinter. I wish we could whisper to each other through the roots of the trees to know you are safe and well when you get there." "Those old tales of connections across our communities would be so lovely if they were true", replied Nilan as he looked across at his Queen. She was strong and upright, yet seem vulnerable at this exact moment in time. "Wife, don't worry about me", he replied. "I have Farrender looking after me, and we have lots to discuss on the journey. Perhaps, you could spend time with the Library Key Keepers to look through the old tales to see if there is any truth in what you describe. It would be incredibly useful to be able to communicate in such a way, although I can hardly comprehend how it would work." Torcas smiled and saw that Nilan had offered her a task that she would have pleasure in progressing. She knew that Nilan gave plenty of credence to these old tales, and had a specific desire to investigate the rumours of tunnels connecting the nations in days of old. "Perhaps I will also look at the tales of how our community was connected underground at the same time" she said, smiling at him. Nilan looked into her eyes. "Had she read my mind as these things had been wandering through my thoughts?" he asked himself. "What an amazing woman."

"When I return" he said, holding her in his arms, "We can do our trade! You can tell me what you have found and I can update you on all the negotiations with Tukerland. I can even update you on how grand Delcant's Elder house has become, and if he truly is trying to create a second capital in the Decinter region." Whilst he intended his comment be said with light humour, both Torcas and Nilan knew that his comments were tinged with a fear that things were about to change. "Let's hope that Farrender is mistaken" said Torcas, "and that all things will be as they should be. Neither of us really like Delcant, but we must give him the benefit of our impartiality until proven otherwise" she added. "Quite right" said Nilan, "I will make the necessary enquiries. It will be quite difficult for him to hide such a structure if what Farrender says is true, although I am sure that Delcant will come up with some excuse as to the reasons for any growth at the Elder house anyway."

It was almost time to meet up with Farrender and the team leaving for Decinter. Torcas kissed Nilan lightly on the lips and said "Go well and go safe my husband." As he lingered over their intimacy he replied "Stay well and remain safe my love." They parted from their embrace and he returned to his final preparations. A short while later Torcas stood at the entrance to their home. The leaves and the structure of the Paltir building were starting to change colour. Whilst Nilan was away that change would continue and the ice white transformation of this loving home would be well on the way to its winter protective coat before he returned.

And so Nilan, Farrender and a small team of helpers began the long journey to Decinter. Allowing for the travel there and back, and a number of days of negotiations, Nilan was all too aware that he would miss Torcas just as much as she would miss him. Perhaps more, he thought. With the Autumn sun just over the horizon their horses gently cantered down the road and onwards in their journey south. Autumn would linger with them as they journeyed to Decinter, and it was expected that they would return just before the HiberWatcher Selection and the Winter Festival. "There is a lot to do and a lot to think about" mused Nilan. Was he being overly concerned about the future or was there very valid reasons for his fears to be increasing? He pushed these concerns away, as much as he was able, knowing he would have to wait and see. "Time will tell all things" as his father used to say, adding that "to worry about such things ahead of time, is as pointless as trying to hold back the snows." The snows were coming and time would tell what future the Hiber Nation was facing as it went into sleep. Normally, that thought was refreshing and reassuring for Nilan. But this year he was not sure. Something he just couldn't pin down was worrying him and he couldn't seem to lose that worry, as much as he tried to follow his father's advice. He tried to push it out of his mind and let the warm Autumn dawn refresh him as they continued on their journey.

As he disappeared into the distance the smile on the face of Torcas dropped away. She was worried and didn't know why. She felt that things were about to change and that the stability she had known for many years was decidedly at risk. She felt it and could almost touch the fear that she kept trying to push away. She would, she decided, approach the Library Key keepers; it would keep her busy and she may possibly find some comfort in the old tales. For some reason a few lines from an old poem kept coming back to her. They did little to salve her concerns:-

"The HiberWatchers watch, and the sleepers sleep

The Queen protects them all in her keep

Winter falls, and deep cold it does bring

And the world will refresh when we wake in Spring"

"Queen Mountain hears when trouble is near

Hiber Trees talk and move if they sense fear

Roots so deep can bring news to those who love

And long tunnels open up new roads from above"

She couldn't remember the rest of the poem, it was lost in some poem learnt somewhere when she was young. She couldn't even remember where she had heard it. However, it gave her both comfort and concern to remember it now. Try as she might to remember the rest of the poem, the other verses would not come to her.

Chapter Seven

Delcant still wasn't sure how he was going to explain to King Nilan the growth of the Decinter Elder house and associated buildings. It wasn't just the opulence of the palatial building that he had constructed, it was the fact that it was much larger than any of the other eleven Elder houses across the nation and was almost as large as the building that housed both the King and Queen as well as the Elder Council. Delcant had also contrived to have a variety of trees from each Hiber community incorporated into the extensive structure that he was now sitting in. It was easy to see how it could be viewed as a direct competitor to the Capital, that of the First Family and Elder Council in Paltir. And the truth was that is exactly what Delcant wanted it to be. However, how was he going to justify this to King Nilan was his immediate and most pressing concern. By fair means and not so fair means he had kept his own local council members subordinate to his leadership, and they had kept quiet about the cost in trees and labour that his vanity had cost his local community. He hadn't totally quelled the disquiet of the wider population though. He knew that his popularity hung by a threat and the Winter Festival this year must be one that showered the Decinter community with awe and wonder. If he achieved this, they may forget his indulgences and not look too closely at what had been neglected as a result of his largesse in extending what he saw as his home; not a community building purely held in trust by the local Elder for all of the community. Anyway, ultimately, he would fall back on that exact fact; this wasn't his actual home, he was just able to live in it whilst an Elder. But he knew that he had absolutely no plans to step aside from this role, none at all.

The Nicenter community Elder, Caltan, was present in the Decinter local council chamber with him. They were discussing the forthcoming delegation arriving from Paltir and also the warrior group that was due to arrive from Tukerland. There was so much to do and Delcant was pleased that his long years of grooming Caltan into an unquestioning and totally loyal fellow Elder had been so beneficial. He wouldn't be present at the negotiations but was a useful sounding board for his plans. All Delcant had learnt in the process of moulding Caltan to his will, he had also employed in bringing Lorsern under his influence. This had been somewhat more difficult as Lorsern was not an Elder, and the distances between Paltir and Decinter were not inconsiderate. However, the regular meetings that Delcant had to attend at the full Elder Council meant he could devote time to cultivating this future Elder. His brows furrowed as he thought of this issue and his annoyance built suddenly. Elder Farrender was determined to spoil his plans. What was particularly annoying was that Farrender was very influential in the Council and with the King and Queen, more than Caltan or Delcant. Delcant had no idea why Farrender would want to step down and hand her privileged position onto another person. Delcant would never willingly give up the position and the perks he enjoyed as an Elder.

That said, Delcant was pleased that Farrender was stepping down. Their dislike for each other had grown over the years. Farrender was a barrier to progress, as far as Delcant deceived himself. The truth was that Farrender was a barrier to Delcant's progress. He wanted to be the most influential Elder in the Council. He wanted to see his own personal wealth, in land and property, multiply tenfold. Ultimately, he wanted to turn the Council into a subordinate body, totally compliant with his plans for greater integration with his 'friends' in Tukerland. Living so close to Tukerland over the years had left Delcant envious of the warrior elite that he had come into contact with. They had no problem with a vast gap in wealth and property between the leaders and the wider populace. Their animosity towards anyone who got in their way was only balanced by their fear of their leader Sargern who ruled the country with a very firm and bloody hand. Delcant convinced himself that he could operate in that environment despite having no real physical presence himself. His lack of physical prowess had been balanced by a brilliant and devious mind. He found that his ability to manipulate people allowed him to use the strength of others in place of his own.

Over the years, Delcant had cultivated a friend of sorts with the Tukerland warrior called Grasby. At first it was a just a relationship of convenience born out of discussing trade options each year. However, during those discussions Delcant and Grasby had begun to explore opportunities of extending trade beyond the norms agreed year on year. Of course, Delcant wrapped these opportunities into arguments that such extension of trade would benefit both nations. The truth was that Delcant cared little about the wider benefit to either nation, so long as his personal benefit, wealth and influence increased. Delcant was so confident in his own abilities and intelligence that he gave no thought to the fact that he had met his devious equal in Grasby. What he did not realise was that it was Grasby who had cultivated the friendship for his gain, not the other way round. And when it came to the depths he would plunge to achieve his aims, Grasby was prepared to go further, deeper and bloodier than Delcant could have ever imagined.

For Grasby, Delcant was a useful pawn in his overall plan to usurp Sargern at some point. He was prepared to play the long game and, over the years, it was true that Delcant had proved to be a very able, but weak, partner in this matter. It was Grasby who had planted the seed in Delcant's mind that the Decinter building wasn't grand enough for such an important Elder. It was also Grasby who had started to suggest areas of trade that would normally not even be considered for discussion. Grasby knew that Delcant had influence across the Hiber Nation, but he didn't know that he also had opposition. Delcant had been very effective in hiding this fact. So, it was a surprise to Grasby that Delcant had, somewhat nervously, updated him that King Nilan had been added to the delegation this year. Delcant had tried to say that this was a measure of respect that the King had in Delcant. However, if the same had happened to Grasby he would have been very concerned that Sargern didn't trust him. Then he reflected that Sargern had placed his son into the Tukerland trade team and that suddenly made him more uncomfortable. Both he and Delcant had issues that needed to be addressed, Grasby thought. Time remained of the essence. If either side of the ruling elite began to have any idea of what Delcant and Grasby were really planning they would immediately remove both from the negotiations. More importantly for Grasby, Sargern would, more than likely, also remove Grasby's head as well.

Grasby had arranged to visit Decinter prior to the main trade team meeting. He had sold this to Saltock on the basis of him needing to establish accommodation and logistical issues. He didn't really care if Saltock believed him or not. This lack of respect for Saltock could prove very costly in the long run. However, Grasby needed to have confidential talks with Delcant to ensure they manoeuvred the meeting in the way that they both wanted. Or, realistically, to gain everything that Grasby wanted; all other considerations were secondary. Grasby approached the border with the Hiber Nation through the "Decinter Gap", as the closest passable trail into the Hiber Nation was called. In winter that gap would fill with snow and ice and the Hiber country would disappear under that ice. However, in Autumn it was a beautiful and not too strenuous a journey for Grasby. As he moved across the plains of Tukerland he still marvelled at the size of the mountain range that surrounded this Hiber Nation. Even though many miles away, he could also see their central mountain or "Queen Mountain" as they called it. It was so vast it looked almost within touching distance. The twelve mountains surrounding this central mountain appeared to be an impenetrable barrier in Winter and could be easily defended in warmer months. It surprised Grasby that Sargern had maintained cordial relationships with the Hiber Elders over the years. Why didn't he look with eager eyes on such amazing potential? "Well, if Sargern didn't want more, then I do", thought Grasby. He smiled to himself as he drew closer to the Gap. He knew he would be met by Decinter guards at the crossing point. However, they knew him quite well and he didn't expect any delays.

A few hours later, Grasby was on the doorstep of Delcant's increasingly grand home, located at the centre of Decinter. He had to admit that the home did look beautiful in the Autumn sun. The new trees that had been used created a hue and a vibrancy that could not be said of any of Tukerland's dwellings. All that would change if Grasby had his way with the trade negotiations. And if they didn't go his way, well, he would just take what he wanted in due course. "Or", he thought to himself, "I may just move in here." It would be no hardship for him to build a garrison within the nation that he intended to fall under the full influence of Tukerland in due course. It could even be a place where he could continue to destabilise Sargern if that was what was needed. All these malicious thoughts served to make Grasby warm with the excitement of what the following days would bring.

Delcant met Grasby at the threshold. "Well met Warrior Grasby" he said, his voice was an octave higher than he planned. This quavering voice betrayed the nerves in Delcant, "I trust your journey was uneventful." Grasby felt that he had to continue to play this appearance of friendship for some time longer and replied "It is excellent to see you Elder Delcant, your home and your girth grow every time we meet." It did no harm to belittle Delcant at the same time as praising him, thought Grasby. It was a fact that Delcant enjoyed his food and it was not the Hiber vegetable diet that was driving this growth in around his middle. Grasby knew that Delcant had developed a taste for cooked flesh. Whilst this was forbidden within his own community, Delcant spent enough time over the border in Tukerland to satiate his carnivorous desires. Grasby was surprised that Delcant's kinfolk hadn't noticed how the usual slight but athletic profile that tended to describe Hiber folk was at odds with Delcant's increasingly bloated figure.

"Please come into dinner" replied Delcant, appearing to ignore the slight that Grasby had started the encounter with. "We have some excellent victuals and beer ready for you" He then added, "We thought they would be a most welcome end to your journey". "Indeed" replied Grasby, "A short repast would be a most pleasant interlude before we enter into our discussions for the forthcoming meeting. I am particularly looking forward to some of your renowned cheese, I hope I will not be disappointed." As he looked across to the dining table, he could see that he was most certainly not going to be disappointed with the spread that Delcant had laid out. "I am sure you will be most happy with the humble table we have provided" replied Delcant, knowing full well that it was a meal fit for a feast. As they sat down, only Caltan remained in the room. The Hiber folk who worked in the Elder's home quietly left the room and closed the doors. In his characteristic style, Delcant did not acknowledge their hard work and ignored their departure.

Grasby launched into Delcant, "Do we have a problem? I was most displeased to hear the short notice addition of King Nilan to the trade team." He then smiled at Delcant, in a way that meant Delcant felt he was looking into the eyes of a hungry beast. "Not at all" Delcant quickly replied. "Just take it as a measure of the interest that our Elder Council has in ensuring a positive meeting." "But", growled Grasby, his mouth partially filled with a mixture of bread and of cheese, "the extra trade we had so carefully planned could come to naught." "Not necessarily so" replied Delcant. "We just need to put on a united front and explain the benefits of what we are recommending." As he then began to think of the risks, he continued, "But we always said that we needed to move slowly in these issues. If our trade team and subsequently the Hiber Elder Council get any appreciation of the scope of our actual plans, they will close all discussions down."

Grasby held Delcant in his gaze, and intentionally made Delcant squirm in his seat "What is your plan then?" he irritably replied. "I had thought we could have made extensive progress, particularly on extending the trade to Hiber trees and to Hiber livestock. I am guessing you have laid the ground out for these discussions." Delcant looked furtive in his response as he replied, "Unfortunately, no agreement was made at the Elder council, and I wasn't able to expand the discussion as much as I had liked." Before he could say more Grasby interjected, "And, as a result of this, the King has joined the negotiations. On any level, Delcant, this doesn't look good." All the warmth had left Grasby's voice and demeanour.

"All is not lost" said Delcant as he tried to recover the situation, and his confidence. "King Nilan has not been involved in trade negotiations before and we should try and win him over to, at least, an agreement to discuss the potential for extension of trade. Also," he continued, "I hope you have control over the young Saltock, in order that he sees the benefit of what we have discussed. Of course, if Saltock isn't under your control, we may have a problem." Delcant's subtle challenge to Grasby was immediately noted. "Saltock has much to learn about trade and about how to get what he wants" replied Grasby. "He will look to my direction in these issues." "If that is the case" retorted Delcant "We have little to worry about, and we can can continue with our wider plans. Once trade extends, the benefits will be for all to see."

Grasby looked intently at Delcant. Was he that naive to believe what he was saying? Grasby knew full well from Delcant's prevarication that Delcant had not received the support of the Elder Council. By experience, he knew equally as well that Farrender was a formidable negotiator and that any attempt to extend the discussions would be very difficult. In part he respected Farrender as a worthy opponent, but he looked forward to the time that he could dispose of this snivelling excuse for a person he was currently talking with. Grasby relaxed somewhat as he thought through the myriad of options that were available. If trade could not be agreed then it would have to be forced. If that was to be the case, he would have to manufacture a reason to force the trade, one that was compelling to both the Hiber Nation, to Sargern and also to the warrior elite at Tukerland. He started to put his mind to what those options could be as it was clear to him that Delcant's usefulness may be coming to an end.

"Let's put these concerns out of our head for this evening" Grasby said, intending to lighten the mood that had turned decidedly threatening - to Delcant that is. Grasby still needed to have Delcant's support when the trade negotiations commenced in a few days time and he said, "I will leave in the morning, and will return to Tukerland. When you next see me, I will be with our delegation. If anything changes in the interim, you must try and get a message to me." "Of course" replied Delcant, pleased that Grasby's mood appeared to have changed. "I will ensure you are fully updated on anything of concern or note." Which is the direct opposite of what Delcant was actually thinking.

Delcant was a coward, he was devious and self-serving, and he was fully aware of this, embracing those character flaws and regarding them more as strengths. He was aware that Grasby would view their relationship as potentially at an end if Delcant couldn't deliver what he had promised. And he was fully aware that Grasby could make it personally terminal for Delcant if he thought he have been double-crossed by Delcant. It added to the weight of concerns that Delcant was trying to manage now. But, at least Grasby had revealed the depth of his disrespect of Delcant, and that was useful. Grasby was powerful, but he was not devious as Delcant, and Delcant had time to work out options that would reduce any life limiting risks that Grasby may have been considering to use against him. The stakes had increased and Delcant knew he had to be equal to the task or his plans would shatter and he may not live to regret the decisions he had made.

Chapter Eight

Queen Torcas hoped that the journey was going well for Nilan, Farrender and the trade team. She would not know for sure until they had returned. The next couple of weeks would need to be spent ensuring that plans for the Winter Sleep were progressing correctly. Once Nilan had returned, the HiberWatcher Selection would take place and there would be the Winter Festival. The trade goods would have been exchanged and the migration of all the Hiber people across the ice bridge into the caverns of Queen Mountain would take place. This process took place each year, and it was a massive exercise. She would have preferred both Nilan and Farrender to have been present with her in Paltir. Whilst all communities were equal, the fact that Paltir was closest to Queen Mountain, and that the Elder Council met there, meant that the coordination fell to the Paltir community to burden the majority of the planning. Under normal circumstances this was hard enough. However, the concerns so vocally raised by Farrender in the Elder Council were very much in her mind and her own intuition caused her to be much more concerned than usual.

Farrender, much to the annoyance of Lorsern, had left Sartora to act as Elder in her stead. This sent a very powerful message that Sartora was her preferred choice as her successor to the role of Elder of Paltir. Torcas could see why Farrender had made this decision. Sartora was a very capable and personable individual. She was intelligent and used her skills very effectively as part of the local council under Farrender's guidance. She treated all she met with respect, affording the necessary dignity to all she engaged with. It was of concern that the relationship with her husband was subject of rumour and speculation. However, no relationship was perfect and that didn't stop the two of them having brought a very well-adjusted child into the world. Torcas did not know Altera very well, but the limited knowledge she had of her made her to think that Altera had all the same positive characteristics of her mother. Sadly, the same could not be same of Lorsern. As she had experienced in the most recent Elder council meeting, Delcant had made no secret of his wish for Lorsern to be considered the next Elder for the Paltir community . Delcant was highly persuasive and was influential with a number of the Elders. However, what Delcant had seen as strengths in Lorsern, Torcas saw as potential weaknesses. Lorsern was clearly effective in his role within the Paltir local council. Any task he undertook, he delivered upon very effectively. However, he was not concerned about how he achieved the result, and often left people feeling as if they were of no value to him.

Torcas decided to leave Sartora and Lorsern to sort out their differences whilst Farrender was away. For her to interfere could be perceived as showing partiality and that would not be well received at the next Elder Council and would undoubtably be exploited by Delcant. She was certain that Lorsern and Delcant would make the most of any potential favouritism shown by the Queen. What she could do, however, was invite both their children to meet with the Queen. Torcas was known to have great interest in the schooling of children across the nation. It would not be unusual for her to ask to meet with students to catch up on studies and the general pressures of being a young person almost at adulthood. That way, neither Sartora nor Lorsern could think that either potential Elder was in higher estimation by their Queen. And the fact was that Torcas didn't really know either child that well and so it would be good to meet them. She hoped that Maltas was not like his father, but meeting him would let her know either way.

Torcas wrote a note to Jandray, who she knew due to his longstanding role as teacher and Chair of the Hiber Teacher network, and sought his permission for two of his students to meet her at a convenient time. Torcas could have just directed this to happen, but that was not her way. In all things she remained humble and respectful of everyone's individual role. She knew that Jandray would not oppose this request at all and she hoped he would be honoured that both children she wanted to meet were from his class.

After she had penned the short note to Jandray she decided that she would arrange to meet the Hiber Key Keepers. As they were both at every Elder meeting she knew these two elderly souls very well. No one knew quite how old they were, but no one could remember a time when Kindross and Kian were not the Key Keepers. Whilst long life was not uncommon amongst the Hiber peoples, these two had taken that longevity to a new level. No one remembered what their original names were or which Hiber community they came from. When they took on the role of Key Keepers they were allocated their honorary names and over time that is all they answered to now. Kindross and Kian lived for their role, and for each other. They were a kindly couple and were on hand, at all times, to provide support as requested by the Elders. At some point a selection would be needed to replace this elderly couple. However, the apprenticeship would be long and arduous and not many would welcome the sacrifice that Kindross and Kian had made in the cause of protecting the Hiber Library.

Holding the keys to the history of the Hiber Nation was both an honour and a great responsibility. Only Elders were allowed into the full library and then only under the watchful guidance of one of the Keepers. A careful record was kept of each visit by an Elder, and also a record of what they had researched. However, in the main, most Elders chose not do the actual research themselves. They would seek the views of Kindross and Kian and they would undertake the research on their behalf. This worked well for most Elders and for the Key Keepers. Whilst the library was warm and cosy, it was deep underground and was vast. Elders generally had no idea where to start their research and were glad that the Keepers undertook the work on their behalf. Torcas had regular meetings with the keepers. She felt it was important to meet with them even when she had nothing to ask. That way she was able to offer support to them and not only go to them in her hour of need. Kindross and Kian respected this and always looked forward to meeting with the Queen.

Torcas approached the entrance to the library. This entrance was imposing. Like most of the structures within Hiber buildings the doors were made of living timber. These timbers had been expertly intertwined to make an impenetrable entrance to those without permission to access the inner rooms. The Queen had learnt that, whilst there were physical keys to the library, the Key Keepers actually used spoken words when they accessed the inner rooms of the library These words were whispered into the doors by the Key keepers. At their voice the door, or rather the branches in the door, opened to allow access to the library within. "If this is possible", thought the Queen, "then the old rumours of being able to communicate over long distances through the trees may not be just a myth after all." Only the Key

Keepers knew the words to utter to bring the doors open. In time, they would pass these words onto new Key Keepers and they would go into retirement themselves. They were so old that there were no retired keepers for them to follow. The first task for the new keepers would be to generate new words to open up the doors and to protect the physical keys that were only used in an emergency. This process would ensure that only two keepers would have full and unchaperoned access to the library.

The earliest documents in the library were chiselled on stone. Later documents were etched on parchment and this medium was still in use. The parchment was made from the flesh of plants grown specifically for the purpose in the Hiber Nation. It was known for its longevity and its ability to prevent deterioration from the ravages of time. Parchments were usually bound with twine to form books that were then stacked on shelves created by an intricate web of branches that spread out across the library walls.

Torcas awaited the arrival of the Keepers. She didn't have to wait long. The door began to open, the branches moving sufficiently for the two keepers to emerge from within the library complex. "Queen Torcas" announced Kindross as he stepped forward, "A real pleasure as always." Kian added, "I have just taken out your favourite cake from the oven, perhaps you will join us for a time of light refreshment." "That is so kind of you" replied Queen Torcas, "A distraction from the issues at hand will be most welcome." She then followed the keepers into a small room located just inside the main doors.

The room was comfortable and warm. In the corner, as well as the hearth, there was a large stove. Sitting on top of the stove was a sizeable cake that looked like it was asking to eaten. "Is that a Hiber sweet cake?" asked Torcas, looking over towards the stove. "I can smell the fruit and the honey from here I think." "It always was your favourite" replied Kian. "I thought I might tempt you with it." "Perhaps up to half the nation for a slice" Torcas laughed freely. It was so good for Torcas to be in this safe place. Kindross and Kian asked nothing from her and gave so much of their time, interest and wisdom. Only Nilan knew how much she had begun to rely on this haven of peace and relaxation. And he encouraged her to take this time away from all the stress of her First Family role. On reflection, this was probably why he had suggested that she carry out some research whilst he was away. It wasn't just to take her mind from their separation, it was to encourage her to go to her safe place and to relax with people who had her best interests at heart.

For their part, Kindross and Kian valued Torcas as much as she needed them. They had never had children of their own. It was not a conscious decision, the miracle had just not happened for them. Over the years Torcas and Nilan had become like children to them. They felt it was their role to support the Queen and King as much as they could whilst still maintaining their impartiality at Council. What made Torcas special to them was that she would seek to carry out her own research. She liked nothing more than poring over old parchments, even older stone tablets, in her mission to discover issues. It was a privilege that the Key Keepers did not give to many people.

Kian looked into Torcas's eyes as she passed a generous slice of Hiber cake over to her. "What is troubling you my dear Queen?" she asked gently. "I can see in the deepest part of your eyes that there is worry and sadness there." In the dimly lit room, Torcas wondered how Kian could see anything and Torcas always had an ability to mask her feelings from most. However, those barriers were of no use to the wisdom and kindness of Kian and Kinross. "I will not pry and you can keep those concerns to yourself, but we are here to help if we can." As was his way, Kindross said very little, but looked across at both Kian and Torcas. With a loving nod he left the room to give Kian and Torcas some privacy. "You have an unnerving way of seeing into my soul" said Torcas. "But, as usual, you are correct. I am worried about Nilan and about the trade negotiations this year. As you will remember from our recent Elder Council meeting, Delcant is pushing for greater trade and Farrender has raised significant questions over Delcant's true motives." She stopped for a second to savour the cake that was in her hands. For a few short seconds she was transported to her childhood, sitting at her own family hearth, listening to her Grandmother recite tales of old. Then her concerns enveloped her again.

"Delcant is a devious person" replied Kian. "Sadly, he does not embrace the true characteristics of an Elder. Kindross and I also see a change in his external physique as well. If we didn't know better we would think he had become a meat eater. The widening of his waist and his ruddy complexion lead us to this suspicion." "If that were true", exclaimed Torcas "It would explain his interest in extending the trade talks. It is clear that Tukerland would love us to export our livestock. What concerns me, and also Nilan, is that if Delcant has started to make promises to the Tukerland elite it will cause Nilan significant issues at the trade negotiations." "I fear your concerns are accurate" replied Kian. "I know this is probably not what you want to hear but Kindross and I have also discussed this. We need to be honest with you. It has been many years since we have encountered the discord in Council that Delcant is creating. And, whilst our role in Council is purely advisory, we both feel that Farrender is absolutely correct in her views." "Does that extend to Farrender's obvious dislike of Lorsern?" Torcas asked. "Unfortunately, yes, my dear" Kian replied as she brushed a stray lock of hair from Torcas's concerned face. "Again, we tend to support Farrender in the view that Sartora would make a much better replacement Elder than Lorsern when that time comes."

There was an odd look on Kian's face as she said this. "There is something you are not telling me" said Torcas. "I can see it, and I can feel it." Kian's manner changed back to her usual demeanour and she gently replied, "Sartora is a regular visitor to us. As you know, she is not allowed into the library like you are. However, she spends much time with us and has learnt many of our ways. In fact, the only person who spends more time with us than you or Sartora is Jandray." She continued, "Jandray is such a wise man that he would make an excellent Elder. However, his love is for learning and teaching, he would never wish to be considered." Torcas considered carefully what Kian was saying. "Didn't Sartora spend time as a student of Jandray? Wasn't she one of his first students, when he wasn't much more than a boy himself?" "Yes", replied Kian "And now Sartora's daughter is also being tutored by him." "Jandray speaks fondly of Altera" explained Kian. "He is convinced that Altera and Maltas are the brightest of their generation" she continued. "He is also quite sure that the whole of his class are part of a group that they think is secret, and who meet at Sartora's home." Kian decided to continue, even though she was concerned that she may be betraying a confidence. "Jandray is convinced that the group is harmless, but he is sure they are planning some surprise. He isn't sure what, but he feels it will be harmless, and maybe even good for the community. He tells us that Altera and Maltas are experimenting very effectively with leadership and that could bode well for their journey in life."

Torcas finished her cake and resisted the temptation to ask for another slice. Perhaps she could take some away and she consoled herself with this thought as the last crumb left the plate. Despite all the tension she felt at the moment the cake, together with the warmth of the room and the kindness of Kian and Kindross, had gone some way to putting her more at ease than she had felt for some time. "It is interesting that you mention Jandray" she said, looking into the fire whilst she spoke. "I have just sent a note to him before I came to visit you." "Oh, yes, may I ask why?" replied Kian. "Well, as you know Farrender and Delcant are at odds over the successor for Farrender when she steps down. Nilan and I cannot be seen to be supportive of either Sartora or Lorsern as a potential Elder, so I thought it would be good to meet their children. It would not raise any questions as I have always had a great interest in schooling across our nation, and I know Jandray quite well."

Just as Torcas was explaining this to Kian, Kindross walked back into the room. "Queen Torcas was just mentioning that she is planning on having a meeting with Altera and Maltas, both are students in Jandray's class." "Well now" replied Kindross. "That is a coincidence. Wasn't Jandray only talking about those two students the last time he was here? It was at the same time he was asking about the root of a poem that he had stuck in his head." That reply appeared to trigger a memory in Kian. "Of course", she said, as though she suddenly realised the importance of the request. "Jandray was asking about a poem he used to hear when he was a small child. How did it go?" Before Kindross could reply, Torcas said in a quiet voice:-

"The HiberWatchers watch, and the sleepers sleep

The Queen protects them all in her keep

Winter falls, and deep cold it does bring

And the world will refresh when we wake in Spring"

"That is it, that is it", how did you guess?" asked Kindross, with a quizzical look. "Jandray told me that he couldn't get the words out of his head and he was looking to find the remainder of the poem." "Yes" Kian added, "Jandray was looking at setting homework for his students to see if they could explore the poem, but he thought he should come to us first in order that he could actually find the old poem himself. That way, he could assess their findings with the actual historic source of the poem."

"I remembered that verse recently" said Torcas, "But I also remembered a second verse"

"Queen Mountain hears when trouble is near

Hiber Trees talk and move if they sense fear

Roots so deep can bring news to those who love

And long tunnels open up new roads from above"

"Isn't that strange?" Torcas added, "that both Jandray and I have been thinking about that poem." She stood and clasped Kian's hand. "However, whilst the poem should be reassuring to me, I cannot help wonder why those words are coming back to me now." She looked over at Kindross as the three of them stood close to the fire. Despite this, Torcas felt cold. "Is it a sign, an omen that we should be concerned about something?" Kindross and Kian moved together to lean into Torcas. "My dear girl", replied Kindross. "That poem has more verses than you imagine, but it has been lost for many a year. I remember being taught it when I was a child." "Yes" added Kian "Since Jandray mentioned this, we have both been looking through the library to find the full poem, but have not been able to find it yet. We wonder if there is meaning in these words that could be relevant to your concerns, and the concerns we have felt since the last Elder Council meeting." "Unfortunately" said Kindross, "We have not found the poem yet, despite all our searching. It could take many months to find it and it probably won't be found until we wake again in Spring." "Something tells me" Torcas said in a worried voice, "That could be too late. Perhaps I could look with you, at least that would be three pairs of eyes." "My dear Torcas" said Kian, "A thousand pairs of eyes may not be able to find what the library isn't willing to reveal at this time. There is much more you need to understand about the library I think."

Kindross looked at Kian and said, "My dear wife, I think it is time that we revealed to Queen Torcas a little more about how this library works, don't you agree?" "Kindred Key Keeper and holder of my heart, I agree. We knew a time such as this would come." "Queen Torcas, please refill your cup and take another slice of Hiber cake, this is going be quite a long story for you, and one that you will scarcely believe."

Chapter Nine

As Queen Torcas was in her meeting with the Key Keepers, King Nilan was nearing the end of his journey with Farrender and the Hiber trade delegation. They were on the outskirts of Decinter and it was interesting to Nilan that the Autumn warmth was stronger here than in Paltir. But then he was almost as far south in the Hiber Nation as he could get without entering Tukerland. It was known that Decinter held onto the Autumn longer than almost any of the Hiber communities. He and Farrender had been able to have extensive discussions about the looming trade talks. Farrender repeated her concerns that Delcant was not trustworthy and that she only hoped he had not made promises to the Tukerland Leaders that he was not empowered to give. Nilan agreed that it would not look good for the unity of the Elder Council if Farrender and King Nilan had to manage inflated expectations. The Tukerland leaders had learnt much of diplomacy over the years but they were still a volatile nation, and barely a generation away from being a ferocious group of warring tribes.

"How do we progress the meeting, especially if, as you fear, Delcant has made promises beyond what he can deliver, and more importantly, beyond what we want to deliver?" he asked Farrender. "It will be an uncomfortable meeting if we get off on the wrong agenda right from the start." "You are quite right King Nilan" immediately replied Farrender. "It would not surprise me if Delcant has said that it was at his suggestion that you agreed to attend the talks this year. He has also probably given hope that the presence of the King portrays a significant movement in our trade expectations." She quickly added, "Delcant will also use your presence to shift blame onto you and to me if the discussions do not go ahead as the Tukerland elite expect." "I rather agree with you" replied Nilan, his voice intonation betraying the concerns he had. "Delcant, as we have openly discussed, is devious and self-serving and it makes him a slippery person to manage and a person even harder to trust." He sighed as he continued to speak his thoughts to Farrender, "What I don't understand is how the Tukerland negotiators don't see these weaknesses in him too." Farrender replied "You may be mistaken in what you think King Nilan. My experience of the Tukerland warrior elite is that they will have got

Delcant's full measure already. His fawning and self-deprecating approach is not one that they will interpret as strength, only weakness. My concern is that they will, perhaps already have, exploit his weaknesses and his greed." Farrender paused at that point. Even her forthright manner had to be tempered with some kind of balance. "It may be that Delcant is over his head this year and he may welcome an opportunity for us to dig him out any hole he may will have got himself into. Anyway," she said, smiling at Nilan,"You are the King, you are paid to take the blame!" At this both laughed and it diffused an altogether tense moment.

The Elder hall of Decinter soon came into view. It did look grand in the autumnal light, and Nilan noted a range of different tree stock intertwined within the construction. It had been some time since Nilan had visited Decinter but the increased scope of construction was significant. He could see why Farrender had reported on this to the Elder Council. It saddened Nilan to think that someone may also judge him by the scale of the residence in Paltir. Did others look at him and Queen Torcas with envy? Was the building he was used to calling home a good enough reason for people like Delcant to think they needed to have more? Then Nilan reminded himself that they had not extended the Paltir residence at all during their tenure as Queen and King and neither had several generations of their forebears. The building was the earliest constructed in the whole of the Hiber Nation and it had housed many people in the early years, which was one reason for its size. When new communities were planted out across the nation the Paltir residence did not grow but its trees, which were well established by then, remained in place. It was also such a size as to be able to host to the Elder Council and provided the accommodation to the Elders and their retinue when they visited.

"No" thought Nilan."No" he repeated himself. "The Decinter residence is growing beyond what is needed by an Elder and perhaps it does say much about Delcant's plans." He hadn't realised he was talking out loud until Farrender said, "I thought you would agree with my views. It is cold comfort that I may be proved right, especially as these trees could have been planted for other worthy purposes." Looking upon this vast structure, Nilan understood that Farrender had never wanted to trade insults with Delcant, but that the obvious largesse of Delcant had needed to be brought to the attention of the Elder Council. "You did exactly the right thing Farrender. If you noticed this significant growth, what must the people of Decinter think? They will automatically assume that this excess was approved by the Elder Council. Perhaps we need to speak with a number of our kinfolk here to gauge their support, or otherwise, for Delcant." "That would be a wise approach" replied Farrender. "There should be time for such an excursion during the talks, and it may even do us good to have something else to think about if the talks get difficult."

Delcant was striding out to meet the delegation which put a temporary halt to the discussion between Nilan and Farrender. "King Nilan, I wanted to meet you personally and I wanted to give you our warmest welcome to Decinter." It was noticeable that Delcant did not extend the welcome to Farrender, nor did he even look in her direction. "I would hope", exclaimed Nilan, "that your welcome extends to our whole party and not just me." Delcant moved nervously and retained his composure. "Of course, King Nilan, no slight was intended to our esteemed Elder Farrender. You are all most welcome." Farrender smiled thinly, as if there were a nauseous smell approaching her nostrils. However, she was wise enough not to engage in any exchange of unpleasantries with Delcant. "Elder Delcant, it would be a great kindness to show us to our accommodation. Our wayside inns have been such comfort, but I would welcome the home environment that your humble dwelling will provide." Nilan suppressed a smile as he saw the words hit Delcant. His reconstruction of the Decinter Elder house was anything but humble.

Delcant instructed two of the house staff to show Nilan and Farrender to their rooms. Stable hands also led their horses away. "The Tukerland delegation arrives tomorrow, and I had thought we could commence negotiations tomorrow evening over dinner if that is acceptable to you" said Delcant. "It is an honour to have the King present and Sargern, the warrior leader of Tukerland, has already arranged to have his son, a young warrior called Saltock, to lead his delegation." This is the first that Farrender and Nilan had heard of this. Sargern had never sent one of his children before. He was an unknown quantity and Nilan wondered how this would impact on the discussions. "It is not my intention to usurp your role Delcant" remarked Nilan. "Together with Farrender, you will lead on the negotiations and I will only step in to assist where necessary. For that reason, I feel it wise that we three should meet tonight to ensure we are with one voice on our position." "I will arrange this immediately", replied Delcant, "Shall we say shortly after sunset?" "That would be ideal, and will give me time to wash off a hard days ride, thank you so much" said Nilan.

Whilst Delcant was devious, he was no fool. King Nilan and Farrender were accommodated in the most opulent rooms in the building. In fact, Delcant had given up his own palatial quarters for the King. That way, he could say that these rooms were only for esteemed guests. The reality was that Delcant lived in them permanently, and it had been quite a rush for his staff to remove personal effects that showed how obviously it was his main living quarters. Thankfully, from Delcant's perspective, the additional construction that he had undertaken had created many suites in which he could remove himself to. In addition, it meant that the Tukerland leaders would also not feel as though they were in accommodation that fell below their status. Delcant did feel aggrieved. In his own mind, Elders should live in palatial buildings, befitting of their high position within Hiber society. They made the difficult decisions and with that should come privilege and authority as far as Delcant was concerned. And this is where he was diametrically opposed to people like Farrender. It was said that Farrender lived a very frugal lifestyle and her Elder home, within the wider First Family building, was no larger than an average home occupied by most families in Paltir. "Each to their own" said Delcant to himself, "Just because Farrender does not like my lifestyle, that doesn't matter and doesn't make it wrong" he muttered. But truth was it did matter and it did make it wrong.

Nilan sat in his room, or rather his suite. It was much grander than his own suite of rooms at home, but there was something missing. Everywhere he looked he felt that the room was boasting to him. But also, in some strange way, he felt the tree branches were unhappy, like they were holding together a room that was sad, and was not full of life and laughter. Some would think he thought too deeply about trees. Whilst many appreciated the living growth within the Hiber Nation, the majority of the Hiber people had just come to welcome their warmth and protection and tended to forget that they were living entities, almost living beings. As Nilan reflected on this, his mind returned to the old tales about being able to communicate, over the vast distances of the nation, using trees and their extensive roots. Whilst it may only have been a myth, he so longed to be able to speak with Queen Torcas. He hoped that she was spending time with the Key Keepers as he was aware how fond she was of them. Perhaps her research may come up with something that would give life to the old tales.

The short time of rest for Nilan and Farrender flew by. Soon the golden sun of autumn had set and it was time for the meal with Delcant. He was famished following the long ride on the final day of their journey to Decinter but Nilan felt his appetite somewhat suppressed by the thought of sharing food with Delcant. "Needs must" he said to himself as he left the suite that would be his accommodation for the next few days. He hadn't felt it necessary to speak with Farrender as they had spent several days to discussing plans on how to deal with Delcant. So they met in one of the many corridors that weaved around the Elder house, or palace, as Nilan felt Delcant had been busy constructing. Two further members of the house staff escorted the two of them to a small dining room at the centre of the building. As he walked into the room Nilan was in no doubt that Delcant was making a belated attempt at showing more simple tastes. Equally, however, he sure that this wasn't Delcant's usual eating venue. It would have been too humble and lacked the scale that Delcant clearly aspired to. That said, Nilan felt a warmth and comfort in this room that had not been matched in the spacious suites he had encountered thus far.

The furniture was of high quality but was subtle in its expression. The dominant feature was a hearth where a number of comfortable chairs had been placed. They both sat and accepted a mug of Decinter beer from a member of house staff as they awaited the arrival of their host. If Delcant had truly been humble, he would have realised that he should have been waiting for them in the room, and even could have poured the drinks for them. But that wasn't Delcant, he was so used to making the final entrance that he continued this approach, even with the King. "Is this an intended gesture of arrogance?" Nilan mused. He refused to let it sour the meeting at such an early stage and he reminded himself that he needed to rise above the petty ways of Delcant. Nilan could see that Farrender was thinking something similar to him. "Let us show Delcant no reason to believe we are annoyed at his lack of courtesy", she suggested. "A reaction, especially from me, is what he is looking for. If I say anything about his tardiness in attending this meeting, he will have some well-presented excuse." Both Farrender and Nilan were used to Delcant swaying into Elder Council at the last minute, having had some incredibly important matter to deal with.

Delcant eventually joined them. He was not that late, just sufficiently delayed to seek a response. He was somewhat surprised when Nilan said, "Thank you Delcant for giving Farrender and I some extra time to discuss our views, it was most considerate of you." Again, Delcant had been outmanoeuvred. Silently he simmered with anger but remained outwardly composed. "There was a pressing matter at hand, I am sorry for my short delay. Shall we eat?" Delcant's house staff had laid out a simple table of Decinter victuals. "My table is humble" said Delcant, "but I hope it provides sustenance for you." He went on, with uncharacteristic candour, "I thought we could enjoy the best of our food in the Hiber way, before we have to increase the grandeur of the table when our Tukerland guests join us tomorrow." Neither Farrender, nor Nilan had any argument with this, and it humoured Nilan that what Delcant felt was simple food was actual his favourites Nilan had no appetite for rich food, although it sometimes had to be presented on high occasions. What Delcant had provided, almost as a snub to his King, or at least some half-hearted approach at pretending he was humble, was indeed a feast for both Nilan and Farrender.

"Your table is fair" immediately replied Nilan. "I must remember your preferred food choices when we next meet at Paltir." Both Nilan and Delcant knew that Delcant was never happier than when a rich banquet was laid out in front of him. "That still didn't explain his girth or his ruddy complexion" thought Nilan. He put those thoughts to one side and began to enjoy the meal. A Hiber meal did not take place by way of courses presented one after another. What normally happened was that a selection of small courses were presented at the same time. Hiber etiquette was such that you could eat sweet before savoury, or both at the same time. Some would drink wine, some water, and some beer. There was no requirement to follow anyone else. It made for a highly communal and convivial approach to eating together. Even Delcant relaxed as they ate. Conversation was limited to things in common such as plans for the local Winter Festival; to how the plans were progressing for the migration to Paltir and to the safety of the Queen Mountain for the Winter Sleep.

The table was simple but it was also extensive. Several hours passed as the three sat, ate and chatted in a pleasant manner. "If only Delcant could always be like this" thought Farrender. "He can be good company when he tries" she said to herself. But that was one of Delcant's strengths. He was quick to assess how best to treat those in front of him. He knew that a simple table would either give a slight offence that no one would be able to challenge, or show that he was humble at heart. To balance the food against the opulence of the accommodation was a necessary ploy. Looking at the relaxed repose of both Farrender and Nilan, perhaps he had got it right thought Delcant.

The meal drew to a close and Delcant indicated that they sit close to the fire that a member of house staff had built up. Nilan could see that fire cones, now placed on the fire, were from many different Hiber communities. Each nation had a predominant tree variety and their cones burnt with different colours. Even Nilan had not thought of mixing the cones. It must be said the rainbow fire effect that the cones created as they burnt was spectacular. Nilan was mesmerised by the dance in front of him. "Delcant, what a marvellous idea to mix the fire cones, I have not see the like of it anywhere else." Even Farrender was impressed and added, "I don't agree with you on much Elder Delcant, but I can say this, you know how to present a good hearth." Delcant nodded indulgently and enjoyed the praise.

"So, to the matter at hand, Elder Delcant" started Nilan. "We know that there are easy trade options that we can just nod through this year and I am sure that you have all these points covered." "Of course King Nilan, I can assure you that I have made extensive progress already. In the preliminary talks with my contacts in Tukerland, there is an ample supply of Tukerland beer and farming tools to ensure all our excess arable surplus can be traded again this year. If I may continue, the transport across both our nation and Tukerland has been arranged and the trade can take place as soon as we agree it. I hope that this meets your satisfaction." Farrender looked at Nilan who indicated that she should answer. "Thank you Delcant, that is most acceptable, and it is to your credit that this has been achieved in the earlier talks you mention. We will ensure the Council are fully aware of the hard work you have put into this years trade negotiations." Delcant saw no hidden meaning in this reply, and indeed there wasn't one. Farrender gave praise where it was deserved, regardless of her personal views of someone or something.

"Now this leaves the trade issues that may prove difficult" replied Nilan as he looked at Delcant. "What extra areas of trade have Tukerland asked to be considered?" Delcant looked from Nilan to Farrender and then back to Nilan. "King Nilan, Tukerland are renowned for their animal husbandry and they have asked for trade in Hiber livestock. They feel that Hiber livestock, bred together with their own, would provide a sustainable source of stock for them." As he said this, he knew that this would not be at all palatable to the majority of the Hiber peoples. Nilan waited and then invited Farrender to speak "What do you think of this request Elder Farrender?" asked Nilan. He little needed to ask as it was absolutely clear what her answer would be, but it had to be vocalised. "King Nilan, my position is clear on this, and I truly believe I would have the support of almost the whole Council", looking pointedly at Delcant. "If this request was made, then we would have to refuse it immediately. What Delcant doesn't make clear is that, as we know, the predominant requirement of increased livestock for Tukerland is to produce meat products to be eaten."

Delcant felt he had to step in at this point, not least as he was fully aware that he had encouraged a level of expectation in Grasby that this matter would at least be discussed. "King Nilan, it is accepted that our culture does not encourage eating livestock. However, that is not a value or judgement we can place on the Tukerland nation." Farrender responded, "Elder Delcant, this is a well rehearsed argument that you have made time and again at Council. Of course we accept that Tukerland should feed itself as it sees fit, but not with our livestock. Our animals are revered for the support provided to us in the giving of their strength, their fleeces, their milk and their protection. We would never approve of them being traded for slaughter."

Nilan looked upon this situation with a heavy heart. He fully anticipated that Delcant had given a level of expectation with his earlier negotiations that would make the forthcoming discussions difficult. Whilst he had no sympathy for Delcant, it would not be just Delcant who would face the potential backlash from this. And, as he was present as King of the Hiber Nation, it was likely that the ever manipulative Delcant would subtly shift the blame for any perceived change in direction onto his shoulders. He held Delcant in his gaze and asked "What else should we be concerned with Elder Delcant?" Delcant looked into the fire and then over to his King. "Tukerland would also like an active trade in Hiber Tree saplings in order that they can be planted within the Tukerland nation." Again, Farrender spoke up immediately, "Elder Delcant, we all know that Tukerland see trees in a very different cultural manner than we do. We do not harvest our tree stock. Rather we have learnt to work with nature and our buildings are living entities. The wood we burn and the instruments we make are all from branches willingly cast from these magnificent trees. Can you honestly say that Tukerland would treat the trees in the same manner?"

Delcant was fully aware that Tukerland grew and harvested trees across their nation. Their demand for sawn timber was outstripping supply, and re-planting of forests had been significantly neglected during the long generations of war within Tukerland. Sargern had commenced a reforestation programme, but it would be many years before that programme became anywhere close in providing for Tukerland's almost insatiable desire for timber. Delcant weighed his words carefully and replied to both Nilan and Farrender. "Again, it is true that our culture is very different to that of Tukerland. But, if you have seen the amazing buildings they have constructed with wood and iron, you may even see the beauty in their craftwork." King Nilan interjected, "On one level I can see your point about the craftwork of Tukerland artisans. However, they are only one generation away from using all that craftwork to engineer weapons of war. In fact, the risk of shortage of trees in their country is directly related to how they depleted their vast forests for such engines of war." Nilan continued, "There are stories of old that Tukerland trees were very much similar to those we have in our nation. However, over time, they have denuded the growth stock to such a level that trees do not grow with the same vigour or lifespan of our trees."

"If we could trust Tukerland not to harvest their trees, there would be potential that we could trade our skills and our trees with them. But how would we guarantee that they would not just grow them and cut them down?" said Farrender. Delcant thought that there may be a glint of an opportunity here. "Elder Farrender and King Nilan, if we could get guarantees that the Tukerland nation would grow and nurture trees like we do, would this be a basis for negotiations?" Both Farrender and Nilan had already discussed this point and Nilan indicated to Farrender to provide a response. "I think there is potential that we may consider this under strict guarantees. It would have to be tied to a willingness to withdraw any further requests about livestock. Additionally, we would ask that our Tree gardeners remain in Tukerland to train and observe how Tukerland use the trees. Of course, this would also have to be held off until after the Winter Sleep."

Delcant could see that Nilan and Farrender were in agreement. He would gain nothing if he tried to push further. He smiled at both of them and said, "Well, it seems that we do have room for trade in that case." However, in his heart, and in his mind, he also knew that Grasby would not be at all happy with this, and he feared what his reaction would be. Secretly, he dreaded how the negotiations would progress and he just hoped his scheming and devious approach to both Grasby and to his kinfolk hadn't gone a step too far.

Nilan yawned and theatrically stretched out his arms. "Well, it has been a long day, and negotiations will commence tomorrow evening. I suggest we call this informal meeting to an end and we can reconvene at the formal meeting." Farrender and Delcant took their lead from this subtle request to conclude the evening. As the fire still burned with spectacular colours, they left the room and headed off to their accommodation. Delcant felt it likely that sleep would not easily come as he tried to work out how best to manoeuvre the negotiations and the negotiators. It was going to be a very difficult few days. But a flicker of hopeful greed was very much alive in Delcant. He could still make this work, just about!

Chapter Ten

The Tukerland delegation had arrived in Decinter and had been accommodated by Delcant into one of the many suites in the extensive complex he had caused to be built. Saltock surveyed his suite and furnishings, which were very different to what he was used to. It was the first time he had observed the intricacies of Hiber construction. Of course, he had heard about the Hiber trees and how they were trained and woven in such a way that the building was almost a living and breathing entity. It was for this reason that Grasby had wanted to extend the talks to include trade in these Hiber trees. Saltock thought the skills of the tree gardeners, as he had learnt they were called, were superb. They wrought with bough and limb of trees what his artisans did with sawn timber and iron. That is not to say that Tukerland builders were not skilful. Their ability to build huge and resilient structures was beyond anything he could do. If the two groups of artisans could, in some way, work together, there would be no end to what structures could be built. Sadly, Saltock thought that many of his kinfolk, including Grasby, would not appreciate the beauty of these Hiber buildings. They would not understand the symbiotic relationship that allowed trees to remain fully rooted in the soil, whilst providing shelter and warmth. It was likely that all they would want to do would be to grow these magnificent trees and then cut them down.

Saltock was still keen to explore the potential for trade in Hiber trees with the Hiber delegation. Yet he would fully understand the reticence that the delegation would have in agreeing to this if they thought their precious stock would just be grown and harvested, sawn into dead planks of wood, and nailed with iron into immovable buildings without the breath of life running through their walls. Looking at what the Hiber craftspeople had achieved, why couldn't Tukerland try to harness the living craft? It would mean that precious iron deposits could be used for other issues. He wasn't sure that Grasby had even thought of this as an option. And his concern was that, even if Grasby agreed, would he renege on any agreements once plant stock had been delivered to them?

Saltock turned his mind towards the initial welcome meal that was planned for the evening. It would be the first time he would be able to have extensive discussions with Hiber people, other than his limited experience of Delcant. Saltock hoped that they were not all like Delcant, whom he had taken a rapid dislike to. Whilst Grasby and Delcant appeared to have a close relationship, it was clear to Saltock that Delcant was much more the weaker partner. Delcant may have matched Grasby in deviousness and manipulation, but he didn't match him in physical "presence" and malevolence. Saltock knew Grasby could not, at the moment at least, be any threat to Saltock due to the protection of his father. That wasn't the case with Delcant, and in recent meetings that he had observed in Tukerland, Grasby gave the distinct impression that Delcant was an important, but ultimately disposable asset to the Tukerland delegation.

Saltock had not had a pleasant journey from Tukerland to Decinter. The journey was not particularly long, certainly the Tukerland capital was much closer to Decinter than the journey the Hiber delegation had made. What had made it challenging was having to listen to Grasby's condescending conversation all the way through. It was clear to Saltock that Grasby did not welcome having him present in the delegation. Whilst he had kept quiet during Saltock's briefing in the presence of Sargern and the Warrior leadership, Grasby had no such reservations on the journey. "I find these negotiations tedious and frustrating in equal measure" growled Grasby. "If I had my way, we would be informing the Hiber delegation of our requirements, and this meeting would be just to ensure their compliance." A barely controlled anger was clear in his voice. "Pretending that we have to politely request what they are willing to export to us is a sign of weakness, which I do not think is good for the long term prosperity of Tukerland." Saltock, listening to this, thought that Grasby was concerned mainly with the long term personal aspirations of Grasby, rather than any benefit to Tukerland.

"My father brought peace to Tukerland and we have become prosperous as a result of that enduring peace" replied Saltock. "Why would he want to visit war upon our neighbour, when we can achieve what we need through peaceful negotiation?" Grasby looked at Saltock as if he was a naive child. "Son", he said, in a manner that was intended to belittle rather than for any sign of affection, "We have a proud history as a warrior nation. We were born into blood and conflict and our current prosperity is built on this. Your father took the leadership of Tukerland by blood and has held it by force; we should follow his lead and do the same outside of our border." Saltock wondered if Grasby would have been so openly hostile if Sargern had actually been present. But, then again, Grasby was highly intelligent and had tied his response into both faint praise and criticism of Sargern. Saltock did not reply, but noted this conversation and he would report back to his father.

Saltock had wondered if Sargern had sent him with Grasby to learn from him, or to be his eyes and ears in a meeting that Grasby may not fully or accurately report back to Sargern and the Warrior elite. Perhaps his father's intent was for him to learn how not to negotiate, and Grasby looked like he was going to be a good tutor in that respect. Saltock was also comforted in that he knew he had his father's full trust and it was obvious that he was confident that Saltock would report back fully on the outcome of the meeting. He wished that Nirtan was with him on this journey. Nirtan was surprisingly reticent in coming along, despite Sargern suggesting he join Saltock and Grasby. He had informed Sargern that he had too much work in Tukerland to be away, even for a few days. However, he sent Mortarn as his personal aide. Sargern, being aware that Mortarn was loyal to Nirtan and would be equally supportive to Saltock, had agreed with this. Mortarn did not have the physique of a typical Tukerland warrior, and was similar in deportment to Nirtan. All three were of the same age and Sargern had seen Mortarn at Nirtan's side in battle and had no doubts about his fighting abilities.

The main Tukerland delegation was just Grasby and Saltock. Mortarn would be present in Decinter to support their needs but would not actively take part in the meetings. It suited Grasby that his influence was not diluted by the presence of other aides in the negotiations. That way, which was his intention, he would be able to manipulate exactly how the meetings progressed. This was made somewhat more difficult now that Saltock was with him. In fact, Grasby's general belligerence was made somewhat worse as he had almost been relegated to a deputy negotiator, with a much younger warrior usurping his prime role. Grasby only managed to keep this annoyance in check by thinking he had already primed the meeting in his earlier interactions with Delcant and, as a result, Grasby and Delcant would be able to easily outmanoeuvre both the Hiber negotiators and Saltock.

Saltock had been intrigued to hear that the Hiber King, Nilan, had decided to be present at the negotiations. Delcant had made it look like that this was an honour bestowed upon the Elder. Whatever the reason, Saltock was looking forward to meeting the Hiber equivalent of his father. Prior to leaving for the meetings, Nirtan had advised Saltock that Nilan was a man of integrity and he could be trusted in the negotiations. Nirtan did not expand on why he knew this to be the case and Saltock had learnt not to ask when it was clear Nirtan did not want to discuss a matter further. Nirtan had also advised that Elder Farrender, the other negotiator, was equal to Nilan in her integrity, and was a very worthy adversary for both Grasby and Delcant. It struck Saltock that Nirtan viewed Delcant as an internal risk to the Hiber position. That said, even in his limited interactions with Delcant, his devious nature was easy to spot.

Saltock left his suite, with agreement that Mortarn remain until his return. In the corridor he met with Grasby. Grasby did cut an imposing figure. He had dressed in his finest clothes, which were warrior-like in nature, but sufficiently tailored to look like civic regalia. He was a head taller than Saltock and battle scars on his face made him look formidable without him having say or do anything. Grasby was the same age as Saltock's father's, but had not expanded his waistline to the degree that many of the older warriors, Sargern included, had done. At his side, Saltock knew he looked very much the junior partner in these talks. Saltock had decided to wear a set of rather subdued but smart clothing, made of Hiber wool. Although they were cut in the Tukerland style, he hoped that anyone from the Hiber team would note he was trying to pass a positive message to them by the way he had dressed. "Why are you not wearing your civic regalia?" asked Grasby as he looked at Saltock with withering eyes. "We need to project power and force all the way through these meetings." Saltock held Grasby's gaze and replied, "You have more than achieved that I think", in a half hearted compliment that Saltock knew could be construed as nothing but. "I have decided to recognise the importance of these trade talks by wearing a Tukerland garment made from the finest Hiber wool." He continued, "I think your martial prowess and my more modest apparel will bring a good balance to the meeting." Saltock groaned loudly and then muttered "we are not looking for balance. We are looking to inform the Hiber people of our requirements, and to remind them that these are not polite requests." At that point, they were met by Delcant who escorted them to the dining hall.

Delcant had chosen the finest room in the building to host the meeting. It was much more opulent than the room he, Nilan and Farrender had held their meeting the night before. Nilan and Farrender were already present. "King Nilan is looking around the room as if he is seeing it for the first time", thought Saltock. Indeed, both and Farrender and Nilan had not been in this latest extension to Delcant's Elder house. "Delcant, said King Nilan "This room is more than a match for any dining space we have in Paltir." "King Nilan", Delcant replied in a slightly high voice, "It was felt that the negotiations each year needed a room befitting the status of our honoured guests." He continued with his explanation, "This room has recently been completed for that purpose, I hope it is to your satisfaction." King Nilan just nodded with a neutral look on his face. However, the woman standing next to him did not appear to hide her distain for Delcant. Whilst she had not been introduced, it was obvious that this was the Elder called Farrender. Nirtan had advised him that Farrender and Delcant were implacably opposed in many respects.

There was an uneasy moment of silence which Saltock suddenly felt he should fill. "King Nilan, please may I pay my respects to you and Elder Farrender for the long journey you have had. My father passes on his regards and asks that you accept me in his stead." In order to assuage Grasby's obvious dislike for his secondary role, he continued, "As you know Warrior Grasby has worked hard in preliminary meetings with Elder Delcant, and I am grateful for his support in these negotiations." King Nilan smiled at Saltock as he thought of an equally diplomatic reply. "Warrior Saltock, son of Sargern, leader of the Tukerland people, it is an honour to meet you. Sadly, matters of state for both Sargern and myself preclude our meeting in person. However, if he is as eloquent as you are, I am missing a great leader to speak with." He then looked at Grasby who had moved closer to Elder Delcant, "And I also add my thanks to Warrior Grasby and Elder Delcant for all their work on the run up to this important annual event." King Nilan then formally introduced Elder Farrender. "May I introduce Elder Farrender to you and to Warrior Grasby. As Warrior Grasby will be aware, Farrender has been our key negotiator for many years, but she is stepping down from this role soon. I took the opportunity to join her and learn from her before she retires as I will need to support our Elder Council in identifying new negotiators as we move forward."

Delcant looked up and tried to hide his surprise. Was it a mistake that King Nilan had said 'new negotiators' in the plural? "Surely" Delcant said to himself, "He meant just one new negotiator to replace Farrender?" Nothing had been discussed about Delcant's position of negotiator being up for consideration. Grasby looked at King Nilan and also at Delcant. He said nothing, but his look was also one of surprise. Both Grasby and Delcant were distracted by this subtle indication that a change of negotiators may be being considered by the King and the Elder Council. If Delcant was removed it would destroy many years of careful manipulation by Grasby. Equally, Delcant was thinking about how he could maintain his influence in the full Elder Council if he was no longer viewed as the chief negotiator with Tukerland. At this point in time neither Grasby nor Delcant could add to the conversation as it would have betrayed their machinations. It was left to Saltock to reply, "King Nilan, my father will happily accept anyone your Council chooses to represent Hiber interests in future meetings. Should new negotiators be chosen for next year, please allow us to honour Elder Farrender and Elder Delcant for all their hard work over the years."

"So", thought Delcant, "Saltock has also picked up on this issue" and he looked across to King Nilan, hoping that he would rectify the comment he had made. He was very much mistaken when King Nilan replied, "That is very generous of you Warrior Saltock. As Elder Delcant has worked so hard at extending his dwelling, it would be appropriate to hold any festivities to recognise Farrender and Delcant at this palatial dwelling here in Decinter. It would certainly reduce the distance you would have to travel. You have given me much to think about." Delcant's face remained impassive, or at least he hoped it did. He could actively argue that he was essential to the negotiations in future years. However, he was fully aware that the trade between Tukerland and the Hiber communities came from all Hiber communities. There was no logical reason why another Elder could not take on the role. This would significantly, if not terminally, impact on his plans for greater and greater influence within the Elder Council and he would need to think carefully, and quickly, about how to address this.

At this point the group were shown to their seats to begin their meal. As in the way of Hiber culture, the food was served in one sitting. This also had the benefit of allowing all the serving staff to leave the room so that the negotiations could be discussed in privacy. The meal was much grander than that experienced by Nilan and Farrender the night before. Nilan was very happy for this to be the case. He understood it was important to host their Tukerland guests generously, but it also allowed them to show the Hiber produce that would be subject to export too. Meat was missing from the platters and Nilan used this as the opportunity to throw himself straight into the matters at hand.

"Warrior Saltock, you will note that our food does not include any produce from livestock. Forgive me if this is difficult for you, as we know that such food is a mainstay the Tukerland peoples. I hope, however, you will find our food tasty and filling. We have had many years experience in fulfilling all our needs from edible crops, and we are told that some of our plants have a consistency not unlike the food you are used to eating." He then added "But enough of that, let us enjoy this feast and talk of less pressing matters whilst we eat." Saltock was indeed impressed with the food laid out before him. Whilst he ate meat, as all did in Tukerland, he was not at all disappointed with the spread laid out before him. And, to a degree, some of the platters did contain food that was uncannily like meat, both in texture and taste.

Saltock wondered how the Hiber Nation could be so 'connected' to their natural world, bending their own needs to nature rather than forcing nature to bend to theirs. It was a real cultural divide between the two nations, and one that would be hard to ever reconcile with the majority of his kinfolk. But that was a much larger consideration that he didn't need to worry about at this time. The key issue was negotiating ongoing trade. However, unknown to Saltock, Grasby was having parallel, but much more sinister, thoughts. "At some point" thought Grasby, "the Hiber Nation has to become a vassal of Tukerland. It will be our warehouse and our store, and I will be it's master." Those thoughts gave him a malicious warmth and he smiled to himself. "The challenge to my influence in this year's meeting is one I can bear" he muttered to himself. "In due course, I will bend to no one, the Hiber Nation will bend to us or it will break." Delcant was trying to read the situation and could see Grasby smiling to himself. A shudder went up his spine, as he had seen that smile before. It betrayed a cold and heartless interior. Delcant knew he was dealing with a monster, but he could not let go of his own desires to gain greater influence, if not total control, of the Hiber Council in due course. Little did he know that Grasby's intentions were much wider, and far more violent, than Delcant could imagine.

The evening ended in polite conversation and the delegates returned to their accommodation. The following morning it was obvious that Delcant had not slept well. He looked tired and underneath his eyes he had heavy dark lines appearing. By comparison, Saltock had slept peacefully. The food, he felt, had been responsible for allowing him to wake revived and ready to enter into further discussions. Grasby's jowly complexion was hard to read. The fact was that he had demanded a further meeting with Delcant in the early hours of the morning. More by threat than persuasion, he had ensured that Delcant would work with him today to move the meeting to a position that was favourable to Grasby's desired outcomes. It was for this reason that Delcant was short on sleep, even though he had not troubled Farrender nor Nilan with the fact of the meeting, or the content of the conversation that had taken place.

Saltock and Grasby shared breakfast. "No meat for dinner and none for Breakfast" complained Grasby. "Are they trying to break our will?" he said. "The sooner we get home to Tukerland the better." Saltock was very happy with the breakfast fare laid before him and he reminded himself to abstain from meat, at least for some days in the week. He felt nowhere near as sluggish as he normally did after a banquet, and was ready for the day ahead. "I agree Warrior Grasby", using his official title. Grasby had never offered to Saltock a more informal address for him, and Saltock did not want to antagonise him anymore than necessary. Saltock had met with Mortarn after the evening meeting and they had discussed potential ways to progress the impending negotiations. Both had agreed that it would be in the wider interests of Tukerland to limit any forceful negotiations on the export of livestock, at least for this year. Whilst Delcant seemed to be in support, it was clear that Farrender and Nilan would not move on this. Saltock decided not to push this issue, rather he would take the initiative on ensuring this did not delay the negotiations unnecessarily. However, at this time, he said nothing to Grasby and he kept his council to himself.

The secondary issue that was worthy of exploration was the potential for there to be a discussion on a limited export of Hiber trees, under the careful supervision of Hiber gardeners. Saltock decided that he would offer to personally guarantee that the trees would be well cared for, as would be the gardeners. Of course, this project could not commence until after the Winter Sleep that would soon take place. What he wanted to ask, and was not sure of the response, was if King Nilan would agree to Saltock personally taking one tree to assess how it fared in a winter without needing to go into its 'ice condition' that he had heard of. He would have been very interested in the outcome. A small sapling, which couldn't be harvested in anyway, could be the request. This again, he kept to himself. He had no desire to embarrass Grasby, and he did not want an argument over breakfast, even though he may have to unpack that argument on another occasion. It would also serve to expose the pressure he was under from Grasby if the Hiber team saw the two of them at odds. Mortarn and Saltock had discussed this risk but both felt that it would also show that Saltock was his own person, capable of thinking beyond Grasby's entrenched views. It would also send a clear message that he was not part of any clandestine and inappropriate partnership with Delcant and Grasby. The thought of the challenge excited Saltock, rather than troubled him. He continued his breakfast, happy with the task ahead of him.

The four key members of the delegation met after breakfast. Delcant had chosen a smaller room for the meeting and ensured that privacy was maintained. Saltock had requested that Mortarn be present to take notes. Grasby thought this a good idea, and the Hiber delegates agreed. Mortarn had been very concerned, almost nervous at the idea, but had no real choice if he was to maintain his role as servant to Saltock. He asked Saltock if he could remain very much in the background in order for him not to be a barrier to the conversations taking place. With him there, he argued, whilst it could be said that Tukerland and the Hiber Nation had equal weight of numbers, Mortarn was not of sufficient authority to be an equal to Grasby and Saltock. Saltock thought Mortarn was being too concerned, but agreed to Mortarn's request. Nevertheless he hadn't expected Mortarn to wear a hooded cloak similar to those of scribes in Tukerland. He put this to the back of his mind and would discuss this with him later.

Farrender and Nilan appeared fresh and well rested as they sat at the table. It was a particularly large table, expertly crafted from the branches of the living trees in the room. In recognition of the Tukerland delegation, a wrought iron vessel fashioned from Tukerland iron, filled with Hiber fruit, was placed in the middle. In addition, exquisite metal goblets and a jug, clearly of Tukerland origin, were also placed on the table. "Delcant is an accomplished diplomat, even if he is not to be trusted" thought Saltock. Grasby took very little notice of the efforts that Delcant had made and, in fact, he appeared to be glaring at Delcant.

King Nilan, as etiquette dictated, opened the meeting. "Warrior Saltock and Warrior Grasby, we welcome you to this meeting. We note your scribe is present, and in due course we can agree his transcription as being a true and accurate record of this meeting" he said, looking over at the hooded Mortarn, who had placed himself discreetly away from the table. Nilan continued, "Elder Delcant and Elder Farrender are our chief negotiators but I feel that we can probably reduce much of these discussions if we focus on what are clearly issues of concern." He continued into the main business. "For our part, we agree to export to you as much arable produce, wool and cheese as we can spare and we will look to make this trade in the very near future." Without waiting for a response, he continued. "In return, we will welcome a trade in beer and in iron goods that Tukerland have such an amazing reputation for." At that, he looked at Saltock and Grasby. "Are you happy for the detail to be worked out between the wider folk of our nations?"

Saltock looked at Grasby who indicated he had nothing to say and so replied, "That is most satisfactory King Nilan. We have had an excellent year for brewing, and our craftspeople have built up a significant stock of iron goods we are sure will be welcome in your nation." Delcant looked a little less apprehensive as this discussion was going on and even smiled thinly at the thought that, at least, the usual elements of trade had been agreed within the minimum of unnecessary discussions. This still left two significant aspects for consideration, and his smile soon wavered as he waited for these issues to be raised.

"A real concern for us" expanded Nilan "Is your request for export of livestock to Tukerland." A silence spread across the table, and Grasby took a deep breath, waiting to respond. Nilan spoke softly but with confidence. "We feel that it would not be the right time take this request further this year. Our culture is very different to that of Tukerland. We make no criticism in this respect, but we cannot consider to trade anything that would hurt our animals, who are very dear to us and who rely on us for protection." As Grasby started to speak, Saltock indicated with this hand that he wanted to reply in the first instance. The fury that flashed across Grasby's face was barely hidden, as he nodded his awareness of Saltock's instruction. "It is true that I am younger in years that all of you around this table, and I am grateful that Warrior Grasby has allowed my lead on these discussions with his grace and support", knowing full well that the only reason Grasby remained silent was fear of the rage of Sargern if Saltock reported back negatively to him. "I have read much about your culture and have observed some of it first hand over the last couple of days. I agree with your views and we remove this request for export of livestock from this year's negotiations."

Grasby and Delcant were astounded, but Delcant hid this much better than Grasby who could almost be heard grinding his teeth as he tried not to erupt and dispute Saltock's statement. Saltock continued, "We respectfully request the opportunity to revisit this issue at a future meeting next year." King Nilan looked at Delcant, who appeared to be in somewhat of a confused and conflicted state. "Of course we can return to this next year, but I must manage your expectations that our position is unlikely to change." Saltock nodded his acceptance of this.

Saltock continued. "If I may King Nilan" he said slowly and quietly, "I think you may have similar concerns about export of your tree stock. However, I think there could be a middle ground on this. I have not had time to discuss this in full with Warrior Grasby" he said looking over at Grasby and then back to Nilan. "I fully accept your position in relation to livestock and I am learning fast that your views on tree stock is of equal concern to you. I wondered if you would consider providing a limited amount of stock, under the care of Hiber Gardeners at a nursery in Tukerland. I would personally vouch that the trees would not be harvested for wood and would be used to try and replicate living structures, like the amazing buildings you have here in the Hiber Nation."

In the short time that the delegations had been face to face it was clear to Nilan that Delcant and Grasby were in league together. Worryingly, Nilan felt that Delcant was much the junior partner in this situation and the lines etched on Delcant's face betrayed his fear too. Even Farrender, normally combative with Delcant, had said very little, almost as if there was a level of pity in her for Delcant's situation. Regardless, Delcant had got himself into this predicament and it was equally as dangerous for the wider situation as for the current risk to Delcant. It reinforced Nilan's view that Delcant had to be removed from future negotiations. It was not entirely in Nilan's grasp to remove Delcant as an Elder, but he could ensure his role in future negotiations were ended after this round of talks.

Farrender had been observing the interactions between Saltock and Grasby. She was impressed with Saltock's overall behaviour and approach to the meetings. It was at odds with Grasby's barely hidden disrespect for the Hiber position, and was also very different from the nervous mutterings of Delcant. She felt it time to speak up. "With your permission King Nilan, may I speak?" Nilan nodded his consent and she continued. "I very much appreciate that Warrior Saltock has taken us to the heart of the issue so quickly. It says much for his integrity, for his statesmanship and also for his respect for our long held cultural views. I would support Saltock's request, but I would ask that he makes time to visit one of our tree surgeries to discuss his plans with our most experienced tree gardeners. We could do this prior to the Winter Sleep this year and set plans in motion for a project when Spring arrives."

Looking across at Farrender, Nilan could see the benefit in this recommendation. The oldest and most established tree surgery was based within the Paltir community. It would mean that Delcant did not have to be involved, and it would ensure Saltock would experience the best hospitality that the Hiber people could bring. If Grasby had to attend with him, so be it, but at least the Hiber delegation would be agreeing to meet the Tukerland delegation halfway. "Thank you Elder Farrender" replied Nilan. "I think Warrior Saltock's request has a great deal of merit and I will approve this course of action." Even Delcant seem to relax at this point, and he was thinking that it would give him the opportunity to continue to destabilise Farrender when he went to Paltir to continue the negotiations. Grasby, on the other hand, was not at all satisfied with this outcome. That said, Grasby was always ready to quickly changed tactics and he realised that he could make valuable use of a visit to the Hiber capital. Grasby looked to Saltock and indicated he would like to add to the conversation, which Saltock immediately and graciously acceded to. "Warrior Grasby, who has so ably led us to agreeing much of what we have discussed thus far, wishes to speak." In truth, Saltock thought that Grasby would argue against the proposal and began to prepare for this.

"In view of the request by Warrior Saltock, and the support of King Nilan and Elder Farrander" he said, pointedly ignoring Delcant, "I would support this visit and I would be happy join in this meeting. I think we first need to return to our Warrior Council to ensure their agreement, and then we could commence a journey to Paltir; arriving a few days after your own return." Saltock looked across at Grasby and tried to disguise his surprise. "Grasby is not supportive of this, and he will not want this to work, so there must be an ulterior motive to his agreement" Saltock thought to himself. But a return to Tukerland would allow him update his father, and more importantly perhaps, to gain advice from Nirtan on how to progress the negotiations.

"It is agreed then" said King Nilan. "We will conclude the next round of meetings in Paltir and our staff will progress all the agreed elements of the trade negotiations. Upon our return home, we will prepare for Warrior Saltock and Warrior Grasby to join us in Paltir, after they have briefed their Warrior elite. If the timing is right, you will both be able to join our Winter Festival and observe our Selection of the HiberWatchers. We can explain all of this at our next meeting." Looking around the table and seeing no dissension, he continued, "If we leave tonight, we can be back in Paltir in a few days, and our Tukerland colleagues have a much shorter trip back to their homeland. Given the time they will need to get agreement from their fellow leaders, I would think that we can reconvene in about a week's time." Delcant was looking more and more energetic and relaxed until Nilan continued, "It is clear that Elder Delcant is needed here in Decinter to manage the logistics of the trade we have agreed and to oversee the migration of his community to Queen Mountain for the Winter Sleep. For that reason, it is unfortunate that he will not be able to join us in Paltir."

At this, Delcant began to speak. "King Nilan, I'm sure that my presence would be more beneficial advising you in Paltir, and I am happy ensure our local Decinter leadership group can cover for me in my absence." Nilan smiled at Delcant and replied to him. "Thank you for that kind offer, Elder Delcant, but I will decline and I look forward to updating you personally on how things progress when we next meet." King Nilan rose from the table. All present took this as an indication that the meeting had concluded. Surprisingly, Warrior Saltock took a step towards King Nilan and clasped his hand in the Hiber way and said "Thank you King Nilan, it was a privilege to meet with you and Elder Farrender, I look forward to meeting again." Then he turned and started to leave the room. No one missed the fact that he had not even looked at Elder Delcant or Grasby as he did so. To Farrender who was watching carefully, it was a message that Saltock wanted to give loud and clear; he was in charge, and had got the full measure of Grasby and Delcant.

"Your usefulness was exceptionally limited in the meetings" growled Grasby to Delcant as they left the room together. "In fact, your usefulness in our continuing partnership is, perhaps, coming to an end." Grasby then walked back to his rooms, like a man who had encountered a rare defeat. Delcant knew that this would made him a more dangerous adversary indeed. Delcant thought to himself "Perhaps it is better that I am not part of the next meeting", as he watched Grasby walk away. "I can plan my next steps, away from the gaze of both Grasby and King Nilan, plans that will ensure I survive this situation, regardless of the wider outcomes." He smiled to himself and walked to his rooms.

Chapter Eleven

Queen Torcas met with Nilan as soon as he arrived back at Paltir. Nothing needed to be said at that moment. They just enjoyed the presence of each other as they walked back to their rooms, set within the wider complex that housed the Elder Council and other departments necessary for the running of the Paltir community. It struck Nilan that these living walls had been growing for centuries. Within them they had protected and nurtured the nation. It was a massive, sprawling complex; both welcoming and functional. The scale was beyond anything else across the Hiber Nation. However, thought Nilan, it was clear that Delcant was constructing in Decinter a vanity project to copy, or even usurp, this building. There was no denying the opulence within the Decinter building. However, to Nilan, it was missing something. He couldn't quite put his finger on what that was other than the trees and their walls projected a kind of sadness. The atmosphere in the smaller rooms were similar in feeling to the Paltir rooms. However, where Delcant had sought to impress with the spacious meeting rooms, it was as if the trees were more captive than willing partners in providing a building for the Decinter Elder.

"So, how did the meeting go?" asked Torcas as they walked through the complex to their private quarters. "Was Farrender correct in her criticisms of Delcant?" Nilan audibly sighed and turned to Torcas, holding her hand lightly. "In every respect" he replied. "Delcant has built a complex to rival this beautiful building, but it is missing something. It is very grand but, I know it may sound strange, the walls shout out their sadness." Torcas and Nilan were so attuned to each other that she could immediately sense what Nilan was trying to articulate. "If the inside of the building is not happy, if the people are not happy, then the walls will retain and reflect this. As much as our history breathes through the walls we are walking past now, so the trees will be suffering in that building if Delcant is as we think." Nilan nodded his agreement, "There is no doubt that Delcant is a good host, and he has harnessed the skills of the tree gardeners in his community, but he has not included the spirit of the Hiber people in the building." The weight of his disappointment was obvious, and he continued, "It is a glorious but sad building that is all I can say."

This was not the mood that Nilan and Torcas wanted around them after their enforced separation. In order to lighten the conversation Torcas explained that she had spent time with the Kian and Kindross in the Hiber library. As she explained her conversations to Nilan, he smiled and said, "I am so pleased that you were able to have some time of comfort whilst I was away. I have a feeling that the poem you mention may provide some comfort to us if we find the original scripture." Torcas added, "It was interesting that our conversation drifted to Jandray and to Sartora, both of whom are highly regarded by the Key Keepers." Torcas then explained her plan, which had not occurred yet, to meet with Maltas and Altera. Nilan agreed, "I think you are wise indeed not to meet directly with Lorsern or Sartora, we cannot give the supporters of Delcant any reason to think we favour either of them." As he reflected on this he said, "But, having seen Delcant in his home environment, I think it is clear that we need to disconnect him from future trade negotiations, and we need to carefully consider a replacement for him as Elder." Torcas looked carefully into Nilan's eyes as she had not expected this from Nilan. "Are you saying that Farrender is so accurate in her views that Delcant is a greater risk to the Hiber people that we thought?" "Sadly" Nilan replied slowly, "I think it not only true, but Delcant's aspirations may reach much further than any of us imagined."

Torcas and Nilan had not realised that they had stopped in the centre of the corridor as they discussed these issues and they decided to continue the conversation in their rooms. They quickly walked the remainder of the way in silence, eventually entering their main living area. In contrast to that of Delcant, the Queen and King enjoyed humble quarters, and the walls seemed vibrant and welcoming after what Nilan had experienced in recent days. A member of house staff brought a simple platter of bread, cheese and wine whilst Torcas and Nilan remained silent. Torcas thanked the staff for the food and when they were again on their own Nilan poured the wine into two cups. As he passed the wine to Torcas, he kissed her and said, "But there are hopeful matters to discuss too." This comment lifted Torcas's spirits and she took a sip of the wine. "Please do tell me about this more positive aspect of your time away." Nilan then explained that the majority of trade agreements had been concluded satisfactorily and he had left Delcant to manage the details of what had been agreed. He then covered the issue of livestock trade and the agreement to shelve any discussion on this. Finally, he covered the request by Saltock to host Hiber tree gardeners in Tukerland as a limited project.

"Can this Warrior Saltock be trusted?" asked Torcas. "I think he can", replied Nilan, "But I would welcome your own perceptive views on this matter. I have invited Saltock to join us here in Paltir to discuss the project further. Assuming that he gains the permission of his father and the ruling elite in Tukerland, he will be with us in a few days time. I was hoping we could accommodate him here and he may well even stay for the Selection and for the Winter Festival." Nilan then added, "Unfortunately, it is likely he will be accompanied by a Warrior called Grasby, who appears in league with Delcant. However, I fear that Delcant has gotten himself into a precarious and possibly dangerous relationship with a violent man." Torcas welcomed Nilan's openness in his views. "So, what makes you think that this Saltock can be trusted?" she asked. "He is the son Sargern, who brutally took control of the Tukerland nation. Does his son follow his father?" Nilan could appreciate his wife's concerns. "Saltock is reasonably young, not much older that Maltas and Altera. He is tall, of the Tukerland way, but he is slimmer than the broad physique that many of his kinfolk have. More importantly, he had a humility and a perception of diplomacy that I have rarely encountered in Tukerland leaders. It was clear to me that he and Grasby have differing views on how the trade meeting should have progressed. That said, whilst he was diplomatic and also sensitive to Grasby's more belligerent attitude, Saltock was confident and had a maturity not to be expected in one so young."

"He clearly impressed you" said Torcas as she looked across at Nilan. "I look forward to meeting him. Perhaps, if he is a similar age to Maltas and Altera, we could arrange for him to meet our younger folk too." "I hadn't thought of that" said Nilan. "It is an excellent idea. Our future is in the hands of the next generation, and forging early links, possibly friendship, would be a wise move. What little I have heard of Maltas and Altera from you, I have no doubt that you view them as leadership potential in the future." Torcas laughed freely. "Are my views that transparent? You are right, I feel that they will have a significant part to play in the future of our Hiber Nation, and I think the Key Keepers feel that too. Although they didn't say as such, it was just that they were very open to me almost mentoring them." "My Queen, the Key Keepers are as aware of your wisdom as I am" Nilan said, smiling back at her. "I look forward to seeing how Altera and Maltas find the Tukerland warrior."

Nilan and Torcas settled into conversation and continued to enjoy their time together. In a few shorts days they would be hosting the Tukerland leaders and also overseeing the HiberWatcher Selection. Just enjoying this time to reflect and to enjoy each other was a welcome distraction. Both, without directly saying anything to each other, were holding worries that they didn't want to trouble each other with. But for now, those troubles could wait.

Chapter Twelve

The Selection was about to commence at the Paltir community. Excitement was growing across all Hiber Communities, each of them having sent representatives to Paltir for this event. As soon as the Selection had taken place, the Winter festivals would take place in each community. It wouldn't be long before winter snows began, the Ice Wall would appear, the ice bridge would form and it would soon be time for the migration into Queen Mountain for the Winter Sleep. However, there was still so much to enjoy before the Hiber people went into this annual time of rest. The excitement in Paltir was heightened as a result of hearing that two warriors from Tukerland would be in attendance at the celebrations. No one could remember a time when warriors from Tukerland had been present at a Selection and also the subsequent festival. Grasby and Saltock had been easy to spot when they had arrived. Grasby cut an imposing figure in his warrior regalia; tall and muscular, he looked like a giant to most people in the Hiber Nation. Alongside him, the youthful features of Saltock. Equal in height, but slimmer than Grasby, he had again dressed in clothes made of Hiber wool. The cut was very different to that of Hiber clothing, but he wore it well. Tailors all over Paltir were rushing to copy the outfit he wore.

Maltas, Altera and the Mountain Keepers society had met up ready for the Selection. Each had done their part in placing Jandray's name into the local selection process. Maltas and Altera had received word that Queen Torcas wanted to meet with them and that they would also meet with Warrior Saltock. "Does the Queen know of our conspiracy?" wondered Altera. "Is this the reason for her wanting to meet with us?" Maltas was less concerned. To the group he said, "Isn't it really good that Queen taking a direct interest in students and wants to know about how they meet outside of class? Whilst we cannot expect the Queen to meet all of us, it is my intention to update her that our class friendship is harmless, positive and entirely due to the excellence of teaching by Jandray." "I agree" added Altera. "We need to ensure that we praise Jandray to the Queen, without giving any idea that we have tried to bypass the random nature of selection." None of the students cared to dwell on what would happen to them if it was discovered what they had done. The embarrassment to their families would be the least of it. But all present knew that the impact would be felt most profoundly on Maltas and Altera, as their parents were highly influential in the Hiber Nation. That embarrassment could translate into long term damage to the reputation of their parents and to their own future. For this reason, all the students respected that Maltas and Altera had the most to lose and if they were willing to risk that then so were the rest of them.

Traditionally the Selection would commence at midday, when the winter sun would be at its highest. It would be presided over by the King and Queen. Each community would be represented at the selection, mostly with their Elder also in attendance. Delcant was not present on behalf of Decinter. Some of the Elders had thought this odd, but were sufficiently placated by the explanation that Delcant needed to progress the trade negotiations and had been given special dispensation by the King to miss the Selection. Only Delcant, Farrender and Nilan knew that he had been instructed to remain in Decinter. Delcant was not going admit this to anyone and hoped that that most would see it as a positive affirmation of the King's support to Delcant.

All the nominations had been brought to the main Paltir Meeting Hall. They had been placed in the Selection chalice, a large round vessel which was now full to the brim with small strips of parchment. The Elders present ensured that the parchments were carefully and thoroughly mixed in the chalice. A surprise honour was given to Warrior Saltock when the King and Queen asked if he would actually pull out the two names who would be the HiberWatchers during the forthcoming Sleep. Whilst Saltock did not fully understand the importance of the HiberWatcher selection to the Hiber people, he was sufficiently aware of the honour that was being bestowed on him. "It is my privilege and honour to be asked" he said as he accepted the role. "I would like to learn more about the HiberWatchers in due course if that is acceptable."

Queen Torcas replied "Of course Warrior Saltock, it is heartening indeed to have your interest in our culture and our history. I have arranged for you to meet representatives of our younger folk after the selection. They have been studying our history in their final year of school. Their teacher is held in particular high regard. He has made no secret of not having any interest in entering the Selection each year, so his teaching is very unbiased and I trust that this has been passed onto his students." "I will enjoy meeting these students" said Saltock and looked across to Grasby. "Will you join us Warrior Grasby?" Grasby replied immediately, "I would feel like a grandfather in a pen of children" he growled. Realising that this may have sounded rude and inconsiderate by Hiber standards he added, "I am happy for you to take the lead on this. However, I understand that there is a particularly good variety of beer that is brewed here in Paltir. I would be grateful to visit the brewer and discuss the differences between Tukerland and Hiber beers." King Nilan, ever the diplomat, stepped in. "That settles it, Queen Torcas will host Warrior Saltock and the students and I will join Warrior Grasby in the search for the best beer." Even Grasby allowed a smile to cross his face at this point. "You will be a most welcome drinking colleague" he replied "But I doubt you will change my views on the best beer."

A sense of quiet began to descend on the hall, tinged with a vibrancy of excitement. Most of the 'Mountain Keepers' society had been able to join in the crowd at the selection. Jandray, who showed little interest in the selection, was not present. Sartora was making a rare appearance with her husband Torpast. Lorsern was present, but seemed somewhat isolated as Delcant was not at the Selection. King Nilan called for silence in the packed hall. "It is the time", he said, "for our two HiberWatchers to be chosen." As he looked round at the expectant crowd he continued, "As we have honoured guests from Tukerland with us this year, finalising this years trade negotiations, we have asked Warrior Saltock if he would pick out the names of the HiberWatchers for this winter." Some of the Hiber folk were surprised, but not at all concerned. The focus of the event was learning who the HiberWatchers would be; who picked them out was secondary.

Saltock approached the front of the stage that had been set up ready for the Selection. He was an impressive and imposing figure as he walked across to join King Nilan. Many of those in the hall noted his clothing was made of Hiber wool, and a murmur of support for his choosing this material was clearly audible in the room. Saltock was not sure if he was expected to say anything and looked towards

King Nilan, who whispered "you may say a few words if you want to." Saltock surveyed the room. He could feel the excitement amongst those present, and was strangely moved by it. This event was looked at with humour and also distain in his country. His folk did not understand the historical relevance of this event and dismissed it as a pointless process. Tukerland warriors knew the mountain passes were cut off under a deep blanket of ice and snow when the Hiber Nation went into their sleep. What need they had of anyone remaining awake was questioned by those who had any remote interest.

Saltock slowly placed his hand into the Selection Chalice. He could see that it was full of small pieces of parchment. King Nilan had explained that it was expected he mix the parchment pieces round with his hand for a few turns until he took one piece of parchment. As he did this, he could feel all the eyes in the hall focussed on him. "This really is important to these people" he thought to himself. His hand grasped at one piece of parchment and he withdrew it carefully and held up high above his head. King Nilan indicated to him to open the parchment and to read out the name contained on it. Saltock was more nervous than he would have liked to admit. One of his biggest fears was that he would mis-pronounce the name on the parchment. Hiber names were different in style to that of Tukerland names. He had learnt that Hiber people did not have a "family" name, rather the community they were from was their family name. His worry was that this could lead to a need to be quite inventive with their given names.

"The name of the first HiberWatcher is Torpast" he announced loudly. On reflection he realised that this was probably too loud by Hiber standards. There was an immediate outbreak of shouts and applause from those in the hall. Two who were not applauding were Sartora and Altera. They had no idea at all that Torpast had decided to put himself forward for selection. Torpast who was standing next to Sartora looked across at her. She did not know what to say and so Torpast, to break the silence between them said, "Sartora, I know we have become estranged in recent times, and I know you think I devote far too much time to my work than my duties to you as your husband." Tears were filling in Sartora's eyes as he continued, "I know that you have had the privilege of being a HiberWatcher before we met. So, I decided to put my name forward for selection as I hope that it will give me time reflect on our family. It is my desire that when you wake from sleep you will find that I am changed person." As his voice became full of emotion too he said "I love you Sartora, and I love our daughter, I will watch over you and all of our peoples, and I will be waiting for you all in Spring." Sartora grasped Torpast's outstretched hands and they pulled together in a warm embrace, in front of the whole hall. When the crowd saw this, knowing nothing of the troubles within their relationship, they loudly applauded these actions of a loving couple.

The applause rose to a crescendo before slowly dying down. Altera made her way to the stage and climbed on it. She ran to her father and mother and joined the embrace, tears streaming down her face. Her father, through his tears said, "When Spring comes, I am stepping down from much of my work, and I will be at your mother's right hand when, as we hope, she takes over as Elder." Sartora looked at Torpast quizzically. "We have never discussed this, and I thought you were jealous of the aspirations that Elder Farrender had for me?" "Not at all" he replied, "for some time Farrender and I have been discussing at length what an excellent candidate you will be." Sartora looked over to Farrender who was standing near to the Queen and King. Farrender was watching the family embrace, and Sartora felt that she could almost see a tear in her eye too, as she smiled at her. "What a lovely gift that Torpast has given me" Sartora thought, "I can hardly wait for Spring" she said to herself, as she continued in the warm embrace of her family.

Saltock realised that it was time to draw out the second name. He returned to the front of the stage and put his hand back into the Chalice. He stirred the pieces of parchment carefully. After a short while, which to those in the hall felt almost as long as their winter sleep, he withdrew his hand with the final piece of paper and announced "The name is Jandray." This time the room remained silent. Many of those present knew Jandray through his role as teacher and he had always showed little interest in this event; proven by the fact that he wasn't present as his name was called out. Saltock was surprised at this lack of reaction to Jandray's name being called. However, he did not know this person and had no idea why there was such a difference in reaction. His confusion was interrupted as King Nilan held up his hand to speak. "Dear Hiber people" he said. "As you know the selection has been concluded and the two names have been drawn out". He looked into the vessel, and

Altera's heart jumped, would any of the other pieces of parchment have opened up and showed Jandray's name? King Nilan continued speaking, "Warrior Saltock is aware that only an individual can nominate him or herself and only they can add their name into the selection." "Oh no, The King has found out" Altera thought as she began to panic. She frantically searched the room for Maltas and any of her fellow students. If they were there, she couldn't see them. "We are going to bring disgrace on all of us, and I will destroy the happiness of my mother and father." She looked mournfully over at Queen Torcas. Altera had so looked forward to meeting with her and Warrior Saltock, and that meeting would now be to decide her punishment.

Altera was still in a fog of despair as King Nilan addressed the hall. "What many of you will not know is what we do with the parchments that are left after selection, and Warrior Saltock certainly has no idea about our traditions and the importance we place on this selection." Altera felt that King Nilan was talking directly at her "So, for the first time we have decided to do in public, what is normally carried out in secret after the event." Altera was so sure he was going to say that the names were opened to ensure no tampering had taken place and was getting ready to seek forgiveness when he suddenly took hold of one of the candles on the stage. He put it into the selection vessel and the parchment papers began to burn. "Each year, after selection, and to ensure the anonymity of those who put themselves forward for selection, we burn the parchments." As the flames rose out of the vessel, King Nilan indicated to Saltock to repeat the two names. Saltock took a deep breath "Torpast and Jandray" he said.

Saltock expected the applause to start immediately, but the silence remained in the hall. "Have I said the name correctly?" he thought and looked at it again. "JANDRAY" was the clear name on the parchment. Unknown to Saltock, both those chosen were from the same community. It was very rare for two HiberWatchers to be chosen from the same community. It was viewed as very auspicious if this happened, and a cause for great celebration for the community concerned. What Queen Torcas hadn't said to Saltock was that amongst the more superstitious Hiber folk it was also said to portend momentous issues for the Hiber Nation. Slowly, the applause began, as the importance of this selection was realised. The Paltir representatives were jubilant that this honour had been bestowed upon their community. Jandray was a well known and well-liked member of the community. Those who knew him also knew that he had always said he would not put himself for selection. Queen Torcas was confused, but delighted, that he had changed his mind.

The people in the hall started to chant Torpast and Jandray's name. Torpast was on the stage and he was looking forward to congratulate Jandray too. However, as the crowd looked around them, it was clear that Jandray was not in the room. "Typical of Jandray", thought Queen Torcas. "He would be so sure that his name would not be chosen, he has not even attended the selection." Queen Torcas walked towards Torpast, Nilan and Saltock. She lifted her hands indicating her desire to address those present. "Many of you will know Jandray, who is a well loved teacher of many years standing in our community" she explained. "Those same people who know him will also know that he is a humble man who does not like recognition of any sort. It is my guess that he had no expectation he would every have been chosen and so is probably at home, preparing lessons for his students. Two of his students are here, that I am sure, and some others may be in the hall. In fact, by strange coincidence, one of his students is Torpast's daughter. I think that this makes the selection very special on many levels. I am only pleased that we did ask Warrior Saltock, someone who knows hardly anyone in our nation, to have made the selection this year. It is a double honour that he has chosen for us, and it has brought an alignment of random events that will go down in Hiber history." As Torcas raised her gaze across those present, she continued, "I am sure that Jandray will learn soon enough of the honour that has been brought to his door, and I look forward to seeing him here tonight at the winter celebration."

Altera's heartbeat barely subsided. They had got away with it, their conspiracy was safe underneath the embers of their parchments that now lay as ash in the bottom of the selection vessel. "So what would Jandray say?" she thought to herself. "Would he decline the honour, would he say that he hadn't put his name forward, what would happen? The other nominations were burnt, and there would be no time for another nomination process." So many questions, and all the answers lay with Jandray.

Chapter Thirteen

Indeed, Jandray was blissfully unaware of the events unfolding at the Selection. Queen Torcas did not realise how accurate she was in her thoughts. Jandray was putting the finishing touches to his lessons for the next few days, where he would go into more detail about the Winter Sleep. One of his favourite parts was explaining how the HiberWatchers were introduced to the only other beings that were awake in the Hiber Nation during the sleep. Two Hiber hounds were identified as 'Watch Hounds'; to remain awake as companions for the HiberWatchers. These hounds were identified for their size, for their loyalty and for one other attribute. During late Autumn all Hiber hounds began to develop a winter coat. It was said by some that the Hiber hounds knew themselves who were to remain awake. This was because a small number of the hounds began to develop white coats, of extra thickness to the rest of their pack. It was the white coat that was so different from the usual rich coats that the hounds normally grew. The normal dark fur of the hounds were lustrous in colour, almost like the leaves on the trees. In fact, hounds were almost impossible to see when amongst the natural foliage in the Hiber Nation.

It was believed by many in the Hiber Nation that the white coat only developed in those hounds who knew that their natural colours would be at odds with the stark white world of winter and that, somehow, their instincts knew when they were to be chosen. There had never been a time when two hounds were not found with coats starting to lighten at the commencement of Autumn. By Autumn's end, these two hounds would be virtually full white in colour. Whilst Hiber hounds lived amongst the Hiber people, they were still wild creatures, and were not domesticated pets. In return for shelter and food they formed a strong bond with their Hiber hosts and many generations of hounds could be traced back through the same families. No one could explain why the fur of only two hounds changed colour and only for one season. The following year, two different hounds would find themselves in this position. It was almost as if they had their own selection event. The two Hiber hounds would be present at the festivities this evening. Whilst Jandray had no real interest in the selection, he was always amazed to see the Hiber hounds. During

Autumn he made it his mission to try and identify the potential hounds that would transfer into this unnaturally light colour. They almost always came from the Paltir region and Jandray had correctly identified the pair for several years.

This year he had been tracking a brother and sister from a litter that had a history of providing Watch Hounds. Whilst they were not normally given names, as he had observed them, in his mind he had named them. The male had a wide chest and deep brown eyes. With a coat that was not fully turned yet, he looked older than his years. Jandray had called him Winterclaw. His sister was of slighter build, but had an energy that was hard to define. She had one deep brown eye similar to her sibling. However, her right eye was as blue as the sky on a winter's day. He had called her Snowblue. Jandray really hoped that Winterclaw and Snowblue were the Watch Hounds. All he had seen of them made him feel that it was their destiny to fulfil that role in the Winter sleep this year.

Jandray's peaceful reflections about the Watch Hounds was shattered by a loud banging noise coming from the front door. His mother slowly walked down the hallway to open to the door and Jandray followed closely behind. When she opened the door both were momentarily stunned by the large crowd on their threshold. Amongst the crowd which Jandray could see were very excited he spotted some of his students. "Why are you all here knocking on our door?" Jandray said. The noise from those present had got louder as soon as they spotted him and he had to shout to make himself heard, "I said, why are you all here, shouldn't you be at the Selection? If you want to make such a noise, go and cheer on the new HiberWatchers." At that the group became even more animated and they started chanting his name "Jandray, Jandray, Jandray." "What in Hiber Nation is this all about?" he thought. Then it slowly dawned on him. He looked over at his mother and it was clear that she was thinking it too. "Mother, you didn't put my name forward did you?" She tried to reply above the noise, "No, Son, I have always respected your wishes, but you could have told me that you were nominating yourself this year. You will be an excellent HiberWatcher, I am so proud of you." "But…." he started to formulate a reply before he realised that she would not be able to hear him above the every increasing noise from the crowd who were chanting his name.

Jandray looked around at the excited faces. "If it wasn't me or mother who put my name forward for selection, then who would do such a thing?" he said to himself, whilst his heart was racing and his logical brain was trying to keep up. "Someone must have put my name forward, against all the rules, and totally at odds with the selection being totally voluntary" he thought to himself. As he looked around the group outside of his home, he then realised that there were quite a few of his students within the crowd. "No, they couldn't have" he thought. "They would not have put my name forward, surely?" As he carefully looked at each of his students, there was something in their demeanour that made him unsure of his immediate views. He knew that they had a harmless 'secret society' and met up frequently outside of class. He also knew that Maltas and Altera were the leaders of this group and they were a highly intelligent couple of students. "To usurp the voluntary nature of the selection, even they wouldn't go that far would they?" However, his heart told him otherwise.

The crowd suddenly went quiet and split into two groups. At the rear of these groups another figure had appeared and walked towards the door. It was Elder Farrender, together with Torpast, Sartora's husband. "Jandray and Mother Tasren, please forgive this intrusion. We had expected to see you both at the Selection." Tasren's face remained impassive and she looked across to Jandray. Elder Farrender looked towards Jandray and smiled. "I think you may have guessed by now that your name was picked out of the selection vessel as one of the two HiberWatchers for this year. Torpast is here with me as he has also been chosen." Jandray did not know Torpast that well, he had always seemed to be so busy, and rarely attended any of the school events that took place over the year. Jandray had seen the sadness in Altera's eyes when only her mother had turned up to the school to these events. That said, at this moment, Torpast seemed happier than Jandray had ever seen him before.

What could Jandray do? His mind was racing. He absolutely knew that he hadn't nominated himself. And he was sure that his mother was telling the truth. That left his students, and if he made it clear that he had not nominated himself it would force him to voice his suspicions that his students had done it. And if they had he had no idea what kind of trouble that would bring on them. "Was I complicit in this?" he thought to himself. "I actively encouraged the students to think creatively, and I have done nothing to stop their secret society." Following this line of thought it was obvious to Jandray that any complaint about the selection would damage his students and would also harm the reputation of the school, and of himself. Looking at Torpast, it would also damage his role as HiberWatcher as, if Altera was part of this conspiracy, it could be viewed that Torpast was party to it too. Jandray closed his eyes as he tried to think of an appropriate response to Elder Farrender and the group around her, which showed no sign of getting smaller. If anything, the throng outside his door was getting larger.

"Elder Farrender" Jandray said. "I am sorry that I was not at the selection. It completely slipped my mind that I had put myself down for the selection this year. I had thought it would be something that would be good for me to be able to teach my students about in later years. However, I had no expectation at all that I would be chosen." As he tried to bring some level of excitement to his voice, he found that he was more apprehensive than excited, but he continued, "It is an honour to have been chosen as HiberWatcher. I assure you that I will do my duty and will endeavour to be a worthy choice." Farrender looked relieved when he said this, "Perhaps she had thought I may decline it" mused Jandray, but he was sure he could never have put his Elder into managing such a dilemma.

Elder Farrender spoke to Jandray, and also addressed the crowd at the same time. "Torpast and Jandray will be our guests of honour at the Winter Festival tonight and they will meet the Watch Hounds that have chosen to keep them company during our Winter Sleep." A cheer rose up from the crowd as Farrender spoke to Jandray in a low voice, "Don't let tonight's festivities slip your mind" she said, and then turned and began to walk away. Torpast took Jandray's hand "It will be a privilege to Watch over our nation with you this year Jandray. I have never told you how much I appreciate what you have done for Altera whilst she has been your student. I have much to reflect about during Winter, and I would value your views on how I can reconnect to her, and how I can rebuilt my relationship with her when our loved ones awake in Spring." Torpast also turned to leave, and as he did so he said, "It is such a great privilege for Paltir to have both HiberWatchers chosen from within their community. I cannot remember a time in recent history when this has happened."

As he said this, a few lines from an ancient poem charged into Jandray's mind. However, they were not comforting in the least:-

"When the HiberWatchers are close in Hiber sense

Winter can be severe and storms intense

Be careful to watch each other as well as the sleeping

And work hard to ensure that at Spring there's no weeping"

Jandray tried to put these words out of his thoughts, and remembered that he had been mulling over this poem in recent weeks. At first he could only remember one verse. "Why is this extra verse coming to me now?" he wondered. There was clearly more lines to this poem than he could remember. Jandray wasn't sure where he could find them but the most obvious place would be in the Hiber library. Little did he know that he wasn't the only person being troubled by lines of this poem!

Jandray prepared for the inevitability of his preferred humble status being elevated to that of Hiber-wide celebrity. His only comfort was that he hadn't sought this honour and this recognition. Rather, a person, or persons had nominated him. Having his suspicions but unable to act on them he decided that he had to embrace this moment. Tasren had come to him after the crowd had dispersed from outside the front of their home. "Son, this must be your destiny" she said to him in a voice that was full of pride. "If you didn't nominate yourself, someone else saw your honesty, integrity and potential to make an excellent HiberWatcher." Tasren could see that Jandray was resigned to what was to happen but could also tell that he was not pleased to have found himself in this position.

"Son, I would gladly have nominated you for the HiberWatcher selection years ago. But I always respected your wishes. I will add that your father, if he were here, would be very proud of this moment." Jandray looked across at Tasren with a note of surprise, his mother rarely talked about his father. "I know that you have always wanted to know about your father, but it is still painful for me and I am still not ready to tell you the whole story." As tears started to flow Tasren continued, "Your father and I were very much in love. However, when he left, he didn't know I was pregnant." As she continued, she held Jandray's hands, "If he had known, perhaps he would not have left. However, he needed to make a choice, free of that emotional pull." Jandray noticed the pain in his Mother's voice as she spoke and realised how frail she was becoming. "There are reasons that I cannot talk about at this time, but in due course, I feel the story will be told, and I hope you love me enough to respect both your father's reasons for leaving and my decision not to prevent him."

Jandray hugged Tasren and replied, "You have been my father and my mother, and I have lacked nothing." As he continued to hold Tasren, enjoying the familiar scent of her hair he said, "Of course I would like to know about my father and why he left. But I don't feel any the less for this vacant space in our family." As their embrace continued he whispered "In due course and in good time, I look forward to you telling the story, and whatever it brings, I will always love and respect you." As they parted from their embrace, Jandray was certain that the time for telling that story would come, and it would fill a gap that had always been there, but it was a gap that had not left a void in him as worthwhile soul in the Hiber Nation. His mother had ensured she had poured enough love into him to ensure that. "Mother, let us prepare for the festival. It is the last thing I expected to be doing this evening, but we may as well enjoy the event now that it has come to pass. I may have an exciting story to tell you in Spring, perhaps we can even swap stories." As Jandray tried to make light of the situation his mother looked at him in the way only a mother can do and said, "Perhaps so, my son, by a warm fire when spring brings all things back to life, perhaps so."

As Jandray walked off to his bedroom to find suitable clothing for the evening, his mood considerably lightened as he remembered that the Watch Hounds would be presented at the event. He hoped that he had correctly identified the two hounds that would be accompanying Torpast and himself. For reasons that he could not understand he had a compelling feeling that Winterclaw and Snowblue would be central to the winter watch this year.

Chapter Fourteen

Torcas was pleased to hear from Elder Farrender that she had met Jandray and he was going to be present at the evening's celebration event. Before this event, however, Torcas still had to host the meeting with Saltock, Altera and Maltas. Grasby had already left with Nilan to visit the Paltir brewery and Torcas was just arranging a light meal to be enjoyed with her guests. She was grateful that Nilan had taken Grasby away for the afternoon. It was clear that Grasby was very different to Saltock. "Were those in Tukerland mostly like Grasby or were they like Saltock?" she thought. She hoped that they were like Saltock but feared the opposite was more realistic. It was a subject that she would try and bring up discreetly at the meeting.

Saltock also really looked forward to a short time away from the overbearing and malevolent atmosphere that permeated anywhere near Grasby. He was certain that whilst his father was the ruler Grasby was no physical threat to him. However, he was also certain that Grasby was a real threat to continued peace with the Hiber Nation and that his relationship with Delcant was not beneficial for either country. He would value Nirtan's advice on this when he eventually returned to Tukerland. Nirtan and Mortarn would have had time to fully assimilate their views on the trade negotiations which they had hurriedly discussed prior to Saltock leaving with Grasby to attend Paltir. Saltock thought he should try hard to put his concerns to one side and concentrate on the forthcoming lunch, and the meeting with two students that Queen Torcas had arranged. He remembered her saying that there was only a few years difference in their ages, and he looked forward to having time with people close to his own age. Being the son of the ruler of Tukerland did not give him this opportunity much, even amongst his own kind, and he wondered if it was making him prematurely older than he actually was.

A member of house staff knocked on the door to his room. As he looked around him he noticed that these rooms were nowhere near as opulent as the ones he had been housed in at Decinter. However, the walls and the room itself seem to breath a kind of peaceful and relaxing tone that he had not experienced in Decinter. He followed the house staff out into the corridor, walking slowly, taking in all the structure around him. This building really was a living entity and its roots seem to exhale a continuing peaceful presence that he had found in his own room.

Saltock was taken to a small dining room, again nothing near the size of the room the negotiations had taken place in within Decinter. However, the atmosphere was much more positive, with decor that was muted but very natural. "There definitely is a strong Hiber culture" he thought, "a culture that is mirrored in this building." One that was distinctly different to Tukerland, but no less important he felt. There was none of the regal and warrior type relics like those that adorned Tukerland buildings. The walls themselves, united into a collage of hues and shapes, were all clearly very much alive with leaves and branches. He very much hoped that his project to host Hiber gardeners and a small stock of trees would be approved next year.

Queen Torcas was standing by the fire with two people standing next to her. They had their back to him; although Saltock could see that one was male and one female. They were modestly dressed compared to Queen Torcas, and all three were head and shoulders shorter that he was. Saltock was reminded that the Tukerland folk were, in the main, much taller than anyone he had met in his limited travels across the Hiber Nation. However, to contrast this, Hiber people tended to look lithe and healthy; even their older kinfolk had not surrendered to a widening waistline that was common amongst Tukerland people. Saltock had begun to enjoy Hiber food and was not missing meat at all. In fact, if he was asked, he felt had gained more energy from the Hiber food than he did from eating his standard Tukerland diet.

As he approached the small group, Saltock was not disappointed to see the spread of food across a nearby table. Whilst he did not miss meat in his meals he still had a capacious appetite, and his breakfast fare had now worn off. He resisted the temptation to head directly for the table and walked up to Queen Torcas. The two figures with the Queen turned towards Saltock as he approached. The young man was the first to speak, "Warrior Saltock, it is an honour to meet you. I am grateful to our Queen for this opportunity." Maltas was tall by Hiber standards, but he barely reached the shoulders of Saltock and had to look up to meet his gaze. "So you must be Maltas" he replied. "Queen Torcas has spoken very highly of you and your parents." In fact Queen Torcas had not really commented much on Maltas's father, but had been complimentary about Maltas and his mother. Saltock was pleased to have heard that Maltas was very little like his father who, he knew from Grasby, was an acolyte of Delcant.

Saltock then turned to address the young woman in front of him. As he looked down towards her face, he was struck by her lustrous brown hair. It was in a plait, that Saltock had learnt was a traditional Hiber style amongst Hiber woman. She then looked into his eyes. For a moment, Saltock thought all the air had been sucked out of the room. He could barely breath as he looked upon the beauty of the young woman in front of him. "Warrior Saltock, I am Altera, and I am honoured to meet with you" she said, seemingly unaware of the impact that she was having on Saltock. At first Saltock did not know how he would manage to reply, but he knew he must say something. In what he hoped was a neutral tone, that did not betray his intoxication with this vision in front of him he replied, "The honour is all mine, I understand that your father will be a HiberWatcher this year. I hope you are happy that I picked his name out." Altera laughed lightly and suddenly Saltock could breath again. "My father certainly surprised me, and also my mother I think, but he is so happy to have been chosen." Saltock, recovering his composure replied, "And I have heard that your mother is also highly regarded amongst the Hiber Elders." He stopped himself before he added "and may be a future Elder."

Altera, without showing any pride said, "It is indeed a privilege to have a mother such as mine. She has always allowed me space to express myself, and I hope that she will be proud of me in due course." Even if Altera hadn't noticed the impact that she was having on Saltock, Queen Torcas had spotted the unease with which Saltock was holding himself. "This is a turn of events" she thought to herself. "A Tukerland Warrior lost for words in front of one of the brightest young women in the Hiber Nation." She couldn't help but wonder what the offspring of such a union would do for the two nations. She quickly put these thoughts out of her mind and decided to speak, to at least put Saltock back at ease. "Shall we sit and eat? It will be so good to speak openly and freely over this humble fare." It was like Torcas had thrown a lifeline to Saltock who was quickly drowning in the beauty that he had found in front of him. "That would be a very welcome distraction" he said out loud. He then realised that his silent answer had actually been voiced and added, "a welcome distraction to the rumbling in my stomach that is." All four laughed and followed Queen Torcas's lead as she sat at the table.

The food had a calming effect on Saltock's mind, if not his heart, which was still racing. Whilst he was used to the emotions that coursed through his body during training in the warrior halls of Tukerland, the feelings he was having right now were quite alien to him. He had never met a woman in Tukerland that had even remotely taken his breath. Yet, here he was, sitting near a woman only a couple of years younger than him, slight in stature by Tukerland standards, and he was barely able to string a coherent sentence together. He was drawn to her, and felt that she must have been aware of his attention, no matter how discrete he was trying to make it. He looked over at the young man, Maltas. Was this her boyfriend? It didn't seem so to Saltock. They were very comfortable in each other's company, that was plain to see, but it looked more like a friendship than anything else. And Saltock wondered if he was catching a hint of a smile in Maltas's eyes when he looked over to him? The fact was that Maltas was very aware of the impact that Altera was having on their guest. It made him smile as Maltas had never seen Altera in any other way than that of a sister, and it was interesting to note that Saltock was in some kind of awe of his friend. Typical of Maltas, there was no envy or jealousness as he watched Saltock. Rather, he felt that there was an inevitability that a relationship may develop. Looking over at Queen Torcas, Maltas felt that she was thinking the same. "Isn't it interesting?" thought Maltas to himself, "Altera is possibly the most intelligent person in this room and is the only one that isn't aware of the influence she was having on this young warrior."

Saltock had to concentrate to prevent this situation making him feel uncomfortable whilst at the same time so excited. He consciously moved his attention to Maltas and said to him, "What will all the Students think about your teacher being chosen as a HiberWatcher this year? Do they have the same fondness as you and Altera clearly have for your teacher?" For a moment Altera's face was etched with worry. "Does this warrior know what we have done?" she said to herself, trying to ignore her inner fears. "No, he cannot have any knowledge" and she endeavoured to push that fear back down. Maltas replied "I am sure that all our fellow students will be surprised that Jandray nominated himself and equally pleased that he was chosen", with not a hint of irony in his voice. Altera looked at Maltas and noted his confidence of reply, a confidence that she still needed to recover, after her fears of being exposed at the selection. Queen Torcas added, "I, and also King Nilan I think, was surprised that Jandray had nominated himself. For many years he had been adamant that he would not put himself forward. He is a highly intelligence man, but also is very humble, and I feel the celebrity status he has had thrust upon him will not sit comfortably with him." Saltock was recovering his composure but was still very much aware of the beauty that he saw in Altera. He said, "I look forward meeting this teacher, hopefully this evening. He sounds like someone who one could learn a lot from." In a guarded, almost saddened voice he said, "Humility is not something that is very apparent amongst most of my kinfolk, and is generally perceived as weakness." His candour surprised those present as he continued, "However, I am learning that it is a trait valued in the Hiber Nation, and one that should be treasured I feel."

Queen Torcas decided to take the conversation in a different direction and started to expand upon the potential for the project that Saltock had requested of King Nilan at the trade talks. "My husband was so pleased that most of the trade negotiations progressed without difficulty. He was particularly interested in your proposal that some of our Hiber gardeners spend time in Tukerland growing a small nursery of trees." Saltock was not sure if Maltas and Altera were aware of this project, but saw that it was a measure of Queen Torcas' comfort with them that she mentioned this. "Yes, Queen Torcas" he answered. "Having now experienced the marvellous structures you are able to achieve with trees that continue to grow and strengthen has been enlightening to me. As you probably are aware, my folk had only considered the Hiber trees for harvest into wood. If I can show them even a hint of the wonders that can be achieved with living branches and roots, I think I can get the warrior elite to understand the benefit of this kind of tree cultivation. A cultivation that works with the living structure of the trees, rather than just cutting them into inanimate pieces of wood."

Saltock's answer was more mature than Queen Torcas would have expected from one so young, and one that may have been under the influence of warriors such as Grasby. However, she was quickly beginning to see that Saltock was very much his own person. "Is he part of a new generation that could bring our nations closer together?" she thought as she looked at him. Then she looked over at Altera and thought that she could definitely see young people like Saltock, Altera and Maltas being central to the positive future of both nations. Comforting as these thoughts were, she was in no doubt about the mountain to climb if the Tukerland elite were more like Grasby than Saltock. "I do hope that your project is approved by the Elders" Queen Torcas said. "I don't think I am betraying any confidences of my husband, when I say that he and I are in favour of exploring your request positively." Saltock was so pleased to hear this from the Queen. Grasby was certain that King Nilan had only feigned interest to end the trade talks on a high note. But then again, thought Saltock, Grasby was judging King Nilan by his standards, which were never positive and were generally self-seeking. Saltock felt that taking this project forward slowly and carefully would pay significant dividends for both nations in the longer term.

Queen Torcas looked towards the entrance of the room, as King Nilan and Warrior Grasby walked in. "Husband, and Warrior Grasby, it is a pleasure to welcome you to our meeting. How did your visit go?" she asked. King Nilan looked at Grasby who immediately replied "It is clear that your brewers are very skilled in their art and perhaps we need to discuss the exchange of brewers in future negotiations" he laughed. It was rare to see Grasby in a happy mood thought Saltock, but the beer must have been good. "Perhaps the Hiber beer helps relax the drinker" he thought to himself. In typical Hiber style King Nilan quickly added, "Tukerland beer is still excellent, but both Warrior Grasby and I wondered what a hybrid of the two hops would bring to a draught of beer. So yes, perhaps we may explore this in the future."

All seem to have gone well in both meetings. Saltock had enjoyed meeting Maltas and Altera, even if the feelings that Altera had created in him had not been expected. Warrior Grasby seemed more relaxed than at any time Saltock had experienced. Queen Torcas noticed this too and thought "Perhaps my concerns are nothing, and the poem that is haunting me is unnecessary." Unfortunately, if she could see into Grasby's mind, her concerns would not have been assuaged. It was true that Grasby was relaxed, and had greatly enjoyed the afternoon with King Nilan and the brewer. However, the source of his enjoyment was born out of the plans he was making that would see the Hiber Nation as no more than a vassal of Tukerland. His scheming would need still need to be developed further but now, more than ever, he was convinced that the Hiber Nation should be the free and unfettered store room of Tukerland, and he was sure he was the warrior to deliver this. Saltock was just a youthful annoyance and he would be swept away in due course, as would his father.

King Nilan explained that it was only a short while before they were all expected at the evening festivities. If the seasons were as normal, it would be highly likely that the sky would deliver a light show that would be both beautiful and inspiring, and it even may begin to snow during the evening. As they made their goodbyes, for very differing reasons, all were looking forward to the evening ahead.

Chapter Fifteen

"Could there really be any chance of knowing Altera better?" thought Saltock. Since the afternoon meeting he could think of nothing else. He needed to see her again and was desperate to spend more time in her company. So far there was nothing to indicate that she would have any interest in him at all. Saltock started to dress for the evening festivities. As he was much further North than his own country he was glad that King Nilan had arranged for a Hiber coat to have been tailored for both Saltock and Grasby. Saltock would wear it this evening, he had tried it on and it was warm and incredibly comfortable. Whilst Saltock had fur lined clothing, he had opted not to bring them out of respect for the Hiber culture. Grasby had no such sensitivities about him and had brought a selection of fur lined outer garments. Grasby had said that he would not "demean" himself by wearing inferior Hiber garments. It would made the difference between the two guests even more stark. But, in a way, Saltock was happy with this and he thought that so was Grasby.

Unlike the selection event, tonight's festivities were in Paltir's main square, situated directly outside of the Queen and King's residence. Fire baskets were lit around the square, both at floor level to bring heat to those nearby and also atop outstretched boughs of nearby trees. Saltock still couldn't comprehend how the trees provided the cones that were used for heat and light across the Hiber Nation, and were even used to house the fire baskets; yet still no harm came to the trees. It really was a thing to behold. There was very little, if any, smoke emanating from the cones and even outdoors their scent was not diminished, giving a refreshing aroma to the air. In Tukerland, the seasoned timber used for burning did not give off much smoke, but many burnt unseasoned wood and smoke was a familiar feature on the skyline of Tukerland communities. "We have so much to learn about living with nature, not against it" thought Saltock. "Even the Winter Sleep seems to be sympathetic to the need of the land to rest from cultivation and continued use."

A large crowd had started to gather in the square. The excitement Saltock had seen at the selection earlier that day was magnified tenfold at this evening event. Food was available at stalls throughout the square and Saltock couldn't see any money changing hands. It seemed as though this event was a massive sharing meal for those present. It had been explained to Saltock this festival was being repeated across every community in the Hiber Nation. Saltock looked forward to meeting Jandray, the other HiberWatcher he had chosen at the Selection event. He was also aware that a further selection had now taken place and two hounds had been chosen to accompany the two HiberWatchers. This interested Saltock, but more so Grasby who was renowned in Tukerland for breeding Tukerland war hounds. Grasby was aware of the Hiber hound breed and was keen to assess their strength and potential for cross breeding. Saltock knew that Grasby had wanted this discussed as part of the trade negotiation on livestock and that he was particularly annoyed when Saltock had closed that aspect of talks down.

In order to maintain the facade of being a united delegation of Tukerland warriors, Grasby and Saltock arrived at the square together. Grasby in his warrior styled fur coat and regalia was dismissive of the Hiber coat that Saltock had chosen to wear. "It looks like you are trying to be one of these people" growled Grasby "Just remember who you are and what you are." "And what is that?" Saltock replied with a hint of aggression in his voice, more than he expected to be there. "Who am I ?" "You are a warrior of Tukerland, amongst a naive group of farmers and gardeners; you are physically stronger than those around you and so is Tukerland." "I thought I was a guest of these people" Saltock immediately retorted "and a representative of our ruler, my father, has that changed?" Grasby looked at Saltock and saw, perhaps for the first time, the look in Saltock that Sargern had given many men before he had them removed from his presence; forever. Grasby was not long-lived amongst a warrior nation by being rash and loose tongued, and he decided he must immediately de-escalate the tension between the two. Time would come when this upstart would be put in his place thought Grasby as he found words to reply to Saltock. "I am only saying that you need to remember we are two nations of very different cultures, and you will do well to remember this." Saltock saw that this was as much as an apology that he was ever likely to get and matched his words accordingly. "Well said, Warrior Grasby, I have watched you well, and I will continue to learn from you." Grasby saw the dual meaning in Saltock's reply and decided not to answer.

Queen Torcas and King Nilan emerged from their residence and walked onto the square. It was amazing to both Saltock and Grasby that neither had any formal entourage of guards around them, which was totally at odds with how Sargern and the warrior elite acted in public settings in their nation. The wider community in Tukerland saw the warrior elite often, but never close up and never without a barrier of heavily armed guards around them. When he was younger, Saltock had thought that this was a relic of the warring days of competing tribes. However, as he became more familiar with the day to day politics of Tukerland, he realised that the safety of his father and those loyal to him could not be taken for granted; an obvious presence of guards was one of the many ways that the power elite preserved their status. This was another very noticeable difference between the two cultures; one that had taken power by force, and one that enjoyed authority by mutual consent.   To Grasby, it continued to confirm his view that the Hiber Nation was no match for Tukerland, and could easily be subdued if there was the will to do it. After the earlier conversations with Saltock he decided to keep these views to himself.

"Good evening Warrior Saltock and Warrior Grasby" said King Nilan. It was not lost on either Saltock or Grasby that Nilan had made a subtle indication on who he felt was the more important guest. Grasby bristled with anger but remained silent. "Warrior Grasby, I hope you have recovered from our afternoon visit to the brewery, I wanted to show you a couple of different beers this evening if you would join me." This had the intended effect on reducing Grasby's anger and he even managed a tight smile as he said "I see that there is Tukerland beer here too, I look forward to some home comfort as well."   Saltock saw how Nilan was managing Grasby and was impressed at how the King had found common ground with a man who clearly was totally different in outlook and culture to the person that was Grasby. Saltock said, "I hope you forgive me if I ask that I spend more time with the students that I met this afternoon, there is so much more that I would like to discuss with them, I hope they can introduce me to their teacher and their fellow students."   Queen Torcas answered "Of course Warrior Saltock, when the formalities have concluded the festival will go well into the night. I am sure that Altera will ensure you are hosted for the evening"; smiling enigmatically at Saltock.

Just as Queen Torcas was finishing her sentence she saw Altera, Maltas and a number of other young people heading across the square. Alongside Altera was Jandray and his mother. Jandray was deep in conversation with Altera and Maltas and both of them had a serious look on their faces. Torcas wondered to herself what would be so serious at such a time of festivities. However, she reminded herself that Jandray took his role as teacher and mentor very seriously and maybe he was discussing something of importance with them. Jandray, with his mother, arrived at the front of the square and slowly approached the King and Queen. "Jandray, thank you so much for coming this evening, we missed you at the Selection" the Queen said. "And please, Mother Tasren, do stand by my side during the formalities; you have indeed honoured our nation with bringing such an important teacher to us." Tasren almost physically grew with pride at being recognised by the Queen. Tasren smiled fondly and then looked over to King Nilan. Missed by everyone, there was a meeting of their eyes and something unspoken passed between them. The moment passed and Jandray moved to stand at Torcas's side.

Saltock wanted to speak with Jandray, but was fixated by the beauty of Altera. Once again he found himself barely able to speak. Instead of trying to say something, he just smiled and said nothing, leaving King Nilan to make the introductions. "Warrior Saltock and Warrior Grasby, please be introduced to our HiberWatcher, Jandray, a man of great intellect and wisdom." Jandray looked at the floor, feeling uncomfortable at the accolades that Nilan was giving him. Jandray said nothing but just took the Warrior's hands in the Hiber way. Maltas moved away as Altera's parents arrived at the group. He was happy to do so, this small group of elite leaders would need to oversee the formalities, before he, Altera and their fellow conspirators could meet up and enjoy the rest of the evening. And he was, unlike Altera, already very much aware of how Saltock was taken by Altera. Again, his emotions were that of a brother to Altera and he was comforted that, in his heart, he knew that Saltock could be a great match for the fearless and intelligent Altera.

The two HiberWatchers were brought to the small stage that had been set up at the far end of the square, nearest the entrance to the Royal residence. King Nilan and Queen Torcas stood either side of them. As culture dictated, both Nilan and Torcas had white coats around their bodies, and garlands made from autumn flowers and leaves that had carefully been woven into matching crowns.   Torpast and Jandray stood side by side. Both were similar in stature; Jandray was only a couple of years older than Torpast, who had not been in Jandray's first class, but had started his courtship with Sartora during their final year of school. Torpast had remembered that Jandray looked impossibly young as a teacher, and reflected on how chance had brought them to this point after many years. Torpast knew that Altera was very fond of Jandray, and it was his intention during the long winter to seek Jandray's advice on how to re-establish his relationship with his daughter. Torpast was fully aware of Jandray's integrity and he was certain that any conversations they had would remain confidential. It was for this reason, he was so pleased that Jandray had been chosen as his fellow HiberWatcher. Anything that would help repair his relationship with both with wife and his daughter would be so welcome. It would make the winter ahead more bearable, knowing he had so much to look forward to in Spring.

Silence descended on the crowd like that of the hint of snow that was gentling falling down. It was seen as great fortune if snow actually fell at the festival. The crowd were looking up at the sky as much as they were at the stage. However, many were hoping that the snow clouds would clear as a further event was seen as even more important; the Winter Lights.   Each year, prior to the Winter Sleep, on clear evenings, the Hiber Nation were treated to an amazing natural light show. Hues of red and green, in fact all colours of the rainbow, were shone across the night sky for several hours on the evenings that they appeared. Hiber tradition said that if the sky was full of this light show on the day of the selection and the festival, it was an important sign for the sleep ahead of them. The only person who was hoping that the light show did not appear tonight was Torcas.   She had continued to be tormented by fragments of the poem that she had heard as a child. She still had not been able to locate the original poem and she was aware that Kindross and Kian were still searching the library to find the origin of the poem. However, as she stood on the stage, another fragment of the poem came to her

"When the snows do fall on HiberWatcher Day

And the lights in their brilliance put on their display

It shall mean an event of great import

A Spring awakening of a different sort"

Now, there were three verses that she could remember, and two mentioned or at least indicated changes in Spring. Torcas couldn't help but wonder what these changes would be and her heart told her that there was a threat to the Hiber community within these verses. Why was she remembering them now? She had been Queen for many years and this poem had never come to her until now. There seemed to be an alignment, and not in a positive way, that was taking place. Two HiberWatchers from the same community is not something she had ever experienced. Tukerland guests at the selection was another event that had not taken place before. She hoped that the Winter Lights would hold off for at least this evening, and she looked longingly into the sky. As she did a snowflake landed on her brow. She looked out across the square, and could see the flakes falling gently down, picked out by the lights flickering across the square. There were shouts of excitement arising from those gathered and she tried not to betray her concerns. She put a mask of a smile on her face and held her hands high to catch the snow flakes. To most present, the snow was a great addition to the overall spectacle of the selection, to her it only brought a sense of dread.

As the snow continued to fall, light but persistent, it started to clothe the buildings, the square and all those present in a winter layer of sparkling ice. Hiber snow did not melt quickly and it didn't quickly seep into the warm outer garments of those assembled. For that reason it was welcomed as a crisp dusting of a benevolent early winter. Only those who had been HiberWatchers in the past saw the massive outpouring of snowy blizzards as Winter took hold on the dormant nation. Only they had the privilege to see the nation slowly disappear under a huge protective blanket of this snow. The majority of the nation were only able to experience a light snowfall, enough to cover everything with a thin cold white coating, but not sufficient to prevent daily activity, especially the migration to Queen Mountain. If the snow continued this evening, it was likely that the ice bridge would also be forming and the Ice Wall would start to appear. This really would begin to indicate the advanced nature of the year, and would ensure that everyone would turn their thoughts to closing down their homes and moving to the protective caves which would host them over winter.

As if they had chosen this exact moment, a pack of Hiber hounds appeared at the rear of the crowd. Two of them detached from this group and began to walk through the crowd. Their white coats were totally at odds with those of the rest of the pack, all of whom still had their lustrous dark coats. The snowy winter frosting of their fur had the impact of almost making them invisible to their surroundings. Those Hiber folk nearby quickly stepped out of their way as the two Hiber hounds walked towards the stage. It was a thing of beauty to see these hounds walk purposefully away from their pack and through the Hiber folk. Jandray looked across at the movement of the crowd and saw the hounds coming forward. At this distance he could not tell if it was Winterclaw and Snowblue, but he really hoped that this would be the case. Grasby seemed particularly taken by the spectacle and his eyes were drawn to the two hounds walking slowly away from the larger pack of hounds that were sitting silently at the rear of the square. Tukerland hounds were larger than these hounds, but would not have had the discipline to walk without lead and handler like these two regal animals were walking. "I need to have at least one of these hounds" he thought to himself. How he was going to achieve this, he still had not worked out. "Even Sargern doesn't have hounds as amazing as these two" he thought.

As the hounds neared the stage, Jandray could see that his hopes had been realised. It was the two hounds that he had been monitoring over the year. Only he knew them as Winterclaw and Snowblue, and was unsure if he should remain silent over the names he had given them. He went to his knees and both the hounds immediately came to him and nuzzled into his body. The crowd went wild at this scene which had never happened before. The connection between the HiberWatcher and the Watch Hound was strong, but nothing like what was being displayed this year. Jandray called over to Torpast, "Come, brother HiberWatcher, kneel before our loyal friends." Torpast moved towards Jandray hesitantly but was encouraged by Jandray that there was nothing to fear. "Come, these hounds will be our guides, our company and our protection in the coming Winter" Jandray said. Torpast overcame his nerves and knelt alongside Jandray. Winterclaw moved from Jandray and gently sniffed at Torpast. He looked over to Snowblue who moved away from Jandray and did the same. Then both nuzzled into Torpast as they had Jandray.

Torpast had never been in such proximity to such hounds, always too busy with work to notice such animals in other years. To him, it was almost a metaphor for this disconnection from Sartora and Altera. These two hounds had entered into his emotions and given their loyalty to him, at the behest of Jandray. He hoped something similar would occur to be accepted back into his family in Spring.

Sartora looked upon the situation with tears streaming down her face. She had never seen Torpast perform such a humble act. In recent times he had barely had physical contact with her or Altera, and he had been increasingly emotionally distant. All this had changed in a matter of hours. Her heart was almost breaking at the thought of the husband she had lost, now re-discovered, only for them to be separated again for winter. Altera was holding onto her closely and broke away from her. Altera walked slowly to her father. Starting to take on their protector role, Winterclaw and Snowblue looked up at Altera, but they seemed to sense the connection. Altera knelt at her father's side and hugged him tight. The tears spoke more than any words could say.

This emotion was totally lost on Grasby, who was now looking at Sartora as she stood alone. He had heard all about this woman from Delcant and knew she was a threat to his overall plans to have a compliant Elder in Paltir. Sartora was striking, beautiful even, in appearance and he could see the similarities in her daughter. Unlike Saltock, however, Grasby had no interest in the beauty of either the mother or the daughter, he saw them purely as threats. Sartora needed to be neutralised as part of his plans. Delcant had promised that Lorsern would be a compliant partner in destabilising wider Elder resistance to Grasby's plans. Grasby laughed to himself when he thought that Delcant deluded himself as being a partner to Grasby. He would only ever be a disposable tool for Grasby, a tool that would be discarded as soon as his usefulness was at an end. Grasby's lack of awareness that Sartora or Altera could be viewed as attractive by Tukerland standards meant that he did not notice the look on Saltock's face as he was gazing across at the young woman kneeling next to her father.

Saltock was aware that this display of emotion between Altera and her father was something that would never have been understood in his nation. However, he could see that Grasby was taking more interest in Sartora than anything else, and this attention troubled him. He knew that Grasby would have no physical interest in this woman; she was devoid of the martial attributes that Grasby favoured. "What is Grasby's interest here?" mused Saltock. "It will not be anything positive, other than to progress any self-interested position for Grasby" he thought. Saltock was aware from an early age that any form of emotion was perceived as a weakness to be avoided. To him, however, watching Altera with her father and mother had sparked a hunger for that kind of relationship with a future child of his. More so, the vulnerability being displayed by Altera made her more attractive to him than ever. He wanted to protect her, and to comfort her. Mostly, he wanted to know more about her and for her to know more about him.

The two HiberWatchers stood, and Altera returned to her mother's side. She glanced over at Saltock and could see something in him that she couldn't describe. "That young Warrior unsettles me" she thought, but it also gave her a feeling that she did not understand. She had always been close to Maltas and thought that their platonic feelings were all that were to be had in such a relationship. Seeing her mother and father so deeply express their love for each other, it reminded her how uneducated she was in matters of the heart. She had noticed a few times that Saltock was paying attention to her, more than others around him, but she just dismissed any thoughts about this. However, the hint of concern in his eyes that she could see as she had been at her father side opened emotions that were confusing to her. The only person she would be able to confide in would be Maltas and she decided to approach the subject with him at some point. She also looked at Grasby. The two warriors were so different, and not just in age. Grasby was looking at her mother, and his face betrayed a suppressed anger. She apprehended that Grasby was a threat to her mother and she did not know why. There was just something in his manner and bearing and she was only pleased that the sleep would come soon, and that Grasby would be gone from their land. She was not so happy to think that she would not see Saltock again though.

The festivities continued into the evening. Those on stage mingled with the crowds, although Grasby made excuses and returned to his rooms. He still could not be comfortable with the level of contact with the wider community that the King and Queen really enjoyed. Saltock did not seem disturbed by it either. Grasby was keenly aware that he would pay a significant price, his life even, if Saltock was injured in anyway. However, it was clear that there was no risk to Saltock in this environment so he left him to his own actions. "Enough babysitting for one day" he said to himself as he left. Saltock was pleased, even relieved, that Grasby had left. It would allow him to relax and enjoy the Hiber way of festival, which was very different to their own Tukerland gatherings. In some ways, there were similarities. Beer freely flowed, as did food. However, the atmosphere had remained pleasant and convivial. By now, in Tukerland, fights would have broken out and many would be nursing more than superficial injuries, in the name of a good time. He saw Altera and decided to try and speak with her

"Hello Altera, it must be a great honour to have watched your father this evening" he said. Altera looked into Saltock's eyes as she began a reply. Saltock felt she was searching his soul and he was unarmed in this search. "If truth be told" she replied "I have not been close to my father until today. He has been so busy at work recently and I feared that it was damaging his relationship with my mother too." Altera halted, not realising how candid she had been with a total stranger. She felt she had to continue, "But today my father opened his soul to us and sought forgiveness. He put his name forward as HiberWatcher in the hope that he would be chosen and would then take all Winter to reflect on how to rebuild his role in our family." As she was speaking, Altera started to weep. Saltock was unsure what to do and held out his hand to her. Suddenly, Altera fell into his arms and sobbed. Whether it was his stature, his concerned look, or the fact that she would never see him again she wasn't sure, but at this moment, Saltock was a rock she wanted cling to. Saltock looked around him, thinking the whole square would be looking at the two of them. In fact, only Maltas was observing them, and he was smiling.

Altera eventually broke away from their embrace and apologised, "I am sorry Warrior Saltock, for my familiarity, please forgive me." Saltock just looked at Altera and replied "I must admit, in Tukerland, we are not given to an open display of emotion, but I am learning that this is not necessarily a good thing." He touched her hand and said, "I hope that next year I can visit again and we could learn more of each other and our cultures. I look forward to hearing how your father changes in relation to you and your mother." Altera was gaining her composure and not wanting to let go of his hand replied, "I would like that very much, perhaps it will be so."

As they were talking the clouds had cleared and the steady fall of snow had ended. There was a shout from within the crowd, "Winter Lights, Winter Lights". The shouts were taken up by all present, making it deafening, even by Tukerland standards. Saltock looked to the sky and was silenced by the beauty of what he saw. Tukerland had snow in winter, but never anything like the lights above him. He could almost touch the colours like they were a garment hanging in front of him; a multi-coloured coat swinging and swaying as far as the eye could see. The most vibrant colours appeared to centred over Queen Mountain, almost like it was a crown dancing over the mountain. Saltock had never seen anything like this and he felt he would be unable to give it justice if he was asked to describe what he saw and what he felt. Looking at Altera he could tell that the light show was having the same effect on her and all those around him. He looked over to Queen Torcas who she looked like the only one who was not enjoying the display. He almost felt there was fear in her face as she watched the sky.

Chapter Sixteen

Several days had passed since the selection event and the Winter Festival. Grasby and Saltock were preparing to leave in the next few days. Grasby had indicated that he wanted to meet up with Delcant in Decinter on the journey back to Tukerland. His excuse was that he wanted to confirm that all the trade aspects agreed at the meeting in Decinter were progressing effectively. Saltock was not sure that his motives were as honest as this. He had witnessed how Grasby and Delcant were similar in their self-seeking and devious natures. However, he had also seen that Delcant was in fear of Grasby, and whatever they were in league for, Delcant was much the minor party. Saltock put these concerns to the back of his mind and concentrated on enjoying the last few days he would have in this nation that, if he were honest, had captured his imagination. And one of their folk had captured his heart. Saltock had not had the opportunity to meet or speak with Altera since the Winter Festival. To his great pleasure, he had been invited to the final event in the Winter proceedings, that of visiting the Ice Wall. By sunrise the following morning any Hiber folk who wanted to, would make their way to the Ice Wall at the foothills of the Queen Mountain. The journey from Paltir would take several hours on foot so it would commence that evening. Even Saltock was surprised at how long it would take to get to the mountain. Due to its vast expanse it seemed much closer than it was.

Grasby had decided not to visit the Ice Wall. When it was suggested to him by Saltock all he said was "Why would I want to see a wall with names that are of no interest to me and watch the formulation of an Ice bridge to the inner sanctum of a Mountain that I have no intention to visit?" Grasby knew only part of that statement was true. He did have no interest in the Ice Wall but one day he would enter the Queen Mountain for entirely different reasons to those of the Hiber folk. In fact, the Winter Sleep would be relic of the past if his plans came to fruition. "Warrior Grasby, I intend to learn as much as I can about this nation so I can give a full report back to my father. I hope you agree that at least one of us should go." Grasby did not have a sufficiently good enough retort in return and agreed that Saltock should go. Grasby decided that he would make use of the time whilst Saltock was away by trying to meet with Lorsern to ascertain if Delcant had been accurate about his potential as a willing acolyte of the Tukerland warrior.

Saltock met up with King Nilan at the entrance to the royal residence. Queen Torcas would not be joining the expedition, but both Torpast and Jandray would be attending as would their Watch Hound companions. To his surprise, Altera and Maltas would be attending. Another two students were also joining them. Saltock learned that one was called Dasbran. This had been at the specific request of Jandray. Dasbran was related to Delcant, but the similarity ended there, as far as Saltock could see. Jandray explained to Saltock that Dasbran had a love of the mountains and it would mean such a lot for him to have the opportunity to visit Queen Mountain on the eve of the Winter Sleep. King Nilan immediately agreed, knowing that it balanced any criticism of his decision to request that Delcant remain in Decinter and not take part in the hosting of Grasby and Saltock in Paltir. More importantly for Nilan, it sent a strong message that he was still, overtly, supportive of Delcant and his wider family.

The other student joining the group was Junstern. She was the only other student in Jandray's class who had a relative that had been a HiberWatcher. Her mother had been a HiberWatcher and Jandray had asked that this be recognised by allowing Junstern to visit the Ice Wall to see her mother's name. This was agreed and Junstern was so excited at the thought of her first visit to the Ice Wall. "So" she whispered to Altera, "Quite a large number of our secret society will be present on this visit." Altera looked at her sharply and indicated that she should be careful not to speak about the society. She could still remember the fear that she had at the selection when she thought their conspiracy had been discovered. Realising that Junstern was only making conversation, she softly added. "There will be plenty of time to talk was as we walk along, and I will be so pleased of your company." The mood was lifted and Junstern smiled back.

It was only a small group that assembled to make the journey. There were representatives from each nation present, and they were prepared for a brisk, challenging walk to the Ice Wall over the next few hours. Another dusting of snow had visited the nation earlier in the evening, and it made for a spectacular, if cold, horizon ahead of them. Jandray walked up to where Altera and her fellow students were standing. "I have the intention of speaking with all of you as we make this pilgrimage" he said, with a face that was set and impassive. "Don't think you have got away with this" and he walked away. Instead of just Altera feeling concerned, now there were four worried faces as they began their march. "I knew that Jandray would suspect us" groaned Maltas. "I could feel that he was looking straight into me as he spoke." "I think that goes for all us" replied Dasbran "But he hasn't declined the HiberWatcher role so perhaps it is a price that we have to pay." Altera said nothing, and just reflected on how to deal with the conversation when it came.

Saltock stood out against the group due to his height. He had kept his Hiber coat on but he was very aware that he was much taller than any of them. He hoped the Hiber humility was having an effect on him; that they would see past his physical stature and would focus on Saltock as a person. This was not a response that was natural for someone from Tukerland, who would normally have relished having a physical height advantage over whoever he or she was with. Saltock decided not to stoop, however. This was his physical frame, and he needed to own it; he could not, and would not apologise for it. King Nilan was comfortable with him, but those who had not really met him until now, were less at ease. He could sense it, but it gave him a purpose. "Another test of my leadership" he said to himself. "I need to try and gain their trust, and belay any concerns they have that we are all like Grasby."

The group were treated to another display of the Winter Lights as they made their journey to Queen Mountain. If anything it was more vibrant than the display on the evening of the Winter Festival. The whole group stopped on more than one occasion to watch the swirling dance of light. As they moved closer to the mountain, the lights seem to be magnified in shape, colour and intensity. Dasbran explained that, as they moved closer to the mountain, they were gaining height and they would experience the full majesty of the lights. He seemed to know a lot about mountains, and the group naturally accepted his explanation. It was a hard and energy sapping walk for most of the group. Only Saltock, hardened by the extensive fitness training required of all warriors in Tukerland, didn't appear at all fatigued by the journey. It was as if the journey to the mountain energised him in some way. Altera noticed that during the journey he was carefully spending time with everyone in the group, speaking to them individually and it was clear that they were becoming more comfortable in his presence.

Altera had little chance for conversation with Saltock and had spent most of her time chatting with Maltas. "You must see the impact you are having on him" was all Maltas said. "Even you are not that dim to ignore the fact that this giant of a person is like a nervous child in your presence." Altera turned to Maltas as they walked, although she slowed her pace so that both were a little behind the main group. "I don't know how to explain it" she said quietly "And please do not laugh at me." Maltas touched her shoulder gently and said, "Let me say it for you. This Saltock has gained your interest too hasn't he? On some level that you have never experienced before, you have connected with him." Altera remained silent as Maltas continued, "You are all mixed up, your feelings are all over the place, and you cannot really put into words the feelings you have when you are in his presence." Altera breathed a sigh of relief, if anyone could read her thoughts it was Maltas. "How do you know this?" she exclaimed. Maltas smiled and simply replied "Because I have had the same conversation with Saltock and he has said exactly the same." At that, Maltas increased his pace and moved up towards the main group. Altera matched his pace and Maltas said, "There is a reason for this I am sure, and I do not think Saltock will be anything other than a positive addition to your life." He then added "And for some reason, I think we may all need his support and strength at some point."

Jandray had wandered through the group and was near to Altera and Maltas. Both Watch Hounds were ahead of the main group, either side of Torpast. During the short days since the festival, Torpast had been inseparable from both of the hounds. Jandray had decided to take a risk and he had told him of the names he had given the hounds. Torpast thought the names fitted perfectly and he was often seen kindly stroking the fur of both of the hounds as they walked along together. "The time has come" Jandray said to both Altera and Maltas "to be open with you." As he was walking he managed to give the impression that he was staring directly at them, even though his eyes were steady on the trail ahead. "I know that you, somehow, had a role in nominating me for the HiberWatcher role this year. I also think that all the students followed your lead." As he breathed loudly with the exertion of the journey and holding a conversation at the same time he said, "I have had time to work out what you did. Each of your secret society friends put my name in the selection pot of the individual Hiber communities. This dramatically increased the opportunity that I was chosen this year." It was almost a relief to Altera that Jandray was saying this and she tried to reply. "I haven't finished yet" Jandray said, holding up his hand. "You were very lucky that tradition has it that the nomination parchments are burnt each year, as this means your conspiracy will not be uncovered." With a hint of anger in his voice he continued, "Most importantly, you have prevented someone who wanted to be HiberWatcher from having the opportunity to do so this year, and you have thrust that responsibility onto a person who never wanted this burden." Maltas was downcast and he looked upon Jandray with guilt. Altera was equally despondent as Jandray continued to talk.

"That said", Jandray added. "Being a HiberWatcher is an honour that my mother always wanted me to explore. I initially thought she had nominated me but she promised me that she hadn't and I believed her as she has high integrity, unlike some around me." The verbal lacerations continued, "You have betrayed both the trust of our Hiber communities and my personal trust. It is only for the sake of your families and their good name, especially your parents, who are significant leaders in the Paltir community, that I have not said anything, and I won't say anything." An audible sigh of relief escaped Maltas when he heard Jandray's reply. "But", Jandray said, lightly holding both by an arm and pulling them closer to him. "There is a price to pay for playing with my life like this. Always remember that you placed me as a HiberWatcher, you will always be partially responsible for whatever happens to our communities. You have interfered with the very core of our culture, and you will need to reflect on this if you are called upon to support our nation. It may be this year, it may be in twenty years time, but you have that responsibility. That is my price. And may I add, your 'Mountain keepers secret society' will have to pay that price too. Are we agreed?" His tone and manner as he added this last sentence left no room for any answer other than what Maltas and Altera said, almost at the same time. "Agreed, Teacher Jandray, it is agreed." Jandray then increased his pace, and walked away from the two of them. Just as they thought their ordeal was over Jandray looked back and quietly said "I will play may part as HiberWatcher to the best of my ability, you keep your word to the best of yours." He then disappeared to the front of the group.

"It doesn't feel like much of a game anymore does it?" breathed Maltas. Altera didn't immediately answer. Maltas continued, "We will need to call the Society together and update them that Jandray has uncovered our 'clever' plan, and he has called on our loyalty as the price we pay for breaching both our culture and Jandray's right to a quiet life. Despite the fact that we know he will be an excellent HiberWatcher, I now realise that I have not respected a man who has done nothing but good for us, and I am ashamed." Altera looked across at Maltas and replied "I agree, but I cannot help feel that we made the right choice and that Jandray has a role to play that we have no awareness of at the moment."

King Nilan gave a shout as they neared the giant lake that surrounded Queen Mountain. It was still dark, but the reflection of the Winter Lights could be seen, not only in the sky, but also on the surface of this lake which was starting take on the sheen of frozen ice. There was a particularly vibrant corridor of light that could be seen across the lake. As they came to the edge of the lake, it was obvious that the ice bridge was forming and that the lights were reflecting more clearly and with greater luminance at this part of the lake. Saltock could not understand why more people of the Hiber Nation didn't want to see this amazing sight. It was almost like the whole of the view was one swirling and swaying host of heavenly colours covering this land. King Nilan said "We will camp here until just before sunrise, and then we will carefully test out the ice bridge. It will still take us an hour to cross this expansive lake. If we time this correctly, we will see the sun rise onto where the Ice Wall should be." Even King Nilan couldn't answer was how the new HiberWatcher names would be etched onto the Ice Wall. For all his knowledge of the Hiber Nation, he had no idea how this happened. All he was sure about was that there appeared to be a symbiosis between the land and the Hiber people. Perhaps the truth was hidden in the library and perhaps Kian and Kindross could answer, but whether they would was a very different matter.

Saltock took the opportunity to try and speak with Altera, "I am sorry to say that there is nothing as beautiful in Tukerland." He suddenly realised that his comment could be read more than one way as he was speaking to Altera and his discomfort was intense. However, Altera saw the embarrassment in his face and came to his rescue. "Yes, the Winter Lights and their reflection on the ice bridge and the lake are a thing to behold." Saltock tried again. "I cannot fully express what this vision is to behold. When I go home and I am asked, I will struggle to find the words." "There is one more spectacle for you to experience" she said, looking directly at him, "At sunrise, the first rays of the sun will light upon the Ice Wall. You will then seen the names of all the HiberWatchers etched into the ice, and you should see the most recent will be my father's name and that of Jandray." She continued to look upon Saltock, even his height seem diminished in vast landscape around them and she said "It is a true mystery as to how flowing water remembers the ice names etched on them, and an even greater mystery as to how the names are added each year." As she was saying this, she became aware of Junstern standing near her so she raised her voice slight and said, "Junstern's mother has her name on the wall, and it will be a source of great pride for her to read it." Junstern looked across at Altera, her eyes filled with pride and said "I can hardly wait, it is such an honour to be here."

King Nilan indicated that it was time to start to walk along the Ice Bridge. It was still quite narrow, but appeared fully formed on this narrow slip. Before the Winter Sleep commenced the whole of the lake would freeze over. This 360 degree bridge would allow the communities to flow into the mountain from all directions, quickly allowing the full migration of Hiber people and all the living things into the mountain. "Be careful" King Nilan said. "This small strip of ice appears fully formed, but do not stray to the right or to the left. Stay on this narrow band and make your way across the lake." Whilst not quite single file, the bridge was still only wide enough for two to walk side by side. As was tradition, King Nilan walked up front, alone. He was the leader, and it was a mark of respect to the Queen Mountain that he approached first. He was followed by the HiberWatchers who, in turn, were followed by the Watch Hounds. The rest of the group followed, with Saltock walking alongside Junstern. "How does it feel to be about to see your mother's name on the Ice Wall?" Saltock asked as they walked along. Junstern's excitement was palpable, "I was so grateful that I was allowed to join the group. Of course, my mother has seen it this close up, and she and my father made the journey, almost as a pilgrimage, a few years ago. However, I was viewed as too young to make the journey, or to fully understand the importance of experiencing the Ice Wall this close up." Junstern continued to speak to Saltock, "Of course, I have seen the name from a distance as we have crossed the ice bridge to our accommodation for the Winter Sleep, but we do not have time to stop and study the wall at that point. And by the time we wake in Spring, the Wall has returned to being a waterfall." Junstern finally added, "Soon I will be an adult, and will be able to put my name forward for selection if I wanted to. In fact, I am not that much younger than my mother was when she was selected." Saltock could see that Junstern was not much younger than he was, and was impressed that she was already thinking of adulthood and service to her community. "I look forward to you pointing her name out to me" he said as they continued to walk along the bridge.

The far side of the lake was getting closer, and the Ice Wall could be seen shimmering in the winter lights which were now starting to fade. The 'door to morning', as Hiber folk called it, was just starting to open. The sun was not in view, but the sky was changing from darkness into different shades of blue. There was a slight red tinge starting to appear and it started to overtake the Winter Lights as daylight began its march on the day ahead. Soon the group were at the foot of the Ice Wall. Saltock had not known what to expect, but he certainly had not expected the sheer size of the wall. It was as high as the eye could see, and looked like it was falling out of the sky. This reminded him of how Queen Mountain reached into the clouds. From this close, there was no chance that he could see much higher than what was really just the foothills of Queen Mountain. Dasbran, unbeknown to them all, except Jandray, was the only person who had scaled into the high peak of Decinter mountain which wasn't much higher than the foothills of this mountain in front of them all.

A silence descended on the group. None of them needed to be told that sunrise was almost upon them. The sun climbed high enough into the sky that the uppermost parts of the Ice Wall began to glow. Although it was only frozen water, the wall had taken on the shape and consistency of the most precious crystal. From this distance it looked similar, but on a much grander scale, to the ice in Winter that dressed all the trees who had bent their will to constructions across the Hiber Nation. Saltock was not ready for the sheer size of the names as they clearly began to appear on the wall. Nothing that he had seen in his life in Tukerland could have carved names of this scale by hand. He was certain that, even if he was on the distant side of the lake from where they had just traversed, he would still be able to see the names. Saltock recognised only two names on the extensive list that was etched into the frozen mass. The names of Torpast and Jandray were inscribed as the last two in the list of names stretching high up the Ice Wall. These names shimmered and had a three dimensional perspective to them. All the colours of the earlier Winter Lights seem to be reflected from within the names. "There she is" shouted Junstern, and she instinctively grabbed Saltock's arm. He followed her hand that was pointed to a position several names higher than Jandray and Torpast. There he saw, in equally vibrant outline, the name Jalper. Saltock started to count the names on the Ice Wall, but they were to numerous to mention. The higher ones were harder to read, but it was clear they were of the same scale as that of Jandray and Torpast's inscriptions.

Jandray didn't realise how much it moved him when he saw his name on the Ice Wall. He wondered if it would have struck him as lacking humility to be pleased to see his name on the wall. However, having seen it, he felt a great deal of pride that his name was inscribed on Queen Mountain, almost like she knew him and was saying that she wouldn't forget him. Torpast was equally proud and the two of them just stood in silence as the magnitude of both the inscription and their HiberWatcher role became very real in that instance. Jandray knew that there was an intense period of instruction to be received from the Hiber Library Keepers upon their return. All HiberWatchers were sworn to secrecy for life about what they learnt of their role. It helped that Jandray knew Kian and Kindross well, and they had been so supportive of him in his teaching role. He was looking forward to receiving and assimilating this information on this return. He looked at Torpast and said, "Now the real work begins; I have no real idea what the HiberWatcher must do, and we need to study hard when we return." Torpast nodded his agreement, too taken in with the occasion to say anything else.

King Nilan called the group to order. "I hope you have all found this journey as rewarding as I have. As you know, I have made this pilgrimage for many years now, and it never ceases to fill me with a sense of awe and wonder." He could see from the faces of all those in front of him that they felt the same. "But now it is time make the long journey back to Paltir. Torpast and Jandray have only a very short period of time to receive instruction on their roles from the Hiber Library Key Keepers and soon we will all be back here on our way to the protective chambers deep beneath the Queen Mountain." At this, he turned and started to walk back towards the Ice bridge. "If we make good time today, we should be home in time for a late supper" he said with a smile, "and that supper will be served in our hall, with Queen Torcas present." The thought of supper filled everyone with something to look forward to as they began the walk home. It would take several hours, but supper was a marvellous prize to fix their thoughts upon.

Saltock was aware that this was his last day within the Hiber Nation this year, although he was already making plans to visit as soon as Spring arrived. He intended to make time to chat with Altera on the way home. The proximity that they had shared on the journey to this point still warmed his heart, and he was now certain that Altera was very much part of the future he wanted for himself. At some point he would hope to gain the courage to ask Altera if she felt the same. If he could have read Altera's mind, he would not have had any concerns at all. He had awakened emotions and feelings in her that she could not articulate. Only Maltas remotely understood that a connection had been made between her and Saltock. More importantly, Maltas encouraged this and he was her closest friend. She felt that the Winter Sleep would feel like an eternity and she couldn't wait until spring.

Chapter Seventeen

The early winter sun began to rise on the final day of Grasby and Saltock's visit to the Hiber Nation. Their moods couldn't have been more different that morning. Grasby was keen to leave, whilst Saltock's heart was heavy at the thought of not seeing Altera for several months. Their journey back together from Queen Mountain had fostered a growing emotional connection between them and Altera took to holding his arm as they walked along. After last night's supper, she had leaned into him and they had embraced. He so desperately wanted to kiss her but it did not seem right at that time. So a deep embrace had sufficed and they had said their goodbyes.

Maltas had visited Saltock early in the morning and said that he had come at Altera's request. "Altera could not bring herself to see you again this morning", he said sincerely and with an emotion brought about by his brotherly love for her. "However, she wanted you to know that she will hold you in her dreams this winter and hopes you will do the same." Despite his sadness, this message lifted Saltock's mood. "I ask you to tell Altera that she will always have a friend in Warrior Saltock of Tukerland", he hesitated and then said, "And please tell her that I will count every day of her sleep until we can meet again. Be assured Maltas, I will be a friend of all those of the Hiber Nation." Maltas smiled at Saltock, and was unconcerned that this new friend towered above him, and also had feelings for his best friend. "Somehow", replied Maltas. "I cannot help but feel that we will need that friendship." As he said this, Grasby entered Saltock's room. "I am ready to leave" he gruffly announced. Saltock felt his anger rise at the unwelcome intrusion into his room but maintained his composure. "I was just thanking Maltas for spending time with me during our visit, I am ready for the journey whenever you are."

Maltas bowed to Grasby and to Saltock, and left the room. "Why are you bothering with these peasants?" said Grasby. "They are just a means to an end, that end being keeping our brave nation fed; they are merely our neighbouring storeroom and you would do well to remember this." Saltock decided to say nothing but thought to himself "There is a strength in this land and these people that you would do well not to underestimate." Saltock had carefully packed the Hiber clothing that he had been wearing during the visit. He immediately missed the comfort of the garments, especially the coat. However, he knew he had to leave as a Tukerland warrior and so he placed on his normal clothing. It was not as war-like in style as Grasby's outfit, but it was obviously Tukerland in its overall outfit. He hoped Altera would not see him like this as he felt it could be a physical barrier at a time when they had only just started on the journey of their relationship; one that Saltock had hoped would continue next year.

Grasby had not wasted his time whilst Saltock had been on his journey to the Ice Wall. He was pleased with the outcome of the meeting with Lorsern. He would not have been so pleased if he had known the young man that had been talking with Saltock so intensely when he had walked in was Lorsern's son. Delcant had been useful, and uncharacteristically truthful, in his description Lorsern. It was clear that Lorsern was in league with Delcant to gain greater influence within the Elder Council. It was also obvious that Lorsern had a streak of greed that Grasby could feed for his own benefit. Delcant had chosen his apprentice well and Grasby considered whether Lorsern could possibly replace Delcant in due course. Ultimately, both were disposable as far as Grasby was concerned. Lorsern had told him of the concerns that Elder Farrender was vocally supporting Sartora to replace her as Elder. "That woman Farrender does not like me, nor does she value what I have done for our local community" Lorsern had said, noticeably missing off her formal title as Elder, in a way that displayed his intense dislike for her. It was untrue, though, that Farrender had not recognised Lorsern's abilities. However, she had also seen his weaknesses, his arrogance, his immodesty when seeking praise and his deviousness; surpassed only by Delcant and his greed. "Sartora is the key barrier to me being the obvious successor as Elder of Paltir when Farrender steps down" said Lorsern. "Elder Delcant fears that Sartora is very highly regarded by the Queen in particular and her influence is significant within the Elder Council."

These issues were of minor concern to Grasby in his wider strategy for the subjugation of the Hiber peoples. However, having Lorsern within the Elder Council was important to his short term plans. He needed both Delcant and Lorsern in position in order that this strategy was not delayed next year. He would have to give it some thought as to how to neutralise this risk. "In my country, I could get rid of this Sartora in a number of ways" he said to Lorsern, with a fierce look on his face. "None of them particular pleasant for her, but all of them permanent." Lorsern looked horrified. For all his failings, he was not willing to be party to murder. Lorsern still had a faint glimmer of humanity in his twisted soul. And he was much more sceptical than Delcant of any equal partnership with this warrior. Lorsern was quickly becoming very aware that his part, and that of Delcant, in Grasby's schemes could be equally terminal for both of them. "I will have no part in any risk of harm to Sartora" he said with a defiance that did not match the fear that was welling up inside of him. "Whatever your plans are to help 'neutralise' this threat, it will not be life limiting to her." He wasn't sure his mask of confidence would last much longer, but he continued, "There must be other ways that Sartora can be removed from the choice of Elder, ways that do not include her permanent demise."

Grasby was surprised at this spark of rebelliousness from Lorsern. It was a character trait that Delcant never had displayed. It was mild by Tukerland standards, but it did earn Lorsern a modicum of respect in Grasby's view of him. Grasby needed to keep Lorsern happy with the role he was going to play, especially as he did not know the tangled web of deceit and betrayal he would be forced to engage in as he descended further down the path of Grasby's plans. He looked at Lorsern carefully and attempted to soften his voice. "Of course, Lorsern, I will accept your views and I will consider a different approach, one that removes Sartora as a risk to your aspirations, but one that keeps breath in her body." He bared his teeth in a twisted smile as he said this, and really didn't care if Lorsern believed him or not. The fact was that Lorsern had given him an idea that he hadn't thought of earlier, and he would revisit all the options in his mind on the long journey back to Tukerland.

Saltock could see that Grasby was lost in thought as they stood together in the room. "Is something on your mind Warrior Grasby, is there anything you would like us to discuss on the journey home?" Grasby quickly returned to the moment. He should have realised that Saltock was very perceptive, mature beyond his years. Having had the opportunity to closely observe Saltock over the last few weeks, Grasby knew full well that Saltock would never agree to any of the plans that Grasby was considering, and would probably try and destroy them if he did get any idea. Grasby had other close warrior 'friends' that he could trust with his ideas, and they were waiting none too patiently for him to make his move on Sargern. Ironically, it was Grasby who had persuaded these warriors to bide their time as he had visions of a much greater prize. "No", thought Grasby to himself. "Saltock has no place in the future I am planning, a future that will see me remove his father, and will bring riches to me beyond anything that can be imagined." Grasby looked over at Saltock. "Well, at least you look somewhat like someone who comes from Tukerland, but your clothing still does not show the warrior in you." Sufficiently pleased with this disparaging note he then added, "Warrior Saltock, my mind was on returning home, that is all. Unlike you, this nation has not put leafy roots round my legs and branches in my brain. This backward nation that cannot even stay awake all year round are at risk of sapping my energy. Let's go home."

Saltock did not have any inclination to respond to Grasby. In some way he was correct, more than he realised. Saltock did feel the living nature of the Hiber Nation in his body; he felt the energy emanating from their love of community and their relationship with the creatures, plants and trees around them. He was excited at the thought of managing the Hiber tree project, and was even more excited about seeing Altera again. "If the journey home is in silence, then that will please me" he thought, looking at Grasby's wide back as he strode ahead and into the square. "And I rather think that it will suit Grasby too." Both Saltock and Grasby took to their waiting horses and rode out of the square.

Saltock consoled himself with the thought of meeting up with Nirtan and Mortarn. Together they could discuss all that had happened and how Sargern was going to be briefed. More than ever, Saltock was convinced that Grasby was hatching a plan. His father would be much more aware of who supported Grasby and whether those plans extended to being a risk to Sargern. Even if Grasby's plans were only against the Hiber Nation, Saltock now felt he had a responsibility to this nation. He knew he was viewed as naive by Grasby's standards, but this responsibility was one he was willing to argue for, and even fight for if necessary. At the same time as Saltock was having these thoughts, Grasby was mulling over a range of plans for the future; a future that would see Sargern and Saltock removed from any hold over him, permanently!   Back to Tukerland via Decinter, one warrior to continue in his conspiracy, one to brief a father on the outcome of the talks. Neither quite sure of the future,   but both knowing, for very different reasons, that the fate of the Hiber Nation was at the centre of their hopes and aspirations.

Chapter Eighteen

As Grasby and Saltock rode away from Paltir on their journey back to Tukerland, Torpast and Jandray were walking to the home of the Hiber Key Keepers. From the limited conversation they had already had with the Key Keepers they were aware that they only had a few short days in which they would be entrusted to read the 'Ways of the HiberWatcher' scriptures. These 'Ways' had been written over generations and much of them had remained unchanged for centuries. Where situations had arisen that the Ways did not cover, additional notes of guidance had been carefully agreed with the HiberWatchers from that year, and added to the Way Scriptures by the Key Keepers. The 'Ways' were amongst the most important documents in the library. The Elders knew of their existence but were not party to the full content. Only the Key Keepers and the Queen and King had the authority to access these scriptures. When the Winter Sleep commenced, the HiberWatchers would have access to the Ways, having carefully removed them from the library and taken them to their quarters in Queen Mountain. They would then be able to use the time they had over Winter to refresh themselves of the contents of these scriptures. But, prior to the migration to this location, they would also be given the privilege to access all the other tablets, parchments and books held within the library. As with all HiberWatchers before them, they would give a solemn undertaking not to reveal anything that they discovered.

At Torpast's request, and with the approval of the Key Keepers, the two Watch Hounds - now openly called Winterclaw and Snowblue by both Jandray and Torpast accompanied them to the library. The bond between the four of them was growing fast and this boded well for the winter ahead. "I wonder what will be expected of us" said Torpast. "I had imagined that our only role was to ensure that our borders remained sealed throughout the winter, and we have little control over this." Jandray was thinking the same thing. "Once everyone has entered into sleep what would need to be done?" he said before continuing with, "I guess one of the key roles is to ensure that everyone has entered into sleep. I think that Winterclaw and Snowblue may have a significant role in this. Their ability to sense movement will help." "I hadn't thought of that" agreed Torpast. "Perhaps we will learn the secret of how we enter into the sleep?" he said with a quizzical look. "When I was younger I thought that there would be a secret draught that we all took, but as I got older, I learnt that one minute I was laying awake next to my family and the next minute it was Spring." He laughed out loud, "the only reason I knew that any time had passed was the fact that my father, indeed all the men, had grown a beard during the Winter Sleep." Jandray smiled back at Torpast. It was the Hiber way to be clean shaven, and so for the menfolk to awake with a beard was a source of much amusement amongst Hiber communities.

"I have also heard that the sleep regenerates us all, and that this is the reason why our elderly folk live to a ripe age, with few ailments" said Torpast. "Now that makes perfect sense to me", answered Jandray. "To be in a state of sleep for the whole of winter, away from the ravages of deep ice and snow and intense cold must assist our bodies to relax and recuperate. All these things will be made known to us in due course. And we will need to know how we are going to eat during Winter"; this statement eliciting a laugh from both of them. "Absolutely" replied Torpast, "I can shave during Winter, but I would rather not have to go on a fast when Spring comes as a result of overindulgence over the next few months." Jandray could see that Torpast kept himself in fine shape and said reassuringly, "I don't think that will be a problem, but I will stop you eating too much if your waistline starts to expand like Delcant's." At this both of them laughed again. They were getting comfortable in each other's company and the risk of loneliness that Jandray had anticipated would be mitigated by a friendship that could last for the rest of their lives after being HiberWatchers.

The two novice HiberWatchers were now at the door of the Library. "I must admit to you" said Torpast, "I have not visited the Key Keepers very much before. I have had no aspirations to be an Elder and gained what little research I needed via Elder Farrender who I know is a frequent visitor. That said, I know that Sartora visits here often and speaks highly of Kian and Kindross." Jandray replied, "I have visited here often. I think you will find this a most welcoming place. I am hoping that there is Hiber cake too!" As he said this, Kian opened the door to the warm and comfortable inner dwelling that she and Kindross called home. There was the unmistakable aroma of freshly baked Hiber cake and Jandray could not help being pulled back to memories of being at his mother's knee on an Autumn evening, waiting for the cake to come out of the oven. "I thought the two of you may like some cake and a warm drink before we start" said Kian. She guided them to the side of the fire, where Torcas had been sitting only a few weeks earlier. "Please take a seat, Kindross will join us shortly."

Kian looked over to Torpast and said kindly "You are too infrequent in blessing us with your company Torpast. I will not betray any confidences but I have seen your wife and she is like a young woman in the early stages of love. Whatever has occurred between you in recent days has removed some of the weight she had on her shoulders." Kian said this in such a way that Torpast did not see it as criticism and it made him reply, "If what I said does anything to repair my neglect of my family in recent years, then I am grateful. I nearly lost everything that I hold deal in the pursuit of things that are not important in comparison to the love of a family." "Well said" replied Kian. "I do understand that during winter you hope to reflect on how to rebuild the relationship with your family. I will admit, Sartora has said as much, and it is this intention in you that has given her such hope." Torpast was fighting back his tears and answered "I have no idea of what is required of me as a HiberWatcher, but with any spare time I have, it is in my heart to listen to the silence, to learn from my mistakes and to prepare for Spring." Kian gently brushed a tear from Torpast's eye, her age allowing her to do this act like a loving grandparent would console a child. "I hope that you can achieve this, as it is a worthy intent" she replied.

Looking to the other seat, she spoke to Jandray. "And how many times did you tell me that you would never put your name forward for selection?" Jandray wasn't quite sure how to answer, he had never lied to the Key Keepers and he wasn't going to start now. "Being selected was a surprise to me, in fact I was so certain that I would not be chosen, I didn't even attend the selection event." Jandray hoped that this answer would suffice. Kian looked at him and studied his face. "She can see right through my equivocal answer" he said to himself. However, suddenly the intensity of her stare softened and she smiled, "Sometimes things happen for reasons that are not clear at the time, and then become more transparent at a later date. Queen Mountain clearly has plans for you Jandray." Kian turned away and went to small table where she had laid out some plates and the Hiber cake. She cut two generous slices and returned to Torpast and Jandray. "Here" she said, "To build up your strength before we commence." As Kian said this, Kindross walked into the room. "Torpast and Jandray, welcome to our home, and to the gateway to the Hiber library. I see that Kian has already offered you some sustenance before we commence your training." He walked over to Kian and stood close to her. "We only have a short period of time together, but we hope that we will equip you sufficiently for the role ahead. You are the latest HiberWatchers in the long history of our folk who have taken on this honourable and important role. We are privileged to be able to share with you the knowledge of many generations of HiberWatchers."

Kindross then looked across to Kian who said "Our intention is to open your eyes and your mind to a world that very few people of our Hiber Nation see. You will remain awake and alert throughout a severe winter, one that will show you levels of snow, ice and storms you never thought possible. You will see our nation disappear under a massive depth of winter covering, and you will realise why it would be impossible for anyone to survive it for long." She noted the alarm on Torpast's face and her approach softened accordingly. "Alongside this severity of cold and snow, you will have the privilege of seeing a world of extreme beauty. You will see how the mountain range, and our Queen Mountain stand alert like guardians throughout the winter. And you will know that all living creatures, human, bird and animal are under your care. Even the fish in our lakes dive the bottom most parts of their habitats and join us in the sleep that we undertake." Jandray hadn't thought about the fish and other aquatic life that was abundant in the Hiber Nation. Their life was equally sacrosanct, they were not viewed as food and were part of the rich ecosystem in the Hiber Nation. Kindross then spoke, "It is probably best if we cover the basics of the Ways of the HiberWatcher and then answer any questions afterwards, what do you think?" Both Torpast and Jandray nodded their agreement.

Kian started to speak. "You will need to remember the following basic instructions that guide all the Ways of the HiberWatcher. The details underpinning these instructions are to be found in the Ways of the HiberWatcher scriptures that you will take with you to Queen Mountain from the Library. You will also be given a key to the library for emergencies which, in itself, is a privilege that only HiberWatchers have. Of course, you will return the key to us in Spring."

"So, here are basic instructions, I will tell you about each one of them over the next few days, but you need to understand the entirety before we commence, as they are interconnected. Here goes:

1. All life is important. You are to guard the nation, with all your strength.

2. You will use the hidden ways to ensure the entrances to Queen Mountain are secure.

3. You will ensure that the HiberWatcher patrols the Hiber caverns regularly to ensure all are safe.

4. With the help of the Watch Hounds you will ensure that nothing enters into Queen Mountain once the sleep commences.

5. You will use your time during winter to research the Ways of the HiberWatcher, ready to add to them if appropriate.

6. Unless absolutely necessary for the protection of the sleepers, you will not leave the sanctuary of Queen Mountain.

7. Only in dire emergency will you read how to wake the nation early."

After Kian had recited these instructions she continued, "Kindross and I will take time to explain each of these instructions in turn. However, don't worry if you forget the detail underneath of these instructions. They are all written down and can be found in the library. It is critical that you remember these instructions, if nothing else, is that understood?" Both Jandray and Torpast nodded their agreement, but clearly had questions. "Hold onto your questions for now" said Kindross. "I know your attention will be on phrases like 'hidden ways' as they tend to jump out to you. Also, the final instruction about 'waking the nation' is equally exciting. Let me point out to you both that this particular instruction has never, in our long history, been acted upon. However, there is a guide showing how to do this, should you need it. It is sufficient for you to know that this is only to be used as a last possible option."

Kian added, "As indicated by Kindross, the instructions on waking the nation early has never been acted upon. As a result there is no supplementary information on this matter."

The Key Keepers were accurate in their understanding that Torpast and Jandray would be immediately drawn to some of the instructions that that Kian had recited. Jandray was deep in thought. The instructions had reminded him of the verses of a poem that he had been thinking about over the last few weeks. It seemed like a different age when that first verse came into his head as he was preparing lessons for his class. Now a further verse emerged and it he had no idea where it came from. It was like it had been released from it's own deep sleep:-

"From afar, others look on the Hiber, safe in their sleep

And they plan to enter the Mountain sanctuary keep

These others will have help from Hiber within

But the plans they do make are not supported by their kin"

Jandray felt a finger of icy cold reach into him and he suddenly shivered. This verse, similar in style to the earlier verse he had remembered, had a much darker context within its words. Could there be a risk to the Hiber Nation this year? Perhaps he was just feeling vulnerable as he considered the immense responsibility he was taking on. For some reason Jandray was certain that this verse was also part of a much larger poem. Had something happened in the distant past that had led to this poem being written, or was it prophetic in nature? He decided to speak with Kian and Kindross about his concerns. He would do this on his own; there was no reason to transfer what could be totally irrational fears onto Torpast.

Kian's recital of the HiberWatcher instructions had brought a sombre mood upon both Torpast and Jandray. This was not unusual; each year the new HiberWatchers were allowed to understand things about the Winter Sleep that they had probably never even thought of before. Most people across the Hiber communities thought the HiberWatcher selection was just a part of Hiber history, the roles only in place to raise the excitement of the Winter Festival. Many said that it was just a relic of a bygone age; that the HiberWatchers had little to do over the Winter months. The only risk they would face was boredom. To a degree, Jandray had thought this and it was one of the reasons that had helped him decide never to put his name forward for selection. But, since that selection had taken place Jandray had become much more aware of his surroundings. It was almost that he could hear the trees in his home breathing and he could feel a presence that he had never experienced before. Torpast had changed too. Since his decision to put his name into the selection he had also become more aware that he was right to regret being out of 'place' with his family. Something had awakened in him that made him realise that his family was more important than many things he had been focussing his efforts on. For Torpast, this difference, this wakening of awareness, was liberating. For Jandray, this awakening made him fearful for winter.

Kindross stood up from his chair. "I think that is enough for one day don't you my dear Kian." "Looking at the faces of Torpast and Jandray, I think you are quite correct" answered Kian. "Please go and enjoy time with your loved ones for the evening, and return here in the morning." Torpast stood and made to leave, "Are you coming Jandray, perhaps we can walk together?" Jandray made his excuses and said, "Please go ahead without me, and would you take Winterclaw and Snowblue with you, I have something I need to discuss with the Key Keepers. I will join you at your house shortly. Unless I am mistaken, I would think that my class will be ensconced in one of their meetings and it will fun to break into it." Jandray had previously told Torpast about the 'secret society' that his class had created and the fact that they hadn't realised he was fully aware of their meetings. "That will be fun" said Torpast. "Perhaps we can enter our home quietly and hear if they are talking about us." At that he made to leave and the two Watch Hounds followed him out. Snowblue kept looking round at Jandray "You will be fine, Snowblue, I will be with you soon."

When Torpast had left, Jandray did not need to say anything, as Kindross said "Kian and I could both see that you were distracted at todays instruction, would you like to share what is troubling you?" "It may be nothing" replied Jandray "but a number of verses of an old poem have come to me in recent weeks. Another verse came into my head as you were going through the instructions." Without saying anything more, Jandray could tell he had sparked interest, even worry, in the faces of Kian and Kindross. "Please do repeat the verses if you can still remember them" gently asked Kian. As Jandray repeated the lines of the poem, Kian sighed audibly. "Dear Kindross, I feel we must explain to HiberWatcher Jandray that he is not the only one to have been troubled by this poem." She indicated to Jandray to sit. "We won't keep you long dear" she said. "Queen Torcas, as you may know, is a regular visitor to our library. Like you she has an avid interest in our history. Recently she also remembered some lines from a poem. It seems like fragments of a very old poem have been woken in you both. We have tried to find the original text, which may even be so old it is inscribed in tablet form." Kindross continued the discussion, "Both Kian and I have had sleepless nights trying to find the poem, but we still have not been able to locate it. The verse you have been burdened with is the most worrying yet, and we do not know the full meaning of the poem." At that, Kian went to a small cabinet and drew out a piece of parchment. She wrote on the parchment the words that Jandray had said, and then passed it to Jandray. "As you will see, we now have a few verses, but we feel there are more to found." She smiled reassuringly at Jandray. "Let's read them through together, because they bring reassurance as well as worry:

"The HiberWatchers watch, and the sleepers sleep

The Queen protects them all in her keep

Winter falls, and deep cold it does bring

And the world will refresh when we wake in Spring"

"Queen Mountain hears when trouble is near

Hiber Trees talk and move if they sense fear

Roots so deep can bring news to those who love

And long tunnels open up new roads from above"

"When the HiberWatchers are close in Hiber sense

Winter can be severe and storms intense

Be careful to watch each other as well as the sleeping

And work hard to ensure that at Spring there is no weeping"

When the snows do fall on Hiber Watcher Day

And the lights in their brilliance put on their display

It shall mean an event of great import

A Spring awakening of a different sort"

"From afar, others look on the Hiber, safe in their sleep

And they plan to enter the Mountain sanctuary keep

These others will have help from Hiber within

But the plans they do make are not supported by their kin"

"It is very interesting that these verses have been revealed in some kind of order to both you and Torcas, without you both knowing it" said Kindross, looking at the parchment. "The most recent verse is, perhaps, the most concerning." Jandray looked up form the parchment and said, "However, looking at the other verses, it does start to make more sense. There is almost a rhythm of expectation in the poem." "That is a good way of describing it" said Kian. "I understand what you are saying. The poem is almost leading us to an understanding that there is a threat to the Hiber people, but that there is safety and protection all around us. What we don't know is if this threat is something that has happened in the past and this is just an historical memory, or if something more sinister has meant that our land, perhaps Queen

Mountain even, is revealing this poem to you and to Queen Torcas."

Jandray looked across at Kian and Kindross. "Has anyone else previously experienced this? Torpast certainly has not mentioned anything. But I know that all HiberWatchers have been sworn to secrecy. Is there anything in the Ways of the HiberWatcher that describe something like this happening before?"   Kindross looked at Jandray and said, "You are a great student Jandray, and it doesn't surprise us that you would be thinking of this. We have already researched the Ways after Queen Torcas had spoken to us. There is nothing obvious that we can find that indicates this has happened before. And, of course, our long years as Key Keepers means we would know of anything over the many years of our service." Both Kian and Kindross also looked troubled. Jandray replied "I don't know why, but I feel there are more verses to come, whether they will be revealed to me or to Queen Torcas or to someone else, but there is more to come."

At that point, the three agreed to end the evening and to let Jandray catch up with Torpast. There were still a few more days to go before the sleep commenced. Jandray wondered if more verses would be revealed, and if those verses would give hope.

Chapter Nineteen

Grasby and Saltock returned to Decinter and were met by Delcant. Later, Saltock would regret not remaining with the two of them when they said there were going to discuss some practical aspects of the earlier trade negotiations. However, Saltock was sufficiently wearied by Grasby's presence over recent weeks that he was pleased to be released from further meetings with him. Delcant was an unpleasant character in Saltock's mind, and quite unlike most Hiber people he had met. Saltock decided to take the short ride over to the Hiber community of Octurn. King Nilan had asked if he would take a message to an innkeeper called Ertin. He also added that Saltock would find no better hospitality in the whole of the Hiber Nation. With Delcant's willing permission, Saltock joined with a couple of Decinter folk to accompany them on the journey. Delcant thought what good fortune it was that Saltock would be out of the way whilst he and Grasby honed their plans.

As Saltock rode away, Grasby walked up to Delcant. "That boy warrior is all too interested in your traditions" he said menacingly. "I am pleased that he will not be present whilst we finalise our plans; I have a few ideas of how things can be progressed." Delcant replied, "I have also had chance to think through such issues. I think there is a clear path to realising our plans; laying the ground for further work next year." Both walked back into the palatial halls of the Decinter building that Delcant had so blatantly built in recent years. King Nilan had not challenged Delcant extensively over the construction, but Delcant knew he wasn't pleased with what he had seen. "His displeasure was voiced in refusing my attendance at Paltir" he felt, not saying this out loud, as he still needed to ensure Grasby had no reason to be concerned over Delcant losing any of his manipulative control within the Hiber Elder Council.

Grasby said to Delcant, "I met with Lorsern, your acolyte, and he updated me on the risk that this Sartora woman poses to your plans. That risk is one that we both share. If she stops your plans in the Elder Council, it will impact on our overall vision for the future." "I agree" said Delcant, "Farrender is committed to supporting

Sartora as her successor. As she is the retiring Elder, she will have most influence on this choice. Lorsern is not well liked by Farrender, but he is critical to our longer term strategy. Having a 'friend' in the Paltir community is essential going forward." Grasby narrowed his eyes when he said "But Lorsern has a defiance that I have not seen in you, Elder Delcant." Delcant did not know whether this was a threat to him or a compliment to Lorsern. Grasby continued, "He insists that he will have no part in any harm coming to Sartora, which makes my initial plans to neutralise her influence somewhat more difficult." Delcant had no desire to see harm come to Sartora either. The difference, however, was he really did not care too much as long as he could assure himself that blood was not on his hands. "There is a way" said Delcant. "But it will need help from some of your colleagues, and will need you to 'host' Sartora if the plan comes to fruition."

Grasby did not like much about Delcant, but he valued his devious mind. "Tell me what you think we can do then" he said. "And be quick about it as I am getting hungry. This lack of meat over recent weeks as made me agitated; although I note that you seem to be enjoying Tukerland fare. I hope there is a way you can provide some real food for me now that your King and Saltock are not present." Delcant smiled and bowed slightly "I have arranged for some Tukerland food to be ready for you after our meeting, I am sure you will be pleased with it." Grasby grimaced in what was meant to be a smile and said, "Well, if your plan is the only thing in the way of that meal let us be on with it." Delcant took a deep breath and said, "You would need to choose a small band of loyal warriors, as close to the physical appearance as Hiber folk as you can find. I will take these with me into the Queen Mountain as part of my community. You will need to choose these warriors carefully as we cannot have people who are head and shoulders above the normal height of our peoples." Grasby was staring at Delcant intently; "Go on, that can be easily arranged." Delcant continued, "I have sufficient knowledge of the workings of our nation and our culture to know that the sleep will not effect your warriors. All they have to do is pretend to sleep as they see our kinfolk sleeping. When all are asleep, there will only be the two HiberWatchers awake, and they have also have to check on the other caverns as well. It should not be too difficult for your warriors to take Sartora. Whilst she is in Queen Mountain she will remain asleep. However, when she is removed from the protection of the mountain she will awake." Delcant did not actually know if this forced awakening would kill Sartora and he wasn't really worried about this risk. If she died, it was not on his hands, and it rather solved the problem. He would remain asleep and would be able to deny all knowledge of the situation.

Grasby considered the outline plan that Delcant had placed before him. "That is all well and good" he said, "but my understanding is that the entrances are all blocked and it would be impossible to get out of the mountain, or do you have plan for this?" Delcant smiled and replied "There are secret passages or 'ways' as the HiberWatchers call them. The warriors would need to find one of these in order to leave the mountain." Grasby's interest was growing. "So, you know these 'ways' then?" he replied. "Not exactly, but the HiberWatchers do. Your warriors will need to be skilled as trackers. They can follow the HiberWatchers along the Ways and I am sure they will eventually lead you to an opening high in the mountain as they carry out their role in checking the various sleeping chambers. The HiberWatchers also need to survey the snowfall, to ascertain when the fury of the late Winter storms subside; signalling that Spring will soon be on its way. I will find a way of providing a stock of food for your Warriors. But they will need to take some food with them, as it could be many weeks that they will be within the mountain, and also a long trek back to Tukerland."

Grasby considered this and replied, "Again, we can do this, some of our warriors are excellent in tracking, and also at ensuring they are not spotted. We are not at war with any of our old Tukerland states, but some of us older warriors do keep an active monitoring of our neighbours." "There is one final hurdle to overcome" said Delcant hesitantly. "What is it?" hissed Grasby. "As you probably know by now, each HiberWatcher has a loyal hound as a companion. These Watch Hounds are intelligent and extremely sensitive to any threat to their HiberWatcher. Your trackers will need to be able to avoid these hounds too." "Yes, I have met the two hounds chosen this year" said Grasby. "They are fine beasts and I would really like to see how we could cross breed these with our Tukerland hounds. I would particularly like to see if we could replicate the winter fur that these two hounds have grown. In fact.." he continued "..I am as interested in these hounds, as any obstacle to your Elder Council issue."

It was clear that Grasby was thinking through this final problem "I may achieve two objectives if we manage to take not only this Sartora, but also one of the hounds. I can split up our group of warriors to ensure that the other hound cannot follow two tracks, yes that would work." Delcant was not as confident as Grasby and said, "How will you do this? The Watch Hounds are very fierce and are always with one of the HiberWatchers." Grasby didn't blink when he replied, "The HiberWatchers are casualties to the cause of our plans, if they need to be dealt with then they will be dealt with, do you want to know the detail?" Delcant really didn't, and looked to the floor. "I thought you wouldn't" said Grasby. "Leave the detail to me, just get my Warriors into the mountain, provide a stock of food and then go to sleep. By the time you awake it will be all sorted out." Delcant worried that it would be so, and the 'sorted' would not be pleasant.

Saltock was nearing Ertin's Inn. It turned out that he would be the only guest as his companions had plans to meet friends in Octurn. With the annual migration taking place imminently the inn was closed. Ertin was also preparing for the journey north to join all of the Octurn community in their migration to Queen Mountain. Just being out of Grasby and Delcant's malevolent and devious presence made Saltock feel much better. At least when he was back in Tukerland he wouldn't have the daily assault on his integrity that both these two had brought over recent weeks. He was also looking forward to discussing all he had learnt with Nirtan and Mortarn. He would welcome their wise advice on how to approach his father with a full update, without overtly criticising Grasby. Sargern was secure in his leadership, but Grasby was a warrior who had many friends in the warrior elite. He could make things difficult for Saltock and for his father if he chose to. "Yes, there is much to consider, and to consider carefully" thought Saltock to himself.

As he approached the door to the Inn, Saltock was met by a man who immediately introduced himself. "By your size, and the fact that we are closed to guests, I am guessing you are Warrior Saltock. I am Ertin, and it is my honour to host you at my humble inn" said Ertin, bowing to Saltock. "Please let me introduce my son, Ocsend, to you. He has just returned from school in Paltir and saw you at the

Selection. He has been brimming with stories about the two great Tukerland Warriors who towered over all around them." Ocsend was of similar height to Ertin, but was much slimmer in stature. Ocsend also bowed before Saltock. "Warrior Saltock, it is a privilege to meet with you. We were so pleased you picked out our teacher, Jandray, during the selection; he will make a fine HiberWatcher." Saltock smiled at Ocsend who, in reality, was only a few years younger than him. "It was a real honour that I was asked to take part in the selection" he replied. "And I also met some of your fellow students as well. Maltas and Altera were specifically allocated to host me." Ocsend's smile betrayed more than friendship at the mention of these two names. "Maltas and Altera updated us all about you." Suddenly realising that it may seem discourteous to be thought of talking about Saltock, he hurriedly added "It was all extremely complimentary."

Ertin looked across to Ocsend and said, "Please ensure there is food and beer ready for our guest, it is only a short journey from Decinter, but I have heard that Tukerland Warriors have a voracious appetite." Saltock's hunger stirred in him at the reminder of food. "I hear that you brew the best beer in the Hiber Nation, and that is straight from the King." Ertin looked like he would erupt with pride and said "King Nilan was a regular visitor to our inn when he had less responsibilities. If it were not impertinent, I would describe him as a friend, but I am unsure if I could use that term of a King." Saltock replied, "Knowing what little I know of Hiber culture, but having spent some time with your King, I think he would be humbled to hear that you would call him friend. Being in his position can be lonely; I am learning that I as enter into leadership within our nation."

Saltock followed Ertin into the building, having to bend his head to ensure he didn't hit the door threshold; low by Tukerland standards, but perfectly adequate for Hiber folk. The entrance hall opened into a warm and inviting area, with a large fire in one corner. There were several high backed chairs facing the fire, and Saltock could see that some of them were already occupied. "Ertin, I see that you have other guests here, I hope I am not disturbing you?" Ertin looked at Saltock and replied "Perhaps you may want to join them by the fire, these guests have recently arrived and, if you are in agreement, I will serve food and beer to all of you in front of the fire." Saltock looked over to the fire and replied, "That would be most acceptable, I have learnt that Hiber folk are easy to talk with and it will be a distraction from thinking about my tasks ahead when I return to Tukerland."

As he moved closer to the hearth, Saltock could see that there were three persons sat in front of the fire. He wondered who these fellow travellers were and if they would be good company. On hearing Saltock approach, one of those sat in the chair turned slowly and looked over to him. "Warrior Saltock, what a surprise to see you here" and then began to laugh out loud. The other male also turned and said, "The beer is superb, you need to catch up, we are already ahead of you." Saltock was lost for words as he realised that Nirtan and Mortarn were in front of him. "How.....Why....Who" was all he could say. "Warrior Saltock, son of Sargern, lost for words, now that is something to tell" said Nirtan and he grasped Saltock's arms in welcome. "Are you not pleased to see us?" "Very pleased" said Saltock, "I am just lost for words to see you here, what is afoot?" Nirtan's smile faulted a little when he said, "There are things we need to discuss, all will be clear in due course, pull up a chair. Mortarn is not wrong when he comments on the quality of the beer. We will wait for Ertin, our fellow conspirator before we tell you our tale." Saltock was surprised that Nirtan used the term "conspirator" and began to say something. However, Ertin returned at that moment with a tray heavily laden with food. Nirtan added, "I know you will have lots of questions, and I hope that we can answer them. Let's eat first as I think we will talk long into the night." Saltock nodded his agreement. A third guest had been sat cloaked and hooded. At that point he stood up and said "Well met Warrior Saltock, I hope you enjoyed your time in Paltir." The hood fell from his shoulders and King Nilan smiled widely as the three Tukerland Warriors, The King of the Hiber Nation and their host began to eat. Saltock was in a daze and wondered just what this night would bring.

After several draughts of beer had been supped, and much of the tasty Hiber food had been consumed, Nirtan said, "So, it's time to answer some questions that are undoubtedly chasing round in your head. Firstly, when I say 'conspiracy', take the term lightly, there is nothing we will discuss that in any way challenges your father; quite the opposite." Saltock was somewhat relieved to hear this and noticeably settled into his chair. "There are relationships going back many years that we need to bring you up to speed on. Under no circumstances are you to discuss what we tell you with anyone. Grasby has loyal friends in places you would not believe - even amongst your own family I am sorry to say." "I am no friend of Grasby" replied Saltock. "I have had the chance to observe him closely in recent weeks. His behaviour with Delcant is concerning, and his dismissiveness of the Hiber folk was demeaning to his Warrior status. More importantly, he is clearly planning something with Delcant, and possibly others. I have heard that he had been in extensive discussions with someone called Lorsern in the Paltir community. I have met Lorsern's son, who I have come to like and trust, but he has warned me not to trust his father. He was uncomfortable saying this to me, but I was grateful for his candour."

Nirtan looked at Saltock and said, "Grasby and Delcant are indeed in league with each other. Grasby also has a number of warriors in Tukerland who support him, although we don't know how aware they are of his plans. What we do know is that, whatever Grasby is planning, it will not be in the interests of the Hiber folk; and will not be in the interest of Tukerland in the long run." The conversation had taken on a serious overtone, and the warmth of the hearth did nothing to prevent a chill in the air as they spoke. Nirtan looked at Saltock and said, "You will not be aware, until now, that King Nilan and I have known each other for many years. How we know each other is for another day. However, until his royal duties curtailed it, we met regularly here at Ertin's Inn. Our intention was to ensure that each nation had an effective communication channel; in addition to those of the annual trade talks. When Delcant and Grasby took a leading role in those talks in recent years, this extra level of communication proved invaluable. Why do you think that Sargern sent you to the trade talks this year? I have been directly updating your father about a number of concerns we have. He cannot directly challenge Grasby at the moment as we are not fully sighted on his aspirations; nor are we sure of the level of support that Grasby has for them. All we do know is that whatever Grasby is planning, it will only serve his own selfish ambitions."

"I am grateful that my father is aware of the risk that Grasby poses; I had rather thought he had put me in place to ensure he had a trustworthy ear at the talks, and I am reassured that my concerns about Grasby are accurate" sighed Saltock. "I was going to meet you in Tukerland to discuss how I should present those concerns to my father. It sounds like he will not be surprised at what I report, and my report will only confirm such fears you already have. Please go on, as I fear you have more to tell me."   Nirtan looked towards Mortarn and continued to speak to Saltock in hushed tones. "We have learnt that Grasby is unsatisfied with the outcome of the talks. He wants to destabilise the Hiber Elder Council by helping Delcant place a compliant Elder into the Paltir community when their current Elder steps down." Saltock interjected, "I have met Elder Farrender and she is a formidable person, one that strikes me as being honest and of high integrity."   "Indeed", replied Nilan, "Farrender is a loyal Hiber subject and always has the best interests of the Hiber Nation at the heart of all she does. However, her preferred replacement is called Sartora. Delcant is continually trying push Lorsern forward as a more suitable candidate." "I have met Sartora and she is a trustworthy woman, exceptionally gifted in leadership from what I could see" replied Saltock. Ertin smiled and tried to lighten the conversation by saying, "I think you have met her daughter too, and she made an impression you."   Saltock laughed out loud, "I have no secrets here, that I can tell. Yes I will admit, here and now, that I was knocked over by the beauty of her daughter Altera. It has gone no further than an embrace and I fear my father will want me to partner a more appropriate Tukerland warrior, but I left part of my heart in Paltir."

Ertin had not shared this piece of information with Nirtan and Mortarn, mainly as he had only just heard about Saltock and Altera from his son. Nirtan and Mortarn looked at each other and Mortarn said,   "Does this complicate matters?" Nirtan could see that Saltock had already asked himself the same question but was uncomfortable that someone else would ask.   Nirtan never treated Mortarn as a servant,   but Saltock was surprised that Mortarn would be so candid.   Nirtan answered slowly and he was looking at Mortarn rather than Saltock when he replied "Some have made great sacrifices in love to protect the peace between our two nations." And then he stopped. Silence descended over the four before Ertin said, "Perhaps that it is a complication that will have to work itself out. Right now there are more pressing matters to address."   Remembering his friend was now King, Ertin added, "I am sorry King Nilan if I have spoken out of turn." "No, you have put us back on the right road Ertin, as you always have done so before. Ertin is right, the more pressing issue is how do we deal with Grasby and Delcant, without anyone knowing that we are meeting up."

Mortarn had remained silent, but Saltock could feel he was looking at him during the silence. Nirtan could also see a pain behind Mortarn's composed exterior. He had known Mortarn all his life, and Mortarn had always been at Nirtan's hand. Saltock could see the loyalty between these two, but he could also see that Mortarn carried a sadness, or a memory of a sadness, around with him. Was Nirtan's comment about sacrifice directed at Saltock and his fledgling relationship with Altera, or was it directed at Mortarn? Saltock thought that the most obvious sacrifice was that Mortarn had always remained a servant to Nirtan; and it was this sacrifice that he was alluding too. He put these thoughts out of his mind and concentrated on possible solutions to the matter at hand. Mortarn said, "We know that Delcant is central to any of the traitorous designs that Grasby and he are planning. I recommend that we place someone into Queen Mountain in case he is planning on an attack from within." "I was thinking that too" said Nirtan, "but all Hiber folk who enter will then fall into sleep. There are rumours that you can avoid the sleep, but then they would soon be discovered by the HiberWatchers, or would starve through lack of sustenance." Saltock looked at Nirtan and was surprised at the level of detail he knew about the Hiber Nation. But he had also been surprised that Nirtan and King Nilan had been meeting up, for how many years, he didn't know.

King Nilan replied, "There is a way that this could be done. It would be dangerous and it would still be extremely likely that whoever we identified to do this would be caught by one of the HiberWatchers or, more likely, their Watch Hounds." Saltock remembered the amazing creatures, Winterclaw and Snowblue, and couldn't help but smile at the thought of those magnificent animals. Nirtan could see the smile on Saltock's face and said, "I guess you have met this year's Watch Hounds. If they are like the ones in the past, they will be prime examples of their breed." Again, how did Nirtan know this detail thought Saltock. King Nilan continued, "There are certain privileges that I have as King, one of these is access to the Hiber Library. What most people do not know is that amongst the many tunnels or 'ways,' as we call them, within Queen Mountain, there is a secret way that links the library to Queen Mountain. Only the Key Keepers and the HiberWatchers can use that tunnel; it allows the HiberWatchers to use the library during the Winter. If we could bring someone to Queen Mountain, and then they secrete themselves within the Library, they could at least be on hand if something untoward occurs. The first place the HiberWatchers will go if this is the case will be to the Library. They would do this to research any possible answers within our rich historical records. Our person could then make contact with the HiberWatchers."

"I will go", said Saltock rising out of his seat. "I have no fear of the danger and if it will protect the Hiber people's it will be worth it." King Nilan smiled and replied, "And how will we hide the fact that you are head and shoulders taller than any other person migrating to Queen Mountain; or how would you ensure that people of Paltir who saw you at their Winter Festival would not spot you?" Saltock sat down and realised that The King was right. Nirtan asked, "Who can go then? King Nilan and Ertin are already attending and the rest of us are from Tukerland, it leaves no obvious options." Mortarn took his turn to stand. "Nirtan and King Nilan, I will volunteer for this. I am not tall by Tukerland standards, and I am not known across the Hiber Nation." At that point, Saltock could see that Nirtan appraised Mortarn with a strange look, one that he could not decipher. "Ertin can take me with him when he leaves for Queen Mountain. King Nilan will have to find a way to get me, unnoticed, from the Sleeping cavern to the tunnel back to the Library. If he can do this quickly, the chances of anyone spotting me will be limited." "This could work" said Ertin. "Our community is one of the furthest from Paltir and from Queen Mountain. There are many in our community who are unknown to our other Hiber communities. If Mortarn is with me, they will just think he is part of our community. I am sure no questions will be asked." Nirtan was less certain of the plan. "My loyal Mortarn, I am unsurprised that you offer, but this is not without risk. We have no idea what Delcant and Grasby is planning and you will be on your own, with no means of gaining additional help. Even if you meet the HiberWatchers, how will they know to trust you?"

"Gaining the HiberWatcher's trust is the least of my concerns", Mortarn replied. "I think that this will not be too difficult, as long as King Nilan mentions something to them." King Nilan looked up. "A kind of password?" he said. "No", said Mortarn, a verse from a poem I think would be appropriate."

"But others, too, are awake and are friends of the Hiber kin

When they are needed they too will be found within

A Hiber heart or two they will be seeking whilst there

And Queen Mountain will unify these hearts in this endeavour"

King Nilan stood up and grasped Mortarn by the shoulder. "You, too, have had an awakening I see. The Queen has been troubled by aspects of a poem that she has been remembering. I think you have just added another verse." Saltock and Ertin looked at each other, not knowing the importance of what had just been said. However, Nirtan seemed to understand the significance but was deep in thought. "That poem is as old as the Hiber Mountains" he said, "and it gives both comfort and concern." "Torcas feels the same", replied Nilan, "But we cannot ignore the fact that Mortarn clearly is the one who has been chosen for this task." Nirtan, still uncertain, looked across at this dear friend and said, "Mortarn, are you sure?" "I have never been so sure of anything since a decision I made many years ago" he replied. "So be it" said Nirtan and sat down in silence.

During the remainder of the evening the four laid out their plans. Nirtan and Saltock agreed that they would come up with a plan to answer any questions about why Mortarn was not at his side. It would not be unusual for Mortarn to be in the far reaches of Tukerland, under orders from Nirtan, and it was felt that not too many questions would be asked. Ertin would take Mortarn with him and he and King Nilan would provide the opportunity for Mortarn to be guided to the library. It was felt too risky to introduce Mortarn to the HiberWatchers immediately and the poem, quickly passed to Jandray, would have to suffice. "Jandray is one of the most intuitive and intelligent people I know" said Nilan. "He will understand not to say anything and, when the time comes, he will understand that there is reason to my actions."

Eventually the plans were finalised. Ertin and Mortarn would leave for Queen

Mountain in the morning. Saltock would meet up with his Decinter travelling companions and would return to meet up with Grasby. Nirtan would make his own way back to Tukerland, and would await Saltock there. King Nilan would also make his own way back to Paltir. The only one of the group who wasn't at all concerned about the plans was Mortarn. He seemed totally at ease, even excited at the thought of this mission. "I have not seen Mortarn like this before" Saltock said to himself, "but then again, I have not seen Nirtan and Mortarn being friends with a King, so I must not be surprised."

Chapter Twenty

The final days before the Winter Sleep was due to commence flew by for Jandray and Torpast. Jandray, Kindross and Kian decided that Torpast should be made aware about the poem. Torpast hadn't had any verses come to him and he wondered if the poem was historic, rather than prophetic. "Perhaps it is a lesson to ensure that we take our roles as HiberWatchers seriously, and not rest on the fact that nothing untoward has ever happened during the sleep" he said, hoping to reassure Jandray. Jandray replied, "Perhaps that is it, Torpast, that would make sense", hoping he was concerned for nothing. Kindross and Kian had also updated Queen Torcas on the verses that Jandray had added. She wasn't so confident that this was just a relic of a story from generations ago. "There must be a reason why Jandray and I are remembering these verses this year" she said to the Key Keepers, "I cannot help but think that they have been sent to us to ensure we are ready, for what I don't know, but ready none the less." Kian and Kindross had still not been able to find any further links to the poem within the library. "We have asked Torpast and Jandray to spend time in the library prior to the sleep, to try and find the original document, perhaps that will help us." Torcas added quickly, "As long as that gives us time to reconsider this issue when we wake in Spring. Something tells me that there is a risk to our nation, and that Queen Mountain is warning us to be prepared."

Jandray and Torpast had continued to receive instruction from the Key Keepers. They had been given access to the Hiber Library and were preparing to transfer with them the maps that covered the routes within Queen Mountain for when the nation moved into its protective caverns. They would have a key to the library, and one of the hidden ways outlined by Kian was a tunnel from Queen Mountain back to the Library. The Key Keepers had used this tunnel to take Jandray and Torpast into the heart of Queen Mountain. They were familiar with the cavern that hosted the Hiber Nation, but had never been into the other caverns for the Hiber animals and birds. They were even shown the highest 'way' where they would find a window to the outside world during the winter period. The hidden ways linked all these caverns together. Jandray and Torpast were lost for words at the magnitude of the sanctuary that was within Queen Mountain. Kian and Kindross mentioned that there were many other caverns within the mountain that they had not entered. "During winter you may have time use these ways to explore this vast 'underground country' within our country" said Kian. "If you research the Ways of the HiberWatcher, you will find that some of this great subterranean landscape has been mapped out by your predecessors, but I am sure you are likely to be able to add to these maps."

As Kian was talking with them she added, "If you have time, visit the 'Forest under the Mountain' during Winter, it is a spectacle to behold. As it is within the warmth and protection of the mountain, the trees do not turn to ice. Each community and their distinct colour of tree is represented in this forest and it is said that all trees trace their roots to this forest. Legend has it, and the poem seems to reflect this, that all trees across our nation are linked by their extensive root network to this forest." The Forest was one of the secrets known only to the HiberWatchers and to the Key Keepers. Kian went onto explain,"You will hardly be able to comprehend the vastness of the Forest within Queen Mountain. The roots tap into hidden nutrients, and the rocks above provide a kind of light, not dissimilar to the Winter Lights. Kindross and I have made many visits to the Mountain over the years and we remain overwhelmed by the majesty of it all. It is one of the main honours bestowed on you as HiberWatchers to be able to witness this incredible 'country' within our country. But remember it is wild, and the forest of trees do not bend to our will like the cultivated ones above land. That said, no harm will befall anyone who enters Queen Mountain with an honest heart and transparent soul, you will do well to remember this." Kian's thoughts seemed far away for a few moments, as if wondering what to say next. She looked at Kindross and he nodded his agreement. "Within the Mountain, there are ways not even known to us. Some that we have never had chance to map or ascertain where they lead. The maps we have given you will provide little help if you stumble into one of these ways, so be alert in your exploration." Kindross said, with a note of caution in his voice, "It may be enough that you just experience the vastness of land beneath Queen Mountain without seeking out ways of uncertainty." Torpast and Jandray remained silent and realised that they had more to learn than they had ever imagined.

Above ground the ice bridge had now fully formed, with the whole of the lake surrounding Queen Mountain now a vast sheet of ice. This allowed a steady stream of Hiber folk to commence their journey to the cavern. Each community knew their entrance, which was easily spotted by an avenue of trees symbolic of their community. These trees surrounded the entrance and had not taken on their icy cloaks, unlike all the other trees across the nation. It was tradition that each community entered through their own entrance. Once inside one of the twelve immense tunnels, naturally sculpted out of the rock, they followed a downward sloping path, worn smooth with generations of feet passing over it. It was still a considerable walk to the main cavern of sleep. What the Hiber folk passing through the main entrance didn't realise was that as soon all the community was safe inside the protection of Queen Mountain, the trees would gently fold across the entrance and they too would take on icy sculptures in readiness for winter. They would form an impenetrable barrier to the outside, a final defence, in addition to being buried under a deep coating of ice and snow.

Eventually, all the tunnels emerged into the main cavern. It was large enough to host all the Hiber peoples and all they had needed to bring with them was a limited amount of bedding. The floor was of a construction that was difficult to explain, the Hiber folk called it "Sleep sand"; it was springy underfoot and soft and warm to the touch. A thin blanket laid over the floor was all the folk needed to prepare themselves for the winter's sleep ahead. As this was an annual event only the youngest amongst the population did not know what to expect. Nevertheless there was still great excitement as folk met up from across the communities, many who had not seen each other since last winter's sleep. There was no hierarchy within the sleep cavern, and no distinct areas for the communities to bed down in. Naturally, each community filled the areas closest to the tunnels through which they had travelled, but the more adventurous wandered across the whole cavern in search of friends. It was an easy migration, in some respects, as nothing was needed for the Winter ahead. In their sleep, they would want neither food nor drink. When they awoke in Spring, they would break their fast, using the limited stores that had been brought to Queen Mountain for that purpose. Then they would make their way back to their own communities, and food stores also made for this purpose provided food enough to sustain them on the journey back to their homes. Once home, each community would open up its own stores and life would return to normal, feeding on last year's stored crop, whilst they worked hard to plant for the next harvest.

Elder Delcant had entered the cavern already and was looking around him carefully. It had not been easy bringing the small group of Tukerland Warriors in with him, and he was continually concerned that they would be discovered. Whilst Grasby had chosen this small band of warriors to fit in with the physical size of Hiber folk, they were still tall by Hiber standards. Delcant knew that he would fall asleep just as all the Hiber folk would. His research in the Hiber Library had indicated that the warriors would not be subject of this sleep. It was a mystery as to how it happened but, at the correct time, a sense of peace would descend over the whole cavern. The roof, illuminated by ways that no one really understood, would dim and sleep would descend upon all Hiber folk. The Tukerland warriors would not be effected by this event so they would have to feign sleep. Delcant's worries were manifest. "Will the warriors even bother to stick with the plan or will they just kill me and the other Elders in our sleep?" He knew that Grasby was not to be trusted, and the carefully laid out plans that he had agreed with Grasby could just be a tissue of deceit to ensure Delcant continued to support Grasby. "It is too late now" Delcant said to himself. "I have made decisions that I cannot retreat from and I must see this through." In an effort to raise his spirits he said to himself, "If Grasby does stick to his plans I will not have any blood on my hands, only Sartora will be directly effected, and the way will be clear for Lorsern to take over as Elder of Paltir community."

What was not clear to Delcant was how the Tukerland Warriors would move around within Queen Mountain. Delcant knew that the main tunnel entrances would lie under heavy accumulations of ice and snow. However, his research had revealed that there were other secret passages that would lead to the surface, above the ice and snow. Delcant also didn't know how they would avoid the HiberWatchers discovering them, and he didn't really want to know. He suspected that he would actually have their blood on his hands, and this thought made him weak with regret. He had, against all Hiber tradition, learnt the addictive taste of animal flesh, but he still wasn't prepared to accept that he would be party to the murder of a Hiber person.   The final concern that Delcant had was he would not know if the plan had worked until he awoke in Spring. He could have asked the Warriors to wake him too, but if he couldn't return to a state of sleep he could be identified as part of this conspiracy, or he could starve to death. Neither option was particularly attractive to him. Delcant reassured himself that he had worked hard to ensure Grasby supported all that had been carefully prepared. This incursion into the Winter Sleep would allow the Tukerland warriors to fill out gaps in their knowledge which could then be used at a future time. The Elders of Hiber would not be able to track back to Delcant the disappearance of one of their own, and the devious conspiracy to manipulate the Elder Council in time for next year's trade talks.

As the Hiber folk migrated into Queen Mountain, all the animals and birds were finding their way into their caverns too. Soon the Hiber Nation would be devoid of life outside of Queen Mountain. The Hiber food stores had been checked by each community and all was ready for the Spring awakening and the subsequent festivities. Queen Torcas and King Nilan had arrived into the cavern. The King had been busy for the last few days and he had not been seen much across the sprawling Paltir building that was their home. King Nilan and Queen Torcas took time to speak with friends from across the Hiber communities. Nilan particularly wanted to speak with Ertin, whose hospitality at his inn was still something that he thought of often. He found Ertin with a fellow member of the Ocsend community, who was slightly taller than him, but of the same age. "Ertin, my friend, welcome to you and your colleague. It has been too long since we have enjoyed your fine inn and your unsurpassed hospitality; I miss it greatly." Ertin beamed with pride and replied, "King Nilan, perhaps you will join us next year and we can spend a few evenings catching up, I have a new beer I would like you to try." King Nilan smiled at Ertin and nodded his agreement, "Well, if that isn't something worth waking up for, I don't know what is. I will definitely look forward to visiting, and I may persuade Queen Torcas to join us." Nothing more was said, and then Ertin looking across at Queen Torcas Ertin replied, "that would indeed be an honour for me host both you and Queen Torcas, an honour indeed."

Nilan and Ertin parted company and Nilan headed back to where Torcas was speaking with the HiberWatchers and the Key Keepers. "May I join you?" Nilan asked as he moved closer to this group. "Of course, husband, you are most welcome. Kian and Kindross were just checking that Torpast and Jandray had transferred the necessary books and maps from the Hiber library ready for winter." "I hope you have also checked the food store too" Nilan laughed. "You will find a good book may be appetite for the mind, but not the stomach." "Indeed King Nilan" replied Jandray, "The store is full and Kian has kindly prepared a stock of Hiber cake too, which is most kind of her. We have also checked that there is sufficient stock of food for our loyal Watch Hounds too." Torpast quickly added, "It was totally unexpected by me that I would grow so fond of Winterclaw and Snowblue; and so quickly." He realised that he named the hounds in the presence of the King and began to stutter. King Nilan could see the discomfort that Torpast was in. "So, you have named the Watch Hounds this year Torpast, isn't that a step outside of tradition?" Nilan decided to put a stern look on his face whilst he said this, enjoying seeing the turmoil in Torpast. It didn't surprise him that Jandray came to his rescue. "King Nilan, it is I who stepped us both out of tradition. I was so taken by these two Hounds that I had been observing over the year. I was convinced they would make as superb pair of Watch Hounds for the HiberWatchers; I just didn't realise I would be one of them."

Queen Torcas could not let Nilan create further discomfort for Torpast and as she looked at him she said, "Forgive the King, he is only playing with you." At that Nilan laughed and put his hand on Torpast's shoulder. "The names are chosen well, and perhaps we should have a naming ceremony for Watch Hounds in future years, what do you think my Hiber Key Keepers." Kindross looked at Nilan and replied "All tradition commences with one initial action, I think that it would be very appropriate for Jandray and Torpast to start this new one." "That settles it, then" replied Nilan. "Torpast and Jandray, you will be responsible for preparing a naming event for the Watch Hounds next year." Nilan then said, "Please forgive me, I need to speak with a few more of our folk before sleep descends upon us." Just as he was about to leave he leaned into Jandray and Torpast and quickly said something to them. Jandray, surprised at this stood back but remained silent. After a few seconds, he simply nodded and said, "Torpast and I understand." Torpast did not understand at all, but nodded his agreement.

Young and old across the mighty cavern started to lay out their blankets on the warm ground. The light from the roof above started to dim. It was obvious to those who had been through this ritual over many years that the time for sleep was coming near. The youngest of the communities were already releasing themselves into sleep, and yawns were barely stifled from many who were starting to lay down. Some of the older ones, worn down by age, were smiling at the thought of the regenerative strength that the sleep would have on their ageing bodies; and the thought that they would awake refreshed and revived for another year ahead. It was a strange factor of the Winter Sleep that all who slept also woke up. The Hiber folk were not immortal; the older folk did pass over in later life, but not during the Winter Sleep. The sleep was one of excitement and comfort, there was no fear of the future as they slept. Well, only one was in fear, and Delcant had good reason to be. He had set in motion an attack on the very heart of The Hiber Nation and he wondered how Queen Mountain would deal with him in due course. Delcant was devious, and he knew he had interfered with the natural way of things. If he knew of the poem that was being heard by Torcas and Jandray, he would also known that Queen Mountain was aware of his traitorous behaviour.

Tradition dictated that the HiberWatchers stood on an elevated position at the far end of the main cavern. This location had rooms that the HiberWatchers would use as their home for Winter. This place was called "Hiberwatcher's Rock" and from it The HiberWatchers could see across the multitude of bodies that were beginning to fall into sleep. Jandray wondered if the sand had something to do with the sleep, or if it was something in the air. What had not been explained, until now, was why Torpast and Jandray would not be subject to those forces that brought on this sleep. Kian and Kindross were amongst the last to take up their sleeping positions. Before they did they approached the HiberWatchers and their hounds. "Hiberwatcher's Rock is special, and you need to remember this. Where you are standing is the only place in this cavern that is not subject to an environment where sleep will fall upon you. You need to stay on this rock for several hours or you, too, will fall asleep." Kindross continued the instructions. "When all have fallen asleep, a very mild glow will appear on the roof above you. It will not awaken the folk, but it will allow you to see across the cavern. Across the other caverns, and the hidden ways, a similar glow will light your way. When all are asleep, you will need to enter both the lower and higher caverns to ensure all other living creatures are equally secure in sleep. It is a scene to behold I can tell you; one of utter peace; again an honour only bestowed on the HiberWatchers." Kindross continued, "After this, you will need to use the hidden ways to get to the upper slopes of Queen Mountain. There, over coming weeks, you will see the Hiber Nation disappear under its protective blanket of ice and snow. Also in early Spring, you will see this icy covering melt away and you will be the first to see the New year ahead of us."

"Remember" said Kian. "You have brought the most important documents with you from the Library. However, as you know, there is a way that leads back to the Library should you need it." She looked intently at Torpast and Jandray and added "But do not forget to heed the instructions. The Library is far beyond the lake of Queen Mountain, so be careful to keep a watch on our communities. We strongly recommend that only one of you leaves the actual mountain at any one time, always leaving one HiberWatcher and one Watch Hound to protect our nation." At that point both Kian and Kindross took their leave of the HiberWatchers and stepped down onto the floor of the cavern. They lay down next to each other and were soon entering into sleep.

"This is it, then" said Torpast. "I have had a very special time with Sartora and Altera today. We are all so looking forward to our future next year." Looking across at Jandray, and taking his arm he said, "Sartora knows I am going to use this time to reflect on being a better husband and father. I would welcome your advice on this over the Winter." Jandray was surprised at the honesty of Torpast, but had learnt that there was much more to this person than he had first imagined. "I have never been married" he replied, "but Sartora was one of my first students and I know her well. Altera is, arguably, my most gifted student. Whatever I can do to help you, you can be assured of my support brother Torpast." "We are to be brothers" smiled Torpast. "I like to think of us as that, more than being fellow HiberWatchers." Jandray was surprised about how he had begun to feel about Torpast. The bonds of brotherhood between them had grown strong over this short period of time. He knew that Torpast had tried hard to be his friend, and Jandray had reciprocated that friendship. "I hadn't planned on being a HiberWatcher" he said to Torpast, not realising what he was saying, "But, I have gained a friend and a brother from it" he added. Torpast gave him a quizzical look. "You must have planned it a little bit, by putting your name forward, but I understand what you mean. I had hoped that I would have been chosen, but I thought it unlikely. I am fortunate indeed to be chosen this year, and I look forward to our friendship over many years to come."

Both Jandray and Torpast looked across at their kinfolk, as they all commenced their Winter Sleep. The challenges ahead were unknown and were heavy on them at this immediate moment. Neither of them knew what the weeks ahead held for them.

Chapter Twenty-One

Sleep had slowly descended across the vast cavern within Queen Mountain. Throughout this immense sanctuary, as far as could be seen, the Hiber peoples had entered their 'Winter sleep'. Torpast and Jandray were on the raised platform of rock together with Winterclaw and Snowblue. There was nothing for them to do for several hours, until they were certain that the sleepers would not be disturbed. They sat in silence, each with their own thoughts. Many weeks of almost solitary existence lay ahead of them. When both agreed that sufficient time had passed, Jandray had carefully walked through the sleeping bodies and had looked upon his mother, sleeping peacefully with her kinfolk. Torpast had done the same with Sartora and Altera, who were laying side by side. "I promise it will be different" he said, as he looked down on his family.

Together, the HiberWatchers walked through the main cavern, ensuring that all the entrances were now fully closed. Thanks to the advice of the Key Keepers, they knew how to access the tunnels that wandered high into the mountain, and which ended with apertures that allowed the HiberWatchers to survey the outside landscape as it slowly froze. The access points into Queen Mountain that had been used by the Hiber folk would soon be impassable as the snow continued to fall across the empty land of the Hiber Nation. Over the next few days, Torpast and Jandray had never seen such snow, nor experienced such winter ferocity. Blizzards had commenced and they brought fresh accumulations, all day and all night. In fact on some days it had been difficult to work out if it was day or night. All seemed well, however, other than for Winterclaw and Snowblue who seem far more restless than the HiberWatchers had expected them to be. Unbeknown to the two HiberWatchers, the four warriors that Delcant had brought into the Mountain sanctuary had waited until neither of The HiberWatchers were near, and had then disappeared into one of the many other tunnels in the mountain. Using their skills as trackers and spies for Grasby, they were adept in maintaining their presence hidden, and they had brought sufficient stores of food and water to sustain them as they bided their time. Delcant had also managed to bring a stock of food in with him and had told them where to find it should they run short of their own rations.

Over the first few weeks the warriors moved carefully around the mountain, in pairs, to establish how they would get out of the mountain. Argrant was the leader and had been a loyal servant of Grasby for a number of years. It helped that he had an intense dislike for the Sargern clan, especially after Saltock's sister had rebuffed his advances. Trenmant was his second in command but his support for Warrior Grasby was based on a more mercenary level. He had no issue with Saltock's family, and was primarily motivated by the financial reward that Grasby offered for his service. Lanfin and Wardok were the other two warriors in this band. They were chosen for their skills in tracking, and would be needed to help the group plot a way back to Tukerland should they find a way out of the Mountain. Thus far, none had been successful in this venture. "The only way we will find an exit is to follow a HiberWatcher when they leave the main cavern. Delcant says that there are hidden ways that lead to the outside, and the HiberWatchers follow those tunnels in order that they can assess the level of snowfall over winter" stated Argrant. "The only problem is those hounds" replied Trenmant. "I am sure they can sense our presence." "Well, even with the extra stock that Delcant managed to bring into the Mountain, we don't have an infinite supply of provisions, and we have been here several weeks already. We have no idea how arduous the journey home will be and we have to make that food last for the journey back to Tukerland as well" answered Argrant.

Lanfin looked across at Argrant and said, "Wardok and I have found the Hiber woman they call Sartora and we are ready to remove her when you decide the moment has arrived." Lanfin and Wardok were female warriors. Grasby had been keen to ensure that no harm would befall Sartora. Even he had standards, he had told these two female warriors. Lanfin and Wardok were part of the team on merit. It helped that they were very slightly smaller in stature than their male counterparts and had been able to assimilate as Hiber folk and thereby had raised much less suspicion than Delcant bringing four large warriors into the mountain. These two warriors, however, were every bit as ferocious as their colleagues and had little time for, or indeed, any real interest or awareness of the Hiber peoples and their culture when they had been recruited for this mission.

"My understanding, said Argrant, "is that there is a short period of time when the snowfall abates, before it returns with a vengeance in late winter." Keeping his voice low he said, "We must find a way out soon, or it is unlikely that we would survive a journey home in the late winter blizzards." Trenmant replied, "Warrior Grasby is keen that we leave as little bloodshed as possible, and that means we need to work around the HiberWatchers. However, he also really wants us to capture one of the Watch Hounds as well if that is possible." Argrant smiled maliciously and said, "If a HiberWatcher has to befall some kind of accident, a fall, or an unexplained head injury, we could take the hound and be away from this place." Trenmant added, "I have studied both HiberWatchers over the last few weeks. They call each other Torpast and Jandray." Wardok answered, "I understand that these two are both from the Paltir region, as is the woman we are instructed to take back to Tukerland." Argrant cut across the chat. "This is irrelevant, just make sure you take the right Sartora when we leave, I don't want to face Warrior Grasby with the wrong woman having been kidnapped!" Trenmant looked at the other three and said, "The one called Torpast spends most time with the female hound which he calls Snowblue. Grasby would particularly reward us if we brought breeding stock back with us", he smiled greedily "That probably settles it then" replied Argrant. "Trenmant and I will look for an opportunity to incapacitate this HiberWatcher called Torpast, and you two can prepare to take the woman. Remember, our problems won't start with her until we leave Queen Mountain. If Delcant is right, and I hope for his sake that he is, she will remain asleep until we remove her from the confines of this mountain, and even then it could take some time for her to awake."   They all agreed that their plans must be put into place soon, and they bedded down for another restless time of sleep. "It is so ironic" thought Lanfin. "Here we are in a measureless cavern full of a whole nation sleeping peacefully, and I have barely had any rest during the time we have been in here." She kept her thoughts to herself and tried to find a comfortable position to rest, but she knew that sleep would not easily come.

Torpast and Jandray had settled into a routine of checking throughout the various caverns of sleeping humans and creatures. Each single tour of the caverns could take several days as they were that large. By agreement, one HiberWatcher and Watch Hound remained in the main cavern, whilst the other toured the mountain. Jandray particularly liked to visit the tunnel that took him to the high aperture and window to the outside world. He was mesmerised as he surveyed the frozen landscape below him. In between patrols they still had plenty of time to spend hours talking, and also discussing what they had read in the Ways of the HiberWatcher. So far, nothing had occurred that would merit any addition to the material they were reading. Tomorrow it would be Torpast's tun to commence the tour and also to assess the snow levels. He had really bonded with Snowblue, and they were pretty much inseparable. Torpast could often be found talking intently to Snowblue and, to all intents and purposes, it looked like Snowblue was listening. Jandray hoped that Snowblue would remain close to Torpast when Winter ended. Although not viewed as domestic pets, such hounds often struck up a generational relationship with various families, so it would not be unusual if this happened with Torpast and Snowblue. Jandray knew that Winterclaw was too independent to be tied to one location, and he was fully aware that he would be fortunate to see Winterclaw from a distance once Winter was over, and he returned to his pack. Jandray was comfortable with this. It was as if Torpast was transferring his love and attention, which would have been bestowed on his wife and daughter, onto Snowblue for this period of time. As he looked on, Jandray thought it boded well for the future.

Both Jandray and Torpast settled into the evening. Jandray would take the first watch to allow Torpast to sleep. Then, when Jandray also had enjoyed the opportunity to sleep, it would be morning and Torpast would commence the now familiar route that The HiberWatcher would need to undertake during their patrol. Jandray decided that he would take a longer watch, as he would have little exertion over the next few days, and Torpast would have a continuous journey ahead of him. The ways of the HiberWatcher did not preclude both sleeping at the same time, but they felt happier knowing that one of them was alert whilst the other slept. This couldn't be maintained all the time, due to the continuing need to rotate the patrol. However, they had additionally realised that it was healthy for both of them to have companionship in between each rota of patrol. Jandray used his solitary time in the main cavern studying the Ways, and reading other documents covering the history of the Hiber peoples. It was fascinating what he had discovered and he made a note to ask how much of this history could be shared with students next year.

The morning arrived, and Torpast prepared to leave. He went to the stockroom that had been filled with supplies for the HiberWatchers. They had decided to ration some of the more 'luxury' food items, such as the Hiber cakes that Kian has kindly cooked for them. However, a tradition had arisen where they would each share a slice of Hiber cake before their patrol commenced, and then would share another slice when they safely returned. As they savoured the cake Torpast said to Jandray "The weeks are passing much faster than I had thought. If what Kian and Kindross told us is correct, there will be a break from the blizzards, before they come back in late winter. I am looking forward to looking out over our nation without the view being hidden by these storms." "Me too" said Jandray. "You should just about reach the high tunnel pass as the snows cease. By the time you are back, and my tour commences, I may also just about catch the last of the clear sky before the hard final phase of winter returns." "My brother and my friend" replied Torpast, "I will put extra effort into my steps so you will have plenty of time to make that patrol." At that he got to his feet, dusted the few crumbs of cake from his clothes and headed on his way. Snowblue followed him closely. "See you soon" he said. "In a few days." "That you will, that you will" said Jandray and stood to grasp his shoulders "Goodbye, Torpast, stay safe and enjoy the view."

As Torpast started his patrol, he was unaware that he was being watched. "We will have to work quickly" said Argrant. "The HiberWatcher Jandray will expect his colleague back in about three days. If I have got his measure, he will be compelled to look for him when he does not return in that time. So we need to incapacitate his colleague and await Jandray to leave the cavern. As soon as he does, we need you," looking at Lanfin and Wardok, "to handle this Sartora, and then meet up with us." "Hopefully", Trenmant added, "we can meet up near to an exit whilst the HiberWatcher is searching for his friend. There are many caverns he will have to search in, and so we have a good chance. All we need to do is follow the other HiberWatcher, hope he leads us to the surface, deal with him, subdue his hound, and then wait for you to find us." Wardok looked at Trenmant and said, "Your smell is so potent, I would be able to find you in the dark with a blindfold on. Tracking you is the least of my concerns, I only hope you can track the HiberWatcher without alerting his hound." Trenmant made for a reply but was cut off by Argrant. "Remember, the hostage is the priority, the HiberWatcher is expendable, and the hound, well that would bring an extra bounty that we would all benefit from." Argrant and Trenmant prepared to follow Torpast. They had already established part of the patrol route, so would not need to risk being seen moving immediately after the HiberWatcher left the cabin. But they would have to be very careful not to raise any noise whilst they were following Torpast and, more so, whilst following the hound.

Torpast, completely unaware of the risks that lay in front of him, was lost in his thoughts as he started his patrol. He and Jandray had enjoyed exploring the HiberWatcher Ways, and they had both found many different routes through the mountain. Each time, when they had returned, they compared their routes with those already indicated on the maps made by previous HiberWatchers. So far they had not discovered any new routes nor had they had time to visit the forest. That really didn't matter to Torpast. For him, to be walking along routes that only a tiny band of fellow HiberWatchers had passed was an honour. In the tradition of previous HiberWatchers, he and Jandray had both scratched their names on the walls of the tunnels. It was amazing to both of them to read names of previous HiberWatchers, who they knew nothing about. They memorised certain names, and then they looked them up in the HiberWatcher literature. It helped them pass the time, and both felt part of a brother and sisterhood that could be traced back over thousands of years.

Many hours passed but Snowblue was still unsettled as she walked alongside Torpast. They had checked all the sleeping chambers for the animals and birds and now they were walking towards the access tunnel to the high platform were Torpast could assess the snowfall. Snowblue was continually looking behind her, sniffing the air. On occasion, she would leave Torpast and trot back down the tunnels they had just walked through. At one point, she chased back up the tunnel to the Torpast's side and knocked into the back of Torpast's legs. "Are you OK, Snowblue?" Torpast said as he crouched down and looked into her eyes. Since they had met, a strong bond that Torpast had not thought possible, had grown between them. Torpast could almost see the concern in her eyes and her low growl, almost like she was trying to talk. "We are fine, Snowblue, there is nothing to be worried about, perhaps it is just the mountain moving." Suddenly out of the darkness a figure arose, and then another. Torpast, having seen no one for several weeks, could not apprehend what these ghostly figures were. The first figure seem to throw something towards him, and then he realised, too late, that it was a net. Suddenly Snowblue was snarling and snapping as it covered her. Torpast tried to pull the net from Snowblue, but was taken off of his feet by a massive force of one of the figures launching themselves over the net and directly at Torpast. He was knocked to the ground with such ferocity that he lost his breath and couldn't even shout. He heard Snowblue howl in pain and this brought him to his senses.

The Hiber folk were not combative in any real sense. However, years of work in an agrarian setting had made them lean and strong. Even Torpast, who was now more of an administrator than a farmer, retained the strength that came from enjoying the outdoor life of the Hiber folk. However, he was no match for the person in front of him. He may have melted with fear if he had known he was facing a Tukerland Warrior such as Argrant. But he had no idea who this apparition was, or even if it was real. There was nothing in the Ways of the HiberWatcher that had described anything like what he was facing. Torpast fought back with all his strength and tried to rise to his feet. The fact that Snowblue had been silenced raised an anger in him that he had never experienced before. He pushed out at the attacker with all his might, and to his surprise, the attacker fell back. This was his opportunity, he could run and his knowledge of the myriad of tunnels that he and Jandray had explored would mean that it would be possible that he could lose these attackers. He could try and get back to Jandray and warn him. "Jandray may be under attack too" he breathlessly said to himself. "How many of these attackers are there?" he thought as he struggled to compose himself. But he couldn't leave Snowblue; such a loyal companion. He had to try and get to her, to see if she was hurt, or worse. He went to step over the body that was in front him but didn't see the other figure that was leaning over the net which clearly had the outline of Snowblue beneath it. As he ran towards her, his legs went limp and the faint light emanating from the ceiling began to dim. Argrant had recovered and he smashed his warrior club on the back of Torpast's head. A crack resounded in the small tunnel; Argrant had heard that death noise before. Torpast collapsed just as he was at the edge of the mound that was Snowblue's body and fell into unconsciousness.

Argrant and Trenmant stood up. Argrant had blood seeping down his forehead. He wiped it with his hand and then leant against the tunnel wall. "That HiberWatcher had a strength that I wasn't expecting" he said to Trenmant. "Our plans will have to change rapidly, I had hoped that we could just incapacitate the HiberWatcher, but I think my blow fell much heavier than I planned. He looks close to death." "At least I was able to silence the hound more successfully" replied Trenmant. "The net immobilised her and I was able to use a less forceful blow - our monetary reward is secure" he grinned at Argrant. "Perhaps it is best that this peasant dies, he will not be able to say what happened and the blow to his head may look like he just fell." "That may be so" said Argrant, "But let's drag him into this side tunnel and position his body like he slipped." Trenmant and Argrant grabbed Torpast's body, trying to avoid the clothing made bloody from the open wound to the back of his head. They carelessly dumped him in the nearby side tunnel. Neither checked his body for life. As far as they were concerned, they didn't care if he was alive or dead, and Argrant was sure that the blow, and the amount of blood lost, meant that this unfortunate HiberWatcher would not survive.

They returned to the tunnel. Trenmant took a muzzle from his pack. "I anticipate this hound will be none too happy when she awakes" he said. Then he roughly forced the muzzle around her snout and tied it tight. "Be careful not to suffocate her" said Argrant, and bent down to ensure that her airways were free. They then wrapped Snowblue into the net. She was heavier than they anticipated and it took two of them to carry her. "Let's hope that we have covered sufficient distance that this tunnel leads to the outside" said Argrant. "If not, we could be going round and round this mountain for ever." Argrant had an uneasy feeling that the Mountain was angry that he had spilt blood within her sanctuary. Tukerland warriors were not comfortable underground, despite many of their kin being miners for the iron ore that wrought their weapons and tools. Most warriors couldn't understand how the Hiber folk willingly committed themselves to this period of sleep each year. It had not been easy for Argrant over the last few weeks, and he longed to see sky and breathe fresh air. "I can sense a change in the air" said Trenmant "We are certainly moving uphill and I think that we may be on the right track."

As they laboriously carried the unconscious hound, they focussed on the walk ahead of them. After an extensive climb, they could see a dim light ahead of them, different from the glow that came from the rock ceiling. "We are there, I think, almost there" said Argrant. The tunnel soon opened into a large space, and in front of the men was the unmistakable vista of sky and mountains. Both blinked with the brightness of the light ahead of them. They dropped their heavy load and walked to the edge of the small cave that had opened up. In front of them, all they could see was the peaks of the Hiber Mountains. All trace of the Hiber civilisation was buried under snow and ice. Both were lost for words but, eventually Argrant said, "We need to get underway as soon as the others arrive. Our pace will be slow as we will all be carrying burdens and it looks like our route will be perilous. If the snow holds off, and if we get clear skies, we should be able to navigate away from this barren landscape and return home."

Neither Argrant nor Trenmant knew if their colleagues had successfully taken the woman Sartora. They would have had to hide close to the main cavern to allow sufficient time for the other HiberWatcher to become sufficiently concerned that his colleague had not returned. How soon that would be was not clear. The longer the HiberWatcher held off from looking for his colleague, the harder it would be to navigate through the snow and ice, especially if the late Winter snowstorms commenced. However, both teams of warriors had sufficient rations to wait for a few days. What concerned Argrant was that there would be no food available from this winter landscape once they left the mountain; they would have to be very careful with whatever provisions they could carry for their journey home. Argrant and Trenmant retreated from the cold air of the mountain exit and decided to hide in a nearby adjacent tunnel. It was just a matter of waiting now. The muzzle would keep the Hiber Hound from biting them, but it would be hard to ensure the hound stayed silent once it woke up. They spent some time binding the legs of Snowblue and wrapped her back up in the net. She would be uncomfortable but would pose no risk to them. Neither Trenmant nor Argrant wanted to be the ones to loosen the final cords when this hound was finally unbound. They only hoped that she would initially be hampered in her actions by stiff and swollen joints from the immobility her body had been forced into. After they had carried out this task, they tried to make themselves rest. Sleep did not come for Argrant, but he could see that Trenmant had no such difficulties. "Hurry, fellow warriors, I want to be out of here as soon as possible" he said to himself.

The day arrived when Torpast should have arrived back at the main cavern. Jandray had expected him early in the morning, but was not unduly worried at first. However, when he hadn't shown up by late evening his concerns began to rise. Winterclaw was pacing backwards and forwards, uttering low growls towards the tunnel that Torpast and Snowblue would have used on their return to the main cavern. Jandray knew that he should not leave 'unwatched' those under his care, but an inner feeling kept telling him that he had to go and see if Torpast was in trouble. "Winterclaw, we need to go and find Torpast and Snowblue" he said. It was as if Winterclaw knew what he was saying and started to make for the tunnel. Jandray took a last, lingering look across the cavern and hoped that Queen Mountain would forgive him for leaving his post. He then made to follow Winterclaw who was racing ahead up the long tunnel.

Lanfin saw the second HiberWatcher leave the cavern. She pushed Wardok, who had been sleeping, "Quick, our opportunity is here - the second HiberWatcher has left." Wardok sprang to her feet and they both quickly, but carefully, stepped through the sleeping bodies in front of them. They found Sartora easily, having already spent many hours deciding the quickest way to get to her, then planning how to move her before meeting up with Argrant and Trenmant. They had a net similar to the one that their colleagues had used on Snowblue. Carefully they bound Sartora by her hands and feet and put a piece of cloth around her mouth. As she was in deep sleep it was easy to manipulate her to do this and then they lifted her above the other sleeping bodies. As soon as they reached the entrance to one of the many tunnels out the cavern, they placed Sartora down. They then rolled her into the net, and fashioned a way of carrying her, suspended between the two warriors. Sartora wasn't heavy, but they had no idea how far they would need to carry her. Wardok was as good as her word, and her tracking skills soon picked up the tunnels that their fellow warriors had travelled. In places they could see where Torpast had tracked off into other tunnels and they could see where Argrant and Trenmant had waited. "You cannot really smell Trenmant, can you?" said Lanfin. "Not from this far away", she smiled "But, as they were behind the HiberWatcher Torpast, they have not been too careful with their own tracks."

The two warriors, carrying their burden between them, made haste along the tunnels. They wondered if they would meet the other HiberWatcher, but they had watched the way he had left the cavern and then chosen a different tunnel to follow in their efforts to meet up with their fellow warriors. "I think the HiberWatcher knows which way his colleague should have returned", said Lanfin. "If that is the case, and if Argrant has done his job properly, we should not come across him or that hound. I don't fear the HiberWatcher, but that Hound could be a ferocious adversary." They made good progress and were soon closing in on where Torpast had been attacked. Wardok looked at the wall and saw a partial handprint that looked like it was recent. She drew closer to the wall. "This is blood" she said, "they must have had to use more force than they had planned." As she was studying the wall, Lanfin looked down a nearby tunnel. She then moved carefully along this tunnel. Suddenly her foot touched an obstacle and she looked down to see the body of Torpast. His face was covered in blood and it looked like he was close to death. She knew, as a warrior, that she should finish the job that either Argrant or Trenmant had visited upon this poor man. In Tukerland, it was viewed as a warrior requirement to despatch those close to death to prevent further suffering. As she leant in to deliver a death kill, something seem to press heavy on her soul. It was almost like the mountain walls were crying out for her not do this act. She stopped and reflected that this HiberWatcher would soon be found by his colleague. If it was in his pathway to survive, it wasn't for her to prevent that future. She looked down on the body of Torpast and could see that he had a serious head injury. Without thinking she unbound some wraps of material that were round her arms. She then carefully bound his wound. Not knowing why she was doing this Lanfin quietly spoke to the wounded HiberWatcher. "Your fate is now in the hands of this Mountain and your colleague" she said, and then returned to the main tunnel.

"Anything down there?" asked Wardok. "Nothing" quickly replied Lanfin and then said, "We must be close, this blood is either from one of our colleagues or from the HiberWatcher. If it is from the HiberWatcher, they must have disposed of him." Lanfin knew that Wardok would have despatched the HiberWatcher immediately. She also knew that she would never be able to mention this to anyone again. Wardok could not see her face. If she had, she would have immediately seen the strange expression on Lanfin's face. "Let's go then" Wardok said. "With luck, we can meet up with our warriors before the HiberWatcher and his hound gets scent of us. At some point he may well join this tunnel from the others he is searching."

They lifted Sartora and headed up the tunnel.

Eventually Wardok said, "I think I can sense a change in the air. And also a subtle change in the light." "I agree" replied Lanfin, "We must be close, but we still need be careful, we don't know where the other HiberWatcher is." As she said this, there was a slight movement in her peripheral vision. "What's that" Wardok whispered", "I can see movement and I think I am close enough to smell that Warrior Trenmant." As she said this, two figures appeared from a tunnel adjacent to the main tunnel they were walking up. "It's about time" grinned Argrant, "We wondered how long you would be, or if you would be able to find us." "I told you I could follow that obnoxious odour of Trenmant anywhere" Wardok answered back with a smile.

"More importantly, I see you have our hostage, is she harmed?" immediately asked Argrant. "Not at all" answered Lanfin,"Although she may well be very stiff when she awakes, with all the bindings on her." "Not unlike our dear Watch Hound here" agreed Argrant, "I am not taking any risks with those fangs when she wakes." Argrant then said, "Did you find the HiberWatcher? I had to despatch him as he was surprisingly strong." Wardok looked over at Lanfin as she answered, "No, there were a number of adjacent tunnels near to a bloody hand-mark on the wall, but we did not see a body. Where did you dump him?" "Not to worry, he was close to death" said Argrant. "He was surplus to our needs, and Grasby was not too concerned if the HiberWatchers were more than just incapacitated. Come and look over this desolate place. We now have to try and cross this mountain range and get back to Tukerland. Hopefully, we will be well on our way home before the next winter snowfall that Delcant told us happens at the end of winter." All four warriors stood at the mouth of the cavern and wondered how they would cross this wasteland of ice and snow.

"We may not have long to make our move" said Wardok. "We left the cavern soon after the other HiberWatcher, who was clearly becoming concerned for his colleague. He took a different tunnel but he may not be far behind. He has the advantage of having the Hiber Hound who may pick up our scent across this myriad of tunnels. Unless there are other places to view the landscape that we are looking at, it is likely he will come to this point soon enough." "I've been thinking", said

Argrant, "the only benefit this snow gives us is the usually impassable mountains have been filled with months of snowfall. We may be able to navigate our way through easier than we think and, in due course, our tracks will be lost under new snowfall." All agreed they were ready to go. Lanfin and Wardok lifted up Sartora's lifeless body, still in deep sleep, whilst Trenmant carried Snowblue over his shoulders. This allowed Argrant to plot a route out of the cavern entrance. As soon as they stepped from the rock, the snow gave way and they sank up to their waists. The snow then stabilised and they felt ice under their feet. They had a hard task to push on through the snow. Even Argrant felt his strength fading very quickly in the harsh terrain. "We have to get out of sight of the cave entrance" he said. "If we can then make some form of shelter in this snow, we can carry on after we have rested. We cannot risk making a fire at the moment, but will need to soon enough or we will all succumb to these temperatures."

They pushed on slowly, realising that their tracks would be easy to see until new snow fell and covered their steps. Grasby had told them that there would be an automatic assumption that Tukerland was responsible for trespassing on the Hiber Nation's place and time of winter refuge. However, he was unconcerned and told them just to leave as little evidence as possible pointing that way. In the arduous conditions Argrant forgot the bloody handprint he had left on the wall. However, Lanfin did not forget that she had, uncharacteristically for a Hiber warrior, bound the HiberWatcher's wounds, and this action could present real problems for Grasby if the HiberWatcher was found. She knew that her compassion could be a problem and she wondered what would happen to her if her act of mercy was discovered "It is too late to worry about this now" she said to herself, "That HiberWatcher's death is not on my heart and not at my hands. I am much happier with that." She still couldn't shake the impact that the mountain had visited upon her. She had felt the mountain 'talk' to her, to almost plead for her mercy, and she had given it. "Perhaps the Mountain will forgive me in due course and grant me mercy if I ever return." She mulled these thoughts over in her mind as she traced the steps of the warriors in front of her.

Chapter Twenty-Two

Jandray ran as quickly as he could through the tunnels leading to the caverns where the animals and birds were sleeping. There was no sign of Torpast. Winterclaw started to bark and ran towards the tunnel leading to the highest cave exit in Queen Mountain. "He has to be up there" thought Jandray, sure that Torpast would have headed that way to check on the conditions outside as he had been so keen to see the landscape in clear conditions. Jandray had difficulty keeping up with the pace of Winterclaw as he ran ahead of him. Suddenly he heard a loud howl followed by barking coming from further up the tunnel. "Winterclaw must have found something" he said to himself and Jandray picked up his pace. In doing so, he ran straight past the entrance to the tunnel where Winterclaw was barking. He heard the howl again and began to retrace his steps. It was coming from a side tunnel, one that he did not remember ever exploring before. He could see a faint outline of Winterclaw's white coat. He ran on and then saw the crumpled body that Winterclaw was standing near.

Winterclaw's howl had now descended into a low whine and he was pushing against the body of Torpast which was laying across the rock floor. "Torpast" he cried "What happened?" There was no reply and Jandray crouched down and gently touched Torpast. There was no sign of life in Torpast. However, as he got closer to his body, Jandray could see that there was dried blood on Torpast's face. He put his hands under Torpast's head and he could feel that it was wet. He pulled Torpast carefully into his chest and cradled his head. He could see that his own hands were covered in Torpast's blood. But he could also feel that there was still some heat in Torpast's body. "He isn't dead"; a glimmer of hope lifted in Jandray's heart. He could also see that there had been an attempt to bind Torpast's wounds. These bindings were wrapped round the back of his head and partially covered his eyes. They were wet to the touch and it was clear that Torpast had a grievous wound. Jandray wondered if Torpast had fallen and then had been able to bind his wound, but this did not seem possible. It was more realistic that someone must have hurt him and then bound his wounds. "But why would they bind his injured head if they had meant him harm in the first place?" he thought. Jandray tried to remain composed, pushing the fears back down that had risen from the bottom of his heart. There was still the harsh final few weeks of late winter to survive and he could see that Torpast was very seriously injured. Jandray's logic kicked in. He would have to carry Torpast back to the cavern and then see if he could tend his injuries. He would then have to think about what to do next. Were the assailants still in the mountain; would they come for him too? All these thoughts were going through his mind when Winterclaw barked and ran up to the tunnel exit. Jandray carefully laid Torpast down and ran after him. "Where is Snowblue?" he suddenly thought. "Has Winterclaw found her?"

Winterclaw ran up the main tunnel to the high pass exit out of Queen Mountain. As he followed, Jandray thought that Torpast would probably have been heading to this location too. He arrived at the entrance and looked out over the Hiber landscape. He surveyed a view of immense desolation but also of great beauty. It was a clear day and the sky was a deep blue against the crystal outline of the mountain range that was buried deep in snow. However, his attention was drawn to a clear track in the snow, leading from the exit. Winterclaw started to run down the track but Jandray called him back. Reluctantly, Winterclaw stopped and looked at Jandray. He was torn, he had the scent of Snowblue and wanted to follow it. "Stop, Winterclaw, we have to try and save Torpast." Jandray could see that the track weaved far into the distance, before it disappeared over a ridge of ice that was still standing proud on the landscape. He could not see beyond this ridge. In the distance was the Mountain Keeper range, with their summits visible in the winter sun. It was clear to Jandray that this track had been made by a group of people who were probably heading to find a way past the mountain range. "That could only mean they were heading for Tukerland", thought Jandray.

Jandray could not see any imprints of Snowblue's paws anywhere near the entrance, nor on the track itself. As much as he wanted to run with Winterclaw down this track, he knew that his priority was to save Torpast. Winterclaw took a final look down the track and raised his head, letting out a long deep howl. He then turned and trotted back to Jandray. "We will find Snowblue, I promise you", Jandray said before he turned back into the tunnel, not knowing that Sartora had also been taken.

Jandray returned to where Torpast was laying in the tunnel. As carefully as he could, he lifted Torpast into his arms. The weight of his injured colleague meant that Jandray had to stop frequently to rest. He laid his friend's injured head into his chest and tried walk as fast as he could without Torpast's head moving too much. He was still warm which was the only hope that Jandray had at the moment. His slow pace meant that it took several hours for Jandray to return to the main cavern where the Hiber folk were still in their peaceful sleep. The light from the ceiling was slightly brighter here and he was able to take a closer look at Torpast's injuries. He carefully unwound the bindings from his head. He could see that there was an extensive injury at the rear of his head, and this was the source of the loss of blood. "If these bindings had not been applied he would have died", thought Jandray. However, it still did not make sense to him that someone would attack Torpast and then bind his wounds. Again, Jandray wondered if Torpast had fallen and had tried to bind his own wounds. Looking at the bloodstained bindings, they did not appear like anything that he had seen Torpast carry. The extent of the blood on the bindings made it difficult to see what they were made of.

After he had bathed the wound and cleaned Torpast's face, Jandray carefully replaced the bloodied bindings with strips of cloth he was able to find in the HiberWatcher store. There was no sign that he would regain consciousness, but Torpast's breathing had stabilised. It was obvious to Jandray that he had to do something; there was no way Torpast could stay here in the cavern until Spring without risk that his condition would deteriorate. Jandray decided that he would carry Torpast to the Hiber Library. It was a long way to travel, but he thought that he may be able to make Torpast more comfortable there. He would remain in the cavern for a few days until the Winter snowstorms commenced. He hoped that this would mean no one would be able to re-enter Queen Mountain. The only logical way that someone could have gained access was the same way as they had left thought Jandray. Over the next few days, he visited all the sleeping chambers of the Hiber folk and the animals. He returned to check on Torpast and noted no change, but at least he appeared no worse. He did his best to force a little water into Torpast's mouth. He wasn't sure if he had been successful at all. Jandray left Winterclaw to guard Torpast and then returned to the exit tunnel, high on the side of the mountain. The late winter snow had commenced, and the tracks leading away from the mountain had quickly disappeared. The blizzard conditions would make it impossible that anyone could return to the mountain via that route. Jandray thought it was now time to try and take Torpast to the Hiber Library. He hoped he could make him more comfortable there, whilst also trying to find any help possible from information stored in the library.

Jandray fashioned a stretcher of sorts from equipment he found in the store and then carefully placed Torpast upon it. He proceeded to drag this improvised stretcher along the 'way' to the Library that he and Torpast had been shown by the Key Keepers several weeks earlier. Winterclaw remained at his side but was clearly still agitated by the disappearance of Snowblue. The journey took many hours to undertake and Jandray had to stop several times out of sheer exhaustion. As he neared the entrance to the main library, Winterclaw began to bark and ran down the tunnel. "If there are more attackers here, I will barely have the strength to defend myself", Jandray thought. However, the idea that he may lose Winterclaw as well made him carefully put down the stretcher and run after his loyal hound. Winterclaw's barking had ceased, and this made Jandray even more concerned. As he entered the room where he and Torpast had enjoyed the hours of instruction from Kian and Kindross, he could see that Winterclaw was sitting next to a darkly clothed figure. "Don't fear me, HiberWatcher" said the hooded person in front of him "I mean you no harm."

Winterclaw looked at Jandray and then at the hooded figure and returned to Jandray's side. "Who are you, and why are you here?" said Jandray slowly. "My name is Mortarn, and I am here to help you and your colleague; there is a lot to explain. You being here means something has gone wrong, of that I am sure. Where is your fellow HiberWatcher?" Jandray replied, "My brother HiberWatcher has been seriously injured, I am unsure if he has fallen or has been attacked. He is need of more care than my skills can bring him, but how can I trust you? It seems that Queen Mountain has had invaders and you could be one of them." "If that were the case" replied Mortarn, "we would hardly be having this conversation. Take me to your HiberWatcher so I can see what assistance I may bring." He then looked at Jandray and said:-

"But others, too, are awake and are friends of the Hiber kin

And when they are needed they too will be found within

A Hiber heart or two they will be seeking whilst there

And Queen Mountain will unify these hearts in this endeavour"

"That verse is part of a poem that King Nilan said to me just before the Winter Sleep commenced. Verses from that poem have been troubling my thoughts over recent weeks. I am unsure how you would know of it. Step into the light so I can see you and put your hands out so I know you have no weapons" demanded Jandray. The figure moved out of the shadow and took down his hood. "See, I mean you no harm" he repeated. "If I had, your Watch Hound would not be so quiet, don't you think? It has been many a year since I have seen such a fine Hiber Hound, I had almost forgot the beauty of the winter coat of those who accompany the HiberWatchers during winter."

Mortarn looked into Jandray's eyes and said, "There is a lot to discuss, but I think it should wait until we have have attended your injured HiberWatcher. Is it Torpast or Jandray who has been injured?" Jandray looked at this mysterious figure who seemed to know a lot about the Hiber people. "It is Torpast that has been injured, he is on a stretcher a short way down the corridor." "Then let's go and get him, we can build up the fire and I can seen what can be done for him." Jandray didn't know whether to trust this stranger, but felt he had no choice. The only thing that partially reassured him was Winterclaw's docile approach towards this stranger. Jandray knew that the Hiber Hounds would protect their HiberWatcher to the death and Winterclaw was a prime example of his breed. Yet, Winterclaw was happy to let this man approach both Torpast and Jandray.

Between the two of them, they managed to get Torpast onto a bed in an adjacent room within the Library. Jandray thought that this must be where Kian and

Kindross lived during the year. Torpast removed the bandages from Torpast's head and explored the injury. "This was no fall" he said. "This looks like it has been caused by some form of instrument, the cut is too deep and the edges of the skin are also too cleanly cut for an injury caused by a fall." Jandray said, "I found him near a high exit from Queen Mountain. There were tracks leading away from the exit. However, those tracks are now under snow. Someone must have gained entry into the Mountain for some reason and were disturbed by Torpast." Mortarn did not reply; but just shook his head and continued to examine Torpast. Jandray looked on, and Mortarn carefully felt around Torpast's head and neck. "Your HiberWatcher colleague has had a serious blow to the back of the head, most definitely at the hands of an attacker. Did you bind his wounds? If you did, it is this that has saved his life. However, I am not certain when or if he will regain consciousness."

"Someone had tended to his injury, but these are fresh bandages that I have placed on his wound" replied Jandray. "I wondered if he had been able to do it, before he fell into unconsciousness." Torpast looked at Jandray and said, "I doubt that he would have been able to bind his injury, it is too severe. That is something we need to think about later. The priority is that we need to keep him warm. He will have to be fed liquid whilst he remains unconscious. It won't be easy to keep him both hydrated and nourished, as he will have no way swallowing." "How are we going to do this?" asked Jandray. "Sadly, I have experience of such injuries and also how to keep someone from starving whilst they are unable to eat" replied Mortarn. "We will have to fashion a tube and very carefully place it down his throat. If I get it wrong, I could end up suffocating him by putting liquid straight into his lungs. Even if I succeed in placing the tube correctly, there is no guarantee that it will work, the body has a strange way of knowing when to survive and when to give up."

There was no choice in Jandray's mind; after several weeks of close friendship, he saw Torpast as more than a fellow HiberWatcher, he was a brother. "Why couldn't have this happened to me?" he said out loud. Mortarn looked at him as Jandray said "This man has a wife and family, and was full of hope for his future after this Winter. It seems cruel that he may not experience the reality of that hope." Mortarn said nothing and continued to tend Torpast. "I have a mother who I love dearly, but other than that, no one close who would miss me. If anyone has to die, it should be me." Mortarn replied "No one has to die, and you will not help by giving up. Go and consult the Ways of the HiberWatcher, it may be that we consider waking his wife early in case he does not survive until Winter's end." Jandray was astonished that Mortarn was mentioning parchments known only to the Key Keepers and to the HiberWatchers. "I see what you are thinking", said Mortarn. "For now it will suffice for you to know that I am aware of all of the Ways of the HiberWatcher, and I am very familiar with the culture and traditions of the Hiber people. All I will say is that Kian and Kindross would want you to try and help as much as you can. Read the guidance on how to wake someone, and then we can discuss if we want to do it. That, in itself, is not without risk, and there will be a reckoning for you in front of the Elder Council when they wake."

Jandray's logical mind was struggling to comprehend all that was happening. Torpast was seriously injured; someone had done this to him after breaking into the sanctuary of Queen Mountain. Also, Snowblue was missing. What more could go wrong? "I will still need to check on those sleeping within the caverns" he said. "How will I care for Torpast, research the Ways, and do my patrols?" "One thing at a time" Mortarn replied. "By my reckoning, Late winter has commenced, so the route out of Queen Mountain will be blocked from any further attempt to regain entry, if indeed the sanctuary had been breached from that location. However, it may be that this attack came from within." Jandray was incredulous at this remark "Who would want to attack a HiberWatcher, and how would they have awoken to do so? I have checked the Ways, and nothing like this has happened before." With an understanding of the confusion that he could see in Jandray's eyes, Mortan replied "Let us deal with what is in front of us first and we can discuss these things. I don't expect your trust at the moment, but I promise you that I only have Torpast's immediate needs at the centre of my thoughts at the moment. Let me try and establish a way to feed and hydrate him as I have explained and then we attend to the other matters you raise. I recommend that you establish how to wake his wife and then, after you have returned to Queen Mountain, you can patrol the caverns to ensure everything else is in order. Then you can also consider if we need to bring his wife back here."

Mortarn's gentle reply helped Jandray see the logic in what he was saying. He replied, "I remember there is instruction on how to wake the whole nation, but there are also very clear instructions not to do so until there is a dire emergency. Without doubt this has to be a dire emergency, as envisaged by those who wrote the ways. If we can wake a whole nation early, then we must be able to wake one person." Mortarn answered, "I think you will find that if you place Torpast's wife on the elevated rock where you have been surveying the main cavern, she will soon start to wake." "How do you know about such things?" said Jandray. "All in good time" answered Mortarn. "Check if what I have said is true and then I suggest you head back to Queen Mountain."

Jandray had to do something. He didn't know this man and he couldn't fully trust him as a result, but he didn't appear to want to cause him harm and he knew another part of the poem that had been in the minds of Queen Torcas and Jandray. He stood and said, "The Ways scriptures are in the main Sleeping Cavern, so I will go back immediately. I will have to take a risk to just briefly check the Hiber cavern and then I will return, with Sartora if I can. Even so, it will be late tomorrow before I return." Mortarn looked across at Torpast, "Sartora, so that is this poor man's wife. That helps, I will speak her name to him, it may reach into his unconsciousness and guide him back." Mortarn stood, "Take your hound with you, Torpast will come to no additional harm under my care. I only hope I have something more positive to tell you on his condition when you return." Jandray quickly grabbed some food and drink, and also fed Winterclaw. He took one more look at Torpast and then made to leave the library to head back down the tunnel "Thank you" he said to Mortarn. "But we do need to talk at length when I return." With nod of his head, Mortarn answered, "Of course, it will be a long story but Winter has not lost its grip on this nation yet, so we will have time. I will hope I can tell that story to both you and Torpast." At that, Jandray left and prepared himself for the long walk back through the tunnel to Queen Mountain, Winterclaw at his side. As he walked away, he looked back and hoped that this mysterious Mortarn was true to his word, and that Torpast would be alive when he returned.

After several hours of brisk walking, Jandray returned to the main cavern within Queen Mountain. It all looked just as he had left it, with no obvious signs for him to worry about. He started reading the Ways of the HiberWatcher. After extensive reading, he did find a passage that outlined how someone could be brought awake by carefully bringing them Hiberwatcher's Rock. So Mortarn was right, thought Jandray, there is much to his story that I need to know. Jandray did not think the time had come to wake all the Hiber folk, and so did not read the carefully bound and sealed instructions at the back of the parchment book on how to wake the whole nation. It was clear from how it was sealed that the expectation for this act to take place was only as a last resort. For all the problems and pressure that Jandray was under he was, at least, grateful that he would only have to account for waking one of their folk. It was fortunate that Jandray had spotted Torpast routinely walking past the sleeping forms of his wife and daughter over recent weeks. For that reason, Jandray did not need to scour the immense cavern looking for her.

He headed off into the direction that Torpast had taken. When he arrived at the rough location, Jandray looked around him. Soon he found Altera. Interestingly, Maltas was laying close to her, and it almost looked like they were brother and sister. However, he could not find Sartora. A sense of dread started to creep up on him. Near to where Altera was laying, there was a gap on the floor. A blanket was on the ground that he would have expected to have been placed there by someone about to sleep on it. But all he could see, was the faint outline of where a body had slightly depressed the soft earth of the cavern floor. Suddenly, all was frighteningly clear in his mind. Sartora had been taken. Whoever had assailed the mountain had done so to take Sartora. But why would they want Sartora? She wasn't an Elder. If someone wanted to harm anyone, surely the Queen or King would be the target. As carefully as he could, Jandray ran to where he knew the King and Queen were sleeping. He couldn't suppress the sigh of relief when he saw the outlines of both their bodies, in situ, and clearly still deep in their Winter sleep.

Jandray knew he only had one choice. He lifted King Nilan carefully and put him over his shoulder. Nilan was a heavy load on Jandray's tired frame, more so than Torpast had been, but he managed to carry him to the Hiberwatcher's Rock. He placed the sleeping body of his King on ground in front of him and waited. Several hours passed, and there was no change in the condition of King Nilan, who appeared heavy in his sleep. Jandray was impatient to return to Torpast, but all the Ways had said was that any person on Hiberwatcher's Rock would not sleep, or those sleeping would wake when placed on the raised platform. After what felt like an eternity, King Nilan began to stir. He moved slowly and lifted himself to a sitting position. "This doesn't feel right" he said. "The sleep isn't over". His eyes tried to focus and he saw the outline of Jandray in front of him. "Is that you HiberWatcher Jandray?" he slurred. "Yes, my King, I have great need of advice." King Nilan tried to stand, but felt too weak to do so. "Please, a drink, I need a drink to wash this sleep out of me." Jandray ran to the HiberWatcher food store and returned with a mug of cold mountain spring water. King Nilan greedily drank the water and said, "That was nectar, thank you." His eyes started to clear and, again, he tried to stand. This time he was more successful, but then had to lean into Jandray who carefully let him drop into a sitting position.

"What is amiss, HiberWatcher?" said King Nilan. "There will be a reckoning for both of us in Spring as a result of your actions." Jandray, not knowing where to start, kept his words short thinking he could go into more detail later. "King Nilan, Torpast has been assaulted and is close to death. Tracks lead out of Queen Mountain and I fear the attackers have taken Sartora and one of the Watch Hounds with them. I went to the Hiber Library to make Torpast as comfortable as I could and a mysterious man called Mortarn was found there." At Mortarn's name, King Nilan's eyes began to clear. "So" he said quietly, "We were right to have a plan." Jandray looked at him aghast, "what is happening, King Nilan? I must be told." King Nilan looked at Jandray and said, "We must get to the Library, you may have to support me for a while until the sleep leave my limbs. But I need to speak with you and with Mortarn." He tried to stand again, but needed Jandray's support. Together, they left the cavern and headed back down the tunnel towards the library. For several hours, King Nilan said nothing and concentrated on trying to walk unaided. Eventually he was able to do so, but Jandray stayed close to him as he remained unsteady. Eventually they reached the library. Mortarn had heard their footsteps and met them at the entrance.

"Mortarn, it looks like we meet under very grave circumstances" said Nilan. "Yes indeed, the first move has been made in this malevolent conspiracy, and blood has been shed" replied Mortarn. Jandray updated Mortarn, "Sartora has been taken, she must have been the target of the attack. I decided to wake the King to seek his advice." "A wise move" replied Mortarn "and the King will be able to reassure you that my presence here is for the benefit of the Hiber Nation." "Before we all bring ourselves up to speed with our stories, albeit mine is mainly one of sleep, I want to see HiberWatcher Torpast" said King Nilan. "My King, there is hope, I feel" said Mortarn. He then explained to both Nilan and Jandray that he had been successful in inserting a tube to provide sustenance to Torpast. "However, he still remains unconscious, and I do not know if or when he will awake."

The three men went into the room where Torpast had been placed. The air was fresh and Mortarn said, "Kian and Kindross had a good store of fire cones, I had forgotten about the freshness they bring to a room." Torpast was laying on his back, with a number of cushions underneath his head. Whilst there was no movement from him, his breathing seemed deep and regular and Jandray felt that a more healthy colour could be seen in his face than his appearance when Jandray had left him. Winterclaw came in the room and gently jumped onto the bed. He placed his head against Torpast's left hand which was laying on top of the blanket that Mortarn had placed over him. "My fear was that he would suffer an infection and a high temperature caused by his wounds festering. Thankfully, I have been able to keep his head wound free from such infection." "It looks like you have taken good care of him" replied Jandray, "I thank you for this. I only wish that I could have brought him good news, even if he couldn't hear it."

They agreed to leave Torpast and returned to the chairs by the fire in the main living area. It was not lost on Jandray that he and Torpast had sat here in happier times, times that seemed so long ago now; yet only a few short months had passed in reality. King Nilan asked of Jandray "Did Mortarn pass a message to you when you first saw him?" "Yes, he did; a verse which I very much think is part of the poem that has been revealed to us over the last few months." "We owe you an explanation I feel" said Nilan. "It would really help" replied Jandray, "although you being here and vouching for Mortarn is enough for me." "Mortarn and I have known each other many years" answered Nilan, "although our meetings have not been as frequent as we would have liked." Nilan then explained to Jandray the meeting that had taken place at Ertin's Inn. The more the story unfolded, the more Jandray's face took on one of incredulous belief at the thought of The King of The Hiber Nation, meeting with Warriors of Tukerland and then secreting one of these Warriors in the Library. "So you think that Delcant and Grasby are at the centre of any conspiracy?" asked Jandray. "Without doubt they are in league, and not for the benefit of the Hiber Nation" replied Nilan. "Delcant is sleeping in the main cavern" Jandray replied. "I noticed him in my routine patrols." "That is not to say he is not involved. What better way of hiding your intentions than to put plans in place before you sleep. Then Delcant can deny any part in what has happened" immediately answered King Nilan. "I agree, and I also think that it is unlikely that Queen Mountain was assailed from the outside" answered Mortarn. "It is most likely that Grasby and Delcant had worked out a way of bringing someone into Queen Mountain. All they had to do was hide from you and Torpast until they thought the time was right to kidnap Sartora." Nilan considered this carefully and replied, "What I don't understand is why they seriously injured Torpast and then bound his wounds. I don't understand why they then did not try to incapacity you too." "Sadly" replied Jandray, "Perhaps they left me alone to take the blame when our nation wakes up. All the Elders will have is my word about what has happened. We cannot reveal the presence of Mortarn, as he will be just viewed as part of a conspiracy of our own making." "Jandray is correct in this" answered Mortarn "And it will not help if the King of the Hiber Nation is caught up in this either."

Nilan said nothing for a while and looked lost in thought as he stared into the fire. "Delcant has built an Elder house almost as large as that in Paltir. It would not surprise me if he would like nothing more than to challenge my fitness to rule." "But why only take Sartora?" asked Jandray "It doesn't make sense. Surely kidnapping you or the Queen, or at least an Elder would have made a much larger bargaining factor?" "I doubt very much that Warrior Sargern has sanctioned this attack on our nation" replied Nilan. "I agree" added Mortarn. "Saltock would not have been placed in the trade meetings if Sargern had any malicious intent. In fact, Saltock felt that he had been placed in there as Sargern does not entirely trust Grasby." "Well, it appears that he is a good judge of character in that case" said Jandray. "But it still does not explain why they have taken Sartora." Nilan answered "I think there is a simple explanation. Delcant is trying to gain much more influence over the Elder Council. He has made no secret of his desire for Lorsern to succeed Farrender as Elder. With Sartora out of the way, the road is clear for him to get his way. Lorsern has been a willing acolyte of Delcant for some years and will be a strong supporter of any of Delcant's views expressed in the Council. By kidnapping Sartora, he removes that obstacle to his plans, and has a valuable asset with which to use against us in the future."

Silence descended over these three troubled souls, as the enormity of the situation continued to sink in. It wasn't just that Sartora had been kidnapped. The terrible crime meant that the sanctuary of Queen Mountain had been overcome, and what did that mean for next year's sleep? It was clear to King Nilan that Tukerland, or at least some factions within its elite, had plans to destabilise the Hiber Nation. None of them could ascertain the wider purpose at this moment. In addition, and perhaps more concerning, was that they had help from within the Hiber people. Jandray was correct in that the finger of blame would automatically point to him in the first instance. King Nilan announced "I will have to tell the Elders that you woke me following the attack on Torpast and I will have to disclose our friendship with Mortarn, Nirtan and Saltock. It is the only way that Jandray will not be at risk from sanction by the Elder Council." "You cannot do that" replied Jandray immediately. "All the work you have done over the years to maintain a productive conduit to Tukerland would be lost. Grasby would know of our plans, and it would even play into his hands if he manipulated a situation where Warrior Saltock was made to look like a spy for the Hiber folk." "Jandray is right in what he is saying" agreed Mortarn. "We cannot afford for your part in this to be made widely known at the moment." "What do we do then?" asked Nilan. "I think we need time to reflect on our options and decided what to do" said Mortarn. "I will check on Torpast, and perhaps we can revisit our considerations later."

After Mortarn had returned from visiting Torpast, the three of them sat down in front of the fire again. "There are a number of things which are clear" said Mortarn. "I cannot be here when the Hiber Nation awakes, and King Nilan cannot tell anyone that he was awoken early." "In addition", he continued, "None can know of our suspicions of Delcant in the first instance." Nilan and Jandray nodded in agreement. "But that leaves Jandray at the mercy of the Elder Council, and they will probably deprive him of his liberty whilst they try and sort this out." Nilan spoke up, "Jandray will be a pariah, no HiberWatcher has ever been harmed in the past, and the sanctuary of Queen Mountain has never been breached until now. It will be an immensely difficult time for Jandray. If Delcant is part of this conspiracy, he will be at the forefront of attacking Jandray's narrative of what has happened." Jandray replied "I have to stay. If I am missing when the sleep ends, it will automatically lead everyone to believe I was instrumental in the attack and the kidnapping of Sartora. It will play directly into Delcant's hands." "I fear you are correct" replied Mortarn. "But we must have a plan to rescue you from this situation, you cannot just be left incarcerated why Delcant does his best to condemn you." Nilan did not want leave Jandray at the mercy of those who would put all the blame on him but he could see no option. "Jandray, if you are willing, you are going to have to carry this burden on your own for a period of time. I will work with Queen Torcas when she wakes and we will formulate some kind of plan. I trust Ertin totally, and as soon as we can we will have to try and meet at his Inn, together with Saltock and Nirtan to establish if they have heard anything of what has happened to Sartora." Jandray added, "We should remember that one of our Watch Hounds is missing too. If she is not dead then they have taken her too." "That might not be a bad thing for us" said Mortarn. "If the hound surfaces in Tukerland, she will be easy to spot - they are fine specimens; there is nothing quite like them in Tukerland."

The agreement was made, but none of the three were particular looking forward to the immediate future. Mortarn and Nilan would remain in support of Jandray until the very last moment. As soon as it was clear that the Winter Sleep would soon end, Mortarn would leave and make his way back to Tukerland. He would meet up with Nirtan and Saltock and then they would plan how to meet up with Ertin and Jandray, if Jandray could be released from his inevitable incarceration. Nilan would assist Jandray in checking the sleeping Hiber folk and the other sleeping caverns until such time that he would feign waking up with his kinfolk. Jandray would truthfully explain everything that had happened except the role of Mortarn and Nilan. It was then expected that he would be placed under guard as the Elder Council investigated the worst attack on the Hiber Nation for as long as anyone could remember.

Jandray was the only one who was not overly concerned about the immediate future. The poem had been revealed to him for this purpose he felt. Mortarn's additional verse made him even more certain that Queen Mountain herself was ensuring her people would be protected. There was something about Mortarn that also comforted Jandray with a sense of peace. He couldn't articulate why, perhaps it was the longstanding friendship that he now knew had been in place with Nilan and Mortarn. But he could tell that Mortarn was studying him when he thought he wasn't looking. And the level of detail that Mortarn knew about the Hiber people and their culture was beyond what Jandray would have expected. Over the following weeks, Mortarn rarely left Torpast's side. There was still no change to his unconscious state, but his breathing was regular and the colour of his skin was healthy. The head wound was healing, and remained uninfected. They could only hope that he would wake and exonerate Jandray by confirming what had happened to him. Time would tell.

Chapter Twenty-Three

Spring was almost upon the sleeping people of the Hiber Nation. The fierce winter blizzards had stopped, and from the high point on Queen Mountain Jandray could tell that the huge blanket of snow and ice was slowly receding. The last accumulations to disappear would be those around the lake of Queen Mountain. This ice would remain in place for several days after the Hiber folk woke from their long sleep. Looking at the landscape ahead, Mortarn would soon be able to leave via any of the main tunnels at the foot of Queen Mountain. Jandray had suggested that, if he planned it right, Mortarn could leave from the Library at Paltir rather than from Queen Mountain. However, Mortarn had wanted to walk through the journey that Torpast had made, and also he wanted to see where Torpast had been attacked. It was agreed that, with King Nilan, the three of them would carefully carry Torpast back to Hiberwatcher's Rock, thereby removing any suspicion that Jandray had been in the Library. It would be obvious to Kian and Kindross, but King Nilan said he would deal with this. Kian and Kindross would know that Jandray was telling the truth once he had spoken with them. Mortarn would check the route that Torpast took, and then would leave Queen Mountain by one of the tunnels through which the Hiber folk had entered several months before. He would take care not to leave any tracks and would head straight back to meet Nirtan in Tukerland. Nilan would remain awake with Jandray until the very last moment and then he would lay at Queen Torcas's side until she awoke. He would then 'wake' with her and face the inevitable uproar that would begin.

Jandray took Mortarn along the routes that he and Torpast had patrolled over Winter. As Mortarn walked through the sea of sleeping bodies he saw the empty place where Sartora had been sleeping. As they carried on Jandray couldn't help also taking one last look at his mother who was sleeping peacefully. Mortarn was at his side when he did so. Jandray turned and thought he saw something in Mortarn's face as he quickly turned away and carefully walked to the outer perimeter of the cavern. Jandray re-traced his steps through the tunnels and identified to Mortarn the side tunnel where he had found Torpast. There was still clear evidence of the blood loss suffered by Torpast and the unmistakable presence of footmarks that were not Torpast's nor Jandray's. "With the bindings that had been found covering Torpast's wound, and the outline of additional footprints, I have no doubt that Grasby is at the centre of this matter. However, one of these is quite a small print and I would even say that it could be a female footprint" said Mortarn.

Nilan, Jandray and Mortarn had discussed whether to mention the bindings to the Elders when they awoke. Delcant would undoubtably tell Grasby that the Hiber folk were blaming Tukerland and this could create tensions, a situation that Grasby probably wanted to be created. Eventually, it was agreed that nothing would be said about the bindings, nor the tracks leading from the Mountain. It left Jandray's position even more precarious. However, it also meant that Delcant could not alert Grasby to the fact that Mortarn and Nilan were aware of the extent of their involvement in this terrible attack on the Hiber Nation. Also, the warrior who had bound Torpast's wounds would probably be at extreme peril if Grasby found out that aid had been given to Torpast. Even without using this evidence, it would be obvious that the attack had been executed by people from Tukerland. Unless Delcant tried to say that Jandray had lost his mind, had seriously injured Torpast, had hidden Sartora's body and had killed and disposed of a Watch Hound; there would be no other logical explanation. But all agreed that this narrative would not work. If he had done this, why would Jandray let Torpast live, and why would he then stay to face investigation and certain imprisonment?

Mortarn grasped Jandray's arm as he made to start the journey back to Tukerland. "I have no doubt that we will meet again, hopefully in better circumstances" said Mortarn. "I know you have questions of me and you want to know why my knowledge of your culture is so extensive. Trust me, there will be a time when I will tell you my story, but not yet. All you need to know is that I mean you no harm, I have given my life to protecting the Hiber Nation from the excesses that Tukerland could bring to bear. I have to play this role for a while longer I fear." Jandray looked at Mortarn. "Your care of Torpast tells me all that I need to know about you" he said. "You are a man of integrity and, regardless of what happens to Torpast, you have done your very best for him. Go home to your family, and take my thanks with you. I do hope we can sit and talk long about things next time we meet." At that point Nilan joined them. "Mortarn, old friend. You were a friend to my father, and you have been the same to me. We are in your debt. Travel well; I look forward to seeing you as soon as it is safe to do so." Mortarn turned to leave and was about to say something. He thought for a moment and then said, "Jandray, your mother has made a fine man of you." He was about to say more but thought better of it. He turned from the King of the Hiber Nation and the HiberWatcher called Jandray, and slowly walked away.

Nilan looked at Jandray and said, "I feel that the sleep will be over after this evening. Let's talk about how you are going to deal with the weight of accusation that is going come your way tomorrow, I know you can carry this burden. But also know that I am on your side. I will not be able to support you in as obvious manner as I would like, but know that you are not alone." Jandray was reassured by Nilan's words and replied, "The important issue is discovering if Sartora is still alive. I cannot see that the invaders would have gone to so much trouble to kill her, there must be a wider plan which makes her important to Grasby, if he is at the centre of this. For all the distasteful aspects of Delcant, I cannot see he would support cold-blooded murder, but I may be wrong." "Delcant is beyond our help now" said Nilan. "His excess at building a rival complex in Decinter, and his clear attempt to manipulate the Elder Council regarding Farrender's successor, is ample evidence that he has taken a different path." Nilan's anger at Delcant was obvious as he continued, "I have no doubt that Delcant and Grasby are both working outside of their authority. If Saltock is a person of integrity, which I think he is, then Sargern would not have sanctioned what has happened to our nation. We have to hope that Nirtan and Mortarn can shed light on what Grasby's future plans are. I think Delcant doesn't realise how much he has been manipulated by Grasby and how expendable he is to Grasby." Jandray did not want to think about Delcant's traitorous role in Torpast's assault and the kidnap of Sartora. A loyal Watch Hound was also missing, and Jandray knew that Torpast would be equally concerned at this, having formed such a strong bond with this faithful hound.

Nilan and Jandray talked long into the night. Torpast's condition remained unchanged. Mortarn had worked hard to ensure he was as healthy as he could be, and the head wound was healing well. Jandray hoped that Kian and Kindross would be able to use their extensive knowledge of healing to help bring Torpast back to consciousness. If that happened then any suspicion that Jandray was complicit in the terrible events that had taken place during Winter would end. Until then Jandray had no doubt that his role in the events of winter would be under intense scrutiny and suspicion. As morning arrived the lights in the cavern seemed brighter. Jandray decided to check one of the entrances to see if they were becoming fully passable. He reached the entrance and could see that the boughs of the trees that had made a living barrier had now pulled back and that the entrance was open. Almost all of the ice and snow had also disappeared around the entrance. The ice bridge was still in place and the Hiber folk would soon need to return to their homes before this final memory of winter melted, and it returned to being a lake. The Spring festival would begin, stores would be opened, and the beer that had been laid up since early Winter would be drunk. Jandray could picture him sitting in a room, guarded against leaving, at the mercy of the Elder Council's deliberations.

Nilan had decided it was time for him to return to his sleeping position next to Queen Torcas. Nothing more needed to be said between Jandray and Nilan. Both knew that the Spring would bring more concerns and Nilan would need to tread careful steps. He had to remain impartial, at least on the outside. Yet he was unsure how he would remain composed in Delcant's presence. He was sure that Delcant had facilitated this attack on the very core of Hiber tradition, and he was equally certain that Delcant would continue to continue down that traitorous path. Nilan carefully laid himself down, next to Torcas. He was comforted with the thought that he would soon be able to confide in her, and she would provide wise counsel on what to do.

When morning arose, as predicted by Nilan, throughout the cavern the Hiber folk began to stir. At first their breathing changed from shallow breaths of deep sleep to that of waking, with the oxygen coursing through their prone bodies as they slowly started to move their limbs. As morning progressed, the awakening increased in pace and people began to sit up and gently watched their loved ones awake from their own peaceful rest. The first day of the awakening created an energy like nothing that could be described. None could remember what they had dreamed during the long weeks of sleep. However, some could feel that nagging aches had disappeared and they were invigorated for the months ahead. Jandray watched the activity from his elevated position on Hiberwatcher's Rock. Soon the Elder Council would learn that this Winter Sleep had been very different. How they would update their communities was vital if this hopeful, happy and excited atmosphere was not to be spoiled. Once they had been apprised of the terrible events that had taken place, it would depend on the Elder Council on how much would be revealed.

The Hiber folk would break their fast together in the cavern, using stores that had been laid up in Queen Mountain for this purpose. Then they would start to make their way back to their communities before the ice bridge melted. In a few days time, the Spring festival would be held and then the hard work of preparing the land for the seasonal crops would begin. It would be a very busy time for all, and Jandray hoped that the concerns about Sartora would be lost in this rhythm of Spring. However, for the Elder Council, the issues at hand would be more pressing. They would, somehow, have to assimilate what had happened to Torpast and Sartora, and seek answers as to what this meant in the longer term.

As with Hiber tradition, the Elder Council's first meeting would take place within Queen Mountain as soon as all had woken. Teams who specialised in caring for farm animals would visit the other caverns. The Elder Council would then be reassured that all the Hiber folk were well, and also the animals and creatures in other the caverns were awake and returning to their natural habitats. The Council would receive a full update from the HiberWatchers and then, in normal years, the HiberWatchers would leave with Kian and Kindross to discuss any issues that needed to be added to the Ways of the HiberWatchers. But this was not a normal year by any measure. However, Jandray felt it important that the Council met as usual where he could then bring the awful truth of what had happened, without alerting the wider communities. If these communities left having any inclination of what had happened, rumours would be rife. It would be the Elders who would need to decide on what to reveal, and how much.

Jandray was more concerned about Altera than facing the Elder Council. Her mother was missing, her father was unconscious and there was no guarantee that he would regain consciousness. Jandray had decided that he would immediately approach Maltas and Altera, before he had to leave for the Elder Council. It would be a difficult conversation and he knew that Maltas would be an important source of support for both Altera and Torpast. He saw that Maltas had awoken and he walked up to him. Maltas was near to his father Lorsern. However, Lorsern, once he had looked disdainfully upon Jandray, made a quick excuse about needing to speak with Delcant. Jandray thought that this betrayed his possible role in this whole nightmare, but said nothing. At least it allowed him to speak with Maltas alone. "Come quickly, we need to find Altera, she is going to need your help." "Altera will be busy with her mother and getting ready to meet her father once the two of you have been before the Elder Council" Maltas replied. "My father was very keen to speak to Delcant; he told me that the Elder council will be meeting shortly to receive your update on anything that has happened over winter."

Jandray and Nilan had planned what he was going to say and they decided that the briefest of explanations to Maltas would have to suffice in the first instance. "Winter has brought an attack on our nation." He waited for the gravity of his message to sink in before continuing, "I am bringing you into confidence as you will need to support Altera. Her father was seriously injured during winter. He was close to death, but I hope that his condition has stabilised. He is unconscious, and has been since the attack." "Attack……..unconscious.. what happened?" stammered Maltas. "I cannot go into detail but you and Altera need to come with me as no one can know about this until after the Elder Council." "We need to find Sartora as well" said Maltas, not realising that his words would lead to the next message from Jandray. "That is a further matter to discuss, and it will be a massive thing for Altera to understand. During Winter, Sartora was taken from the cavern. I do not know who took her, or where she has gone." Maltas was lost for words. "Taken, what do you mean taken?" Jandray saw the impact of his words on this young man but needed him to not be buried by his confusion. "Come, questions later, we need to find Altera." Maltas looked at his teacher and mentor and could see that he was deadly serious about what he had said. "I will follow you and will give whatever support I can." He dropped in behind Jandray as he strode off to find Altera.

Altera had woken and wasn't too concerned that her mother wasn't at her side. She assumed her mother had gone to find Farrender to see if she needed anything prior to the Elder meeting. Altera was aware of how the Council worked, more than most people of her age. Sartora had openly discussed the workings of the Elder Council with her daughter as she knew she was being trained to potentially take over the Elder role. It was important that Altera knew what pressures an Elder would be under Sartora had said. Altera was also keen to meet up with her father and hear all about his winter as a HiberWatcher. One of her proudest moments was seeing his name on the Ice Wall, a name that would now re-appear on that wall every winter. She was thinking of this when she saw Jandray walking up to her. Maltas was slightly behind him and she could tell from his face that something was troubling him. Before she could say anything, Jandray gently took her arm and guided her away from other Hiber folk that were nearby. "Altera, I have some deeply concerning news to bring to you."

At first, the gravity of Jandray's voice did not register with Altera, but she could see that Maltas's face was a mask of worry. Jandray continued, "Your father was injured during Winter and he is unconscious. It is highly likely that he was attacked and I need you and Maltas to look after him whilst I brief the Elder Council." Jandray was aware that there was no easy way to convey this information to Altera, and he could see from her face that the enormity of the situation was not sinking in. "I am going to take you to Torpast and I need you to care for him. As soon as I have finished at the Council, I, or someone else, will come and help you." Altera remained silent, barely being able to comprehend what was being said. When she found her voice she said, "Mother will want to be there, she will be the best person to care for father. I think she must be with Elder Farrender as she had woken prior to me." Jandray was aware that the next message was going to break this young woman's heart, but it had to be done. "My dear Altera, your mother is missing. During winter she has been taken, I don't know by whom, or where she has gone." Altera sank to her knees and started to cry quietly. "This cannot be true, why are you saying this?" Maltas knelt beside her and held her tightly, "We must trust what Jandray is saying, your father needs you and we must go to him." Jandray was grateful for Maltas's intervention. He added, "Please Altera, I will tell you as much as I can, as soon as I can, but first I need you to come to your father." At that, Maltas and Jandray gently helped Altera to her feet and the three of them made their way to the elevated position of Hiberwatcher's Rock, where Jandray and Mortarn had laid the body of

Torpast.

Upon their arrival, Altera fell to her father's side. He looked like he was sleeping. "What happened to father?" she said. "He just looks like he is sleeping." Jandray replied, "On one of his routine patrols it appears that he was attacked, and suffered a serious head injury." Jandray started to say, "we managed…" and then to stopped himself, but Maltas had picked up on the mistake and looked at Jandray quizzically. "There clearly is more to be told" said Maltas to himself. Jandray started again, "I managed to find him and bring him back to here, where I have cared for him over winter. However, whilst his injury is healing well, he still has not gained consciousness." Altera looked at her father and then at Jandray. "Nothing like this has ever happened before, has it?" "Not that I am aware" he replied. A rush of guilt suddenly overwhelmed Altera. She was to blame, she had come up with idea that Jandray would be nominated by the Watchkeepers society. Had this tinkering with Hiber tradition created this situation where her father was attacked, she asked herself. She could see the weight of the responsibility that was sitting on Jandray's shoulders and that added to her guilt. "Show me what I need to do and I will do it." Jandray was encouraged that this young woman could comprehend that she needed to care for her father, and he carefully instructed Altera and Maltas on how to ensure that Torpast was getting nutrition through the carefully inserted tube in his mouth. "I have fed him each day, and you may need to do this later if I don't return by evening" he said. "Why would you not return?" she replied. Jandray didn't immediately answer and then said, "I must go and brief the Council." He stood and took the arm of Maltas and Altera. "All I ask is that you trust me, whatever you hear." He didn't wait for an answer, turning away from them he headed off to meet the Hiber Council.

Chapter Twenty-Four

The Elder Council had assembled around a large table in the Elder chamber which was located under Queen Mountain. Over recent years this chamber had only been used in a ceremonial manner for brief meetings prior to, and after, the Winter Sleep. However, in the Hiber Nation's long history, the chamber had remained one of the most secure places in the Hiber Nation and had been the centre for Elder meetings in times of uncertainty. Queen Torcas and King Nilan were in attendance. Kian and Kindross, the Hiber Key Keepers were also sat at an adjacent table, ready to take notes of the meeting. Nilan had quickly summarised the gravity of the situation to Torcas on the way to the meeting. She maintained an impassive expression as he updated her on his suspicions that Delcant and Grasby were at the centre of what had happened. "Husband, I think you are right in not revealing your role in tackling this massive attack against our community; Delcant would only use it against you. We are much better providing a facade of impartiality as we work behind the scenes to fight this evil partnership." She then added, "We need to discuss everything in detail with Kian and Kindross who will be essential to these discussions." "My concern at this meeting" replied Nilan, "is what will happen to Jandray. If I don't step in to support him, he will be at the mercy of Delcant and any malicious response Delcant seeks to play out at Council. I know that Jandray is equal to this problem" he added, "but both the anger and the concerns of the Elders will be focussed upon him." Torcas replied, "Husband, we must continue to have faith in the Elders; that they will realise this situation is not due to failings of Jandray, or by Torpast for the matter. Torpast needs constant care at this time. Kian and Kindross are, perhaps, the best people to provide that care. At the very least we can push for Jandray to be incarcerated, if that is the desire of the Council, within the Paltir building in order that he will be close to us."

There was no further time for Torcas and Nilan to discuss their plans as all the Elders were ready for the meeting to commence. Jandray had walked into the chamber and looked around him. Before he was asked to speak, the Elders received an update that all the communities were now awake and were slowly leaving the sleeping chamber. Those Hiber folk who had attended the animals and creatures in the other chambers also reported that they were also awake. The wild creatures were leaving, and the birds had flown already. Hiber folk were guiding the farm animals back to their respective communities as they too left. Tradition dictated that this was not a long meeting. The Elders were usually keen to return to their communities to start preparations for the Spring festival, and all the day to day plans for preparing the land for the sowing of crops. They needed to ensure that all the farm animals were settled back into their fields and barns. The meeting was called to order as King Nilan stood up from his chair. Looking around at all the Elders, he couldn't help but linger in his gaze at Delcant more than he wanted to. Delcant was a master at hiding his true intent and had given nothing away in his behaviour since waking.

"HiberWatcher Jandray, please come forward. We note that HiberWatcher Torpast is not present, shall we wait for him?" asked King Nilan, commencing the agreed subterfuge entirely to support Jandray. "My Queen, King and members of the Elder Council" said Jandray, "It will soon become clear why Torpast is not present. I am sorry to bring distressing news about the Winter Sleep." The Elders, who had been distracted by a myriad of local concerns, suddenly returned their full attention to Jandray. Over the next hour, Jandray carefully explained all that had happened, as agreed by Nilan and Mortarn. Whilst he was talking, Nilan and Torcas looked at all the Elders. Most displayed their horror at the situation that Jandray described. Delcant also played his role well and gasped when Jandray outlined how he had found Torpast seriously injured and close to death. Farrender was physically moved to tears as Jandray explained that Sartora was missing. As he finished his report he said, "Members of the Elder Council, I present myself here as this harbinger of terrible news. Torpast needs immediate care and I ask that you prioritise this. I truly hope that he awakes and he will then be able confirm how he was attacked and, perhaps, identify his assailants."

At first the Elder Council remained silent; stunned by Jandray's report. Most of the Elders, like Farrender, had been part of the council for many years and had never before awoken to such terrible news. Nilan knew far more about the Winter's events, but the repeating of them by Jandray also reinforced his belief that the Hiber Nation had been subject of an attack. If it was of Tukerland origin, this was only the start of a wider plan to destabilise this nation, felt Nilan. Farrender, still visibly moved by the news of Sartora was first to speak. "King Nilan, our priority must be the care of HiberWatcher Torpast and to prepare for an expedition to locate Sartora. We are assuming, on Jandray's update, that she is not within Queen Mountain, but I feel that a more extensive search of the Mountain would be beneficial."   Nilan, knowing that tracks had been seen leading from Queen Mountain, was sure that this search would prove fruitless but would need to agree. "Elder Farrender, I would agree with both your recommendations." As he looked around the room, he could see that all of the Elders were in agreement. "The further matter at hand is how much we tell our local leadership councils and our communities" he said. "Do we restrict the awareness of these terrible events from them until we can fill in more detail of what has happened?"   Elder Fendrix raised his hand, "I think it is imperative that we don't create panic amongst our communities. If Torpast awakes, we will be in much better position to help us all understand what happened to him. It will also allow for the search for Sartora to take place within Queen Mountain. However, if Sartora isn't found before too long, how are our communities going to return to the mountain to sleep; if we cannot confirm they will be safe?"

Fendrix had a very valid point, and all the Elders agreed that now wasn't the time to reveal Jandray's update to the wider Hiber communities. Ospeth raised the matter that all the Elders were thinking. "Is Tukerland behind this terrible situation?" Silence resounded around the room. None of the Elders wanted to entertain the idea that their neighbour was preparing an attack on them. Nilan expected Delcant to speak up at this point but he also remained silent. It was Caltan who spoke; "We met Warrior Grasby and Warrior Saltock in early Winter and the trade talks had gone well. Why would Tukerland wish to invade our Winter sanctuary?   And if they wanted to, how would they do it?" So that was it, thought Nilan. Delcant would work his mischievous plans through Caltan who had been under his spell for some time. Nilan didn't know if Caltan was part of a wider conspiracy of if he was just too close to Delcant to see him for what he really was.   It was at this point that Delcant spoke up. "I agree with Caltan.   What purpose would Tukerland have in attacking us? We know that Queen Mountain is impregnable, so how would they manage to gain entry? Jandray has given no information that would support the notion of external forces at play here." He left his challenge to Jandray's account to sink in. He then continued to try and sew seeds of doubt about Jandray's account. "The only person who can shed light on this matter is Torpast and it appears that, conveniently for Jandray, he is incapable of doing so at the moment. As a result, HiberWatcher Jandray is key to our deliberations." Torcas was waiting for the next words out of Delcant's mouth and wasn't at all surprised when he said, "Jandray, as distasteful as it may be, must be under suspicion at this time. Until we know more I recommend that he is kept under guard and his movements limited."

Farrender immediately stood up and said, "That would be so easy for you wouldn't it Elder Delcant? The person who is most closely engaged with Tukerland is the one who refuses to see their hand in this, and would rather blame one of our own; a man who has served his community and our children for years without any blemish on his character." Farrender, in her typical style then caustically added, "Is it not interesting that Sartora is the woman who is missing; and she was the only obstacle to Elder Delcant persuading us to support Lorsern as my replacement?" Farrender was sensible enough not to damage her position by challenging Lorsern's integrity at the same time as making her distrust of Delcant clear. Nilan was burning to support Farrender. He also felt that it was entirely possible that Sartora was taken for this reason. Without Nilan having to say anything, Farrender had spelled his concerns out to all the Elders. It was a valid hypothesis that Delcant had cleared a major obstacle in his desires for Lorsern to be voted as Elder of Paltir.

Delcant portrayed the role of an injured party and replied, "I don't think that this council will give credit to your assertions Farrender. It is true, I have made no secret that I feel Lorsern would be a worthy Elder, but that is for the Paltir Community to decide." Farrender grimly smiled and said, "Our Elders will remember your support for Lorsern at the last meeting." Torcas could see how this meeting could potentially deteriorate and decided to step in, "The most obvious way to deal with this is to lean on Elder Farrender's good will and ask her to delay her retirement as Elder. This will placate any concerns about Lorsern benefiting from Sartora's disappearance." Delcant could see his plan falling apart. "Queen Torcas, it would be unusual to delay such an appointment further. We have delayed it once already." "But", Queen Torcas replied firmly, "Elder Delcant, don't you think that what we are facing is, at the very least, unusual?" Delcant had no answer to this.

Elder Farrender looked at Queen Torcas. "If I have the support of our fellow Elders, I will agree to delay my retirement as Elder of Paltir until such time as we know the full circumstances of Sartora's disappearance." "This calls for a vote" replied Queen Torcas. "All in favour?" Delcant knew he had been outmanoeuvred on this occasion. However, he consoled himself, it would only delay the inevitable and it would just extend his timeframe for getting Lorsern onto the council. He knew he would have to vote in favour of the Farrender staying in position. His mind raced, and he realised it may actually work in his favour. He would be seen as supporting Farrender, instead of opposing her, thereby somewhat negating her assertions that he wanted her gone from the Council. The vote was taken and it was unanimous. Queen Torcas said, "We thank Elder Farrender for delaying her retirement and I am grateful that it was a unanimous vote", her eyes resting on Delcant.

Delcant then raised his hand, "We still need to resolve the matter of Jandray. I feel that we should all agree that he remains under close guard until this situation is resolved. We could say that he is briefing the Key Keepers on the Winter Sleep, and will return to teaching in due course." King Nilan saw his opportunity, "In support of Elder Delcant, I think that Jandray should be accommodated with the Key Keepers, we had hoped that they can arrange care of Torpast and, if they were willing, they could also ensure that Jandray is available for further discussions with this Council whenever we want." Delcant's face betrayed his dissatisfaction with King Nilan's proposal. However, Nilan had couched it in such a way as to appear to be supporting Delcant. "King Nilan, I was thinking that a more restrictive guard be placed on Jandray." At this Queen Torcas stood up, "Why is this Delcant?", she said, with an edge to her voice. "Do you not accept HiberWatcher Jandray's account of what has happened. I have no hesitation in voicing my belief that Jandray is a man of high integrity and has given a truthful account of what must have been a very traumatic Winter for him." Delcant could see that he did not have much support for his view around the room. Even Caltan, the normally compliant Elder from his neighbouring community, kept his head down and did not make eye contact with Delcant.

Trying to recover the situation Delcant said, "I was merely trying to ensure that Jandray would be safe whilst we examine his account. If Torpast was attacked, as

Jandray indicates, is there a potential risk to Jandray?" It was a weak response, but Delcant thought it was legitimate and could cover his earlier challenge to Jandray's integrity. Queen Torcas answered, "Elder Delcant, you raise a valid point. If people within our nation", speaking directly at Delcant whilst she said this, "were responsible for breaching our sanctuary and are complicit in the assault on Torpast and the circumstances of Sartora's disappearance; the most serious of crimes against our nation will have been committed." Torcas carried on, still looking at Delcant, "I will need to look closely at our history to find anything of comparison, but I think that, should anyone from the Hiber Nation be found to have been involved in this matter, they would be brought before the Council and a recommendation would be made that they are stripped of all they own and immediately banished from our nation."

King Nilan looked around the room and said, "Perhaps we vote on this issue to allay Delcant's concerns about our seriousness in investigating this matter. We can immediately agree the most gravest of sanctions should we find Jandray, or anyone else from our nation, has been plotting against the very core of our Hiber culture." As King Nilan said this, Delcant's heart was racing and he tried hard not to show his fear at being discovered. All the Elders raised their hands in agreement, and Delcant had to join them. The Key Keepers wrote down the agreement, and Delcant wondered if he would survive the investigation. The way that King Nilan had looked at him made his quake in his clothing; "Does he suspect me?" was his immediate reaction; especially as he felt that Nilan was looking straight at him when he had spoken.

Queen Torcas was fully aware that Nilan was backing Delcant into a corner, whilst giving a facade of impartiality. She said to the Council, "We have agreed that Torpast and Jandray would both be placed under the care and guard of our Key Keepers. However, we have not asked them if they have the resources or accommodation to fulfil this request; I would like to hear from them." Kian stood up and replied, "We are at the behest of this Council. I can confirm that there are chambers adjacent to the library that we can make secure and comfortable. They are near enough to our living quarters that we can easily manage this, and they also benefit from being within the additional security that the library provides.

However…….", she looked at Kindross as she said this, "We are not as young as we once were, and would welcome someone to assist in these extra tasks." Torcas, knowing Kian and Kindross so well, could see beyond the request and gave a barely imperceptible nod and replied, "As Jandray's class will not be able to be run in the normal manner, I suggest that we return all students to their own communities until this issue is resolved. It will mean that Altera and Maltas, who I met prior to Winter, could undertake a supporting role. I believe that they would be ideal helpers to the Key Keepers."

King Nilan looked to each of the Elders and then towards the Key Keepers. "It would make sense to agree to the Queen's proposal, and it would be the right thing to do as well. Altera can help in caring for her father. It would also assist in that, if there was any ongoing risk to her, bearing mind what happened to her father and the unexplained disappearance of her mother, then she would be within the confines of our Paltir building, near to help." Looking at Delcant, he continued, "Maltas is the son of Lorsern, who may well be an excellent potential Elder for Paltir, so it would be appropriate that his son provides support to the Key Keepers as they provide a safe and secure environment for Jandray and also for Torpast. He would also be close to his father who works in the Paltir administrative buildings and could seek his help if necessary too."

Delcant did not like the idea of Altera being close to her father, but it was balanced by the thought of Lorsern having direct access to anything that was said by Jandray. He would not have been so delighted with King Nilan's idea if he had know that Maltas was nothing like his father, and was totally loyal to both Altera and Jandray. Elder Delcant stood and replied, "I fully support this idea, and I think it affords the necessary security and protection that we all want."   King Nilan acknowledged Delcant's reply and said, "The Queen and I will take personal responsibility to set up an investigation into this matter and to report back to the Elder Council as soon as possible. With your agreement, I think we should now end the meeting to allow you all to return to your communities."   Nilan could see that all were in agreement. "One final matter, however, needs to be agreed."   All the Elders looked at him expectantly. "As Delcant has had most contact with the Tukerland Warriors of late, I think it prudent that he remains in Paltir to advise me on how best to approach the

Tukerland warrior leadership, in order to agree how best to approach them as and when necessary." Delcant immediately stood and said, "King Nilan, surely I would be better utilised returning to Decinter as soon as possible; I can make myself available to you there and can meet with my Tukerland trade colleagues."

Queen Torcas smiled at Delcant and said, "Elder Delcant, we have seen what serious injuries HiberWatcher Torpast has suffered, possibly at the hands of people outside of our community. We cannot risk any harm coming to you; I think it would be wise for you to remain here." The Elders around the table voiced their agreement. King Nilan said, "Elder Ospeth and Elder Caltan, you can be briefed by Elder Delcant and then please arrange the appropriate support to the Decinter leaders whilst Delcant is helping the investigation here at Paltir." Ospeth and Caltan stood. As was usual, Caltan looked to Delcant before he spoke but Ospeth said, "I am sure that Caltan and I can do this if the Council wills it, our three communities work closely together due to our proximity to Tukerland in the normal course of things anyhow." He added, "And with the growth of the Decinter building that Delcant has managed over recent years, there will be plenty of room for us to visit." All the Elders laughed at this remark; all except Delcant that is. That final remark indicated to most around the table that Ospeth thought that Tukerland warriors were involved in this matter and, by default, that Delcant's freedom to interfere, if allowed to return to Decinter, should be avoided.

It was unusual for someone like Jandray to have had access to such candid discussions as those that had been made. He had remained silent but was even more convinced that Delcant was central to these terrible events. He thought it was masterful how both Queen Torcas and King Nilan had wrapped Delcant into a situation where he would not be free to progress any clandestine meetings with Grasby or anyone else for that matter. Furthermore, he could see that bringing Altera and Maltas into this could be very beneficial. No one would care more for Torpast than his daughter, and it may distract her from the impact of her mother's disappearance. Maltas was a very bright student, and would repeat nothing to his father, Jandray was sure of this. What needed to happen now was to have a plan to expose Delcant, Grasby and anyone else involved. More importantly, it was clear to Jandray that kidnapping Sartora was only part of a wider plan which they had yet to understand.

The Elders left the chamber to begin their long journeys back to their home communities. This left the Queen and King, the Key Keepers and Jandray in the chamber. "Jandray", Queen Torcas said gently, "I think that I speak for all here now, when I repeat that I have total faith in you and your account of what happened this Winter. There is a pressing need for us to reflect on all that has happened. We need to ensure that Torpast is carefully taken to the Hiber Library and that you are also 'guarded' there. With Kian and Kindross's permission, I think we all use the secret tunnel back to the library. It is quicker and will place less physical stress on Torpast's body." Kian and Kindross agreed; and by mentioning the secret tunnel Jandray realised that both the Queen and King were aware of things that he thought only a HiberWatcher knew; but then again, he wasn't sure of anything much any more.

The small group then went to Hiberwatcher's Rock, and met Altera and Maltas. It was the first time that Queen Torcas and the Key Keepers had seen Torpast. Kian gently placed her hand on his forehead. "He appears to have a normal temperature and his body seems nourished; you have done a good job Jandray." Jandray knew he would have more to tell the Key Keepers but he would have to wait on the King's permission. He just nodded at Kian, but he could feel that she knew he had a much longer account to divulge. Jandray and King Nilan carefully lifted Torpast onto the stretcher that had brought him from the library. It was interesting, thought Jandray, that Torpast would return back to where he had been cared for over the latter part of winter. "Altera and Maltas" said King Nilan, "You have the privilege of helping to support both Torpast and Jandray. They will both be under the Key Keepers care for the foreseeable future." As he looked at them he said, "In addition, we are not going back to Paltir the way you came. You are joining us on taking a secret passage that leads from Queen Mountain back to the library. Before we take that journey, you must promise that you never reveal this tunnel to anyone, ever." Altera and Maltas nodded their agreement. Ensuring that the cavern was now empty, Kian led the way to the tunnel and they started their journey back to the library. All were lost in thought as they tried to comprehend what had happened and what lay ahead of them.

Chapter Twenty-Five

It had been a long and frustrating winter for Saltock. When he had returned from the Hiber Nation he was convinced that Grasby's devious plans did not only impact on the Hiber People, but were part of a wider strategy to destabilise his father. More worryingly, he had seen Grasby speaking with his mother, Baltock, on a number of occasions. Saltock loved his mother, in the Tukerland way. Within their culture, Tukerland warriors respected strength above all other things, and the close and loving relationships he had experienced in the Hiber Nation would be viewed as weaknesses in his own country. Only Nirtan and Mortarn seem to show a kind of brotherhood that Saltock had seen amongst the Hiber folk; although this was masked by their master/servant relationship careful portrayed to all around them. The meeting at Ertin's Inn had been a revelation, and he now looked at both of them with very different eyes. During his ongoing meetings with Nirtan it was clear, however, that he remained totally loyal to Sargern. Nirtan had told Saltock that he was sure that Sargern would not be complicit in any plans Grasby had. "But what about my mother?" Saltock had asked. "Why do you ask?" replied Nirtan, to which Saltock replied, "I have seen Grasby and my mother speak frequently since we returned from Tukerland, and their conversations seem serious. However, they quickly turn the conversation to mundane matters when I have tried to get close enough to hear."

"Grasby has always longed after you mother" answered Nirtan, "From well before she chose Sargern as her partner, Grasby had thought they would be a couple. When your mother chose Sargern, it was at the time when it was becoming clearer that he would be the most powerful warrior in our nation." He stopped at that point and didn't seem to want to continue. "I may be young" Saltock said, "But I see the ambition in my mother's eyes. I have thought, as I have grown older that her love for power is greater than her love for my father." "Perhaps you are right" replied Nirtan. "I think that Baltock cares for Sargern but she is, I fear, planning for a time when there will be challenge to Sargern's authority. That challenge could be soon, and she may be manipulating Grasby's previous feelings for her." "If that is the case", replied Saltock, "then is she in league with Grasby; or just preparing to hold onto her power and influence?" "At this time" replied Nirtan, "that is not at all clear, we will have to watch and wait; nothing would be gained by approaching Sargern at this time."

Nirtan had spent the Winter touring the numerous states that made up the Tukerland nation; and had just returned from this long journey. It was part of his normal role as a close friend of Sargern and none questioned what he was doing. Over many years he had proved himself a fierce Tukerland warrior, and was totally loyal to Sargern. During these years, with Mortarn's help, he had set up a network of contacts across these states of Tukerland. Some were friends of Nirtan and could be trusted completely, others were only as loyal as long as Nirtan's coinage continued flow into their hands. One such contact played a dangerous role in being in the pay of both Nirtan and Grasby. Whilst Nirtan was aware of the duplicitous nature of this particular warrior, Grasby was totally unaware of the conduit of intelligence that leaked from within his band of supposedly loyal warriors. It was a weakness of Grasby that he thought that all his warriors were too fearful of the consequences if they challenged his authority; and the consequences for those who may betray him were beyond imagining, in pain and suffering. Grasby had this reputation for good reason. He had no compunction in putting a warrior to death if and when he wanted to. He didn't need to do it often, as the threat of the torture and slow death, used on occasion to show his power, were sufficient to ensure he and his instructions were generally followed without fail.

Nirtan and Mortarn would not reveal the names of the contacts within their network to anyone, not even to Sargern, who benefited from this information they routinely provided to him. Saltock looked around the room they were in within Nirtan's home. He couldn't help but be reminded of the difference in construction of Tukerland houses and those he had seen in the Hiber Nation. He hoped that the project to host Hiber Gardeners in Tukerland would take place this year. His thoughts were brought back to the present as Mortarn walked in. Nirtan and Mortarn were very comfortable in each others presence and Saltock could see that the friendship between them ran deep. After some refreshments, they all sat down. Nirtan had ensured he had loyal warriors protecting his home at all times; there was no risk that they would be overheard.

"Before we start" said Nirtan. "There is part of this story that even you are not aware of Saltock." He looked at him intently and continued, "You need to be fully aware that between Mortarn and I we have an effective network of contacts throughout the states of Tukerland, and your father has benefited greatly from this network over the years. Grasby has suspected someone is coordinating intelligence for Sargern, but has never managed to break into this network." Looking at Mortarn he said, "Grasby's lust for power, and lack of regard for those he regards as inferior to him, is his blind spot. Mortarn generally has acted as the hub for managing this network; and his 'servant' role to me has meant that Grasby has had no idea of how important he is to me, and to Sargern. However, Mortarn has had another role to play in recent months. More about that in a moment."

Nirtan looked back at Saltock and said, "Grasby is far more dangerous than you possibly realise. I have known him for many years, and have been close to him in battle. Like all Tukerland warriors he is ferocious and has no fear. With his opponents he has no mercy and in his mind justice is a quick death, rather than a long and painful one." None of what Saltock was hearing came as a surprise, other than the fact that Nirtan had been in battle with Grasby. Nirtan continued his story. "At the time we fought together, Grasby realised that Sargern's power was on the ascent and so he decided to side with him against other warring factions within Tukerland. Sargern needed Grasby's support, and that of his warrior clan, but Sargern has always been aware that Grasby covets his leadership of Tukerland." Saltock replied, "I had always assumed that my Father did not trust Grasby, and I had hoped that this was the reason he sent me with him in the trade talks." "Indeed, that was the reason", acknowledged Nirtan, before adding, "Grasby saw you as no threat which is why he did not argue against you being part of the talks. I am sure he felt that he could dominate you in those trade talks; a situation that didn't happen and now he probably regrets the fact that you were present."

"What we have been able to do" Nirtan said, again looking across at Mortarn and bringing his voice to no more than a whisper "is connect with someone within our network who has worked hard to gain the confidence of those leaders closest to Grasby. What we have learnt from this is that Grasby had met with his most trusted lieutenant - a warrior called Argrant. He, in turn, had brought a small team together, who were secreted into the Hiber sanctuary at the commencement of their Winter Sleep." "Delcant." was all that Saltock said. "You are right of course", answered Nirtan. "This was only made possible by the traitorous actions of the Hiber Elder called Delcant, someone you know only too well after the extensive trade talks you held with him. However, our contact was able to place one of their trusted companions as part of that team which was secreted into the Hiber Queen Mountain. I have just returned from meeting our contact and need to update you on their news."

Nirtan continued his account. "I have met with our contact and they confirm they were able to place someone into the team that Argrant had been tasked with setting up. This team of four Tukerland warriors were chosen for their stature - so that they didn't stand out too much amongst the Hiber folk, but also for their covert skills and their tracking abilities. Unfortunately, all our contact can tell us is that there are rumours that they returned a few weeks ago, but no one knows where they are. If we push further as to their location, not only will it endanger our contact but also the person who they placed on the team." Mortarn didn't seem surprised by the news. "Is there any hint of where they are?" he said. "At this time no", quickly answered Nirtan, "All our contact can tell us is that Grasby seems very pleased with himself." Mortarn then said, "But I have also heard that Elder Delcant was not with his community when they returned from their 'awakening', which is highly unusual."

Nirtan, Mortarn and Saltock remained silent for a short while as they reflected on the information that Nirtan had managed to find. "We need to find out what happened during Winter; what were the instructions given to the Tukerland warriors, and were they successful?" said Saltock "We must meet with King Nilan if possible" he added. Nirtan and Mortarn both looked at Saltock and Nirtan said, "We know exactly what happened in Winter." "How, if you cannot find this team and your contact doesn't know anything about their whereabouts?" replied Saltock. "This time", said Nirtan, "I defer to Mortarn in this update, but you will remember our meeting at Ertin's Inn." It suddenly dawned on Saltock that he had missed the vital fact that Mortarn had offered to go to Paltir and hide within the Hiber Library, in case anything untoward happened.

It was Mortarn's turn to continue updating the group. "I went with Ertin to the Queen Mountain and met briefly with King Nilan. From there I was able to hide in the Hiber Library. It can be accessed via a secret tunnel, but is still several hours walk from the main cavern. I did not see this band of Tukerland warriors before I went on my way, so they had been chosen well. Nothing happened for several weeks and then, just before the period that the Hiber folk called Late Winter, the HiberWatcher Jandray appeared at the library, dragging a makeshift stretcher. On the stretcher was the unconscious and badly injured HiberWatcher that he called Torpast." "I met both of these men in Paltir and it was I who picked out their names to be HiberWatchers" Saltock said, suddenly feeling a pang of guilt wash over him. Mortarn continued, "The password - in the form of the poem verse that we agreed - worked and this HiberWatcher Jandray accepted I was not his foe. Over the next few weeks, I was able to care for his friend. When I left, he was free from infection, and his wound was healing, although he had not gained consciousness."

Nirtan indicated to Mortarn to continue his story. "It was clear that the HiberWatcher called Torpast had been attacked. HiberWatcher Jandray had found Torpast and then discovered tracks from a high mountain exit, leading away from Queen Mountain. A Hiber woman called Sartora is also missing, as is one of the Watch Hounds. Jandray could only assume that they were taken by those who attacked Torpast. When I had tended to his wounds, I found his head had been crudely but effectively bound by strips of cloth which I believe were similar to those worn by Tukerland warriors. This binding of the wound undoubtably saved him from bleeding to death before Jandray found him." Nirtan watched to see if Saltock understood how this story was unfolding as he then spoke, "What Mortarn has discovered is that Grasby appears to have been successful in penetrating the sanctuary of Queen Mountain; with a primary aim of kidnapping the woman called Sartora. The reasons for this are not totally clear, but Sartora was favoured to succeed Elder Farrender who is due to retire. Why take the Hiber Hound as well is confusing, however." Saltock replied immediately, "I think that this could be the easiest answer within this complex conspiracy. Whilst we were in Paltir, Grasby was very much taken by the Watch Hounds when they appeared at the Winter Festival. I have no doubt that he wanted one as a prize." Mortarn answered, "That would explain, perhaps, why HiberWatcher Torpast was chosen to be attacked. He had become close to the female Watch Hound and they were rarely apart. It may also explain why she is missing too. If she saw her HiberWatcher attacked, she may well have fought the attackers and had to be subdued or killed."

"Where does this leave us?" said Saltock. "It makes no sense to have such a complex plan to only kidnap one woman from the Hiber folk. Why wouldn't they have taken the King or Queen? They would have been a more important hostage and bargaining tool." "I think" said Nirtan, "that Grasby's plans run much deeper and are longer term. He would know that kidnaping a member of the Hiber First Family would cause a greater international incident between the two nations than taking Sartora. He is not sufficiently confident that Sargern would have supported any of this and so has taken someone not so significant in his eyes. More importantly, he can deny any knowledge of this attack; which would be hard to hide if he was keeping the King or Queen hidden somewhere." Mortarn nodded his agreement. "If some of Grasby's fellow warriors knew he had such a rich prize as a King or Queen, it would possibly put him at risk from their desire to achieve a ransom, or a reward for revealing their whereabouts."

Nirtan thought it important for Saltock to understand all that had happened and said, "Jandray and Mortarn agreed to wake the King prior to the ending of the Winter Sleep. King Nilan helped Jandray and Mortarn over the final few weeks of Winter and then returned to the cavern just before his folk awakened. It was agreed that none of his kin should know all that he had learnt, especially that he had been woken from his sleep. We have heard that Jandray has now been placed under protective guard; albeit in comfortable accommodation at the library. No surprise that we also hear that Elder Delcant wanted a more severe form of incarceration." The Elder Council is aware of what Jandray has told them, but not of Mortarn or King Nilan's part in what happened. They have all agreed to keep Sartora's kidnapping secret at this time as it could create panic. Thankfully, King Nilan has also neutralised the despicable Delcant by creating a situation where he has to remain in Paltir for the time being. This keeps him out of direct contact with Grasby - something he may well thank us for at some point. Delcant will be totally dispensable to Grasby in due course."

Nirtan said, "If the HiberWatcher was given life-saving care by one of the Tukerland warriors, we are hoping that it is the one that we had carefully placed in the group. If we can find this person, I am sure that the whole conspiracy will unfold. However, I am equally sure that Grasby will have put sufficient distance between him and these warriors to protect himself." "Don't forget" agreed Mortarn, "Grasby would have no hesitation in killing that whole team if he thought he had a traitor in his midst, or if he felt they would admit their actions were at his behest, so we need to be careful. He won't want to do this, though, as they are the key to penetrating the mountain again. I think that this expedition was only to assess the potential to breach the mountain during the Hiber Nation's winter sleep. Just think what would happen if he had the support for a full scale attack on this nation. They could wake up as subjugated peoples; or they could not wake up at all." All three contemplated the gravity the situation, and all three knew that Grasby's ambitions could lead him to commit murder on a massive scale if that was necessary to feed his ambitions. "We need to let my father know about this" said Saltock. "I do not think that he wants this future for our two nations. I know he sees the trade between us as very positive. If Grasby's plans were successful, he could irreversibly damage the country that provides food for our growing nation. Even if, over the years, we could replace Hiber folk with our own, there would be years of hardship for our peoples, and for what?"

"Grasby has little concern for the majority of our peoples, and absolutely no concern for any of the Hiber folk. As much as Grasby wants to put a wedge between our nations, I feel that we need to stand together, more than ever" said Nirtan. "Mortarn and I have lived through the wars that Grasby and his fellow warriors visited on our own states for many years; we don't want return to that." Saltock stood up and was animated in his reply, "We must tell my father; and get him to stop this madness." Nirtan considered Saltock's reply before he answered, "We need to be careful. Remember what has been said here. Your mother has been seen speaking with Grasby. We must assume that she has some role in this too. She may not have known about it from the start, and probably didn't. Grasby would not have wanted to have presided over a failure. But now that it appears the first part of his plan has been successful, he will carefully plan his next steps. I am sorry to say that it is possible that your mother could be part of a wider conspiracy."

"It still doesn't answer why he would have taken this Sartora", replied Saltock, but then he thought about what he had just said and added, "However, on reflection, when Grasby and I were in the Hiber capitol, it was clear that Sartora was highly intelligent and highly regarded. She would have much information that could inform Grasby about the ways of the Hiber folk." Nirtan's face was one of worry and anger as he replied, "That concerns us too, and I am sure you are right. It makes it even more important to locate her. Grasby has ways of making people talk that you don't want to think about. Regardless of how strong willed she is, I doubt very much she would be able to withhold long from the torture he could bring to bear. She will talk; and she will probably die from the experience."

Mortarn could seen the impact that Nirtan's words were having on Saltock and he said, "I know that you are fond of Sartora's daughter." Saltock's expression told Nirtan and Mortarn all they needed to know. "What is good for us, is that we understand her daughter has been directed by the King and Queen to care for her father. Also, a close friend of hers has been enlisted to help guard Jandray." Nirtan and Mortarn looked across at Saltock. "The important thing is that we meet with our Hiber friends as soon as possible. We will need you to lead on this" said Nirtan. "Mortarn and I will have as much as we can manage trying to find Sartora and also finding a way of protecting our contact in Grasby's warrior team. We will also need to ensure we protect Sargern. I don't think that Grasby has any immediate plans to rise up against him, but we need to be prepared."

"I could seek permission to go to Paltir to progress the Hiber tree project that King Nilan agreed to consider" answered Saltock. "Whilst there I could find Altera, and we could discuss all that has happened." Nirtan thought on this and then answered, "I think it too much of a risk that Grasby finds out what we are planning if you go to Paltir, and you will need to be closer to Tukerland too, as we may need you here at short notice. Mortarn and I have discussed this. We need to get a message to Nilan for him to send someone to meet you at Ertin's Inn. We can cover for you being missing for a short period of time. Also, if you are Ertin's Inn we can get you to return quickly if any suspicion about our real plans are raised." "But who will they send?" replied Saltock. Nirtan replied, "That we will have to discover; thankfully our network also extends to the Hiber folk. Ertin has already been contact and is making the arrangements." Nothing more could be done as far as the three warriors could see. Saltock prepared to leave for Octurn. A cryptic message would be sent to Nilan, but they would not reveal who would attend the meeting; security against the message being discovered by Grasby. They only hoped that time was on their side and that they could find Sartora before it was too late.

In Paltir, the searches throughout Queen Mountain had proved fruitless, there was no sign of Sartora nor of the Watch Hound. King Nilan and Queen Torcas had met many times with Kian, Kindross and Jandray. Altera and Maltas had been fully updated on all that had happened over winter. Rather than press her into depression, the revelation of the extent of the conspiracy had changed Altera into a determined member of this group, caring for her father and fighting to clear Jandray's name. Maltas, ever at her side, continued to be a strong support for Altera, and all could see that they were future leaders in the Hiber Nation.

"We have had message from Nirtan and Mortarn" said King Nilan. "They want to meet; but it isn't safe for Nirtan to leave Tukerland at this time. They have suggested Ertin's Inn, where our last meeting took place." "I think it wise that neither you nor I leave Paltir at the moment" said Torcas. "I agree" replied Nilan, "I was thinking that perhaps we could send a couple of folk who have proved their worth over recent weeks" and he turned to look at Altera and Maltas. "As we have created a situation where the Elders, and more importantly Delcant, think you are helping Kian and Kindross, we can ensure that you can leave for the meeting whilst everyone will think you are continuing your duties under Kian and Kindross." Torcas looked at Altera, "The only problem is that you will have to leave your father's side; but we will ensure he is cared for. Hopefully when you return he will have regained consciousness." "I am ready to leave at your command" immediately replied Maltas, "and I promise to protect Altera with all the strength I have." Altera smiled at Maltas, "And I will leave, although with a heavy heart. The risk is that I may lose my mother and my father; but there are greater things at play than just the future of my own family."

Nilan looked at both these young people and said, "We are unsure who Nirtan will send to meet you, but it will probably be his close friend Mortarn - who has been central to our fight against whatever plans Warrior Grasby has laid. I know you would want to meet the young warrior again, but if Nirtan cannot leave; it may be unsafe for him to leave too. Under his guise as servant to Nirtan, Mortarn has greater ability to manage his movements without raising suspicion." "I think this meeting needs to take place as soon as possible" added Kian. "Each day that Grasby has Sartora could be serious risk to her." Looking at Altera she said, "I am sorry Altera, but in your heart you know that your mother is at grave risk and we cannot hide that from you." "I know that she will only be kept alive as long as Grasby finds her useful" replied Altera, "So time is of the essence and I think that Maltas and I need to leave as soon as possible." "Prepare to leave as soon as you can" answered Nilan in agreement. "There is a group heading to Octurn tomorrow morning, and we can add you to that group. They were part of the searchers that we used in Queen Mountain and they are now heading home. You will not be known to them, so remain silent and do not reveal your names. If pressed, say you are visiting your schoolfriend Ocsend." Queen Torcas looked concerned as she considered the weight of responsibility they were placing on these young shoulders. She softly spoke with Altera and Maltas. "Speak with Ertin when you get to his Inn, We will have arranged with the leader of the group to ensure you get there safe. Ertin will ensure you have a safe journey home when the meeting is concluded." "It's a long journey there and back" said Kian, "so we will not expect to hear from you for several days; please stay safe my dear children."

The following morning, careful to cover their faces with their cloaks, Maltas and Altera met the Octurn group. They were not at all concerned to have two extra in their group and spoke fondly of Ertin's Inn. From an upper window in the Paltir building, both Torcas and Nilan watched as the group left, knowing that the fate of the Hiber Nation rested in their hands, for a while at least. Nothing was said and they turn away as the group slowly disappeared from view.

Queen Torcas sat by the fire in her room and read the poem again, as she had done many times since the awakening: -

"The HiberWatchers watch, and the sleepers sleep

The Queen protects them all in her keep

Winter falls, and deep cold it does bring

And the world will refresh when we wake in Spring"

"Queen Mountain hears when trouble is near

Hiber Trees talk and move if they sense fear

Roots so deep can bring news to those who love

And long tunnels open up new roads from above"

"When the HiberWatchers are close in Hiber sense

Winter can be severe and storms intense

Be careful to watch each other as well as the sleeping

And work hard to ensure that at Spring there is no weeping"

"When the snows do fall on HiberWatcher Day

And the lights in their brilliance do put on their display

It shall mean an event of great import

A Spring an awakening of a different sort"

"From afar, others look on the Hiber Nation, safe in their sleep

And each year they plan to enter the Mountain sanctuary keep

These others they seek to have help from Hiber within

But the plans they do make are not supported by their kin"

"But others, too, are awake and are friends of the Hiber kin

And when they are needed they too will be found within

A heart in more than one nation they will be seeking there

And Queen Mountain will unify these hearts in this endeavour"

It distracted her from her concerns of placing such young Hiber folk at risk, and she wondered if more verses were yet to be found. If she and Nilan had only watched from their window a little longer, they would have seen a lone figure carefully tracking the main group, working hard not to be seen.

Chapter Twenty-Six

The small band of Tukerland warriors had made slow progress across a desolate land of ice and snow that was betraying no sign it would soon return to life. Argrant looked back at where they had exited, high up on Queen Mountain, and knew that as soon as the snows melted it would be impossible to reach that particular place from the outside of Queen Mountain. He was also looking back to see if the other HiberWatcher had begun to follow the obvious tracks they had left in the snow. So far the sky had remained clear and it would be easy follow their route. Argrant wasn't particularly troubled by this thought as his warriors could easily despatch the lone HiberWatcher if he tried to follow. "If I were him, I would not know what path to take" he said aloud to Trenmant who was following behind him. "Do I pursue those who had breached the sanctuary of this mountain and leave all those I have sworn to care for; for the sake of one woman and a hound?" He continued speaking his thoughts, "Or do I stay and protect those still sleeping, and mourn a dead fellow HiberWatcher?" Trenmant replied, "I think that I would not want to be in his position, either way. If this situation was reversed, from a Tukerland perspective, he would be executed, whichever path he took. If he stayed, he would have been blamed for allowing the attack to succeed; if he left and then returned he would be executed for leaving his post."

Argrant stopped to allow the group to gain their breath and said, "However, from what little I know of these people, I do not think that they would execute the HiberWatcher. They do not have the warrior pedigree that we enjoy, and have little fondness for conflict." Wardok replied, "If we don't make good haste he will not have had to follow us as we will perish in this desperate wasteland." Argrant nodded in agreement, "This period of clear skies will soon be replaced by the final snowstorms of winter. We must get back to Tukerland before this happens." He could see that the sheer battle against the harsh elements of this season was already taking a toll on all of them. Once he was sufficiently satisfied that they were out of the view of the high mountain entrance from which they had left, he had called a halt to their journey and they fashioned protection by building tunnels into the snow. These tunnels at least afforded protection from the biting wind. Delcant had provided a stock of fire cones that the Hiber peoples used for warmth, but Argrant knew that these cones would only last them for a few short nights and he wasn't at all sure how long it would take them to get back to Tukerland.

Their journey continued with both the woman and the hound remaining silent for much of the first few days, as the mountain slowly receded into the distance. Then the hound had begun to stir. It could not move easily, and was only able to emit a low growl as far as the muzzle allowed. The woman, Sartora, remained asleep and Argrant had left it to Lanfin and Wardok to ensure she remained alive. The temperatures were such that one could easily succumb to frostbite and death, especially if immobile and not able to generate heat from the exercise that walking would have brought. Nights were long and cold. As soon as the winter sun appeared, they made ready for the day's trudge ahead. There was no way they could have survived the extreme cold that nightfall held. Lanfin had looked upon the night sky which was illuminated with what seem like hundreds of colours dancing in the sky. She had never been in a landscape so beautiful, whilst so inhospitable to life at the same time. Her thoughts wandered to what this country would be like when Spring arrived. Her time within Queen Mountain had changed her. Binding the wounds of the HiberWatcher had been totally at odds with what was expected from her. Yet, she did not regret it and felt that the HiberWatcher had a right to life if that is what the mountain wanted. This feeling that the mountain had called out to her made her unsettled but also gave her a sense of peace. She looked upon the sleeping form of their hostage and feared for what lay ahead of her. Again, these feelings of concern were alien to her; she had always followed orders and was viewed as a loyal warrior. What would Argrant say if he could look into her mind. Wardok appeared to have no such worries, but was stretching in a vain attempt to get some warmth into her tired limbs.

"Let's go" said Argrant, looking into the distance. "Tonight, as a treat, we will light some fire cones to force warmth into our bodies. We have made good progress and I think it will be only a few more days before we get to the border with Tukerland."
"With the depth of snow, it is hard to gain a perspective on where the normal pass through the mountain of Decinter is" replied Trenmant. Wardok, one of the best trackers in Tukerland said, "Look carefully, you can see the Decinter mountain in the

distance. Although much of it is buried under this incessant snow, we should reach it in a day or so." It was clear that Argrant and Wardok had discussed this as both were in agreement that their journey home was coming to an end. "I cannot wait for some real food, beer and warmth - in that order" replied Trenmant; adding "I am sure that this one", indicating to Sartora, "will be hungry too when she finally awakes."

Argrant did not want to deflate the enthusiasm that had begun to build across his group, an enthusiasm that was increasing at the thought of being back in their homeland. However, he also knew that their journey would not end at the border. Grasby had given instructions on where to take their prized possessions, and it was nowhere near any of the inhabited parts of Tukerland close to the border. Good food and drink would be somewhat more distant they had imagined. "I will let them know when we get to the border" he thought to himself, "no point in spoiling their good humour at this time, especially as we have at least two more hard days of travel ahead of us." Trenmant and Argrant lifted the hound together. Now that she had woken, Trenmant was not at all comfortable with carrying her round his neck. So a pair of warriors each carried one 'load' as they continued the heavy slog towards the Decinter mountain.

The hours passed and the winter sun soon left its place in the sky; to be replaced by the chill of evening and the cold night ahead. Now very adept at fashioning shelters in the snow, the four made a spacious hole for their night-time protection. Good to his word, Argrant brought out the last of the snow cones and a small, but welcoming fire, was kindled. Lanfin really loved the smell of the cones; it reminded her of fresh water and open sky. However, that view was not shared by the others who longed for the smoky hearths they were used to. Their kidnapped woman had still not woken from her sleep and Lanfin placed her close to the fire to ensure warmth was able to seep into her body. At Argrant's suggestion, the Watch Hound was placed at her side. Having loosened the muzzle, he had very carefully given Snowblue some food. It was a measure of her hunger that she rapidly took the meagre offerings; even though she continued to bring a low growl to any of them that came close. As soon as she had eaten, Argrant tightly fastened the muzzle back into place. "I would not want to be at the mercy of those teeth" he said. "She is a fine specimen and I can see why Grasby would want one of these hounds." He then looked over at Sartora's body laying next to the hound. "What he wants with this one; that I am unsure. All I know is that the pathetic excuse for a man called Delcant was very keen that she was the one taken, and that was why Grasby instructed us to specifically find and take her." "I understand that she isn't Hiber royalty, or even an Elder" answered Trenmant, "But she must have some worth to Grasby to go to these lengths to bring her under his captive eye."

"What worries me" Argrant said quietly to himself, "Is that only four of us were sent on this mission. Does that mean we are dispensable in Grasby's plans?" Trenmant must have heard him muttering Grasby's name because he replied, "All I care about is the extra coin that he will give us. Although, having carried that hound round my neck for several days, I would think her fur would make a fine winter coat." Wardok laughed along with Trenmant, "If you were to make a coat of this one, I think that Grasby would have your hide too" said Wardok. Lanfin did not engage in the conversation but brushed her hand across the netting within which Snowblue was contained. She could feel the warmth of her body and the softness of her fur. "No" she thought, "This animal is too valuable to be culled for her fur." Argrant noticed Lanfin looking at the prone outline of the hound. "What do you think Lanfin?" Knowing a reply was expected she answered, "I was thinking that I would like to see how these hounds tracked; they would make for loyal companions I feel, if Grasby succeeds in breeding her." "Well said" replied Argrant, "perhaps he will give us pick of the first litter." Lanfin looked over at Argrant and said, "that would be a fine payment indeed, but I pity the Tukerland hound that tries to mate with her." All four warriors laughed at this, and Trenmant replied, "True, those teeth and claws will make it a painful experience for any Tukerland hound that tries."

Sartora kept her eyes closed as she listened to the conversation between the four warriors. She had been awake and alert for several days. At first she had been totally disoriented, but it soon became clear that she was no longer in Queen Mountain and was totally immobile. It had been hard to continue the pretence of sleep during the long journey. By awakening, she had also experienced the hunger that all Hiber folk felt when they awoke in Spring. All she had been able to do was take some snow in her mouth as they had placed her down when the warriors were resting. It had satiated her thirst, but she knew she needed to eat soon. Her heart had lifted when she realised that Snowblue was with her and also apparently unharmed. They would need to escape, but the time to do so was not yet apparent. Even if she could escape from her bindings, she would have no way of getting far from her captives before being caught again. In addition, she could not leave the hound to their mercy. Torpast had really bonded with this Watch Hound before the Winter sleep, and it was almost like part of him was with her in the form of Snowblue. No, she would listen and gain as much information as possible before the warriors knew she was awake. By doing this, it had ensured she already knew that Grasby and Delcant was at the centre of this terrible event. She was only pleased that they had not mentioned Saltock. It was clear to her, if not to her daughter, that Saltock was smitten by Altera. It would have broken her daughter's heart if he had been part of the conspiracy.

The winter sun climbed into the sky and Argrant encouraged his warriors with the thought that they would reach Tukerland by nightfall. Whilst it would be winter there, the snow would be much less ferocious, and they would be able to find easier and warmer places to bed down this evening. It was as if the mountains of the Hiber folk kept all the snow to themselves, as part of protecting the Hiber Nation. What was a desolate wasteland to those looking on, was a protective blanket for the sleeping nation. Argrant dismissed these thoughts and concentrated on the last few hours of pushing through the snow. Sartora continued to pretend she was still asleep, although she had heard little more of use from any of the warriors. She had noticed that one of the female warriors had taken much more care with her than any of the others, and had also taken interest in Snowblue. Soon her hunger would betray her consciousness and she would have to "wake" in order that the warriors would feed her. What had become clear was that she was of some value to this group. If Delcant had wanted her out of the way permanently, surely he would have instructed these warriors to kill her. This gave a glimmer of hope that Sartora held onto. She could see the Decinter Mountain looming large on the horizon, soon she would be taken out of the Hiber Nation and into Tukerland. As she thought of this, the hope faded as she then reflected that it would mean she would be at the mercy of Grasby and these warriors.

"One last push" exhorted Argrant. "The depth of this snow will mean it will be all downhill once we reach the crest of the lowest point of the mountain that is uncovered by snow on this side."   With the energy of ones nearing home, the four increased their pace and soon reached the lowest point of the mountain that was clear of snow. They looked ahead of them and could see the plains of Tukerland in front of them. Snow lay on the ground, but it did not look as deep as the journey from which they would soon be resting. Trees and buildings could be seen in the distance, and smoke was curling from the roofs of those nearby buildings. Without any conscious agreement,   all four then looked behind them.   The vast Queen Mountain could still be seen in the distance. Her size was barely diminished by the distance they had travelled. However, they could see that the snow was deep across this nation, as far as their eyes allowed a view. The whole mountain range seemed to contain all the snow that could possibly be thrown from the sky. As they slowly turned back, each were in their own thoughts as to what lay ahead of them. They almost ran down the steep gradient of Decinter Mountain in their desire to reach home ground. Just as the evening began to bring a deep blue tinge to the sky, they reached level ground. "We are home", cried Argrant. "Let's settle here and we can continue our journey tomorrow." Trenmant looked at him quizzically, "There are homesteads close enough for shelter; surely we can reach them in an hour or so?"   "And how would that make for a secret mission?", replied Argrant. "No, I have instructions to make towards Grasby's private estate. He has made shelter available to us and will give us more instructions as soon as we can let him know we have been successful in our mission."   Trenmant wanted to argue but the thought better of it. Argrant was not the leader without good reason. He was a seasoned warrior and would not stand for a challenge to his instructions. "As you instruct" was all that Trenmant said as they began to make shelter amongst the first trees they had seen since emerging from Queen Mountain.

Chapter Twenty-Seven

Sartora could see that she had left her country and was now in Tukerland. She decided to continue in her pretence of being asleep in order that the warriors wouldn't realise she was memorising her surroundings. If she could escape at some point, she would need to know how to return to the pass at Decinter Mountain. This strange land would need to provide her with fixed points to remember, if she was ever to escape back to home. Her hunger was at a point where she would actually lose consciousness if she did not get sustenance soon. It had been many days since she had actually awoken. She didn't realise that it was only the fact that her body had been at rest, and she had not exerted any energy since waking, that meant she was still able to remain coherent. The limited amount of water she had been able to gain from the snow she had eaten would not be enough to keep her alive for much longer. She only hoped that this band of warriors would reach their intended destination soon.

As soon as the sunrise lifted over the Tukerland plains Argrant instructed them to break camp. "We will be at Grasby's estate within a matter of hours if we leave now. It will feel much easier now we are not pushing against the snow." They carefully avoided the homesteads that were closest to the protective forest canopy and made a wide detour around all the inhabited places in this part of Tukerland. Keeping close to the edges of the forest, they retreated beyond the tree line when they saw any signs of life. Despite the constant effort of moving in and out of the forest, the going was certainly a lot easier than their journey from Queen Mountain, and their closeness to the relative safety of Grasby's estate filled them with energy. Finally, in the distance, the heavily fortified walls of Grasby's estate came into view. Lanfin noted that there seemed to be a lot of activity across the estate, with enough warriors wandering around to make up a small army. Surprisingly, Argrant directed them away from the main fortifications and led them a considerable distance away. A simple homestead appeared, for all purposes looking abandoned. Argrant turned to his band of warriors and said, "This is where Grasby has placed supplies for us. There is ample shelter, and do not be deceived by the dilapidated state; it will give us good protection from the elements. Grasby uses this for a range of purposes, its interior will surprise you."

Argrant was sure that no one would be present in this homestead, but still sent Wardok ahead to make certain. "Grasby has given careful instructions that no one from his fortress is to venture anywhere near this building" said Argrant. "It actually was his family homestead and he has ensured that it remains in good repair despite its appearances. Grasby often stays here and insists on not being disturbed when he does." Wardok soon returned and confirmed that the building and its environs were empty. They quickly walked to the building and entered through the main door. Indeed, the interior was very different from what was expected. It was well appointed, in the Tukerland way, with a large hearth in one corner. Several rooms could be seen down a corridor leading further into the dwelling. "Trenmant, light a fire and let us get warm for the first time in weeks" said Argrant, with a smile on his face. "Have no fear that our presence will be noted, no one will dare come and risk the wrath of Grasby if they believe he is here." Trenmant went to work, using the wood that had already been stacked near the hearth. Soon a fire was burning brightly and its warm glow filled the room. As they started to relax, Argrant said, "We will eat and then I will arrange to get a message to Grasby to meet us here. From this point, I am unaware of what his next instructions will be."

Trenmant had found the food that had been stored within the building, and had started to prepare a dinner for them. "What are we to do with our guest and the hound?" he asked. Argrant replied, "I think that Grasby or Delcant has arranged a stock of food of the Hiber style to be here, both for the woman and the hound. But for me, I want meat and lots of it. Feed the hound carefully and we will then feed the woman when she wakes." The extended sleep of this woman continued to be cause for concern for Argrant. Whilst it was clear she was alive, he had not expected her to be asleep for the whole journey. If she didn't wake, Grasby would immediately blame them for lack of care of her. "I only hope she awakes soon, for all our sakes." he said as Trenmant continued to prepare the food. "I think the time has come that we loosen their bonds. Grasby tells me that there is a strong room down the corridor that he uses for 'guests'; place them in there and we will take turns in watching them." Sartora and Snowblue were lifted up, still in their bindings, and taken into the room. It was a sparse room, with only limited light coming from a window that had iron bars running across it. A simple bed was in one corner. After they had removed the bindings from Sartora, they placed her on the bed. They then removed Snowblue from her captive bindings but left her muzzle loosely fastened. The lack of mobility meant that all four of them could leave the room before Snowblue found her feet. Trenmant threw some food into the room and Snowblue slowly walked towards it. In her hunger, with difficulty, she greedily ate it, despite the obstruction of the muzzle, and then walked back to the bed where Sartora was laying. She sat by her side and looked back at the door. Her growls were absent as she then nuzzled into Sartora in an effort to wake her. "Let's eat" said Argrant. "Don't worry about a guard; she isn't even awake yet." The four warriors withdrew to the main room and Sartora was left alone.

Sartora slowly opened her eyes and tried to sit up. She moved her ankles and her arms to try and get mobility in them. She almost cried out due to the pain that coursed through her body. Snowblue licked her face and she tried to touch her fur, but the pain caused by her enforced bindings just brought more agony. She laid back down and tried to think about what she could do next. Over the hours that passed the blood started flow more freely through her body. However, this only made her hunger more apparent and she would soon have to let her captives know she was awake. She could smell the aroma of food that was drifting into the room. It did nothing to satiate her appetite, however, guessing that it would be meat they were eating. Her thoughts went to what she would do if they only presented her with meat to eat. Would she be able to stomach this, having never tasted such food? She decided it was time 'awake' and she cried out to her captors "where am I?" She could hear the sound of furniture scraping along the floor. There was a flap in the top half of the door that swung outwards and she could see a face looking at her.

"So, you are finally awake" said Argrant. "Where am I?" Sartora replied, "and why am I in this room?" "All will be made clear to you in due course" he replied. "But first, you must be hungry. Don't worry, we have some of your tasteless food." As he said this, he moved away from the aperture and threw a loaf of bread onto the bed. He then called her forward. "Unfortunately, I cannot throw the water at you, you will need to come and get this vessel." Sartora tried to stand up and immediately collapsed on the floor. She tried again, and leaned on the wall as she pulled herself upright. Eventually, she was able to claw her way to the door. "Your bonds have impacted on your ability to walk" Argrant stated. "It will wear off soon enough." There was no threat in his voice, just a weary tone. "Rest while you can, I do not know trials lay ahead of you; but meeting them with food in your stomach may at least help."

Sartora took the vessel and was grateful to find that it did only contain water. She supped it down and passed the vessel back through the hatch. "What is to happen to me, where am I?" she repeated. Argrant said nothing but moved from the door and closed the flap. Sartora carefully walked back to her bed and reached for the bread. She broke into it and began to eat. "If they meant to harm me they would have done it sooner" she said to herself. Even the basics of just bread and a little water raised her spirits. She knew she had to think carefully about what to do next, how to attempt an escape and how to make her way back to her country. But there was so many unanswered questions. From the little that the warriors had said, it appeared that she had been the main target of their kidnapping and this probably meant that Torpast, Altera and the Hiber folk were still safe for now. But what would they want with her? Farrender had spoken with her about Grasby and she had met him briefly in Paltir. Everything about him cried out a feeling of suppressed violence and deep animosity towards the Hiber folk. And knowing that Delcant was part of this attack on her made it even worse. "The closest part of our nation to where I am captive is Decinter; I must find a way to get there" she murmured into Snowblue's ear. "I have to return and tell the Elders who is behind this." She continued to eat at the bread and then carefully secreted some under the bed. "If I am to escape, I will need provisions" she told herself. Lost in thought she laid back on the bed and tried to rub the pain from her wrists and ankles. "I also need to gain strength and mobility if I have any chance of escape." With that in mind, she closed her eyes and tried to formulate a plan to escape from her captives.

The hours turned into days, and Sartora slowly gained back her strength. Snowblue also began to gain back the weight she had lost on the meagre rations she had been fed. Her white fur began to regain its lustre, although she was constantly scratching at the muzzle. Sartora had removed the muzzle on one occasion. However, when her captives discovered what she had done, her own hands were tied behind her back. In addition, Snowblue was pinned down with a heavy net as Argrant and Trenmant had forcibly placed the muzzle back over her snarling teeth. Whilst they had eventually done this with no permanent damage to her, they had been none too careful with the restraints on both Snowblue and Sartora. Snowblue had then been removed and had been put in an adjacent room. Sartora could not see her but could hear that she was alive. As a result of her actions, her only trusted companion had been removed form her, and Sartora bitterly regretted what she had done.

Each of the warriors took turns in stationing themselves outside of her room. Sartora assumed that they could keep watch on both her and the room that Snowblue was in. Now that they knew she was awake, little was said in front of her. On occasions she was left alone when all the warriors ate together, usually in the evening. She sometimes heard snippets of conversation, but nothing useful was gained. If she had heard the full conversation she would have known that Argrant had passed a message on for Grasby to be aware that the mission had been successful, but nothing had been heard back. All that had been received back was that Grasby was tied up at Sargern's stronghold and it would take time for him to make excuses to return to his own fortress. Sartora had tried to engage her guards in conversation but had only succeeded with Lanfin who had started to communicate haltingly with her. The other three said nothing to her during their time at the door to where she was being held. Unlike the others, Lanfin was careful when passing food and water to her and she let Sartora know not to worry about Snowblue. "We are under instruction to let no harm come to either of you" she had said to Sartora. When pressed for what was going to happen, even Lanfin would not say anything.

Sartora had no way of knowing how long it had been since she was kidnapped, nor how long she had been asleep on the route from Queen Mountain. Slowly, however, it was obvious that the days were getting longer. She felt that Winter would soon be over and she should be with Torpast and Altera, celebrating their renewed family relationship. Instead, she was languishing as a prisoner, somewhere in Tukerland. The evening arrived and she was left on her own whilst the warriors had their evening meal. For the first time, she felt that dissension was in the air. Voices amongst the warriors were raised and it seemed like an argument was taking place. Suddenly it all went quiet, and she heard heavy footsteps and a door bang. She wasn't quite sure whose turn it was to guard her until Lanfin's face appeared at her door. As usual she passed food and water to her. "I heard shouting tonight" Sartora said, "Is everything in order?" Lanfin's face was one of confusion and worry. "We have heard that our master is on his way; in fact he will be here tomorrow or the day after at the latest." "I can see you are worried" Sartora decided to push. "Surely it is only me that is at any risk from your master?" Lanfin stared at Sartora "What we have done here is not within the etiquette of our creed" she said. "You may know that we are a warrior nation, that prides ourselves on martial skills. Taking hostages is not something that we do. Historically we have killed each other on the field of battle, but captured warriors are normally traded for our own folk. It doesn't sit comfortably with me that we are treating you in this way; it you demeans me and what I stand for as a proud warrior."

Sartora had not expected such an outburst and did not know what to say. "I have only met two warriors of your nation before, one is called Warrior Grasby and one is called Warrior Saltock. The one called Grasby seemed to bristle with anger and hate, but the younger one impressed all those he met in our country." Lanfin moved closer to the door. "Grasby is the one who had instructed us in our mission and he is the one who will be here soon. He is a ruthless warrior and I fear that he will be harsh in his dealings with you." Sartora looked into Lanfin's face and could see the fear in her eyes. "Why do you follow this man, if he does not display the etiquette that you believe is so important?" "I have been asking myself that recently", she answered. "I was recruited by our leader Argrant, and knew little of Grasby, other than his reputation. Argrant told me that I was needed for my tracking skills and that I would be required to keep a female safe. I needed the coinage he promised to help me through winter so I didn't ask more questions." Sartora was used to engaging with people and she knew she needed to remain connected with this warrior, who was clearly frightened and, more importantly, was having second thoughts about her loyalty to Grasby. "I am sure that there would be a place for you in my country if you were able to free me; you have not seen it other than as winter landscape. I can promise you it is abundant with life during the other seasons of the year." She let this statement hang in the air and could see the conflict in Lanfin's eyes.

Suddenly the flap in the door slammed shut. "That's the answer then" Sartora said to herself in desperation. She began to mentally prepare for the arrival of Grasby and whatever sorrow and hurt he was going to visit upon her. She lay back down on her bed and closed her eyes. If only she hadn't unmuzzled Snowblue, at least she would have company in this sparse room. She knew that she couldn't give up all hope. Grasby wanted her alive; otherwise this group of warriors would not have risked their own lives to bring her back here. It was the emerging fear of what he would do to her that would deny her rest and sleep. Her only consolation was that she was sure that Grasby was not acting in any official capacity. If he had been, she would not have been incarcerated in such a place, she would have been in closer proximity to the ruling elite of Tukerland. Added to this consideration, the warriors had only mentioned Grasby and had not implicated Saltock or mentioned anyone else other than Delcant.

Whilst Sartora was wrestling with these thoughts, she was dragged back to reality when she heard the door being quietly opened. There at the threshold stood the Warrior Lanfin. "Come quickly, the others are sleeping. This is your only chance." Sartora wondered if this was some kind of trick, a false hope to break her will before Grasby arrived. Would she get to the door only to be met by the warriors, ready to throw her back in the room? "Come, this is the only time you will have to escape." Sartora jumped to her feet "Where will I go? I am not dressed sufficiently, even for this mild Tukerland winter." "I will go with you a short way", answered Lanfin, "and I have found some clothing you can wear, but we must go, NOW." Sartora quietly followed Lanfin into the hall, she could see another room with the door firmly closed. "Where is Snowblue?" she asked of Lanfin. "Snowblue?" "The Watch Hound, she must come with us." "There is no time, the others could wake at any moment, we must go without the hound." Sartora looked at Lanfin with fire in her eyes. "I cannot leave without Snowblue; I will stay here and our fate will be decided together." Sartora made to return to the room in which she had been captive. Lanfin grabbed her arm, "Follow close, you will need to ensure she doesn't bark, or we will get no further than the end of this corridor."

Lanfin carefully opened the door to where Snowblue was being held. Sartora knelt down and called her quietly. Immediately Snowblue was at the door threshold. "My loyal hound, please be quiet, we are to leave. I need you to guide me back to Torpast, your work is not finished." Snowblue seemed to understand what Sartora was saying and quietly padded out of the room. She looked at Lanfin but made no attempt to go near her, nor did she growl. "There is an exit at the bottom of this corridor. If I can open it, we can escape without waking the others" she whispered to Sartora. "If they wake, I will create a noise and you must run as fast as you are able to the forest cover, and I hope your hound can guide you from there." "What will happen to you?" said Sartora. Lanfin replied quietly, "I know this landscape better than you and I will be able to travel far and fast away from them." Sartora looked at this unlikely friend and said, "Let's hope that they don't wake, as I would like you to remain with us. I meant what I said about a welcome for you in our country." It was the first time that Sartora had seen Lanfin's mouth turn into a smile. "That is something to hope for" she replied.

The two women, and the Watch Hound slowly walked down the short corridor to the rear of the homestead. Lanfin found the door and gave a sigh of relief when it opened. "Almost there" she said, "we will head directly out to the forest. The tree line is a few short seconds away if we run." They started to move away from the curtilage of the building and then started to run towards the tree line. Just as they though they had made it undiscovered, Sartora heard a cry. "Lanfin, you traitor - Grasby will cut the skin from your body for what you have done." Both Lanfin and Sartora quickly looked behind them. Outlined in the light of the doorway stood Argrant. They both looked back at each other and Lanfin said, "My fate is sealed, we run or I die, and that death will be slow and painful." Snowblue turned and made to run back to attack Argrant. "No", shouted Sartora, "I need you with me." Snowblue stopped and ran back to Sartora's side. For some reason, Argrant had not started to run after them. "I have thrown their boots into another room" she said, smiling despite the threat they were facing. "He knows he will get frostbite if he tries to follow without footwear." Sartora grabbed Lanfin's hand. "You are my saviour, let's go." They started to run, becoming more confident that they would make good distance before the chase began.

Their confidence was to be short-lived as Argrant had plans that did not involve running in the snow. He grabbled for a bow that was located near to the door threshold and quickly placed an arrow. His only concern was which target to choose. The figures ahead were already getting to the extremity of his skill with a bow and both were wearing similar cloaks. Hitting Lanfin was his plan, and then the three warriors would be able to track this Hiber woman. If they were lucky they would not even have to tell Grasby of the involvement of Lanfin; they could say she had left and would meet up with them for her payment later. However, if he hit the Hiber woman, he doubted any of them would survive Grasby's wrath.

The arrow left his bow and flew high on the winter's cold night air. Almost immediately it reached the two figures running swiftly to the trees. Argrant saw one of the women fall to the snowy ground. By now, the other Warriors had joined Argrant at the door. He quickly pulled on his boots and the three of them ran after their quarry.

Printed in Great Britain
by Amazon